About the Auth

Born into a military family in Wellington, New Zealand, Anna's childhood took her to many interesting parts of the world, including Australia, Singapore, Malaya and England. A love of language, reading, writing and acting led Anna to a career in radio as a creative writer and voice-over artist. While taking a sabbatical from radio to pen her first novel, *The Locket* (published July 2023), Anna was diagnosed with multiple sclerosis, which saw her world turn upside down. Now confined to a wheelchair, she continues to create engaging tales of life and love.

Appearances

Anna Hendry

Appearances

Vanguard Press

VANGUARD PAPERBACK

A CIP catalogue record for this title is available from the British Library.

ISBN 978-1-83794-494-1

This is a work of fiction. Names, characters, businesses, places, events and
incidents are either the products of the author's imagination or used in a fictitious
manner. Any resemblance to actual persons, living or dead, or actual events is
purely coincidental.

Vanguard Press is an imprint of
Pegasus Elliot Mackenzie Publishers Ltd.
www.pegasuspublishers.com

First Published in 2025

Vanguard Press
Sheraton House Castle Park
Cambridge England

Printed & Bound in Great Britain

Dedication

I fondly dedicate *Appearances* to my lovely sister-in-law, Carol (Green) Pearce, a born and bred Leominster lass, whose first-hand knowledge and wonderful descriptions of the lifestyle and the area in the fifties and sixties have been both inspirational and invaluable.

Acknowledgements

To Carol Pearce, thank you for providing me with the perfect town in which to set my story. Leominster offered every single requirement that was essential to the plot. My heartfelt thanks to Veronica, Dorothy and the late Flo Green for all the wonderful, informative brochures about Leominster that you sent to me. The little maps of the town's layout and its surroundings have been invaluable to me. I would also like to acknowledge all those who played a part in preparing those great little brochures in the first place. You helped to bring Leominster to life for me as I sat here, twelve thousand miles away in Auckland, New Zealand, writing about a fictional family living in a quintessential English town which I must freely admit I have never had the good fortune to visit. Thank you. I humbly acknowledge and grovel at the feet of the good people of Leominster, Birmingham and the entire county of Herefordshire in the hope that you can forgive any faux pas and screaming errors I have made in the content of *Appearances*. Please accept my deepest apologies. To my beloved family and friends, I must once again say thank you all for your endless support, patience and encouragement. I love you all. Allan, I thank you for all your wonderful ideas about including zombies in the plot. I'm sorry to have let you down again, but thanks for all the guitar and keyboard interludes along the way. They did help…

Chapter – 1

Elizabeth Victoria Anne arrived in this world two years after the end of the Great War, destined to become the adored and pampered only child of Birmingham City Councillor David Pritchard and his socialite wife, Eunice.

A beautiful child with an angelic face and big blue eyes, softly framed with a halo of pale golden hair, Elizabeth led a privileged life.

The home in which she grew up was large and comfortable, and her every material need was generously catered for.

Her parents considered appearances to be of the utmost importance, and accordingly, Elizabeth was well educated, beautifully attired, and at all times, expected to behave like a young lady worthy of her upbringing. Impeccable manners and respect for her elders were drummed into her from the off, and any lapse was swiftly dealt with.

Children were to be seen and not heard, and having no siblings to share her life with, she grew into a lonely, serious young woman, always anxious to uphold her parents' wishes. Her greatest joy came from spending time in the garden with her mother, where she quickly learned to tend the many plants that thrived under Eunice's expert care, while at the same time, she developed a genuine love and flair for the art of flower arrangement.

By the age of twenty, Elizabeth had also acquired a passion for fine art and antiques, which, just like the garden, offered a world in which she could happily immerse herself for hours. A special place that intrigued, fascinated and absorbed her. She enrolled at Birmingham University in order to study Art History and Antiquities and found part-time employment at the nearby Art Gallery. It seemed Elizabeth had found her niche in life.

Her contentment, however, was to be short-lived, as the events of the Second World War quite literally brought her entire world crashing down around her.

On The 25th of October,1940, Elizabeth left work early and hurried home to join her parents for high tea, before they headed out to the Town Hall, where a meeting had been called to discuss how Council might raise funds for the war effort and find ways to boost local morale.

Having waved them goodbye and closed the front door firmly behind them, Elizabeth repaired to the kitchen, where she made herself a fresh pot of tea before sitting down at the large, comfortable kitchen table to study. She seemed to have barely settled into her task when the peace was disturbed by the disquieting approach of a dull, threatening rumble overhead.

The sinister throbbing quickly turned to a deep, menacing growl as aeroplane after aeroplane roared relentlessly overhead, causing the house to shudder on its foundations and the windows to rattle in their frames.

Her teacup danced on its saucer, and feelings of disbelief and utter terror washed over Elizabeth as the sudden, unexpected scream of bombs raining down and the ensuing thunderous explosions shook her to the very core.

She sat paralysed with fear, a sick feeling gnawing at the pit of her stomach, until the screech of an incendiary bomb, which seemed to be directly overhead, prompted her to take action. She frantically threw herself to the floor and then scrambled under the table, where she sat trembling with fear as the house shook violently around her.

Windows exploded in a shower of glass, and it sounded to a terrified Elizabeth that the entire roof was falling in. As the house began to fill with the pungent aroma of smoke and cordite, Elizabeth decided to make a desperate dash for the back garden, where her father had erected an Anderson Shelter just weeks earlier, fervently hoping as he did so, that the need to use it would never arise.

For Elizabeth, the shelter now offered her at least some hope of safety from the thunderous onslaught and refuge from the bitterly cold night air. She drew up her knees under her chin and snuggled under some old woollen blankets and a faded counterpane, which Mother had placed there in an old suitcase. Traumatised, frightened and feeling utterly alone and vulnerable, she shivered with fear, her face drenched with uncontrollable tears, her ears straining for any sound of her parents' return as wave after wave of aircraft attacked.

The night sky glowed an eerie orangey red, and the air was thick with acrid smoke and choking clouds of dust and debris. The deafening roar of aircraft and endless explosions were punctuated only by chilling screams and desperate cries for help.

It was dawn before the mayhem stopped, and Elizabeth felt brave enough to venture out of her shelter. She was relieved to find the house still standing. A section of the roof appeared to be damaged and devoid of tiles, and barely a window remained intact, but it was still there.

By comparison, the neighbouring house was in tatters, with smoke still rising from within and no sign of life to be seen or heard.

"Hello," she called. "Hello. Can anybody hear me? Is anybody there? Hello! Hello! Do you need help?"

Her voice grew louder and louder, but there was no reply. She slowly made her way through the barely recognisable, litter-strewn garden, back to the house, then out through the debris to the street beyond, where she stopped at the gateway and looked about.

The scene of total devastation that met her eyes would haunt her forever. The road and the footpath were strewn with smoking rubble. Firemen and ARP Wardens raged in battle with flames and burning embers. Ambulance and Red Cross personnel bore stretchers and supported the walking wounded. A seemingly endless procession of shocked men, women and children gingerly picked their way through the smouldering chaos.

Elizabeth stood stock still, uncertain of what to do next. Her eyes searched in the vain hope that her parents would be amongst those who were headed in her direction, but even as she scanned the street, a growing feeling of deep-seated anxiety told her they would not return.

A young boy she judged to be around eleven years old, walked slowly towards her. He was pushing a toddler in a stroller, while two other small children clung tightly to his coat sleeves. A little boy perhaps eight or nine, and a girl of five or six.

"I want Mummy,." sobbed the little girl. "I want my Mummy."

The older boy said nothing, and as they got nearer, Elizabeth could see silent tears streaming down his face. All four of the children were covered in grime, and the younger boy shivered with cold and shock while the baby sat dazed and motionless.

"Where are you going?" Elizabeth asked the eldest boy, her heart going out to the little group. He looked at her and shook his head.

"I don't know," he answered, his voice strained and thick with emotion.

"We're just following the others. Do you know where I should take them, Miss? Where are *you* going?"

"I'm going to look for my parents because they went out last night and they haven't come home yet. Where are your parents?"

The boy swallowed hard, and his shoulders shook as the silent tears gave way to gut-wrenching sobs.

"Our Mum died," he wept. "Last night, when the roof came down, she was hit by a big wooden beam. I tried to move it off her, but I couldn't, and then I realised she wasn't breathing anymore."

Elizabeth put a consoling arm around his heaving shoulders.

"Our Dad's joined up," continued the boy.

"He's somewhere in France, I think. How will I tell him what's happened?" His voice trailed off, and his troubled eyes looked pleadingly at Elizabeth.

"What should I do?" he asked her.

"How about we look for help together?"

She forced herself to smile as she looked around the frightened and forlorn little band of children that stood before her. All she knew for certain was that she must do the right thing. That was what her parents would expect of her.

"What's your name?" she asked the eldest boy.

"I'm Charlie, and this is Jack and Betsy and the baby's Tom."

"Well, I'm Elizabeth."

She took hold of the stroller as she spoke.

"Betsy and Jack, you both hold tight to Charlie, and I'll push Tom. Come on, then. Let's find somewhere for you to be safe."

She smiled encouragingly, though inside she felt as lost as the children. She told herself she must be strong; that appearances were everything; that she would find her parents later and they would be proud that she had done the right thing.

They walked on together in silence, stumbling and tripping over obstacles that blocked their progress, until Elizabeth caught sight of a Red Cross truck in the distance.

"There we are," she said, "the Red Cross will help us."

"Will they know where your Mummy is, Miss Elizabeth?" Betsy spoke for the first time.

"I shouldn't think so, but perhaps we can ask them."

"They might know where our dad is too," suggested a hopeful Jack.

Charlie shook his head.

"Only the army will know *that* Jack. We'll have to ask *them*."

They had reached the truck by this time, and as they stepped alongside it, Elizabeth approached a young woman dressed in the familiar Red Cross nurse's uniform.

"Would you be able to help us?" she asked.

"The children here lost their mother and their home in last night's raid. Is there somewhere they can go? A shelter? A school or a church, perhaps?"

The woman looked back at Elizabeth with a weary smile.

"I think the Police are trying to arrange something for displaced persons. Do the children have any other relatives? Are you related to them?"

"No. I just happened upon them. I don't think they have anyone else to turn to. Their father is in France."

A short conversation with Charlie confirmed that there were no other relatives in Birmingham, but they had a Granny in Hereford. The lady from the Red Cross looked thoughtful. She was from Hereford herself. Perhaps if Charlie knew their Grans' address, she could get a message to her later and see if the children could go there. They'd need a place to stay in Birmingham for tonight, at least, though.

Elizabeth didn't hesitate.

"They can stay with me," she offered. "I'm sure my parents will agree. We have a shelter if the planes come back, so they should be safe until proper arrangements can be made."

"Thank you. That would be wonderful. Where are your parents at the moment?"

"I'm not sure. They were out last night at the Town Hall when the planes came over. I imagine they spent the night in a public shelter. Father's an ARP Warden. He's most likely helping somewhere. I just stepped out to search for them."

A concerned look flashed across the young nurse's face. She reached out and put a hand on Elizabeth's arm.

"I'm so sorry," she said, her voice not much more than a whisper, "I have to tell you... it might not be true... but the Police said... and I think they're pretty sure..."

Her voice trailed off, and a feeling of dread washed over Elizabeth.

"Sure, of what? What is it?"

"I think the Town Hall was one of the first buildings hit last night. The Town Hall, The University and The Art Gallery were all destroyed, and the roof of The Council House was damaged by fire. I'm so sorry. I don't know if they've found any survivors, but we can ask the Police or a Warden."

Elizabeth felt faint and tightened her grip on the stroller to stop herself from falling. Her parents, the university *and* her job. Her whole life. *All gone?* Just like that? No. It couldn't be true. Surely not.

"Try not to worry, Miss Elizabeth. I can see a policeman over there. Let's see if he can help find them. Come on."

Charlie took Elizabeth by the elbow as he spoke, steering her in the right direction and urging the Red Cross Nurse to join them. Sergeant Jones, however, could offer no solace. He could only confirm that The University and several civic buildings had been among those destroyed.

The deep concern on Elizabeth's face, and the plight of the children, did however prompt him to call to a nearby colleague for assistance, and they swiftly formed a plan of action. Sergeant Jones and his Constable would check out the children's address and confirm the situation both there and at the Town Hall.

Meanwhile, Elizabeth would take nurse Jenny and the children home to her place to wait away from the bitter cold until the police could get news to them.

The house, with its missing windows and damaged roof, was almost as cold as the outdoors, so Elizabeth and little Betsy searched out some warm woollen blankets while Jenny and the two older boys made their way to the yard in search of something to board up the missing windows.

They returned a short while later flushed with success, carrying a bundle of discarded fence pickets, along with the door and roofing of the garden shed, the latter of which had also relinquished a hammer and a box of nails.

Elizabeth meanwhile had discovered an old camp burner and a bottle of paraffin, which had enabled her to boil the kettle. A tin of biscuits still sat on the table from the night before, and a search of the pantry unveiled tins of condensed milk, tea and cocoa.

By the time the police arrived the windows were boarded up, and the little group was settled at the kitchen table, wrapped in blankets, sipping hot drinks and devouring home baked biscuits.

As he walked hesitantly into the room with slow, deliberate footsteps, Sergeant Jones inwardly marvelled at their calm resourcefulness. The news he and his constable had ascertained was the worst possible for everyone. He solemnly removed his helmet, clasping it to his chest, then nervously cleared his throat as he took another step towards the table. The two young women and their small charges looked up at him hopefully, but there was no real need for him to speak. His troubled expression said it all.

"I'm so sorry," he consoled them in a gruff, kindly voice.

"So sorry."

He confirmed that Charlie was right about his mother's passing and explained to Elizabeth that while no trace of her own parents had yet been found, there was little hope that they could have survived the direct hit on the Town Hall.

The next few days passed in a blur for Elizabeth. Her parents' bodies were uncovered from the rubble, and she was called upon to identify them and make the necessary funeral arrangements.

The kindly Sergeant Jones was a tower of strength to Elizabeth throughout, while Jenny's help was used to find the children's Gran, Ivy.

News of her daughter's passing hit Ivy hard, but she was determined the children should become her first priority. She caught the next train from Hereford to Birmingham in order to escort them home and to make her own funeral arrangements for *their* mother.

Elizabeth and Jenny took the children to meet the train, and as Ivy stepped down onto the platform and the children ran to hug her, she looked at the two young women through tears of gratitude.

"Thank you both so much," she sobbed. "I don't know what would have become of them all on their own."

"Don't cry, Gran. We were fine. I was looking after the little ones before Miss Elizabeth found us."

"Of course, you were, Charlie."

Ivy smiled at him fondly through her tears as Jack and Betsy chimed in with their contributions to the events of the past few days.

"Well, you've all had a very big adventure, I'm sure."

"They have all been very brave and very well-behaved," smiled Jenny.

"And an immense help," added Elizabeth.

"We shall miss them very much when you take them home."

Two days later, Elizabeth stood at the station waving until the train for Hereford disappeared from sight. A huge surge of loneliness suddenly washed over her. Jenny, too, was returning to Hereford with them, and as she slowly made her way home, the reality of her situation hit Elizabeth for the first time.

Then, as she turned the key in the lock and stepped into the cold, empty house, she burst into tears. She sat alone at the kitchen table weeping inconsolably, all the heartache and horrors of the past week playing over and over in her head like the hideous tale of a *Penny Dreadful.*

She finally sobbed herself into a fitful sleep until the loud, frightening whine of an air-raid siren woke her with a sudden start. She pulled herself together then, making the now familiar nightly run to the shelter in the garden in record time. The dark, empty space was strangely soothing, and the solace gave her the opportunity to gather her thoughts. Sitting there, alone in the dark, she formed a plan, and as the sounds of the air raid faded away and the first signs of morning crept over the city, Elizabeth rose wearily to her feet and slowly trudged back across the garden to the house.

Her newly formed plan whirred around and around in her head, gaining momentum with every step she took. Her parents would want her to be strong. To make the most of her current situation, and above all else, to do the right thing.

It had occurred to her as she undertook her lonely vigil in the shelter that, like Jenny, she too could make a useful contribution to the war effort. She may not have Jenny's nursing skills, but she had never been afraid of hard work, and there would be plenty of areas where an extra pair of hands would be welcomed. To start with, she could offer temporary accommodation to those whose homes had been destroyed. With that thought foremost in her mind, she made her way upstairs to make an immediate start in preparing the unused bedrooms.

The broken windowpanes and missing roof tiles would need to be repaired, then if not perfect, the rooms would at least be adequate and secure. A comfortable haven for the homeless. For her part, she would move to her parents' room.

The project kept her occupied for several days, giving her both a sense of purpose and a reason to carry on.

Elizabeth left her parents' room till last. She had kept the door firmly closed, unable to venture through it since that dreadful night when her world fell apart. She paused now at the threshold, took a deep breath and turned the handle. The room was exactly as it had been left. Mother's jewellery box remained open on the dressing table, the slippers she had been wearing earlier that fateful day sat discarded on the floor, and Father's tie hanger lay on the bed, its contents spread across the counterpane like a bunch of colourful ribbons on display at the haberdashery shop. Everything seemed so normal that for one moment, Elizabeth felt the past few days must have been no more than a terrible nightmare. She made her way to the bed and sat for a moment, running her fingers gently over the abandoned neckties, then reached for a favoured blue one and placed it around her neck, carefully tying a knot the way her father had shown her to do with her school tie. She lifted the silky fabric to her lips and closed her eyes, remembering.

The sound of loud knocking on the front door snapped her out of her reverie, and she made her way downstairs, wondering who might be visiting so early in the day. To her delight, it was Jenny.

"I'm back in Birmingham for a few days." She smiled.

"Hoped that perhaps you might like some company."

"Yes, please! Especially if you don't mind helping me prepare the house for displaced persons."

As the two girls caught up over a cup of tea, Elizabeth filled Jenny in on her plans to offer rooms to those who had been left homeless by the blitz.

"I'd like to do more, though," she confided. "I have no particular skills like you do, but there must be something I can help with."

The answer to her dilemma presented itself the following day in a manner she could never have expected. The heart-breaking task of clearing her parents' room completed, the girls had moved their focus downstairs to Father's office, where the contents of a large filing cabinet presented the most challenging task, as they decided which papers should be kept for future reference, and which could be safely discarded. As Jenny reached into the drawer labelled 'E', she pulled out a large manilla envelope marked 'Elizabeth.'

"Here," she said, passing it to her friend, "this is addressed to you."

A puzzled look crossed Elizabeth's face as she opened the envelope and carefully removed its contents. Her eyes scanned the opening line of the first page, over and over, as she struggled to come to terms with what she was reading.

"No," she whispered. "No. It can't be true. No. NO!"

The pages slipped from her grasp, falling silently to her lap, and she stared blankly at Jenny.

"What is it, Elizabeth? Whatever is it?"

"It says that I'm adopted."

Elizabeth gathered the papers from her lap and handed them to Jenny as she spoke.

"I never knew. They never said. I had no idea."

"It says here that you were adopted from the orphanage at Leominster Priory."

"Yes. But why? It doesn't say why."

Elizabeth found it impossible to carry on clearing out the office after that. The revelation burned in her mind and her heart, consuming her every thought. *Why had she been adopted? Why had Mother and Father never told her? Who and where were her biological parents? Did they miss her? Wonder what had become of her?*

Elizabeth felt the rug had been pulled from underneath her. Her whole world turned upside down, and the more she struggled to make sense of it all, the more she felt she was falling into a deep, dark hole. *Who was she?*

"You need to find some answers."

Jenny seemed to read her mind.

"I have an idea. You can say no if you don't like it, but it might help. I saw a poster at the train station on my way here. The Land Army is looking for women to help in Herefordshire, and Leominster is one of the towns they mentioned. It's less than an hour from here, so you could easily come home on your day off if you wanted, and you could visit The Priory Orphanage to see what you can find out about your adoption."

"The Land Army? Farming? Do you think they'd take me?"

"Of course. You're young and fit, and you love gardening. It could be just what you're looking for, to help with the war effort. You'll have accommodation provided and make new friends. Do you think you might look into it?"

Elizabeth stared at her friend, her mind racing.

"You really think I could do it?"

"Of course, I do."

"Oh Jenny, thank you. I should never have thought of it for myself, but you're right. It's the perfect answer all round."

As if to confirm her decision was indeed the right one, just three nights later, as she kept a lonely vigil in the Anderson Shelter during yet another night raid, the house suffered a direct hit and burned to the ground.

Chapter – 2

Elizabeth's application to join the Land Army was received with open arms, and as she boarded the train from Birmingham to Leominster, she could scarcely believe how quickly and dramatically her life had changed.

Sergeant Jones, who had been keeping a fatherly eye on her, insisted on seeing her off, and as the train lurched and pulled away from the platform, he removed his helmet and waved it enthusiastically.

"Take care, Elizabeth," he called. "I know you'll do a grand job."

He had already reminded her that both Jenny and he would always be on hand should she need anything.

As she settled back in her seat, Elizabeth felt butterflies churning wildly in her stomach. Birmingham and all that was familiar to her slowly disappeared from sight, and fear of the unknown threatened to overwhelm her as she wondered what lay ahead and whether she was doing the right thing. Well, it was too late to turn back now, she told herself. There was nothing left here for her anyway. She must be strong and do her bit.

Her anxiety eased a little as she stepped down onto the platform at Leominster. Two other young women who had been seated nearby, disembarked with her, and they all stood around now looking unsure what to do next.

As the train disappeared into the distance, a pleasant-looking woman dressed in a warm tweed coat and sturdy leather boots hurried towards them.

"Are you the young ladies for The Land Army?" she asked cheerfully. "We are so pleased to have you here," she continued without waiting for a reply,

"I've come to take you to your new digs. Grab your bags and follow on. The truck's just through here. I'm Mavis, by the way. Call me Mave. Everyone else does."

She led the way through the station waiting room and ticket office as she spoke, the three girls trailing behind, struggling to keep up with her brisk pace.

"Don't worry," she reassured them as she helped them climb hesitantly onto the back of a small farm truck. "You'll soon get used to it."

Without further ado, she took her place behind the wheel and set the truck in motion.

"Any of you ladies drive?" she asked hopefully but as all three replied "No," in unison, she sighed deeply and shook her head.

"Just have to teach you then. Easy when you know how."

She drove on in silence for a while, and the girls took the opportunity to introduce themselves. By the time Mave brought the truck to a halt, a budding friendship had developed between them.

"Here we are, then. Home sweet home."

As they clambered down to the ground, the girls looked around with interest. 'Home', it appeared, was a long wooden building set in a field on the outskirts of a small village. As she turned to Mave, Elizabeth looked a little concerned.

"I thought Leominster was a market town."

"It is. This is Kingsland. Leominster is just a short drive away. You will be picked up and dropped back daily for work. Otherwise, you can catch the bus to town."

Mave smiled, a little perplexed at Elizabeth's apparent disappointment, and Elizabeth nodded, the troubled little flicker of a frown fading as quickly as it had appeared. She followed the other girls inside then, where they were confronted by rows of bunk beds to either side of the building, with a central wood stove doing its best to keep the winter chill at bay.

"Right ladies, choose a spare bunk and pop your bags down. You can unpack later, but we need to sort out your uniforms before you do that."

The ever-organised Mavis then led her charges to the supply hut, where she busied herself gathering the required measurements from each of them as she handed out the extensive range of items that were considered necessary to cover all eventualities.

There were corduroy knee breeches, woollen stockings and brown leather shoes, neat cream skirts and warm green jumpers. There were Wellies and oil skin macs for days of inclement weather, and even accessories were provided, in the form of beige hats and wide leather belts, but what the girls liked most of all, were the three-quarter length dark beige coats, with their smart white wool lining.

Uniform distribution was completed, and Mavis escorted the young women back to their quarters.

"Right-oh, I'm off," she announced. "You should just have time to get yourselves sorted before the others return and dinner is served. See you all at oh-six thirty hours tomorrow."

As the door to the hut closed behind her, the three girls dropped their clothing bundles on their beds and turned to look at each other.

"This is it then," declared Rita, "no going back now."

"I've never had so many new clothes all at once," confided Dorothy, "and I've never had a coat as lovely as this one."

She held up the new coat as she spoke.

"Who'd have thought," she said, speaking almost to herself as she hung the favoured garment in the locker by her bed, "I never expected all this."

Elizabeth smiled at her.

"Yes," she agreed, "It's all, *most* unexpected."

Little did she know then, how the unexpected would become a regular occurrence in her life over the course of the next few years. While the workload was hard and far from that she was used to, Elizabeth settled into her new lifestyle with total commitment.

Despite her petite stature and ladylike demeanour, which quickly earned her the nickname of Lady Liz, her stamina and determination were admired by all. Whether hoeing or stone picking, building hay and wheat racks, stacking corn, or leading the horses as they ploughed the fields, she toiled stoically. If the back-breaking tasks of loading carts and planting and picking potatoes left her aching and exhausted, she shrugged it off. The nation needed to be fed, and in Elizabeth's mind, she was simply doing her bit. Doing the right thing.

It became apparent from the very first day, however, that time off was a precious commodity and that in order to find the information she longed to know, she would have to forgo a much-anticipated Saturday night movie at the Kingsland Village Hall with the other girls and knuckle down instead to the task at hand.

Having feigned a headache in order to excuse herself from the outing, Elizabeth headed to bed for an early night, planning to rise before dawn and make her way back to Leominster. She slept fitfully until the first sound of birdlife told her morning had finally arrived, then she slipped out of bed and dressed quietly, taking care not to disturb the others.

As she silently made her way out into the cold, Elizabeth hoped fervently that she would find The Priory was open nice and early on a Sunday.

Feeling quite unable to wait for the bus, she struck out on foot, walking at a brisk trot that saw her reach the town of Leominster in just a little under an hour. The Priory Church was easy to find, but to her dismay, the doors were firmly shut, as was the case at the neighbouring collection of Old Priory buildings. A wave of disappointment washed over her.

"Can I help you, Miss?"

The man's voice came from behind her, and she turned to see an elderly gentleman walking towards her.

"Was it the church you were wanting?" he continued as he reached her side.

"Reverend Peter Green," he offered by way of introduction, "Vicar of this Parish."

As Elizabeth introduced herself, the reverend escorted his early morning visitor back to the church, showing her into the vestry and offering her both a seat and a cup of tea.

"Now, Miss Elizabeth, perhaps you would like to tell me what it is that brings you out so early on a cold Sunday morning. I fear it must be a matter of grave importance."

Encouraged by his kindly, caring manner, and with a little prompting on his part, Elizabeth found herself divulging the series of events that had befallen her over the past few weeks. To her horror, she felt hot tears running down her face as she told him of the discovery that she had been adopted from The Priory Orphanage.

"I'm so sorry." She sobbed softly. "It's just that I don't really know who I am any more. Why did my birth parents give me away, do you suppose?"

The Reverend Peter gently patted her hand.

"If you've time to stay for Matins, then directly after the service ends, we shall search for your records."

He smiled encouragingly.

"Now wipe your eyes and finish your tea, my dear. I promise to keep my sermon short," he added with a wink as he offered her a plate of plain wine biscuits.

Elizabeth took a deep breath to calm herself.

"Thank you, Reverend." She smiled wanly.

"You must talk for as long as you wish," she added politely as she reached for a biscuit.

"Is there anything I can do to help you prepare for the service?" she asked, regaining her usual poise and composure. "Perhaps I could lay out the hymn books."

True to his word, the vicar kept his sermon short, and with the last parishioner farewelled, he turned to Elizabeth, who stood waiting patiently inside the church door.

"If you could be so kind as to gather up the hymn books again, my dear, I shall remove my vestments and we'll be on our way to the Old Priory Office, where all our parish records are held."

The revelations divulged by the ensuing search were not what Elizabeth had either expected or hoped for. The adoption papers she had brought with her held scant information, but they did disclose the names of her birth parents, giving her a reliable starting point for her search. She handed the papers to the Reverend Peter, and as he read over them, he drew a sharp breath before peering intently at his young visitor.

"Of course," he said, "I should have realised. Samuel and Anne Harris. I knew them both, and you look so much like her."

He paused.

"It's not a happy story, I'm afraid, child," he continued, "but I can tell you what happened if that is what you want."

Elizabeth swallowed nervously.

"Yes, please," she replied quietly.

Her heart raced as he sat down opposite her. The Reverend closed his eyes, sighed deeply and slowly recounted the tragic details of past events as he recalled them.

Samuel, it seemed, had been a seasonal farm labourer with a talent for sketching and painting. His artworks of Leominster and the surrounding countryside were popular with both locals and visitors to the town. He sold them at the weekly market and they provided a source of income between farm jobs.

He joined up and fought in France in the First World War until he was invalided home after being almost totally blinded by mustard gas. Unable to find work or cope with his new situation, he eventually took the only path he could see open to him. His body was found in the River Kenwater, and his distraught wife, who was with child at the time, found herself both penniless and homeless.

Forced to find accommodation at the workhouse, she eked out a living as a laundry maid. Shortly after Elizabeth's birth, Anne caught pneumonia and passed away herself, leading to Elizabeth's placement at the orphanage.

The Reverend Peter paused.

"Such a tragic story. I'm so sorry, my dear."

He put his hand on Elizabeth's shoulder and she looked up at him, blinking away her tears.

"Thank you," she whispered sadly, "at least I know now that they didn't just give me away because they didn't want me."

"Never, my dear. Never. Come."

He helped her to her feet and led her out to the cemetery, stopping at two simple crosses set side by side in the ground.

"We buried them here together. It seemed the right thing to do." Elizabeth nodded.

"Thank you," she whispered again.

"Perhaps you would like some time here alone," offered The Reverend, as Elizabeth slowly knelt and reached out to gently touch the sad, timeworn little crosses.

"We can talk again whenever you like."

"Thank you," she replied once more as he took his leave.

"Thank you for everything."

For the first time since she happened upon the adoption papers, Elizabeth felt at peace. She had found her birth parents, and while their story was sad, she could rest in the knowledge that she had never been unwanted.

Elizabeth became a regular visitor at The Priory after that, striking up an easy friendship with The Reverend Peter and helping out wherever she could. In return, he shared his memories and did his best to answer her myriad of questions, though he felt instinctively that this young woman, who had been brought up in comfortable, upper-middle-class surroundings, may struggle to come to terms with the reality of her birth right.

Elizabeth did find the truth difficult to accept. Secretly, she had hoped that at least one of her parents might still be there. That their circumstances may have changed, and they would be pleased to have her back in their life. While things were not what she had hoped for, she was still determined to find out all she could about the lives of Samuel and Anne.

She was, therefore, delighted when the reverend found the address where they had been living at the time of Samuel's death. Armed with the relevant information, Elizabeth took herself off in search of Bridge Street, where the old farm workers' tied cottages mingled with what must have been half a dozen public houses. The quaint little black and white cottages were tiny in comparison to her home in Birmingham.

A large number of children played outside in the street, and she wondered where they all slept. Their scruffy appearance unsettled her. A small girl in a thin cotton dress with the hem hanging down stood shivering in the doorway of one of the little houses, watching two older boys kick a tin up and down the street. One of the boys wore mismatched shoes, while the other wore an ill-fitting jumper with gaping holes that were causing it to unravel. They all looked to Elizabeth as though they were in need of a bath.

Further down the street a shoddily clad, tired looking woman with a baby on her hip and another on the way, was calling in her older children for their supper. Their thin little bodies told Elizabeth that the meal would be a meagre affair.

Saddened and dismayed by what she saw, Elizabeth turned to retrace her steps back to the bus stop. She'd not gone far when the door to one of the public houses suddenly flew open, and a young man, smelling equally of both ale and cider, lurched through it. As he staggered into her path, he reached out his arm to make a pass at her. Elizabeth recoiled in horror, wildly swinging her handbag at him in self-defence. He cursed loudly, then as he lost his balance and toppled over into the street, Elizabeth ran off as fast as her legs would carry her.

As the bus slowly made its way back to Kingsland, she sat motionless, her mind churning over and over. The realisation that had fate not intervened she would have been raised in that sad, unfamiliar environment sent shivers down her spine.

By the time she reached the safe haven of her temporary home, she had determined to make the most of the opportunities she had been given.

She would strive to live up to the high standards the Pritchards had instilled in her. Surely Anne and Samel would want that, too. She was not ashamed of them, but the thought of what other people might think should they learn the truth troubled her immensely. She knew the locals called her Lady Liz behind her back and she worried they would mock her if they found out the reality of her situation. The Reverend Peter would, of course, keep her secret safe, and for her part, she would take comfort in the knowledge that she had been both loved and wanted. Samuel and Anne had done all they could. Their lives had been tragic through no fault of their own, and now she must honour their memory and make them proud, just as she must do for David and Eunice Pritchard, who had so kindly and generously raised her as their own. She felt she owed them all so much.

Elizabeth settled into her role as a land girl with a renewed sense of purpose. She helped out at The Priory on a regular basis and became a familiar figure on the streets of Leominster and Kingsland.

On her rare days off, she would travel to Hereford to visit Nurse Jenny and check on Ivy and the children, or she would make the journey to Birmingham to see Sergeant Jones.

She slowly began to feel a sense of belonging. A feeling that was further enhanced when Jenny accepted a position at the nearby Baron's Cross American Military Base Hospital. The two of them would meet up for trips to the market and the movies, or attend the weekly dances that were arranged to entertain the visiting and recovering service men.

As the war raged on, the combination of hard work and a busy social life gave Elizabeth little time to dwell on her past.

Peace, however, brought with it many changes.

Nurse Jenny, who had fallen in love with an American military doctor, was married and sailed away to make a new life for herself in California while the children's father arrived home safely and moved his family, including Ivy, to Bristol for a fresh start.

With the Land Army disbanded, the other girls all moved on too, most of them happily returning home to re-join family.

Elizabeth felt a growing sense of loss and loneliness as one by one her friends disappeared. There were no happy reunions for her, just a stark reminder of all that had been taken from her. She toyed with the idea of returning to Birmingham, but the very thought of it, along with the memories it evoked, filled her with anxiety. Where could she go? What could she do?

Feeling completely at a loss, Elizabeth decided to do what she had done so many times over the past few years and headed off to The Priory in search of Reverend Peter.

He was nowhere to be found, so she turned to the graveyard to find solace instead by the two little crosses she had come to know so well. She sat motionless, her mind in a state of turmoil, until, still unable to find any answers to her quandary, she finally rose to her feet and slowly made her way back towards the bus station.

She'd not gone far down Church Street before a stone in her shoe caused her to stop and remove it. As she slipped the worn leather pump back on her foot, Elizabeth looked up, noticing for the first time that she had paused outside an Art Gallery. A small painting of the River Kenwater caught her eye; its soft, appealing beauty drew her in, compelling her to take a closer look. She caught her breath, and her heart skipped a beat as the artist's signature suddenly seemed to jump off the canvas at her. *Samuel A. Harris.* Her father! The painting was his! Surely, it was a sign that he was speaking to her. Telling her to stay on in Leominster.

A tingle ran through her as she felt compelled to make her way into the gallery. She was determined to make the painting her own, no matter its cost. Elizabeth's conviction that the small framed canvas was sent to guide her gained momentum as she reached the shop counter, where taped to the front of the cash register was a notice reading, *Shop and Office Assistant required.*

A slightly dishevelled middle-aged man approached her.

"Can I be of assistance, Miss?" he asked, smiling pleasantly as he pushed his spectacles back in place.

"Yes, please." Elizabeth's voice was clear and steady, belying the turmoil she felt in the pit of her stomach.

"Firstly, I should like to purchase the Samuel Harris painting of the Kenwater that you have in your window, then I should like to apply for your job vacancy."

The bespectacled gentleman smiled again and nodded as he made his way to the window and uplifted the canvas.

"Here you go, Miss. An exquisite work. You have excellent taste. Samuel Harris is a very favoured and respected artist in these parts."

He handed the little artwork to her as he spoke, and she took it from him eagerly, holding it almost reverently as she gazed at it adoringly.

It seemed to Mr. Rundle, the purveyor, that his young customer was entranced by every brush stroke.

"The painting is a little costly, I'm afraid." He smiled apologetically. "And the job doesn't pay a great deal."

Elizabeth appeared unperturbed.

"That's all right. As long as the salary is enough to live on, then I would love the job if you'd have me. I do have a little experience," she added modestly as she completed her purchase.

"I rather thought you might," replied Mr Rundle.

He led her to the office so that they could talk uninterrupted, and by the time she was ready to take her leave of him some sixty minutes later, Mr Rundle sat in stunned silence, unable to believe his luck. He had been looking to fill the vacancy for some time, and now, quite out of nowhere, Elizabeth had appeared. Not only was she beautiful with charming manners, but her knowledge of art history and her past work experience were, to him, a dream-cum-true! He felt obliged to add another shilling a week to her pay, feeling sure it would be worth every penny to have her on board.

As he showed her to the door and warmly shook her hand, both Mr George Rundle and Miss Elizabeth Pritchard felt the day had come to the perfect conclusion.

'Lady Liz' sat on the bus back to Kingsland, clasping her precious package close to her heart, misty tears wetting her cheeks and a warm feeling of 'belonging' washing over her. A trembling smile touched her lips as she told herself that tomorrow, she would look for a room to rent in Leominster, and next Monday, she would start her new job.

It was on an errand to hand deliver a letter from Mr Rundle to the manager of the nearby branch of Lloyds Bank that Elizabeth first came to the attention of Robert Moncreiff.

He looked up from the huge ledger that lay spread out in front of him as his junior clerk showed her into his office. Immediately struck by Elizabeth's delicate beauty and refined manner, Robert promptly set about making it his business to find out all he could about Miss Elizabeth Pritchard.

She, in return, found Robert Moncreiff very much to *her* liking. He was a tall, aristocratic-looking man with a great deal of presence about him. Though a few years older than herself, Robert was still very young to be a bank manager, which fact only served to impress her further. Following a whirlwind courtship, they married just a few months later. The Reverend Peter took the service, and Sergeant Jones travelled from Birmingham to act as 'father of the bride.'

Elizabeth settled happily into her new life as the wife of a respected bank manager. She enjoyed working for the kindly Mr Rundle, and loved spending her days surrounded by objects d'art, before returning home each evening to Robert.

She felt quite certain that all four of her parents would approve of the choices she had made, but as she stopped off at the butcher's shop one day on her way home from work, she overheard two local women discussing their disapproval of folk from the workhouse.

It seemed they felt any child born there did so out of wedlock and could never amount to anything. They seemed firmly of the opinion that both the workhouse and the orphanage should be closed down to avoid their inhabitants giving the town a bad name.

Elizabeth felt hot and cold all over. She had never felt ashamed of who she was before. Her parents were married, their deaths were tragic, and she herself had done nothing to incur such uncharitable comments.

As the two women departed, still in amicable agreement as to their shared opinion, Elizabeth made a silent vow that nobody should ever find out the truth about her past.

Her fear of being 'discovered' began to overwhelm her. Robert knew the truth, of course, and like the Reverend Peter, he would keep her secret safe, but the thought of becoming the centre of town gossip and a figure of ridicule played heavily on Elizabeth's mind.

What if someone *did* uncover the truth, and it badly affected Robert's position and his ability to advance his career because his wife had come from the workhouse? Perhaps she should encourage him to seek a position elsewhere. *London would be good,* she thought. There were some lovely leafy suburbs where they could live; there would be wonderful opportunities for Robert to advance his career. The secrets of her past would remain just that.

Chapter – 3

Far away in the distance, the Priory bells tolled the hour. The small girl with the pink dress tucked up into her knickers stood stock still and counted the chimes. Five of them. Five o'clock! It couldn't be! It seemed that only a few minutes had passed since the group of children gleefully ran out of the school gates, over the meadow and down the hill to where the river trickled happily over the big moss-covered stones she was standing on.

"Was that *five* chimes? Already? It couldn't be, could it?"

"I don't know. I wasn't counting."

"Yes. It was five."

The colour drained from the small girl's face.

"I have to go. See you tomorrow," she called as she turned abruptly and began to make her way back to the riverbank.

The big, smooth boulders were slippery underfoot, causing her to tread carefully despite her haste. She had just one last slimy green stone to manoeuvre when she lost her footing and slipped, tumbling into the water with a splash. Great whoops of laughter wafted across the river from the direction of a large willow tree where the other children sat lined up on the bent, gnarled branch they had knick-named the Devil's Elbow.

"Don't laugh at her. It's not funny. She might have hurt herself," shouted Joshua Bates as he jumped from his perch on the overhanging branch and waded through the water towards the little girl. They always picked on Hilly just because she was the smallest. It wasn't fair.

"You all right Hilly?" he asked, as he helped the child back onto her feet. She looked at him, her soft brown eyes brimming with tears.

"Yes, thank you, Joshua," she whispered, blinking fiercely to keep the tears from spilling down her cheeks. She couldn't let Joshua see her cry. At almost eleven, Joshua was the eldest, and everyone looked up to him. The others had stopped laughing now, and they, too, came to see if she was all right. They formed a circle around her, and she stood in the middle of them, bravely ignoring the fact that she had skinned her knee and it was bleeding.

"Your Mum will kill you," offered Maisie Cowan.

"Look at your new dress. You've torn it."

Hilary Anne Moncrieff looked down at the pretty pink dress she'd tried so hard to keep dry and shuddered. Maisie was right. There was a big tear right by where she'd cut her knee, and the whole dress was sopping wet and clinging to her like a limp rag. Mother would be furious.

"I'll walk home with you if you like and explain that it was an accident," offered Joshua.

Hilly nodded. She would like that. She'd feel much braver about confronting Mother with Joshua by her side, and Mother wouldn't be so likely to fly into a rage if Joshua was there because she always worried so much about what other people would think. Yes. It would all be much easier if Joshua took her home, she decided, as she sat on the grass and buckled on her sandals. She looked up at him and smiled gratefully.

"Your knee's bleeding. Have you got a hanky or something I can tie around it?"

"Mother always puts one in my bag."

Joshua nodded and handed Hilly her school bag. *Of course, Mrs Moncrieff would make sure she had a hanky,* he thought as he took it from the little girl and tied it firmly around her knee. She was a very particular woman, Hilly's mother. He'd heard his mum say so many a time. He pulled the child to her feet and slung their schoolbags over his shoulder.

"Can you walk all right?"

She nodded, and they set off together across the meadow that led back up to the school. Any other day, Hilly would have stopped to pick big bunches of the wildflowers that grew in great drifts along the way. She would take them home, and Mother would put them in the shiny brass vase that was really an empty shell case Daddy's father brought back from France after the Great War.

Today, though, a little voice inside her told her it would be wisest just to get home as quickly as possible. She was already at least an hour late, and tea would be on the table, and Mother would be getting anxious. Mother worried about everything.

Hilly cast one last look of longing at the bright yellow cowslips that danced merrily in the breeze, then turned and urged Joshua to hurry. She stumbled as they scrambled up the hill, and Joshua took her hand to keep her from falling again as they scurried across the schoolyard. They accelerated their pace even further as they hurried on through the town, increasing their stride with every step until by the time they reached Rylands Road, they were running as quickly as Hilly's skinned knee would permit.

They were hot and bothered and gasping for breath, but a sense of urgency had overtaken them, and they ran on as though their lives depended on it until flushed and dishevelled, they burst headlong through the door of *Elm Cottage* like a pair of startled rabbits.

"Hilary Anne Moncrieff! Where have you been!"

The child froze in her tracks.

"Look at the state of you! How dare you stay out till this time and then come into my house looking like something the cat dragged in! Look at that dress. Brand new, and you've ruined it already!"

"She didn't tear it on purpose, Mrs Moncrieff. Honestly, it was an accident. She slipped over. It's really very lucky that she wasn't badly hurt, though she did cut her knee, as you can see."

Elizabeth Moncrieff eyed up the young boy standing at her daughter's side. She'd seen him around before. He was one of those Bates children, if she wasn't mistaken.

"Yes, of course, I can see that. Thank you, young man." Her voice still had an edge to it. "It's very good of you to see Hilary Anne home, I'm sure, but I imagine your own mother is concerned as to *your* whereabouts this time of day. Or if she isn't, she should be."

Hilly threw an apologetic glance in Joshua's direction, then cast her eyes down at the floor. Despite their frantic dash, her wet hair was still dripping, and it was making a little puddle where she stood. Mother hadn't noticed that yet.

"I'm sure Mum'll understand my being a little late when I tell her about Hilly's accident," Joshua was saying.

"She'll just be concerned if Hilly's all right, that's all ~ and I'm sure she'd be happy to mend the dress."

"Hrmph!" Elizabeth threw him a scathing look, then bristled with indignation as Joshua chose to ignore it and turned his attention to her daughter instead.

"Hope your knee is all right, Hilly. See you at school tomorrow."

"Thank you, Joshua. Thank you for bringing me home."

The door had barely closed behind him before the tirade began. If Hilary Anne thought Mother hadn't noticed the puddle on the floor, she was mistaken, and she needn't think that just because she'd scratched her knee on something, she would get away with coming in late and ruining her new dress because she wouldn't. It simply would not do. Father did not work all hours of the day and night to provide for them, to have *her* go around spoiling expensive new dresses, and she wouldn't get another; she could count on that just as she could count on being sent to bed with no tea. As for letting that Bates boy walk her home! She'd told her before about hanging around with that lot.

Hilly sighed as she made her way upstairs to run a bath and divest herself of the wet dress. *She didn't mean to be troublesome,* she thought, *as she sank into the warm, soothing water and carefully untied the blood-stained handkerchief.* She took a deep breath and slowly lowered her injured knee until it was completely submerged. She held her breath until the graze stopped stinging and wondered why it was that Mother never took any notice when she was hurt or poorly.

Silent tears slid down the little girl's cheeks. She wished that Mother was more like Joshua's mother. Mrs Bates was always kind and cheerful. She couldn't understand why Mother always insisted on calling the Bates family *"that lot"* in a voice that suggested there was something wrong with them. Hilly liked all the Bates family. They were always so nice to her. *Not like Mother*, she thought, with a little twinge of sadness. *Mother can be very unkind when she chooses to be.*

Robert Moncrieff was tired. It had been a long day, and he was looking forward to a quiet evening, but before he even shut the front door behind him, Elizabeth was berating him.

"You're late," she complained.

"It's little wonder your daughter thinks nothing of strolling in whenever it pleases her."

Robert pursed his lips. He put his briefcase on the floor alongside the hall table, collected his mail from the top of the table, and made his way to the kitchen.

"Have you had a sherry?" he enquired.

"Yes. But I'll have another thank you." The words were spoken in such a manner as to convey to Robert the fact that Elizabeth felt she *needed* another sherry to help her come to terms with whatever it was that Hilary Anne had done to displease her. Robert handed her a glass, then sat down at the table and waited expectantly.

36

"That girl will be the death of me."

"What's she done now?"

"Only *ruined* her new dress."

"Oh, is that all?"

"*Is that all?* Liberty lawn is extremely expensive, Robert, as you well know."

"Then dress her in sackcloth, my dear."

Elizabeth scowled.

"There are standards to be maintained, Robert."

"Then dress her in Liberty lawn for Church if you must, but find something more suitable for school. She is an eight-year-old child, Elizabeth. Eight-year-old children spill paint on their clothes and get mud on their shoes."

Elizabeth sniffed.

"A little bit of paint I could wash out, but she's gone and torn a great hole in it."

"Then send it to Mrs Bates for mending."

"Send it to Margaret Bates. It was one of her brats that caused the problem in the first place. That oldest boy of hers marched in here with Hilary Anne, bold as you like and informed me it was lucky, she'd only grazed her knee and torn her dress."

"Why? What happened?"

"I have no idea. They came in here dripping water all over my clean floor, and that boy told me his mother would be happy to mend the dress. I bet she would. At a price, no doubt! And it will never be the same again anyway!"

"*Elizabeth! That is enough!*"

Robert Moncrieff banged his fist down on the table. It was all a storm in a teacup, as far as he was concerned. Of course, Margaret Bates would charge to mend the dress. It was her trade. Whatever did Elizabeth expect? He would pay the bill as he always did, and the dress would still be perfectly adequate for school and play. There was an end to it!

Robert turned his attention to the waiting mail, and Elizabeth sniffed as she took the plates from the warming drawer. It was all very well for Robert. He'd be the first to complain if she allowed Hilary Anne to turn into some kind of wild hoyden.

"Ah! Aunt Hilary would like us to visit," Robert's voice broke in on her thoughts.

"Oh?" the tone of her voice changed.

"Does she say when?"

"Next weekend. She's organising a fund-raising fete for the local church. White elephant, flower show, you know the sort of thing, and could use a few extra hands."

Elizabeth smiled pleasantly at her husband, her previous desire to convey to Robert that she was sorely vexed, curiously tempered by his intelligence.

"We shall have to arrange something for Hilary Anne. She'll only get in the way. Perhaps Miss Winter would stay with her."

"No. Hilly's invited, too. There's to be someone else staying with a child about her age."

"Does Aunt Hilary say who?"

"No. No, she doesn't mention a name." Robert scanned the page and shook his head.

"Old friends from the city she'd like us to meet. That's all she says."

It didn't really matter anyway, thought Elizabeth. Robert's Aunt Hilary moved in such excellent circles that the offspring of any of her acquaintances would surely make suitable friends for her young namesake.

Elizabeth smiled again as she sat down opposite Robert, and he heaved an inward sigh of relief. It appeared the storm had abated. Good old Aunt Hilary!

The delicious aroma of freshly baked bread wafted through the air as Hilly wandered down the street towards Bates Bakery. She paused momentarily to gaze through the little panes of glass at the shelves where Mr Bates displayed his cakes and buns, then carried on around the side of the shop to the back door, where she banged hard on the big, shiny brass knocker. As she stood back and waited for someone to come, a large black cat slowly stirred in the wooden planter box where it had chosen to take a snooze.

"Hello, you." A delighted Hilly bent down and gave it a pat. It purred happily, encouraging the little girl to pick it up, but as soon as her hands reached under it, the cat's demeanour changed. It clawed wildly at her, scratching her hands and her arms, and she sprang back in fright.

"Raven! Stop that!" Margaret Bates opened the door just in time to see what happened, and as the berated cat made a hasty departure, she turned to Hilly.

"Are you all right, dear?" she enquired, putting a comforting arm around the alarmed child.

"Goodness, look at those scratches. You'd best come in, and we'll clean them up."

She led Hilary Anne inside, past the door that would have taken them into the bakery, and past the little room where she worked as a seamstress.

"Josh! Lindy!" she called up the stairwell as they passed it by, "we have company!"

By the time she showed Hilly into the room at the end of the passage and settled her at the kitchen table, all four Bates children had joined them.

"Look what that Raven's gone and done to poor little Hilly," stated Mrs Bates, "and she was only trying to be nice to the silly thing."

"It's only because she's pregnant," explained Lindy kindly.

"Did you try to pick her up? She hates that at the moment, you see."

Lindy Bates was nine years old and already knew what she wanted to be when she grew up. Lindy wanted to be a vet and often hung around the local veterinary clinic after school in the hope that Mr Young would let her help with the animals in his care. She loved to feed them, and sometimes Mr Young would even *pay* her to help him clean the cages.

"Raven will be fine again once she's had her babies," Lindy advised Hilly with an air of quiet authority. She smiled knowledgeably at the little girl who was a whole six months her junior, in precisely the same way that Mr Young would smile at her, causing her mother to chortle fondly and declare that Lindy was nine going on ninety.

Six-year-old John Bates promptly informed Hilly in no uncertain terms that Raven scratched anyway.

"You have only to pull her tail to find that out," he stated firmly as he helped himself to a glass of milk. Lindy threw him a disparaging look and Joshua grinned.

"Susan dear." Margaret Bates turned to her eldest child and smiled fondly. "Why don't you pop along and see if your dad has got any currant buns left? You can tell him I said one for each of you and a nice fresh loaf for Hilly to take home to her mother."

She finished applying some Mercurochrome liquid to Hilary Anne's scratches as she spoke.

"Now, I noticed you had a package with you, dear. Would that be the dress you tore the other day? Joshua told me you'd be needing it mending. How's your poor knee now?" she inquired, prattling on in a kindly manner as she lifted the dress from its brown paper wrapping.

"You really have been in the wars, haven't you?… My word! What a beautiful dress, Hilly; no wonder your mother was upset!"

She ran her hands gently over the soft, fine fabric as she lay the garment on the table to inspect the damage. Her eyes looked lovingly at the dainty print; Margaret found herself wishing she could afford to clothe her girls in Liberty Lawn!

It must be wonderful, she thought to herself, *to not have to worry about watching every penny.*

She carefully lifted the torn edges of Hilly's dress and gently brought them together. There was no fabric missing.

"Tell your mum I'll be able to mend it so as you'll never notice." She smiled.

Hilly smiled back at her.

"Thank you, Mrs Bates."

"Not at all, dear. It'll be ready after school on Monday if you'd like to pick it up then."

"How much will it cost, please, Mrs Bates?"

"It'll be two shillings and sixpence, tell your mum."

"Half a crown! Good heavens!" came a voice from the doorway.

"Daylight robbery! Just as well, I managed to find a nice cob for you to take home."

As he spoke, Matthew Bates placed a brown paper bag in front of Hilly with one hand and a tray of buns and pastries in the middle of the table with the other.

"Little Saturday morning treat," he said with a wink.

The sound of a tinkling bell drifted along the hallway.

"No rest for the wicked." He sighed as he made his way back out of the room.

Hilly watched after him with interest. Mr Bates had an unusual way of walking. He limped and seemed almost to sway from side to side, just as a sailor might, and his right leg, which looked awfully stiff, moved quite differently to his left.

As she reached for a proffered currant bun, the child was consumed with curiosity as to why Mr Bates walked the way he did, but she was too polite to enquire as to the reason in front of Mrs Bates. Perhaps she would ask Joshua or Lindy some other time.

Elizabeth Moncrieff was delighted when Hilly handed her the loaf from Mr Bates.

"Well, that's very good of him, I must say." She smiled.

"He does very well, really, all things considered. It can't be easy for a big, strong man like that to lose his leg. He used to be a farmer's labourer, you know, before the war."

Hilly's mouth dropped open. *Lose his leg*! What was Mother talking about? Mr Bates might have a strange way of walking, but he had *two* legs. That was plain for anyone to see. Mother was obviously mistaken.

"Anyway," continued Elizabeth, "that nice fresh loaf will go very well with the cold meat and cheese I have set aside for lunch. Go and call your father Hilary Anne, there's a good girl."

Hilly was longing to know more about Mr Bates and his 'lost' leg, but Mother didn't mention him again other than to advise Father of his kindness in sending the fresh cob. All she could talk about over lunch was the impending visit to Aunt Hilary.

"You're very fortunate to be coming with us, you know, Hilary Anne," she advised her daughter.

"You'll have a lovely time. There'll almost certainly be pony rides at the fete, and Aunt Hilary has people from the city staying who have a little girl about your own age, so there'll be someone for you to play with."

"What's her name?"

"I don't know, dear, but I'm sure she'll be very nice. Aunt Hilary moves in excellent circles, you know."

Hilly looked perplexed. Mother was always saying that about Aunt Hilary, but as far as she was concerned, Aunt Hilary moved just like everybody else. To say she moved in circles was almost as strange as saying Mr Bates had lost one of his legs.

Hilly couldn't help but wonder if Mother was feeling quite all right, and she said as much to Joshua as they walked to the bakery together after school on Monday.

"Do you know Mother even said your father had lost one of his legs!"

"He did! It happened in the war."

"*No! How terrible!* Well, I'm very glad he found it again because otherwise, he wouldn't be able to walk at all, and that would be awful for him!"

"He didn't find it again, Hilly." Joshua suppressed a grin.

"He has an artificial leg now," he explained kindly.

"That's why he walks the way he does."

"You mean like a pirate's peg leg? How awful! Poor Mr Bates."

A troubled frown creased the little girl's brow.

"Does it hurt him?"

"Sometimes it does. Sometimes, he gets sores where the artificial leg fits onto his stump."

Hilly shuddered at the picture that Joshua's words had conjured up, and they walked on in silence until they reached the bakery, each of them thinking how glad they were to have their own two legs to carry them.

As Joshua let them in through the back door, Matthew Bates stepped out of the bakery to greet them.

"Hello there, you two. Hungry?" he asked, holding out a jam tart in each hand.

Hilly stood rooted to the spot, staring at him. How could he stand there, smiling at them and being so kind as though everything was perfectly normal when he must be reminded every time he moved an inch that everything was not and never would be again? Suddenly, without warning, she flung herself at him, throwing her arms around him and almost knocking him off balance.

"Oh, Mr Bates," she whispered, her voice trembling with emotion.

"Goodness! What's all this?" exclaimed Matthew, quite taken by surprise.

"It's only a jam tart, Hilly!"

She looked up at him then.

"Oh no, Mr Bates, it's not that," she explained, "it's… well… I'm so terribly sorry about your leg. I'd have said something sooner, only I didn't know you see. I do hope it's not causing you too much pain today," she added politely.

Matthew Bates shook with mirth. He would have loved to throw back his head and roar with laughter, but he didn't want to hurt the little girl's feelings, so instead, he motioned his equally amused son to take the little tarts and picked the child up.

"Well it's very kind of you to be so concerned for me Hilly, but I assure you my leg is perfectly comfortable today thank you."

He gave her a reassuring hug, then put her back down and patted her on the head.

"So, don't you go worrying that pretty little head of yours about me. You just go and enjoy that tart before Mrs Bates scolds me for upsetting you," he said kindly.

Hilly looked at him.

"Thank you, Mr Bates." She smiled. Then, a dreadful thought occurred to her, and the smile faded again.

"It wasn't improper of me to mention your leg, was it?" she asked hesitantly.

"Not at all," Matthew assured her. *Funny little Hilly*, he thought.

"That was her mother's influence, of course," he said to his wife as he recounted the episode to her a few minutes later.

Margaret Bates agreed with him.

"She is certainly a very proper woman, Elizabeth Moncrieff."

Margaret joined in Matthew's laughter then.

"Oh, I do wish I'd been witness to it." She chuckled as she took herself off to wrap up the mended dress.

Joshua, meanwhile, had taken Hilly to look at Raven's new kittens, which had arrived overnight and were residing in the drawer at the bottom of Lindy's wardrobe.

There were six of them in all, snuggled up to Raven as she lay curled up on a soft woolly jumper. Three of the kittens were as black as Raven herself; two were tabbies and one a soft pale grey. Hilly had never seen newborn kittens before and was enthralled by them.

"They're so tiny," she whispered as she sat on her haunches, peering into the open drawer.

The little grey kitten opened its mouth and issued a tiny squeak. Hilary Anne was delighted.

"Oh, it's so cute," she cried, "though it sounds more like a mouse than a baby cat!"

"That's a good name for him." Joshua laughed.

"Mouse! We'll call that one Mouse!"

Hilly was delighted when the other children agreed she had come up with the perfect name for the little kitten. She couldn't wait to tell Mother all about it, she thought later as she walked home, the brown paper package holding the mended dress tucked firmly under her arm. She wasn't sure if she should mention that she had told Mr Bates how sorry she was about his leg, though. Mother might think she had spoken out of turn, even though Mr Bates had assured her otherwise. Just think! Mother was right all along. Mr Bates actually *had* lost his leg.

She wondered if Mother was right about Aunt Hilary, too. She would have to watch her very closely over the course of the weekend and see if she really did move in circles.

Hilly almost reached the front gate before she remembered that Mother had given her an extra sixpence to buy a loaf of Mr Bates' bread. She had put the money for the dress in an envelope addressed to Mrs Bates and then tied the sixpence in the corner of Hilly's handkerchief so she wouldn't lose it, but what with all the fussing over Mr Bates' leg, and then the excitement of the kittens, Hilly had forgotten all about it!

The little girl turned abruptly and began to retrace her steps. She ran as fast as she could, her long plaits bouncing up and down on her back and tangling themselves in the strap of her satchel.

By the time she burst into the bakery, long wisps of hair had come free of her braids, and her cheeks were flushed scarlet.

"Oh, Mr Bates," she gasped, "I forgot Mother's bread. Could I have a white loaf, please?"

She fumbled with the handkerchief, freeing the sixpence and placing it on the counter. Matthew Bates looked at her and shook his head.

"I thought the devil himself was after you, the way you came belting through that door." He chuckled as he reached under the counter, then carefully placed a large white loaf into a brown paper bag.

It was the very last white loaf he had and he'd been keeping it to take along to Margaret later, but he didn't tell Hilly that, and ten minutes later, when Elizabeth Moncrieff uttered cries of despair over her daughter's dishevelled appearance, Hilly didn't tell *her* that she had almost forgotten the bread!

"I do hope you'll behave with a little more decorum around your aunt, Hilary Anne," scolded Elizabeth as she brushed the tangles from Hilly's hair.

"We don't want her thinking you're no better than the village children."

Hilly gave her mother a concerned look. *There she went, saying strange things again!*

"Your Aunt Hilary is a very dignified woman. It would cause her considerable distress to think that her namesake was turning into some sort of ill-kempt rustic, so just mind your manners this weekend, please, young lady!"

It occurred to Hilly that Mother always behaved quite differently whenever Aunt Hilary was around, and she was the one person in the whole world whom Mother never spoke badly of.

As Elizabeth neatly secured Hilly's hair with a ribbon and sent her to the bathroom to wash for tea, the little girl wondered why it was that Aunt Hilary had such an effect on Mother. It really was most curious.

Chapter – 4

Hilary St Clair caught the flash of the headlights as the car turned into the driveway of Oak Manor, several seconds before the rumble of the tyres on the red gravel chips announced her nephew's safe arrival.

She excused herself from the little group gathered in the sitting room and strode briskly across the hallway to the front door.

"Robert! How wonderful to see you!"

She ran down the wide, stone stairs and gave him a quick hug as he opened the car door for his wife.

"Elizabeth. It's been far too long!"

She greeted Elizabeth with the same enthusiasm she had shown Robert, but even as she spoke, she found herself wondering how long it would be before the woman started to get on her nerves. She was a woman of classic beauty, Elizabeth, with a flawless complexion and a winning smile, which was of course how she had landed Robert in the first place, but she was highly strung and fidgety, which Hilary found irritating. That, along with the fact she was prone to putting on airs and graces.

"Hilary Anne, there you are!" Hilary St Clair held her arms open wide in welcome as the child alighted from the back seat, and the little girl responded obediently, giving her great aunt a hug and a kiss on the cheek.

"Thank you for inviting me, Aunt Hilary," she said politely.

Her aunt smiled indulgently, noting as she did that the child was immaculately dressed and groomed as always. *She'd give Elizabeth that,* she thought. Hilary Anne was a credit to her. It wasn't until they made their way into the well-lit hallway that she noticed how pale little Hilly looked.

"Are you quite well, dear?" she asked with genuine concern.

"Hilly will be fine, thank you, Hilary," Elizabeth answered on her daughter's behalf.

"She doesn't travel well."

"How beastly for you," sympathised the older woman.

"Perhaps a glass of ginger ale might help you to recover. They say ginger is good for calming the stomach." She took the child's hand and led the way into the sitting room as she spoke.

"Don't you agree, Daphne?" she addressed an elegantly attired woman sitting on the settee.

"Ginger settles the stomach?"

"So I've heard," concurred the woman, taking in Hilly's pallid countenance.

"Car sickness, is it?"

"I'm afraid so."

The woman smiled sympathetically. She had suffered from that very malaise herself whilst carrying Geoffrey. She knew just how unpleasant it was. She patted the seat beside her.

"Come and sit down, dear, till it passes over," she said kindly.

Hilly sank thankfully onto the settee. The room was swimming before her, so she closed her eyes and let her head fall back against the soft, fluffy cushions. Little beads of perspiration pricked at her forehead and settled above her lip, and she moaned softly.

"Grab the coal scuttle!" she heard someone say, and just in time, Aunt Hilary thrust it under her chin.

Elizabeth Moncrieff recoiled in horror! What must Hilary and her guests be thinking?

Hilary Anne!… Really me! You should have asked for the bathroom!
The child whimpered softly.

"There, there, dear." Aunt Hilary patted her soothingly on the head.
"No harm done."

"Poor old Hilly," sympathised Robert. "That was bad luck. Feeling better now?"

Hilly nodded.

"I'm sorry, Aunt Hilary," she apologised, "only I couldn't help it."

"Well, of course you couldn't," agreed her aunt.

The little girl cast two troubled brown eyes in the direction of her mother. *Mother would be mortified!*

Elizabeth *was* indeed mortified, but a quick glance around the assembled company helped to calm her anguish. Everyone else seemed genuinely concerned for her unhappy daughter. She took a quick, sharp breath, swallowed hard and held up her head.

47

"Never mind, Hilary Anne," she said, "what's done is done."

Hilly's eyes opened wide with surprise. She had expected Mother to be furious, yet here she was, being perfectly pleasant.

"I really am most terribly sorry, Mother."

"I know, dear. Now, why don't we go and clean you up."

"Let me come and help you," offered Aunt Hilary's visitor, pulling herself up from the settee and smiling pleasantly at Elizabeth.

"I'm Daphne, by the way," she introduced herself, "Daphne Chatswood. It's Elizabeth, isn't it?"

"Good Lord! How perfectly awful! I haven't even introduced you!"

Aunt Hilary rose from her knees, coal scuttle in hand and surveyed the company.

"Oh well, you seem to be doing very nicely on your own, so I'll just leave you to it while I take care of this!"

"Geoffrey will take that out for you," volunteered the man who had been sitting opposite Daphne.

"What a good idea, William," agreed his wife.

"Of course, he'll do that, won't you, Geoffrey?"

It was only then that the members of the Moncrieff family noticed the young boy standing by the window at the far side of the room. He was a lanky child with a shock of fair hair, and Hilly judged him to be about the same age as Joshua.

"Do I have to?" he complained.

"It stinks. I can smell it from here."

"*Geoffrey!* What an awful thing to say!" Daphne frowned at him.

"You will apologise to the poor little girl and take the scuttle from Mrs St Clair at once!"

Geoffrey offered Hilly a mumbled apology of sorts and sullenly asked Aunt Hilary where she would like him to take the scuttle.

"Follow me," she advised, leading the way from the room with her customary brisk stride.

Daphne, meanwhile, led the way to the bathroom.

"I must apologise for Geoffrey," she said, "the problem is he's been rather bored since we arrived. He's such an active boy, you see, and there's really been nobody for him to spend his time with. He's been looking forward to meeting you, Hilary Anne."

"I don't think he wants to meet me any more," replied the little girl.

Daphne Chatswood laughed.

"Of course, he does." She smiled as she handed Elizabeth a damp flannel with which to wipe Hilly's woe-begotten little face.

"He's brought some games for you to play together."

"What sort of games?"

"Ludo, Snakes & Ladders, that sort of thing."

Hilly smiled happily.

"Oh good, I know how to play those."

"Well, of course, you do, Hilary Anne."

Elizabeth looked at her daughter.

"There. You'll do," she said, running a comb through Hilly's hair and carefully twisting the long, soft ringlets around her fingers until they sat neatly in place.

"Your colour is coming back now."

She turned to Daphne then and thanked her for her kindness.

"Where's your own little girl this evening?" she asked. "Has she retired to bed already?"

"*My* little girl?" enquired Daphne. "There's only Geoffrey, I'm afraid."

"Oh. I do beg your pardon; I must have misunderstood. I thought you had a little girl about Hilary Anne's age."

Daphne shook her head.

"Sadly not." She sighed. "Though I should dearly love a daughter, of course. Especially one as sweet as your own little Hilary Anne."

She smiled at Hilly as she spoke and gently ran a hand over her long, silky hair.

"Such pretty hair." She sighed. "Not like Geoffrey's unruly mop!"

Elizabeth preened herself. Hilary Anne may be a trial to her in many ways, but she did indeed have beautiful hair. Daphne was not the first to comment on the fact.

"How kind of you to say so," she gushed. "It takes a great deal of looking after on my part, of course. I'm obliged to tie it in rags every night to keep it from hanging straight."

"Well, your efforts are certainly not in vain," smiled Daphne as the object of their discussion made good her escape.

"Hilary Anne has quite the prettiest head of hair I've seen in a long time and the manners to match. The child is a credit to you."

Elizabeth waved a hand in the air.

"One does one's best. Though heaven knows there are times when motherhood can be extremely vexing, as I'm sure you're only too aware of yourself."

Daphne laughed in agreement, and they followed in Hilly's wake, chatting like old friends as they made their way back to the sitting room.

The gentlemen rose to their feet as the ladies re-joined them, and as final introductions were made, Geoffrey eyed up Hilly with obvious disdain. He was not at all happy that he had been made to help Mrs St Clair dispose of the contents of the coal scuttle, apart from which he had been led to believe that Mrs St Clair's great niece was his own age and possessed of a spirited nature. Hilly was obviously nowhere near ten years old, and she looked positively feeble to Geoffrey. As far as he was concerned, all girls were feeble. He should have known better than to hope she would be any different.

It was then, with considerable surprise, that he found Hilly next morning sitting high in the branches of a big oak tree that straddled the front lawn. He had ventured outside to kick around his soccer ball and Hilly threw little pieces of twig at him until he felt obliged to stop what he was doing and look up to see where the missiles were coming from.

"Oh, it's you," he scowled. "What're you doing?"

"Watching you."

"Annoying me, more like!"

"No, I'm not."

"Yes, you are. Why don't you go inside and play with dolls or something?"

"Because I like being up here."

"Why?" Geoffrey was scornful. He couldn't imagine why anyone would like to climb trees. He certainly didn't.

"Why don't you come up and join me?" invited Hilly.

"Why would I want to do that?"

"Because you can see for miles from up here. I can see the big house up on the hill and horses in the field over the road... and I can see right down over the trellis into Aunt Hilary's kitchen. Your mother's making a pot of tea, and my mother's putting out some biscuits."

"Big deal!"

"There are some children playing a little way down the lane, too."

50

"Playing what?"

"I'm not sure. They have something they're taking turns riding on."

"What? Like a bike?"

"I told you. I'm not sure. I think it might be a trolley, though I can't quite see because there's a branch in the way. Maybe if you came up here too, you'd be able to see over it because you're taller than I am."

"No thanks."

"Oh, come on."

"I said no."

"Don't you like climbing trees then? Are you afraid of heights?"

"Of course not!"

"It's quite all right to be, you know. My friend Maisie's scared of heights, too."

"I told you. I'm **not**!"

Geoffrey was getting agitated now. He couldn't let this pip-squeak of a girl think he was a scaredy-cat.

"Oh, all right!"

Geoffrey dropped his ball at the foot of the tree and hesitantly began his ascent. His hands gripped the branches tightly as he inched his way up to where Hilly sat happily astride her favourite perch.

"See, I told you. You could see for miles up here," declared Hilly as Geoffrey slowly pulled himself up onto the branch alongside her.

"So where are those other children?" asked Geoffrey in a voice that didn't sound quite like his own.

"Shh! Here comes Mother," whispered Hilly. "Keep perfectly quiet and don't move."

"Hilary Anne!" called Elizabeth. "Geoffrey! There's morning tea ready in the kitchen."

Hilly shook her head at Geoffrey and put a finger to her lips.

"Hilly! Hilary Anne!" called Elizabeth.

Her eyes scanned the garden. She was sure she'd seen the child out here earlier, and Daphne had sent Geoffrey out here with his soccer ball not more than five minutes ago.

Where had they got to, she wondered. Oh well. They'd turn up when they felt hungry.

She made her way back inside, and Hilly let out a long, slow breath.

"That was close. I thought she'd see your ball and find us."

51

"What if she had?"

"She doesn't like me climbing trees. It's not lady-like, you see."

Geoffrey looked at her.

"Neither is throwing up in someone's sitting room."

Hilly agreed he had a point there. She sighed.

"It's very hard trying to be a lady all the time, you know," she informed him.

"Anyway, I think we should go down now before Mother comes looking for us again."

Hilly slid down to the branch below them as she spoke, then turned nimbly so she could grip the branches with her hands to aid her descent. She was about halfway down the tree before she realised Geoffrey hadn't moved.

"Come on!" she called up to him.

Geoffrey sat stock still, and Hilly could see his face had turned deathly white.

"What's wrong?" she called. "Aren't you feeling well?"

Geoffrey didn't answer. Instead, he tightened his grip on the branch until his knuckles were as white as his face.

"Don't look down!" called Hilly, scrambling her way back up to him. Why had he said he wasn't afraid of heights when obviously he was. This was exactly what happened to Maisie Cowan. She had climbed up a tree as happily as you like, but when it came time to climb down, she simply froze with fear.

"It's all right," Hilly comforted Geoffrey as she reached his side.

"It's quite common to get stuck, you know."

"I'm not stuck."

"Then why don't you come down?"

"Because I like it up here."

"No, you don't."

"You'd know, of course!"

"Oh well. If you don't want my help."

Hilly began to descend again.

"All right. Only don't tell anyone, all right?"

Hilly gave Geoffrey an old-fashioned look. Who did he think she would tell? Mother?

"Now it's only getting started; that's the problem," she assured him as she tried to show him what to do.

"I'll hold on to you," Hilly offered, putting an arm around his waist, but he yelled at her to leave him alone.

"Well, I can't help you if you won't let me," she replied firmly. "Would you like me to fetch your father?"

"No, I would not!" Geoffrey was adamant on that count, but after several failed attempts to get him to lower himself to the next branch, Hilly began to wonder if she had any other option.

"You just hold tight," she said finally. "I'll be back in a minute."

"Why? Where are you going?"

"To fetch a ladder. It won't sway around like the branches do and you'll be able to climb down it more easily."

Hilly made a nimble descent from the tree, then ran off across the lawn and ducked around the side of the house to the garden shed as quickly as she could. It would never do to let the adults see her. Mother would blame her for Geoffrey's predicament, and then she would have to endure another lecture.

As she reached the shed, Hilly paused momentarily. She stood on the tips of her toes and peered cautiously through the window to make sure no-one was there, then she quietly opened the door and slipped inside.

She could see a tall ladder leaning up against the far wall and made a beeline for it. Now, all she had to do was get back to Geoffrey without being seen! She was sure she could manage that. The adults all seemed to be inside taking tea, and they wouldn't be able to see her making her way back across the lawn to the tree because of the big rose-covered trellis outside the kitchen window.

Hilly's hands gripped the sides of the ladder, and she lifted it away from the wall, only to discover it was more awkward to handle than she had imagined. She sucked in her breath as it waved menacingly above her head, then as she struggled to get the top of the ladder under control, the other end swung around wildly, sweeping across the top of Aunt Hilary's potting table, and causing a dozen little seedlings that had been carefully prepared for sale at the church fete, to tumble to the floor.

Hilly spun around in horror at the sound of breaking pots, causing the top end of the ladder to smash its way through the window. The little girl froze in fright as the pane of glass showered down in a myriad of tiny shafts onto the cobbles outside.

What had she done! Mother would be furious. Everyone would be furious. Even Aunt Hilary!

Hilly's hands felt clammy with sweat and her stomach churned until she thought she would be sick again. Surely, someone must have heard the window breaking. Any moment now, someone would come and discover what she had done, and she would be in such trouble! She fought back her tears and waited in trepidation, her ears straining for the sound of approaching footsteps, but there was nothing. Nobody had heard! Hilly couldn't believe her luck! She took a deep breath and carefully disengaged the ladder from the broken window. She had the wretched thing under control now, and she must carry on with her mission to rescue Geoffrey. Surely, he would come and help her clean up the mess once she helped him down from the tree, and then she would go and confess to Aunt Hilary.

Never before, in all his ten years, had Geoffrey Chatswood felt so humiliated. It was bad enough that he felt so utterly terrified, but having to be rescued by a girl made his misery thoroughly complete. He clung to his branch and watched as Hilly half carried, half dragged the ladder across the lawn in the direction of the oak.

"Hurry up," he whimpered as she struggled to position it in such a way as to make it easy for him to access.

"Hurry up yourself," came the agitated reply.

"Surely you can get down now."

Geoffrey wasn't at all certain that he could. He still needed to get his feet onto the ladder somehow. Hilly stamped her foot at him impatiently.

"Oh, for goodness sake, Geoffrey, if you don't come down at once, I shall go and fetch your father."

"You promised not to."

"I don't care. I wish I'd just gone and got him in the first place instead of fetching this silly ladder! Especially if you're not going to climb down it anyway. I'm going to be in so much trouble, and it's all going to be for nothing!'"

Geoffrey had no idea what she was talking about. As far as he was concerned, he was the only one in any kind of trouble, and he wouldn't have gone up the tree in the first place if it wasn't for her nagging at him to do so.

The whole thing was *her* fault. He hated her!

Hilly glared at him. Stupid boy! Well, he could just stay up there for all she cared! She had more important things to worry about. She turned on her heel and ran off back in the direction of the garden shed, turning a deaf ear to Geoffrey's screams for her to come back.

As it became apparent to him that Hilly had no intention of helping him any further, Geoffrey's distress turned to panic, his hysterical wailing getting louder and louder until, eventually, his anguished cries drifted through the open kitchen window and caught the attention of the adults within. Not only his own father but Hilary Anne's father, too, came running to see what all the fuss was about.

William Chatswood summed up the situation in an instant.

"Calm down Geoffrey," he said quietly, making his way up the ladder to where his distressed offspring sat rigidly holding on to the branch in front of him, "you're perfectly safe. Mr Moncrieff and I will have you down in an instant. Heavens! You've only to swing your feet onto the ladder."

"I can't! I already tried, and I can't," wailed Geoffrey.

"Of course, you can. It's easy."

William took hold of the child now and encouraged the boy to let go of his hold on the branch and hold on to him instead.

"That's the way Geoffrey," he said, "now just get the leg closest to me onto the ladder ~ here."

Geoffrey took a huge gulp and slowly did as his father said.

"Right. Good boy. Now I've got hold of you, and I want you to hold onto the branch again and swing your other leg over to this side. You can do that, can't you?"

"I'm not sure." Geoffrey's teeth chattered with fright.

"You're doing so well, Geoffrey," encouraged Hilary Anne's father from below.

"I have a hold of the ladder down here, so it won't move. Just bring your leg over now, as your father says, and you'll be down here with me in a trice."

"That's right, Geoffrey," agreed William.

"On the count of three, right?"

Geoffrey held his breath as William counted, and then, somehow, he'd done it! He was standing on the ladder, one rung above his father.

"Well done!" approved William and Robert in unison, and William patted him on the back.

"You'll be fine now, son," he encouraged. "The rest is easy."

Geoffrey's legs still felt a little wobbly, but the further down the ladder they went, and the closer they got to the ground, the braver he began to feel.

"There you go," smiled Robert as Geoffrey finally stepped thankfully to the ground and stooped to pick up his ball.

"I'd forget about tree climbing and stick to soccer in future if I were you," laughed his father.

It was then that Geoffrey noticed they were not alone. His mother was there too, as were Mrs Moncrieff and Mrs St Clair. They had all seen him stuck in the tree like a baby. His cheeks burned with humiliation. It was all Hilary Anne's fault. She'd pay for this. He'd see to that.

"Whatever made you go up there in the first place, Geoffrey?" asked Daphne, running her hand through his more than usually tousled hair.

"You know you've no head for heights."

"Hilary Anne made me do it."

"I beg your pardon?"

"She was already up there, you see, and when I came out to play soccer, she started throwing things at me. She… she *taunted* me and made me climb up to join her. Then, when I couldn't get down, she just went off and left me."

"Went off where?" bristled Elizabeth Moncrieff. She might have known Hilary Anne had something to do with this! Well, she would be found and made to answer for her behaviour.

"Where did the ladder come from?" asked Hilary St Clair.

"I don't know. Hilary Anne brought it."

"Oh?"

"She just stuck it up against the branch and told me to get down because she was in trouble, and it was all **my** fault if you please… and then she just ran off."

"In which direction did she run?"

Geoffrey pointed towards the garden shed, causing Mrs St Clair to nod knowingly and stride off in the same direction, leaving the others to struggle along in her wake. She knew exactly where Hilly found the ladder because she put it there herself just moments before she went in for tea, and she knew that due to its length, it was a cumbersome object with a mind of its own. She had very nearly knocked over some of her seedling pots with it, and if *she* found it difficult to manoeuvre, then how impossible it must have been for little Hilly to control.

As she reached the garden shed, her shoes scrunched loudly on broken glass, and a quick sideways glance confirmed that the windowpane was missing!

The windowpane was missing, and so was the key to the door, which was shut tight. Hilary tried the handle, but it wouldn't move. The door was locked from the inside.

"Hilly!" she called, "unlock the door and let me in!"

On the other side of the door, Hilly froze with fear. She'd hardly begun to clear up the mess she'd made. She couldn't let Aunt Hilary in. Not yet.

"Hilly dear! It's all right. I'm not angry with you. I know you didn't break the window on purpose. Now open the door and let me in. There's a good girl. I only want to fetch the yard broom to sweep up the glass."

Hilly took a deep breath and stood stock still, her hand hovering over the key. Aunt Hilary might not be angry about the window but she hadn't seen her broken pots yet.

"Hilly. I'm waiting."

The little girl gulped and slowly turned the key in the lock.

"I'm so sorry, Aunt Hilary. It was an accident. All of it."

"All of it?" Hilary pushed the door open wide and stood on the threshold, looking about in amazement.

"Good Lord, Hilly! You don't do things by halves, do you?"

"I'll fix it all up, Aunt Hilary; honestly, I will. You see, I've already picked up the plants and put them over here so they can go in new pots, and I'm putting all the broken pieces of pottery in this box. I thought you might be able to use them for something."

Hilary St Clair looked at her great niece's woe-begotten little countenance and suddenly found herself hard-pushed not to burst out laughing. She was quite certain that she would have done so had Elizabeth not chosen that very moment to sail through the door like a battleship at full tilt.

"Hilary Anne!" she ranted loudly, "Whatever have you done now?" Her eyes fell on the mess before her.

"It looks as though a tornado has passed through here! And I suppose it was you who broke the window as well? I *despair* of you, child! You leave poor Geoffrey stranded up a tree! You destroy your great aunt's potting shed! You are a disgrace! Why, for two pins, I'd... I'd..."

Elizabeth was suddenly lost for words. There was none she could think of that would adequately convey her displeasure, so she tossed her head and snorted, her nostrils flaring and her cold eyes staring wildly at her unhappy daughter.

Hilly stood stock still and lowered her eyes to the floor. There was no point in her trying to explain anything to Mother. Mother never listened.

"That's enough, Elizabeth. Shouting at the child will solve nothing." Robert Moncrieff laid a hand on his wife's shoulder.

"I know you're upset, and I quite understand, but I think we need to hear Hilly's side of the story, eh?"

"Oh, that's right! Stick up for her the way you always do," sniffed Elizabeth, turning on her heel and striding from the shed with another toss of her head.

Robert frowned after her, then turned his attention to Hilly.

"Right, young lady. What do you have to say for yourself?"

Hilly took a deep breath and looked up at her father.

"Well, we were just sitting up in the tree watching some children playing down the road when Mother came out to call us in for afternoon tea, only when we went to climb down, well, Geoffrey found he couldn't. He'd frozen with fear, just like my friend Maisie Cowan did one day. I told him it was all right because lots of people are afraid of heights and not to worry because I'd help him, only he wouldn't let me."

"Why didn't you come and fetch me or Mr Chatswood?"

"Because he asked me not to tell anyone. I wanted to because I just couldn't get him down by myself, and I was worried that he'd panic and fall... but I'd promised not to, do you see? That's when I remembered that Aunt Hilary kept a ladder in the shed, so I came to fetch it... only it was very heavy and it swayed around all over the place until I got used to it, and that's how I broke the window and the pot plants. I didn't mean to. It just happened because the ladder was too big and heavy for me. Then, when I finally managed to get it to the tree, Geoffrey wouldn't climb down it anyway."

She stopped and glared at Geoffrey, who, along with his parents, was now standing at the door of the shed listening.

"So, in the end, I just left him to it because I wanted to clean up this awful mess I'd made, before I went and told Aunt Hilary what I'd done... so that she wouldn't think I was *too* dreadful."

She stopped again and rolled her eyes, then looked at her Aunt, who seemed to be having some sort of trouble keeping her lips from trembling. Hilly was horrified. Aunt Hilary was trying not to cry! Whatever had she done!

"I really am so very sorry, Aunt Hilary. I'll clean it all up. I *promise* I will, and I'll replant all the seedlings and do chores to pay for the window."

Hilary St Clair suddenly started to shake, causing Hilly to fly to her side and throw her arms around the older woman.

"For heaven's sake, Hilly! You'll be the death of me, child! Lord! What I wouldn't give to have seen you trying to control that ladder!"

She roared with laughter.

"I'm sure you'd leave Laurel and Hardy out in the cold!"

Hilly was confused. Instead of being angry and upset with her, Aunt Hilary was laughing.

"Well, I don't know who Laurel and Hardy are," she informed her amused relative, "but I wouldn't leave anybody out in the cold. Not even Geoffrey," she added as an after-thought, which for some reason made *all* the grown-ups laugh.

"Why did you have to go and tell them I was scared?" Geoffrey hissed at Hilly through clenched teeth as they followed the adults back to the house.

"Now they'll think I'm a sissy."

"No, they won't. Lots of people don't like heights."

"Like who?"

"Like my friend Maisie, who I told you about."

"A *girl*!"

He sneered at Hilly, then turned on his heel and stormed off, his humiliation complete. She'd be sorry. He would not let this rest. It was all her fault anyway. He wouldn't have gone up the silly tree in the first place had it not been for her! Then, to just go off and leave him like that so that he had to call for someone else to come and help. She might have known the whole lot of them would come traipsing out to gawp at him! Well, she wouldn't make a fool of *him* and get away with it. He'd been right about her all along. She was horrible. Just another feeble girl. No doubt like that Maisie creature she kept prattling on about.

Once her amusement had subsided, Hilary St Clair turned her thoughts to Geoffrey. The poor boy was obviously highly embarrassed by the morning's events, and it was equally certain that he held Hilly responsible for the whole entertaining escapade.

The stormy look on his face as he brushed past her confirmed her suspicions, and she looked back to see how her niece was coping with his outrage.

"Poor Geoffrey," she said as Hilly reached her side.

"I think his pride has been severely wounded."

"He's acting as though it was all my fault," complained Hilly indignantly, "and it wasn't. He chose to come up the tree. I told him not to if he didn't want to, but he insisted. I know Mother wants me to be nice to him, but it's awfully hard, you know because he's not very nice to me."

Aunt Hilary smiled sympathetically.

"In fact, don't tell Mother I said so, but I really don't like Geoffrey at all."

"Our secret," Hilary promised as she removed a piece of twig from her niece's hair and tossed it to the ground. Hilly slipped her hand into that of the older woman and smiled up at her.

"I like *you*, though, Aunt Hilary," she confided, and Hilary St Clair chuckled with pleasure.

Geoffrey, meanwhile, retired to his room to lick his wounded pride. It wasn't right that chit of a girl showing him up like that. He would have got down by himself ~ eventually ~ if she had only stayed and held the ladder steady. He was quite certain of that. But now everybody thought *he* was a stupid sissy, while *she* was wonderful and so amusing! Apart from her mother, nobody even seemed to mind that she had broken the window and the pots. *Little Miss 'butter wouldn't melt'*. He hated her!

A good night's sleep did nothing to assuage Geoffrey's wrath. He glared at Hilly over the breakfast table and scowled when his mother suggested he should look after her at the fete.

"We'll all be busy helping Mrs St Clair with the plant stall and the flower show," she explained, "so you can take little Hilary Anne to the side shows."

"I don't want to go to the fete."

"Oh, you'll have a lovely time, the two of you. There'll be a coconut shy and pony rides ~ all sorts of things."

"Boring."

"Geoffrey! Whatever has got into you this morning. You've been looking forward to this weekend."

"That's before I met *her*!" Geoffrey muttered darkly as he scowled in Hilly's direction.

"Geoffrey!" Daphne was horrified.

"Whatever has poor little Hilary Anne done to incur such disdain?"

"She's a girl! Isn't that enough?"

"Don't be so ridiculous, Geoffrey. You will apologise at once, then go and get ready for the fete."

"I told you. I'm not going." Geoffrey looked at his mother defiantly. Daphne pursed her lips and frowned at him.

"It's perfectly all right, Mrs Chatswood; he doesn't have to come for my sake. I should like to help Aunt Hilary, anyway. I think I owe it to her after yesterday, and Mother says I'm not to have any pony rides or candy floss on account of my appalling behaviour," said Hilly with simple candour.

Daphne Chatswood turned back to the kitchen sink so that neither of the children could see her smile. What a delightful child Hilary Anne was!

Elizabeth Moncrieff, however, did not share in Daphne's sentiments and spent most of the drive home to Leominster the following evening, ensuring that her daughter perfectly understood what a trial she was.

"It simply was not good enough for her to go behaving like a hoyden in front of people like Aunt Hilary and the Chatswoods. Whatever must they think! Poor little Geoffrey was such a nice boy. Hilary Anne should be ashamed of herself for causing him such distress and humiliation, aside from the fact that Mr Chatswood was a very important man in the city and might be in a position to help her father in the future, should he desire to change jobs. It was, of course, highly unlikely that Mr Chatswood would do that now, after the appalling way that Hilary Anne had behaved."

"For Heaven's sake, Elizabeth!" interrupted Robert, "That really is going too far! Anyway, I have no interest whatsoever in working in the city. I enjoy my job, and I am very happy living in Leominster."

"Well, yes, dear, but you don't want to be just a bank manager forever."

"Don't I?"

"Of course, you don't."

"I will be the judge of that, Elizabeth."

The tone of Robert's voice told Elizabeth that she would be unwise to pursue the matter further.

She turned her head and gazed out of the window with a pout. It was all very well his being happy in Leominster, but what about her? And Hilary Anne? If they moved to London, not only could Robert find a more powerful and more financially beneficial position, but *she* could mix with the right people, and Hilary Anne could attend a top-notch school.

Aunt Hilary's late husband, Winston, had made a small fortune in the city before his untimely death. Look how well Hilary lived by comparison to them, with her beautiful old manor house in Malvern, her exquisite clothes, and her regularly updated expensive motor cars.

It really was too bad of Robert to be so selfish. She was tired of his lack of ambition. A long and interesting discussion with Daphne Chatswood had revealed that William was now *the* senior partner in the very same firm of London brokers that Winston St Clair had started up with his great friend, William's father, Charles Chatswood.

William Chatswood took over the company reins on the occasion of his father's recent retirement. Ever since Winston's death, Aunt Hilary had been a sleeping partner and major shareholder in the company, while Charles Chatswood had assisted her in taking care of St. Clair's not in-significant portfolio.

Now, with Charles' retirement, that task had fallen to William, which was how his association with Aunt Hilary had developed.

Elizabeth was certain that William could find Robert a senior position in the firm. He had as good as said so; only Robert, of course, laughed at the idea.

It was so typical of him, thought Elizabeth, as she gazed unseeingly at the passing countryside.

She pursed her lips with a sulky pout and narrowed her eyes as an unattractive scowl creased her brow.

She married Robert because she thought he would *be* somebody who could make something of himself. Well, so he would! She would see to that. She knew exactly how to handle Robert Moncrieff, and if he thought he'd heard the last about moving to the city, he could think again.

Chapter – 5

'All things bright and beautiful, all creatures great and small,
All things wise and wonderful, the Lord God made them all.'

The children's voices drifted across the churchyard in the still morning air, causing the vicar to smile and incline his head in the direction of the Sunday School. He had kept his sermon brief this morning, which resulted in the morning service ending a little ahead of time. He stood now at the door to The Priory, chatting with his parishioners as they waited for their children to join them.

"Talking of all creatures great and small." Margaret Bates smiled at Elizabeth Moncrieff. "I wanted to talk to you about our Lindy's kittens."

"Oh?" Elizabeth raised an eyebrow. It was beyond her comprehension why Margaret Bates should think she would be in the least bit interested in discussing Lindy's kittens.

"She's looking to find good homes for them all you see," continued Margaret, ignoring the look on Elizabeth's face.

"Mr Young the vet has checked them over to make sure they're healthy and all, and well the children were wanting to give one to your little Hilary Anne. There's a pretty little grey one called Mouse that Hilly's particularly partial to, and the children have quite made up their minds that she should have him, only I told them they'd need to see if it was all right with you first before they gave it her."

"Well, that's very thoughtful of you, Margaret," smiled Robert Moncrieff, before his wife had a chance to answer.

"Hilly's full of stories about Lindy's kittens. Mouse in particular. Isn't that so, Elizabeth?"

Elizabeth looked at her husband and nodded.

"Yes, but…"

"It would be good for Hilly to have a pet to care for. Teach her a sense of responsibility."

Margaret smiled and nodded in agreement while Elizabeth eyed her husband with uncertainty.

"I suppose," she agreed hesitantly, "but I wouldn't like it sleeping on her bed."

"Then she shall teach it not to."

Elizabeth sighed. There was a finality to Robert's statement that implied the imminent arrival of a kitten at *Elm Cottage* was now a fait accompli.

A hand patted her on the shoulder, and she looked up to see the vicar smiling down at her.

"What a wonderful thing it is," he enthused, "for a child to learn to care for another of God's creatures."

He folded his hands across his stomach and nodded happily, causing Elizabeth to agree with him.

Of course, there was no harm in letting Hilary Anne have the kitten. What would the vicar think if she turned the offer down? She smiled at Margaret Bates.

"It's really very kind of you and the children to offer Mouse to Hilary Anne, Margaret. We'll make sure she looks after him properly. Won't we, Robert?"

"Lord! I've no doubt she'll do that!" chuckled Margaret,

"I'll send Lindy and Joshua along with him after lunch if it suits you?"

"After lunch will do just fine," Robert assured her, as the door to the Sunday School burst open, and the ensuing flurry of activity caught his attention.

A dozen little voices babbled in unison as the children spilt out into the yard, each of them carrying a cardboard cut-out.

"Look!" cried Hilly as she joined her parents.

"We made cardboard animals today! I made a Mouse! See?"

"Looks more like a cat to me," teased Robert.

"Mouse *is* a cat, Daddy! Mouse is one of Lindy's kittens, remember?"

"Well, so he is! Silly me!" Robert winked at Elizabeth, who shook her head and smiled in spite of herself. As the vicar said, it would be good for Hilary Anne to learn to care for another living creature, and really, what harm would it do to let her have a kitten?

Elizabeth couldn't be certain why it was, but as she walked home with her husband and her daughter at her side, a dreadful sense of foreboding began to hang over her. She told herself it was nonsense to feel uneasy over the simple prospect of having a little kitten in the house but try as she might, she could not rid herself of the feeling that disaster was just around the corner.

By the time the lunch dishes were cleared from the table, Elizabeth's head was pounding.

"I'm sorry, Robert, but you'll have to cope with Hilary Anne's visitors on your own," she informed her husband.

"I need to have a lie-down, I'm afraid. I have one of my heads again."

Robert looked at her and nodded. Elizabeth was prone to migraine headaches. It was her nervous disposition that brought them on.

"Anything I can get you?" he enquired kindly, taking in the glazed look in his wife's eyes and noting the pallor of her skin.

"No, thank you," she shook her head. Past experience had taught her that very little helped to alleviate the pain. She had some tablets from the doctor in the drawer beside the bed. She'd take one of those and try to sleep it off.

Robert poured Elizabeth a glass of water, then escorted her up the stairs to the bedroom, where he hovered anxiously over her while she took her tablet and settled herself comfortably.

He kissed her gently on the forehead and picked up the empty glass before closing the curtains to block the light and quietly letting himself out of the room. Having carefully closed the door behind him, he then went off in search of Hilly so that he could warn her to be very quiet as Mother had one of her heads again.

"Poor Mummy," sympathised Hilly.

She filled the kitchen sink with warm soapy water, and started to carefully wash the plates, as Robert dried them and put them away.

"I wonder why she gets so many headaches. It's not fair, is it? No one else gets headaches all the time. Only Mummy."

Robert smiled sadly to himself. He knew that more often than not, Elizabeth laid the blame for her *heads,* as she called them, squarely on the shoulders of their only child. For his part, he could never understand why Elizabeth found Hilary Anne so vexing. He always found her to be a perfectly reasonable child. Warm-hearted and helpful; obedient in the main. Certainly, she was prone to outbursts of exuberance, which Elizabeth always construed as unbecoming behaviour, and she did tend to lose track of the time when she was off playing with her friends, but surely all children did that. Children should be full of the joys of life, running about enjoying themselves while they can. Childhood was all too short, and Elizabeth worried too much, especially about what other people thought. She was constantly concerned that people would think she was failing in the upbringing of her daughter. That they would find Hilly unruly and raucous, and Elizabeth herself, lacking in her duties. She firmly believed that certain standards must be maintained at all times. It wouldn't do for the Moncrieffs to be thought of as common.

A knock on the back door brought Robert out of his reverie.

"Shall I get that?" enquired Hilly, reaching for a towel to wipe the soapy water from her hands.

"That's a good idea. I think it might be someone for you anyway."

"For me?" Hilary Anne was mystified. Why ever would Father think anyone would be visiting her, especially on a Sunday afternoon?

Robert grinned at her.

"Well, hurry along then, or they might think there's nobody home and go away again."

Hilly threw him an old-fashioned look, but just in case he was right, she hastened her step in the direction of the door, reached eagerly for the handle, and then pulled the door open wide with a gusto her mother would have found unnecessary.

"Josh! Lindy! What are you doing here?"

"We've brought you something," grinned Joshua.

"Show her Lindy."

Lindy Bates cautiously relaxed her hold on the old shoe box she was clasping tightly to her chest and held it out to Hilly.

"What's that?" Hilly was intrigued.

"Lift the lid and see."

"Wouldn't it be easier if you were to put the box down on the kitchen table?" suggested Robert, who had quietly followed his daughter to the door.

"Show your visitors in, Hilly."

"Yes, of course. Please, do come in. It's very rude of me not to have said so already. It's just as well my poor Mother's laid up with one of her heads, or she'd be frowning at me for not minding my manners."

Hilly stood back to allow the Bates children room to pass by her.

"We'll have to be very quiet, by the way," she added apologetically as she shut the door firmly behind them, "Mummy has one of her heads and is sleeping."

Robert Moncrieff smiled wryly as his daughter assumed the air of the gracious hostess. She could be quite the little lady when she felt the occasion called for it, although Robert suspected it was a guise she had learned to assume, rather than one that came naturally. His suspicion was confirmed almost in an instant as the subject of his scrutiny raised the lid on Lindy's cardboard box and up popped a small furry head. As two large blue eyes, an assemblage of long, soft white whiskers, and a tiny squeak greeted her, Hilary Anne Moncrieff instantly reverted to a small excited child right before her amused father's eyes.

"Oh! It's Mouse!" she cried with delight. "You've brought Mouse to visit me!... Why?"

The little face became serious and the smile gave way to a worried frown.

"You're not giving him away, are you?" she asked in a small, tight voice as she picked up the tiny kitten and cradled him gently in her arms. Mouse responded by snuggling happily into her embrace, and the thought she may never see him again filled the child with anguish.

"Well, yes, we *are* giving him away," responded Joshua seriously.

Lindy frowned.

"Don't be so mean, Josh," she chided her elder brother.

"You can see how upset Hilly is at the thought of not being able to see Mouse anymore. It's all right, Hilly," she put an arm around the little girl who was a whole six months her junior and gently stroked the kitten's head.

"We *are* giving him away, but we're giving him to *you*!"

"Oh, *thank you*!"

A tiny gasp escaped Hilly's wide open mouth, and just for an instant, her eyes shone with pure delight. But the moment was short-lived, and the excitement drained from her face as she spoke again in a sad, quiet voice.

"It's really kind of you, and you know that I'd love to have him more than anything, only I don't think Mother will let me keep him. She's not very fond of animals, I'm afraid."

"Your mother knows all about Mouse, Hilly, and has agreed that you may keep him as long as he doesn't sleep on your bed."

Hilly looked at her father in disbelief. Mother knew and had agreed! Well, of course, her parents already knew! That's how Father had known who was at the door before she even opened it!

"Mrs Bates spoke to her at church today," continued Robert, who found himself strangely moved by his daughter's incredulous look, "and with a little encouragement from myself and The Reverend, she agreed we should give Mouse a home."

"Oh dear. That'll be why poor Mummy has one of her heads," offered Hilly with a flash of insight beyond her years.

"She'll be fine by morning," Robert assured Hilary Anne, patting her fondly on the head. "Meantime, I suggest you let Mouse explore his new home while we find a snack for Josh and Lindy."

Not wanting to be found lacking in manners for a second time in such a short while, Hilly immediately put Mouse on the floor and took herself off across the room to raid the larder. There was some Madeira cake left over from lunch, and only yesterday, Mother made some lemon cordial. She reached down some plates and glasses, then added a bowl to their number.

"We can't leave Mouse out," she explained happily. "He needs a nice bowl of milk to make him feel welcome."

Try as she might, Elizabeth Moncrieff could not share in her daughter's enthusiasm for the newest arrival at *Elm Cottage*. She agreed the kitten was a pretty little thing, and it behaved as well as any small creature might be expected to, but her feelings of discomfort remained. No matter how hard she tried or how irrational it might be, she could not look at Mouse without feeling he was about to bring a major catastrophe upon them.

She provided Hilly with a separate cloth to wash Mouse's bowls and made her clean them under the tap out in the yard. She insisted Hilly wash her hands every time she touched the kitten and locked Mouse in the garden shed every night before she went to bed so she could be certain he wouldn't try to sneak between Hilly's sheets. Yet despite all these measures, Elizabeth still felt ill-at-ease about Mouse's presence in her life.

For her part, Hilly couldn't be happier. Mr Jones, the school janitor, gave her a cat basket to put out in the shed for Mouse to sleep in. His old cat had gone to heaven a year ago, he told her, and the basket was, therefore, of no further use.

"Don't you want another cat?" Hilly asked, but Mr Jones said no, and a delighted Hilly happily accepted the gift and took it home to show Mother.

"People are so kind, don't you think?" Hilly asked Elizabeth. "I think they are anyway," she continued without waiting for a reply.

"First, the Bates gave Mouse to me, and now Mr Jones has given me a basket for him."

She picked up Mouse and kissed him on the head, then gently rubbed her cheek up and down his soft, velvety fur.

"This is for you," she told him, holding him over the basket, "now all we need is an old cushion to put in it, and you'll have your very own cosy bed."

Elizabeth bristled.

"Don't kiss that animal, Hilly. Don't put your mouth anywhere near him. You never know what you might catch!"

"Catch?" Hilly was mystified. She'd never heard of anyone catching something from a cat.

"What can you catch from a cat?"

"Lots of things," said Elizabeth firmly.

She was sure she'd read somewhere that cats could pick up illnesses that were harmful to humans. She couldn't remember what exactly, but anyway, it didn't matter. She simply did not like the thought of Hilary Anne kissing the wretched thing like that.

"Put Mouse down now," she continued by way of changing the subject, "and we'll go and see what we can find to put in the basket for him to sleep on."

"Oh, *thank you,* Mummy," smiled Hilly with genuine delight, and Elizabeth suddenly found herself wishing that she could share Hilly's love for the little creature. It would give them something to enjoy together, and there was little enough of that these days. When Hilary Anne wasn't at school or fussing over Mouse, she was hanging around Bates Bakery, and running wild playing with Josh and Lindy, and Elizabeth was none too happy about that either. It wasn't that there was anything wrong with the Bates'. There was nothing wrong with being a baker or a seamstress; they were both perfectly respectable trades, and she was sure the Bates' tribe of children were all very pleasant and brought up well enough in their own way, but the fact remained she wanted more for *her* daughter. She planned to see Hilly mixing with children whose upbringing was a little more refined, like that nice little Geoffrey Chatswood, who had been at Aunt

Hilary's. The trouble was that those sorts of children did not attend the village school. They went away to good boarding schools.

Elizabeth sighed as she reached down an old cot blanket from a shelf in the stair cupboard and handed it to an ecstatic Hilly. She would have to speak to Robert again about Hilary Anne's education. The local school might be all very well for the time being, but after Hilly sat her eleven-plus exams, then things would be different. She simply must make Robert see that. Make him understand that by sending Hilary Anne to the local grammar school, they would be holding her back and spoiling her chances of meeting the right type of people. She would broach the subject again tonight, she resolved, as Hilly dashed off dragging the blanket behind her.

"If you won't consider moving to the city, Robert, you might at least ensure your only child receives a proper education. If we don't put her name down at a good school now, she'll never get in," Elizabeth persisted.

Robert raised his eyes to the heavens, and Elizabeth bristled.

"I'm sure that, as you so rightly say, there's nothing wrong with the local grammar school, but they simply don't get the same calibre of students or teachers as a good public school."

"So, you said."

Robert was bored with the whole conversation. As far as he was concerned, it made no difference. If a child *wanted* to learn, they would, regardless of which school they attended.

"After all," he quietly pointed out, "*you can lead a horse to water, but you can't make it drink.*"

Elizabeth pouted and petulantly stamped her foot.

"Well, I'm afraid I don't see it that way!" She sniffed, refusing to give an inch. "There's more to it than learning to read and write, Robert. She would learn how to behave in polite society and meet the right kind of people. Daphne Chatswood told me she was educated at the Cheltenham Ladies College, and look how well she's done for herself."

It all boiled down to appearances as usual where Elizabeth was concerned. Social status was everything. Robert sighed. He supposed he could see no real harm in putting Hilly's name down for a place at this 'school for young ladies' that Elizabeth was so hot on. *After all,* he thought, *it didn't mean she absolutely had to go there, and at least it would get Elizabeth off his back for a while.* She had been on and on at him about providing for Hilly's future ever since their visit to Aunt Hilary's.

"Oh, all right!" he finally agreed. "Go ahead and put her name down."

"Oh, thank you, darling. You won't regret it, you know!"

To Robert's utter amazement, the moment he gave his approval to her plan, Elizabeth's demeanour changed. *She was like a chameleon,* he thought, as the pout that had dominated her features for the last several days suddenly disappeared and she reverted to the gracious and charming woman he had married. It was funny that something which seemed so trifling to him could be of such overwhelming importance to her. Perhaps he should try harder to understand her yearning for them all to have the very best in life. So long as she understood, he drew the line at moving to London and working in the city. He could do very well for himself right here in Herefordshire. Certainly, well enough to ensure that Elizabeth and Hilly should want for nothing.

Elizabeth lost no time in writing to the school in question. After all, she must strike while the iron is hot in case Robert should change his mind. Not that she really thought for one minute that he would. Robert was a man of principle. She smiled sweetly at him across the table, and he reached out to take her hand. Despite her fixation with appearances and occasional outbursts of temperament, he was still impossibly drawn to her. *She was, above all,* he thought, *a stunningly beautiful woman.*

"Do you think Hilly would notice if we were upstairs when she comes in from feeding Mouse?" he asked with a boyish grin.

"*Robert!*" She laughed and shook her head at him, then pulled away her hand as the back door opened to admit Hilary Anne.

Elizabeth turned her attention to the child, reminding her to wash properly before she sat down to dinner. As the little girl obediently made her way to the bathroom, Elizabeth assumed her most sultry expression and, in a soft, husky voice, pointed out to her husband that there would be no such interruptions once Hilly was away at school.

For once, Robert had no argument with her, and as Hilly sat down to join them, the thought flickered through his mind that perhaps Elizabeth was right after all, and his daughter may indeed benefit from attending a school for young ladies.

Hilary Anne may have washed her hands, but she most certainly had not cleaned her face or brushed her hair. A mixture of dirt and jam was smeared across her chin, and her untamed locks were tangled up with a collection of leaves and twigs.

"Let me guess," said her father, "after school today, you went to the bakery where Mr Bates gave you one of his delectable jam tarts, after which you ran off to the river with Joshua and Lindy and climbed up that tree that overhangs the water."

"How did you know that?" Hilly was incredulous. "Have you been spying on me?"

"Not at all, my dear. It's a very obvious deduction to make, given your somewhat dishevelled appearance. I believe your mother is quite right. A nice school for young ladies could just be the making of you."

Hilly swallowed hard. She didn't want to go away to school. She liked it here in Leominster. Who wanted to be a '*young lady*' anyway if it meant you couldn't run around in bare feet and climb up trees with your friends or cuddle your cat when you wanted to?

It was this very subject that she had been discussing with Josh and Lindy this afternoon as they sat huddled together on the Devil's Elbow. Lindy agreed wholeheartedly, but Joshua seemed strangely envious as Hilly disclosed her mother's plans for her future.

"I wouldn't mind going to a really good school," he announced. "A really good school and then university."

"University? What would you do at university?"

"I don't know," he lied.

More than anything, Josh wanted to be a doctor, though it seemed an impossible dream. After all, where would the likes of him get the money for university.

"I didn't know you wanted to go to university, Josh."

"Neither did I. I've never heard you mention it before."

"No. Well, you needn't go repeating it either, you hear, and especially don't go saying anything to Mum and Dad," Joshua advised his sister.

"You either, Hilly, please."

"Of course not," came Hilly's prompt reply.

"Lindy?"

"No. Not if you don't want me to. Though I can't see why not. They know I want to be a vet."

"That's different."

"How is that different?"

72

Joshua said nothing.

"How?" repeated Lindy.

"It just is, that's all." Joshua felt he had already said more than was wise in front of his sister.

"How about you, Hilly," asked Josh, steering the interest away from himself, "What do you want to do when you leave school?"

"I'd like to work in a flower shop or be an artist," Hilly confided, "only I don't think Mummy would like it very much. She thinks I should just get married to a rich man and do charity work like my Great Aunt Hilary does. That's why she wants to send me away to a posh school. So I'll meet what she calls 'the right kind of people.' Like that horrible Geoffrey boy who was visiting Aunt Hilary. I don't think I'd be very happy if all Mother's *'right kind of people'* are like him."

"Poor Hilly. I'll always be your friend, even if your mother does end up sending you away to a posh school," comforted Joshua, putting an arm around her shoulder.

"So will I," promised Lindy.

"Let's make a pact that even when we're grown up, we'll still be friends no matter what."

"Oh, yes," agreed Hilly. "A secret pact just between the three of us. Only we'll have to hurry and do it now because I can see Maisie Cowan coming!"

The sound of the post arriving caused Elizabeth to wipe the flour from her hands and run to the front door, the way she had done every day for the past two weeks.

A small pile of letters spilt across the floor, and she swooped on them eagerly, scattering them further as she keenly scanned the envelopes in search of the one she'd been waiting for!

It was here at last! A long white envelope postmarked Cheltenham. It even carried an identifying crest on the back!

Leaving the remainder of the mail where it lay, Elizabeth made her way back to the kitchen, fumbling nervously with the envelope as she went. It took several attempts before she finally managed to rip it open, and her hands were trembling so violently that she was obliged to lean her arms on the tabletop to help control them as she removed the enclosed letter and spread it open. An involuntary squeal was quickly followed by an uncharacteristic shout of glee.

"**Yes**!" she cried out loud as she quickly scanned the page.

"*Yes! Yes! Yes!*"

There were still a small number of places available, and the Cheltenham Ladies College was conducting its annual interviews for prospective students in a fortnight's time! They would interview Hilary Anne now, and then, should she pass muster, there would be a further interview after she passed her eleven-plus exams.

A time and date were given for the initial interview, with a polite request to notify the college to confirm attendance.

Her half-mixed scones lying neglected on the benchtop, Elizabeth set about writing an immediate reply, then sallied forth to the post box. Nothing would keep her from taking Hilary Anne to this appointment. *Nothing,* she told herself, as she popped her letter through the slot in the box, then double-checked to make sure it wasn't stuck in the aperture.

Elizabeth's excitement at the prospect of Hilly actually being accepted by such an excellent school as Cheltenham Ladies College grew to fever pitch as the afternoon proceeded.

She couldn't wait to tell the news to Robert and by the time he came in from the office, Elizabeth felt ready to burst.

"Hilly has an interview," she cried out excitedly as she heard the front door close behind him.

"Isn't it wonderful?" she enthused. "I was rather afraid we may have left it altogether too late!"

"Well, there you are then." Robert smiled wearily. "We hadn't after all... and how does Hilly feel about it?"

"I've not had a chance to tell her. The little monkey hasn't come in from school yet. She'll be messing about with those Bates children and Maisie Cowan again, I daresay. I'll be pleased to get her away from their influence."

"Mm," muttered Robert absent-mindedly as he sat down at the table to open the rest of the mail.

"We have to take Hilary Anne to the college two weeks from today for an initial interview."

"Good. Good."

"You'll be able to get away from work then? The appointment is for three thirty in the afternoon."

"Yes, yes," confirmed Robert, but Elizabeth had the distinct feeling that he barely heard a word she'd said. He was obviously preoccupied with something, but she was far too wrapped up in her own schemes to be bothered enquiring as to what was concerning her husband. Whatever it was must surely pale in significance to their daughter's future. It really was too bad of Robert to show so little interest. Well, he will take them to the interview. She would make certain of that!

Elizabeth turned back to the kitchen sink just as the back door flew open to admit Hilly, who, knowing she was not only late for tea but also in a state of disarray, hurtled through the kitchen, intent on getting upstairs without Mother seeing her. On the realisation that she had failed in her quest, Hilly came to a sudden halt in the middle of the room and waited stoically for the tirade to begin.

Elizabeth took one look at her dishevelled daughter, with her mussed-up hair hanging loose, and dirt on both her knees and her dress, and drew herself up with outrage.

"For heaven's sake, Hilary Anne!" she cried.

"Just look at you! Like something the cat dragged in! You're a disgrace. How on earth you expect to be accepted into the Cheltenham Ladies' College when you behave like a... a... *grubby little tinker*, I don't know!"

Hilly blinked.

"I'm sorry, Mother. It's just that we've been celebrating because Josh has passed his eleven-plus exams, and that means he can go to the grammar school instead of the secondary modern!"

She paused for a breath. Surely, Mother would be impressed by that!

"I don't care about Joshua Bates' future education, Hilary Anne. It's *yours* that interests me. Anyway, Joshua Bates will never be anything more than a farm labourer or a baker like his father. Now go and wash up for tea, and for goodness sake, stop scratching!"

Hilly was only too happy to run upstairs to the bathroom to get away from Mother's censure. *Surely, she could have been a little bit happy for Josh,* Hilly thought to herself as she wiped away the grime. Then, of course, she didn't know that Joshua wanted to go to university. Perhaps if she knew that, she'd be a little more impressed!

Hilly raked a hairbrush through her tangled hair and tied it back in a ponytail, noting as she did so that her head was itching again and a large knot of hair had attached itself to the bristles of her brush. Mother would be complaining about the way she got knots in her hair next, she thought, as she made her way back down to the kitchen and sat up at the table.

"You think it's good news about Joshua, don't you, Daddy?" she asked Robert as Elizabeth scooped out the mashed potatoes.

"Mm. Of course it is." Robert smiled at his daughter as he spoke. She wasn't to know that her father quietly agreed with Elizabeth about Joshua's future prospects, or that it was Matthew Bates's financial situation that was currently occupying his thoughts.

"Hilary Anne! For goodness sake!" Elizabeth's voice rang out over the dinner table.

"Stop scratching your head!"

"I'm sorry, Mummy. I can't help it. My head is itchy."

"Lord! Don't tell me you've picked up fleas from that wretched cat!"

"I don't think she's got fleas, Elizabeth," intervened Robert.

"She'd be itching all over if she had fleas. Maybe it's nits."

"**Nits**!" Elizabeth shuddered.

"If you're right, Robert, then the sooner we get her away from this dreadful school and those appalling Bates children, the better. For the time being, Hilary Anne," she turned her attention back to her daughter, "you will not be attending school and you will not go near Joshua or Lindy Bates or any of the rest of that clan. You hear me?"

Her eyes flashed as she spoke, and she grabbed hold of Hilly's wrist so tightly that it hurt.

"Mummy! You're hurting me."

"I don't care! I've had quite enough of you for one day, Hilary Anne." Elizabeth's fingers dug in a little tighter.

"I try very hard to be a good mother to you and teach you how to behave nicely, and all you can do in return is throw my efforts back in my face and come home with *nits* in your hair!"

Elizabeth let go of her grasp on Hilly, got up from the table and ran from the room, her shoulders heaving with convulsive sobs, while Hilly sat frozen to the spot, tears welling up in her soft brown eyes.

"I didn't *mean* to get nits in my hair." She sobbed quietly to Robert, who was uncertain which way to turn.

"Well, of course you didn't," he agreed. "Now, don't go getting yourself all upset. Nits are easy to get rid of."

"Then why is Mummy so angry with me?"

"Well, I think she's just a little over-excited today. Don't you worry. I'll see to her. You eat up your tea and hop into bed; then, in the morning, Mother will take you to see Doctor Evans."

Hilary Anne sat in the doctor's waiting room, quietly inspecting the bruise Elizabeth had made on her wrist. Elizabeth sat next to her, staring straight ahead, wondering how she would tell nice Doctor Evans that *her* daughter had nits in her hair. The very thought of it was humiliating. In fact, she was so mortified that she had been unable to bring herself to even touch Hilary Anne's hair to tie it in rags before sending her to bed, and this morning, she left it entirely for Hilly to tie it up by herself.

She gave a start as the nurse called out their names, then rose to her feet, tugging on Hilly's elbow.

"Come along," she hissed through gritted teeth. "Let's get this over with."

It was obvious to the doctor from the very moment that Hilly and Elizabeth entered his office, that there was a great deal of tension between them, and he guessed at once that the child had done something to set her mother's delicate nerves on edge.

"Well now, young lady." He smiled kindly at Hilary Anne, "What mischief have you been up to?"

"I have nits in my hair," Hilly stated dramatically.

"Oh, is that all?" chuckled the doctor.

"They do have a habit of attaching themselves to heads of beautiful clean hair."

"Do they?"

"Oh yes. The cleaner the hair, the more those pesky little chaps like it."

Hilly sighed with relief. Mother couldn't be angry with her any more. She didn't have nits because she was a grubby little tinker, after all. It was because she had clean hair!

"Let's have a look at the little devils then," continued the doctor, making a closer inspection of Hilly's head.

"Hmmm," he muttered. Then, "Aahh."

Doctor Evans sat back down at his desk and looked Elizabeth in the eye.

"Your daughter does not have nits, Elizabeth," he announced. "I'm afraid it's a little more serious than that."

Elizabeth felt her blood run cold.

"Hilary Anne has ringworm, I'm afraid. Do you have a dog, perhaps, or a cat?"

Elizabeth recoiled in horror, momentarily stunned into silence, her breaths coming in short, sharp gasps and a light sweat breaking out on her pinched, pallid face.

"Now, don't be working yourself into a state," the doctor continued, "You'll only go giving yourself a migraine, and it's not the end of the world."

He smiled encouragingly at Hilly as two huge, frightened brown eyes looked at him enquiringly.

"I'll prescribe some cream that will help to fix it, but you'll need to be careful to wash your hands every time you touch your head because ringworm is contagious."

It was all very well for Doctor Evans to think this wasn't the end of the world, but Elizabeth could not agree. Hilary Anne's hair was currently her only saving grace in the eyes of her much-tormented mother, and now here was Doctor Evans telling her that the child had ringworm. No doubt she caught it from that wretched cat! Elizabeth had been right all along. She knew from the start that that creature spelt trouble; she knew it would bring disaster to their heads. She should have followed her own instincts and put her foot down. Refused to let Hilary Anne have it. Well, it would have to go now, and the sooner, the better. Her thoughts ran wild as she dragged Hilary Anne down the street and all but pushed her through the front door of *Elm Cottage*.

"Go straight to your room," she ordered, "and stay there!"

"Can't I just see if Mouse is all right first?"

"No, you cannot. It's that disgusting cat that's given you the ringworm in the first place."

"No! He didn't," cried Hilly. "And even if he did, he didn't **mean** to! It's not his fault! You can't blame him!"

But Elizabeth did blame Mouse, and once having seen her sobbing daughter to the precincts of her bedroom, Elizabeth donned a pair of rubber gloves and headed outside in search of the poor, unsuspecting animal.

She found him snoozing under a bush in the front garden and gingerly reached to pick him up, holding her head as far away from him as possible, as she placed him into a cardboard box and quickly closed the lid.

Next, she marched down the road to Dr Young's Veterinary Clinic and slammed the box down on the counter. The sight of Lindy Bates gently coaxing a new-born lamb to feed from a bottle did nothing to appease her.

"Hello, Mrs Moncrieff," Lindy greeted her.

"What have you got there?"

"This," snarled Elizabeth, "is that disgusting animal you palmed off on my innocent little Hilary Anne. Your mother told me Dr Young had checked all your kittens to make sure they were healthy. Huh! Healthy indeed! Either your mother was lying, or Dr Young has no business calling himself a vet! Either way, it makes no difference. The harm is done ~ and this animal is going to be put down!"

With that, Elizabeth turned on her heel and would have marched out the door had it not been for Dr Young coming to see what all the commotion was about. He ushered Elizabeth into his office and implored her to calm down and tell him what the problem was.

"I see," he said gravely as Elizabeth finally stopped screaming at him.

"Well, I can understand your being so upset, Mrs Moncrieff, but I can also assure you that Mouse did not have a ringworm before he went to Hilary Anne."

"So now you're blaming *her* for infecting the *cat*! That is ridiculous!"

"No, no, of course I'm not. I'm merely pointing out that the fault does not lie with young Lindy Bates or, indeed, myself. Poor little Mouse has contracted the ringworm somehow since he came to live with you."

"You don't deny the cat *has* ringworm then?" demanded Elizabeth as the vet finished his inspection of the sorely agitated kitten.

"No. Sadly, you are correct. He is badly infected and should be put down for his own sake."

"Well, there you are then!" snorted the righteously triumphant Elizabeth, rising to her feet and sailing from the room.

She stormed from the Veterinary Clinic, like a woman possessed, and almost ran the short distance to Bates Bakery, where she burst through the door with such vehemence that she almost knocked down a startled customer who was unfortunate enough to be in her way.

"How *dare* you!" She spat at poor Matthew Bates.

"How **dare** you!"

She stood poised in front of him, like a cobra ready to strike, her bosom heaving and her narrowed eyes staring wildly. Matthew took an involuntary step backwards, his mouth falling open in utter disbelief, as the very proper Mrs Moncrieff told him in no uncertain terms, and with the aid of some extremely colourful language, what she thought of him, his business, his family and not least of all, his cat!

At the end of her extraordinary outburst, Elizabeth Moncrieff burst into tears and ran back out of the shop in much the same fashion as she had entered it. Matthew stood frozen on the spot. If he hadn't heard it for himself, he'd have never believed it.

"I thought she was going to combust before my very eyes," he told an equally stunned Margaret a few minutes later as she came to investigate the cause of the disturbance.

"Will she be all right, do you think?" asked Margaret, "You don't think we should go after her?"

"No," said her husband firmly. "I think she's best left to herself for now. Anyway, she said '*our lot*' was to have nothing further to do with her or her family. Especially Hilly, poor little mite. I can't help feeling bad about her catching the ringworm and all, and I can't help hoping this doesn't affect our chances of getting that loan from the bank."

An anxious frown flickered momentarily across Margaret's brow.

No. Robert Moncrieff was a decent, sensible man. He'd never let something like this interfere with business matters. She looked at Matthew's troubled countenance and smiled reassuringly.

"Of course, it won't. If we don't get the loan, it'll be because Robert thinks we're not in a position to pay it back, not because his wife feels she has an argument with us. But you're right ~ it's a dreadful shame about poor little Hilly."

As the Bates family gathered around the table for their evening meal, Hilly's misfortune and the fact that they might have been the cause of her hair '*falling out in great handfuls,*' as Mrs Moncrieff had so dramatically informed Matthew, was the main topic of their conversation.

Matthew finally decided they should recall all of Raven's kittens and have them, as well as Raven herself, checked out by the vet.

"Just in case." He smiled at an upset Lindy.

"I'm sure they'll all be perfectly fine, but we shouldn't go taking chances. It wouldn't do for anyone else to catch ringworm from them if it is our cats causing the problem."

"Can we afford to pay Dr Young to check out all the kittens again?" Margaret asked Matthew after the children had left the table.

"We can't afford *not* to," Matthew replied.

"Think what it could do to our business if Elizabeth Moncrieff is right. She threatened to have the Health Department on us anyway!"

Elizabeth Moncrieff stiffly thanked Dr Young and sent him on his way. No doubt he thought he was doing the right thing coming to inform her that all the Bates' cat family were free of ringworms and that the problem had been traced to the barn cats on the farm just along from *Elm Cottage*. Well, if he or anybody else thought *she* was going to apologise to Matthew Bates or any other member of the Bates family, they could think again. Hilary Anne would not have contracted ringworm had she not been given that kitten, and that's all there was to it.

Thanks to the whole sorry episode, *she* herself had been humiliated to the quick and suffered another of her migraines while Hilary Anne's beautiful hair was falling out in handfuls, and much of what wasn't falling out was breaking off to leave a nasty stubble. She would have to wear a hat inside when she went for her school interview, and that would surely be seen as bad manners.

By the time the day of the all-important interview arrived, Elizabeth had been forced to cut off Hilly's long locks in order to help disguise the problem.

Unfortunately, the hat was still required to hide the worst of the damage, and as she walked up the stairs to the college with Hilly at her side, Elizabeth reminded her daughter, for the umpteenth time, that she was not to remove her hat under any circumstances.

"Yes, Mother," agreed Hilly obediently.

"Stop worrying, Elizabeth," chided Robert, who was reluctantly following along behind.

They sat together in silence, waiting to be summoned to the head mistress's office.

Hilly swung her feet backwards and forwards in front of her to keep herself from being bored. She didn't care about this silly interview. It was only Mother who felt it was so important, she thought, absent-mindedly scratching her head through the little boater hat.

"Hilary Anne," hissed her mother, "don't scratch!"

"Sorry."

Elizabeth frowned. Surely, the child understood the importance of this interview. She had spent enough time trying to drum it into her.

Robert sighed and shifted uneasily in his chair.

"Mr and Mrs Moncrieff and Hilary Anne."

The refined voice rang out from the door of an office across the hall from where they were seated. It belonged to a pleasant looking middle-aged woman, who showed them into her office, then sat down opposite them.

Having introduced herself, Miss Dawes picked up a pen and then smiled pleasantly at Hilly.

"Now, Hilary Anne," she asked, "what makes you feel you would like to attend Cheltenham Ladies' College?"

Elizabeth caught her breath and felt her cheeks burn with humiliation as Hilly, with polite and simple candour, informed Miss Dawes that *she* didn't really feel she'd like to come here at all.

Miss Dawes dropped her head to one side and briefly closed her eyes, then, making the smallest of noises at the back of her throat, turned her attention instead to Robert and Elizabeth.

Despite Hilly's embarrassing lapse, Elizabeth soon began to feel the interview was going well. She and Robert quite obviously impressed Miss Dawes with their appreciation and understanding of the school's academic record and social prowess, and Elizabeth made sure Miss Dawes perfectly understood that cost was no obstacle.

For her part, Hilly wished the interview would come to an end. It was hot and stuffy in Miss Dawes' office, and her head was itching. She glanced in Elizabeth's direction and, satisfied her mother's attention was taken by Miss Dawes, reached up and scratched.

"If your hat is annoying you, Hilary Anne, then perhaps you should remove it," suggested Miss Dawes.

"Unless, of course, there is some reason you'd prefer not to," she added as she caught a glimpse of the uncertain expression on Hilly's face.

Elizabeth froze with horror and was about to inform the headmistress that Hilary Anne's doctor had advised her to keep her hat on as she was still getting over a particularly nasty head cold when Hilly decided to offer her own explanation.

"Thank you, Miss Dawes," she said in a clear, polite, matter-of-fact little voice, "but I'm afraid Mother says I have to leave my hat on. On account of the fact I have the ringworm and my hair is falling out. It doesn't look very nice, you see."

Miss Dawes's eyes opened wide, and she bit down hard on her lip.

"I see," she sputtered as Robert threw an anxious glance in his wife's direction.

Elizabeth felt herself go hot and cold all over. How could Hilary Anne disgrace herself and her parents like that? What must Miss Dawes be thinking? Hilary Anne would never be accepted into the Cheltenham Ladies' College now! And with that thought pounding in her head and a cold sweat clinging to her every pore, Elizabeth Moncrieff swayed limply back and forth in her chair until she was overcome by an awful darkness and crumpled silently to the floor in a deep faint.

Chapter – 6

Whether Hilary's ringworm or mother's fainting fit had any bearing on the decision was not divulged, but regardless, the Cheltenham School for Young Ladies proclaimed Hilary Anne to be an unsuitable candidate for enrolment at this stage. Perhaps, in due course, should she pass her eleven-plus exams, they would care to apply again, and she could be reassessed.

Elizabeth stewed for days, and Hilly's life became so unbearable she began to wish she *had* been accepted, even though she longed to stay at school in Leominster with her friends.

Mother of course felt quite certain it was Hilary Anne's inexcusable behaviour in removing her hat and describing her affliction in such detail that was to blame, though ultimately of course, the blame lay with the Bates family for giving Hilly that dreadful cat in the first place!

Hilary Anne spent the next week shut away in her bedroom, her face pressed against the windowpane, hoping in vain for at least a glimpse of one of her friends, but no one came. Of course, Mother had forbidden Joshua and Lindy to visit, and Mrs Bates would see that they obeyed Elizabeth's wishes, but even Maisie Cowan didn't come. She was keen as mustard to see what Hilly's hair looked like, but her own mother had told her not to be so silly.

"The ringworm is contagious, Maisie. You might catch it, and your own lovely hair could fall out," she stated.

Maisie ran to her bedroom and stared into the dressing table mirror to anxiously check the state of her luxurious chestnut curls.

She decided Mother was right. It wasn't worth the risk of losing her own hair. Not just to poke fun at Hilly and her stuck-up Mum. Anyway, with Hilly out of the way, there was a greater chance that Joshua Bates might notice *her* for once! Fancy Mrs. Moncrieff having a go at poor Mr. Bates the way she did! It was the talk of the town that… along with the fact that Hilly was being sent away to boarding school. Well, she didn't care what happened to Hilly anyway. She had better things to do. She looked in the mirror again and pouted her lips, then she ran her hands over her body to smooth the wrinkles from her little summer-shift dress. At just eleven years of age, Maisie was developing early, which pleased her immensely. *She was a lot more grown-up than Hilly and Lindy were,* she thought to herself.

She tied her hair up in a neat little ponytail, grabbed a bright red duffel bag from the hook on the back of her bedroom door, and sallied forth in search of the Bates children, though in truth it was mainly Joshua she hoped to see. With any luck they might have gone swimming at the Sydonia, where all the local children liked to congregate.

She hurried towards Caswell Terrace and the swimming pool, jauntily swinging the duffel bag as she trotted along. The postman turned his head as she passed by him, and she wiggled her hips a little more to show her appreciation of his attention. He grinned broadly and pushed his cap back on his head.

She'll be a handful that one, in a year or two, he chuckled to himself, as he made his way along Hereford Road, and then into Rylands Road.

Not like that poor little mite, he thought, catching sight of Hilly as he turned into *Elm Cottage.* She'd been stuck in that room, gazing out of the window for days now.

He waved cheerily up to Hilly, and she waved back at once, happy to see someone other than just mother and father. The postie waved again as he left and knowing it unlikely that anyone else would call by, Hilly sighed, and returned her attention to the small desk at which she sat. A large pad, surrounded by a collection of boxes and tins of pencils, crayons and pastels, lay open before her. She gazed down at the open page on which she had been sketching the familiar scene of the garden below her.

She sighed again, as she reached for a pencil and deftly added the postman walking up the path, then added his bicycle leaning against the garden gate. She wished she had a bicycle. *It would be such fun,* she thought, *to ride everywhere.* She would put a bell on the handlebar and a pretty basket on the front.

Hilary Anne's daydreaming was suddenly brought to an abrupt halt as the bedroom door flew open, and Elizabeth Moncrieff burst into the room, waving a letter in the air with an exaggerated flourish.

"Well, you are a very fortunate young lady, Hilly," she announced.

"Very fortunate indeed! It seems that entirely thanks to the efforts of your great aunt, you are to be given a second chance!"

Hilly sat bolt upright and waited for her mother to continue.

"Not at Cheltenham, mind you, but equally as good! Better even, more likely than not, and I don't know why I never thought of it myself! You are now enrolled at Malvern Girls College, provided you manage to pass muster, and Aunt Hilary would like you to spend the weekends with her whenever you wish! She attended Malvern Girls herself, of course. It really is the better choice for you!"

Suddenly, being sent away to school seemed a wonderful idea to Hilly, especially if she could spend her weekends with Great Aunt Hilary. Only she did hope that Geoffery boy wouldn't come and visit too often. He was horrible! She looked at her mother and smiled sweetly.

"When will I be leaving?" she asked politely.

"After you have sat and passed your eleven-plus exam, of course," replied her mother. "You will be required to attend another interview as well."

"Oh." Hilly sounded a little disappointed.

"Couldn't I go now?" she asked.

Elizabeth was perplexed at Hilly's sudden change of heart and apparent eagerness to oblige. She expected the little girl to put up a fight.

"You most certainly will not be going anywhere until your hair has grown back, which will probably take at least a year."

Elizabeth shuddered at the thought of anybody at Malvern Girls College catching sight of her daughter in her current state.

"You will be expected to behave with considerably more decorum than you display at present, Hilly, and to apply yourself to your lessons with a great deal more diligence, so you might as well start practising those attributes right now!"

She turned and made her way back to the door, at which point she paused to fire one last rejoinder in her daughter's direction.

"You can rest assured you will be spending less time with the Bates children, too!"

Hilly sighed. It would be two whole years until she turned eleven and she could take the silly exam. *Well, she would still play with her friends until then,* she thought defiantly. Mother couldn't really stop her, and Father would stick up for her on that score. He was always perfectly pleasant to *all* her friends.

As it happened, the two years that followed passed without any further major incidents to upset Elizabeth, although a few minor skirmishes ruffled her feathers like the day Hilly rushed in from school and carelessly tossed her satchel across the kitchen table.

As the air-borne bag shuddered to a halt, it sent Mother's favourite crystal vase crashing to the floor, causing it to shatter irreparably. The vase was full of fresh-picked daffodils at the time, which Hilly tried valiantly to salvage from the myriad of crystal shards that had flown in all directions. To add to her feelings of guilt at having caused such a catastrophe, she then cut her finger as she reached for a stem which had become embedded with one of the sharp, tiny splinters.

Elizabeth declared the injury to be a just reward for her thoroughly silly and reckless behaviour! Her distraught daughter's genuine distress at the situation did, however, soften her mood, and she cleaned and dressed the wound with no more than a mildly disgruntled scolding and a request that Hilly should take a little more care in future!

Hilly heaved a sigh of relief and thought herself lucky to get away with such a mild rebuke. She then doubled her efforts to behave in a manner she thought Elizabeth would find more pleasing, and for a while at least, she succeeded.

Life at *Elm Cottage* settled into a more comfortable existence after that, encouraging Robert to comment one evening how lovely it was to see his 'two favourite girls' rubbing along so well.

For her part, Hilly found herself torn between an eagerness to please Mother and head off to Malvern Girls College, where she would be able to spend more time with Aunt Hilary, and a desire to stay in Leominster, where everything was so familiar. The thought of leaving her friends behind began to play on her mind, and she wondered if it might be best to persuade Mother that Leominster Grammar School was an equally suitable choice. The answer to the whole, vexing question became blindingly obvious to Hilly, however, the day she agreed to let Maisie paint her fingernails bright pink, dust her eyelids with pretty blue eyeshadow, and apply a luscious, rich cherry lipstick to her lips. Hilly thought she looked very glamorous and grown up. Elizabeth, however, thought very much otherwise. She flew into a rage, demanded Hilly remove that *awful muck* from her face at once, and forbade her crest-fallen daughter to go anywhere near the Cowan's house ever again.

The peace between mother and daughter came to an abrupt end and the atmosphere at *Elm Cottage* became strained once more, Elizabeth declaring that the time for Hilary Anne to head off to Malvern, could not come soon enough!

At that point, Hilly gave up all hope of remaining in Leominster and mentally prepared herself for the inevitable. She consoled herself with the thought that she could spend weekends with Aunt Hilary and told herself she would be able to make *new* friends. At least Mother would not be constantly berating her!

Elizabeth's demeanour remained frosty for some time after that, with what she called *Hilary Anne's latest appalling lapse in acceptable behaviour* playing heavily on her mind.

"It's as though she does this sort of thing to deliberately irk me," she complained to Robert.

"Nonsense!" he retorted, "and you really must refrain from constantly whining about Hilly's friends, Elizabeth. Maisie is a perfectly pleasant child, and the pair of them were simply having a little girly fun. I am sorry, Elizabeth. I am tired of your constant nit-picking. Hilly will be off to school soon, and you'll miss her when she's gone. Surely, you can be a little more forgiving until then."

Stunned by her husband's stinging retort, Elizabeth fell into a funk of wounded silence, which lasted for several days and may have continued for considerably longer had not the unhappy perpetrator of all her anguish finally done something that pleased her!

Troubled by her mother's continued hostility and determined to make amends, Hilly applied herself to her schoolwork with added diligence, and her enthusiastic efforts were duly rewarded.

With the news that her troublesome daughter had passed the all-important eleven-plus exam with flying colours, Elizabeth's air of pained, long-suffering melted away like snow in the spring. Her dark, disapproving scowls gave way to warm, sunny smiles, and her past demeanours were finally forgotten.

To her even greater delight, the interview at Malvern Girls College went without a hitch, at which point, Elizabeth was overcome with a new obsession.

With a sense of great importance and an air of great purpose, Elizabeth Moncrieff busied herself to acquire the necessary items of clothing that made up the Malvern Girls school uniform. She felt, however, that perhaps the expense was such that she should please Robert by purchasing garments that would last for as long as possible.

Then, determined that her daughter should not look like 'little orphan Annie', Elizabeth procured the services of Margaret Bates to adjust the oversized skirts and shorten the sleeves of the winter jacket in such a way as they could be sized up again later.

These tasks were duly completed, and Margaret then stitched name tags into each separate item. The whole idea of sending a small child away to boarding school saddened Margaret. She had noticed of late that Hilly seemed a little quiet and withdrawn, and her heart went out to the little girl. Perhaps she would make Hilly something to take away with her.

'Something pretty yet useful,' she thought, *'like a laundry bag. Surely Elizabeth would find that a suitable gift!'*

Elizabeth did indeed approve of the laundry bag and felt obliged to comment that Mrs. Bates was, in fact, a good-hearted woman whose stitching skills were really quite excellent!

Then, every bit as much to her own surprise as that of everybody else, the week before Hilary was finally due to depart for Malvern, Elizabeth decided to throw a farewell afternoon tea party in her honour.

Margaret, Josh and Lindy headed the guest list, and Maisie and her mother, Sally Cowan, were invited. Elizabeth made a plate of dainty sandwiches and a huge Victoria sponge cake for the occasion, and Matthew Bates sent along some of Hilly's favourite jam tarts, as well as a box of his delicious sausage rolls.

Maisie and her mum presented Hilly with a pretty little manicure set to take away to school, while the Bates family gave her some boxed notelet cards so she could write home. Hilary Anne, overcome by the whole affair, burst into tears and promised she would write *every* single week.

The reality of going away to school finally hit home, and it was with considerable trepidation that a few days later, Hilly climbed into the back seat of Robert's little Hillman Hunter and took a long, lingering look at *Elm Cottage*, the only home she had ever known.

By the time they travelled the short twenty-two miles from Leominster to the Malvern Hills, the butterflies in her stomach were making her feel increasingly ill. Her anxiety rose even further as Robert slowly turned into the school's meticulously maintained driveway, where she caught a glimpse of the handsome red brick facade of Malvern Girls College.

The impressive building, which stood four stories high, was then capped off by a row of pretty attic windows, attractively set into the dark slate roof. To the rear of the building, a tall Church spire stood sentinel. Beyond that rose the soft, undulating folds of the glorious Malvern Hills, embracing the entire horizon and providing a stunning backdrop to both the school grounds and their surrounding area.

"Oh, Hilly!" breathed Elizabeth as she turned to the little girl and smiled with delight, "How beautiful it looks! There is so much here for you to sketch!"

She failed to notice the apprehension on her daughter's drawn, pinched little face, and as Robert opened the car door for her, she declared Hilary Anne to be the luckiest child in Leominster.

Hilly swallowed hard and forced herself to smile back. As Elizabeth strode eagerly ahead and led the way up the stairs to the entrance lobby, Hilly hung back, staying close to Robert, who had taken on the duties of school porter.

"What do you think then, Hilly?" he asked. "Perhaps we should leave Mother here and make a run for it!"

Hilly giggled and threw him a grateful look. At least *Father* understood how she felt.

Her anxiety was short-lived, however, as they were warmly greeted by the headmistress and a plump, pleasant girl named Grace, who was one of the senior pupils. Grace offered to show them first to Hilly's dormitory and then on a guided tour of the school. Hilly smiled shyly, and as Grace led the way, she looked about with interest.

"You're down to room with Imogen," Grace told her as they stepped into a pretty little double bedroom. "I think she's due back tomorrow. She mostly spends the holidays overseas. Her dad's in the army, you see, so they travel all over. Which bed do you prefer?" she carried on, barely pausing for breath, "Your bags look rather heavy, and I'm sure your father would like to put them down."

Hilly indicated to the bed nearest the window. Robert placed her bags on the floor alongside the bed, and as Elizabeth gave the room her nod of approval, Grace ushered them back out into the corridor.

She prattled on cheerfully as she led the way around what seemed to Hilly to be a labyrinth of rooms, hallways and staircases. They inspected everything from the bathrooms to the common room, the dining room and beyond. There were classrooms, which included special studios for art and music, and an auditorium where assembly took place each morning. It all seemed very grand! The tour concluded with a visit to the chapel, the sports grounds and the gymnasium. Finally, after a short meeting with the headmistress, Mr and Mrs Moncrieff were offered a cup of tea and a biscuit to fortify them for the journey home. Grace then politely excused herself to give them a moment of privacy in which to say their goodbyes, returning to Hilly's side just as the Hillman Hunter turned out of the driveway.

"Come on." She smiled kindly at Hilly. "Let's get you unpacked and settled in before the dinner bell."

As Robert steered the little Hillman back in the direction of Leominster, he reflected quietly on the day's events. It seemed obvious to him that Hilly was feeling overwhelmed by it all. He fervently hoped she would settle quickly into her new surroundings. He could not fault the school, but his daughter's happiness was his prime concern.

His wife, however, could not contain her excitement.

"Oh, Robert," she gushed, "isn't it wonderful! We couldn't want anything better for her, don't you agree? The building, the grounds, and that lovely little girl, Grace, just exactly the kind of child Hilly should be mixing with! Such beautiful manners!"

"As long as Hilly is happy there, Elizabeth, then I quite agree."

He held back his desire to comment further. Robert was fully aware of what drove his wife's obsession with constantly trying to 'get ahead' as she called it. Her overwhelming need to prove her worth to the world and her fervid belief that every other person she encountered was judging her was deeply embedded in her past.

As he parked the car and followed his wife inside, he hoped the decision they had made was the right one. The house seemed strangely empty to Robert as he poured himself a whiskey and sat down in his favourite leather armchair. Usually, at this time of day, Hilly would be there with him, sitting on the floor and telling him all about her day's adventures. This evening, there was nothing but a resounding silence which seemed to overwhelm him.

He found Elizabeth's constant chatter over the evening meal quite irritating and opted for an early night, only to be haunted when he closed his eyes by his daughter's drawn little face and big, sad eyes as she waved goodbye.

Hilary Anne, meantime, lay alone in her strange new surroundings. She buried her face in the pillow to muffle the sound of her sobs until overcome with exhaustion, she finally cried herself to sleep.

Chapter – 7

The rain lashed at the window in a seemingly endless torrent, making it virtually impossible for Joshua Bates to see anything beyond the wall of water that poured relentlessly down the pane. It had rained for three days now. An endless solid mass of rain not just showers that passed on the wind.

The last time it rained like this, there had been a great flood. The River Lug broke its banks and the waters rose so high that some of the folk who lived down by the mill streams had to be rescued from their upstairs windows. Poor old Mr Taylor drowned as he searched for his missing wife, who was safe up at the Priory the whole time!

Joshua shivered slightly with the cold and dampness as he pushed the memories of that day from his mind and turned his attention instead to the pages of a book laid open on the small table before which he sat, but it was to no avail; his concentration had deserted him. Perhaps he should take a break from his studies for a bit, go and see if his father needed any help in the bakery. At least it would be warm down there.

He scraped back his chair on the well-worn carpet, blissfully unaware that in doing so, he had ripped a hole in its sparse threads; then, with a yawn and a stretch, Joshua rose slowly to his feet. He was sixteen years old now and determined to do well with his 'O Level' exams. He still dreamed of attending university when his college days came to an end, though he hadn't told his parents so. They expected that he would help Matthew in the bakery or find work labouring on one of the local farms, the way Matthew had done before he went off to war and lost his leg.

Like his father, Joshua now stood over six feet tall, and while he had no fat on his bones, he was strong and wiry. *Just the right build for a farm worker, everyone kept telling him, but not if he could help it,* thought Joshua, as he pulled open the bedroom door to be greeted by the delicious aroma of freshly baked bread wafting up from below.

He closed his eyes and drew in a long, deep breath, savouring the warm, familiar redolence, then, without further ado, bounded down the stairs, taking the last three in a single leap, and made his way along the passage to the bakery.

"Need any help?" he enquired of Matthew, who was busy transferring loaves from an oven tray to a large flat basket.

"Not really," replied his father with a sigh, "this endless rain's keeping the customers away. Old Jim Stephens is the only one I've seen all morning."

"Got a boat then, has he?" quipped Joshua, helping himself to a currant bun, but Matthew offered no response. Instead, he picked up a soft white cloth and began to polish the countertop with slow, deliberate movements.

It seemed to Josh, as he watched, that the more his father rubbed, the more preoccupied he became, until by the time Margaret's voice drifted down the hallway calling them to lunch, he was so completely lost in thought that he failed to hear her.

"You coming then?" asked Joshua, heading for the door.

"Mm?"

"Lunch is ready."

"Oh."

Matthew dropped his cloth onto the counter and followed in his son's wake, completely forgetting about the wholemeal loaf that Margaret had requested earlier to accompany the soup for lunch.

He looked at her blankly when she asked what he had done with it.

"The loaf, Matthew?" repeated his wife, casting an anxious eye in his direction. It wasn't like Matthew to be forgetful.

"Oh, I'm sorry, my love."

"I'll fetch it," offered Joshua as Matthew sat down with an audible sigh and watched Margaret ladle the soup from the big stockpot she had placed on the table.

Sensing her husband had something to say, Margaret set the ladle to one side and gave him her undivided attention, but Matthew stared unseeingly in the direction of the stockpot and said nothing.

He waited for Joshua to return with the loaf, then took it from him, cutting it into a neat row of evenly sliced pieces, and it wasn't until he carefully set the knife down on the breadboard that he spoke again.

"I've been thinking," he finally announced, clasping his hands together in front of him and looking at each member of his family in turn to be certain he had their attention.

"Thought so," piped up young John as he helped himself to a slice of bread and dipped it into his soup.

"Hush, John!" admonished Margaret.

"You were saying, dear?"

"Well, I've been busy baking this morning as usual, but what with all this rain, there's nobody venturing out ~ apart from old Jim Stephens."

Matthew paused and slowly stirred his soup.

"Now Jim was telling me," he continued, "that the millstreams have merged with the river again, only this time there's melting snow as well, making things worse than ever. They're moving out the folks down Bridge Street and taking them up to Baron's Cross. So, what with that and business being slow and all, I was thinking maybe we should shut up shop for the day and send everything up there. They'll be needing food, poor souls."

"So, they will," agreed Margaret, "and you're quite right, my love. There's no sense all those fresh loaves and pastries going to waste when hungry mouths want feeding."

It occurred to her, as indeed it had to her husband, that they could ill afford to be giving away a whole day's bake, but no sooner had the thought entered her head than she banished it. What was one day's income by comparison to what those poor souls down by the mill streams would lose before this day was out?

"It's not much of a loss for us," Matthew assured her as if reading her mind, and she nodded in firm agreement.

"Have you given any thought yet as to how we'll get the bake up to Baron's Cross?" she asked, her mind now fully concentrated on the practicalities of the exercise.

"I'll take it," offered Joshua.

"We can pack it up all water-tight and fill the delivery basket on the bike, and I'll take it up there this afternoon. *It's not that far!*" he added as a worried frown settled on his mother's brow.

Margaret was none too happy at the idea of her eldest son out on his delivery bicycle in this weather, but Joshua could see no cause for alarm.

"C'mon, Mum! How many times have I done deliveries in the rain?"

"Not rain like this, Josh. Not when there's a storm raging and the river's all swollen, washing the banks away and turning farmland into sea."

"Don't worry, Mum. I'll be fine."

Margaret sighed. She had to admit she could see no other way of transporting the bread to where it was needed most. It would be churlish to stop Josh from going because of some silly, irrational fear on her part.

"All right!" she finally agreed, determined not to let her own reservations stand in the way of those in need.

"We'd best get you sorted."

Margaret fetched a roll of plastic sheeting from her sewing room and delved into the cupboard under the stairs in search of Matthew's old army groundsheet, then made her way to the bakery.

As she stood at the counter cutting large squares from the roll of plastic, her feeling of apprehension mounted. Try as she might, she could not dispel her fears, and she watched with growing anxiety as the preparations for Josh's mission unfolded around her.

Matthew stood alongside her, placing a selection of bread, buns, cakes and pastries into paper bags, which Susan then carefully parcelled up in the pieces of plastic.

Joshua and Lindy then stacked the bundles into the big basket that was fixed onto the front of the bicycle while young John, having been sent out to the shed in search of rope, spotted the old tin baby bath hanging from a nail on the wall, and came up with the clever idea of turning the now discarded tub upside down and tying it over the top of the bundles for added protection. This was done. Joshua covered the entire basket with the ground sheet, and Matthew helped him to secure it with a length of good sturdy rope. Lindy then unearthed an umbrella with a broken handle, the remainder of which was still intact, so they rested the open brolly over the whole load and tied that in place, too.

As they stood back to admire their handiwork, and Matthew congratulated the children on a job well done, Margaret looked on with a deepening sense of foreboding.

It seemed to her that the load was far too large and unwieldy, and she felt obliged to say so, but Josh gave the basket a good hard shove to prove it was perfectly secure and laughingly told her it would do fine.

"Don't fret, Mum. It's perfectly all right," he said with an encouraging smile, which did little to dispel his mother's fears. He buttoned up his oilskin coat, then pausing only to give Margaret a reassuring hug and a kiss on the cheek; he wheeled the laden bicycle out of the back door and along the path to the gate.

"Take care," Margaret called after him.

He answered her with a wave and a dull ring of the water-logged bell, and then he was gone, leaving Margaret to stand anxiously on the doorstep offering a fervent prayer for his safe return until long after he disappeared from sight.

Sally Morgan's knitting needles clicked merrily as she sat by the fire enjoying a break from her chores. In front of her on the hearth-rug, a little boy played happily with his building blocks, and alongside him, a young Jack Russell pup lay curled up in his basket, enjoying the warmth from the fire.

The dog pricked up his ears as a gust of wind rattled the window, then, with a stretch and a yawn, rose slowly to his feet and shook himself from head to toe before making off in the direction of the kitchen.

"Toby wants to go out, Mummy. I can hear him scratching at the door."

Sally sighed as she put aside her knitting. *It was time she checked on the hotpot she had prepared for tea anyway,* she thought, as she followed after the little dog. Alex would be in before long, looking for a good hot meal to help overcome the chill.

"Off you go then," she encouraged the little dog as she opened the kitchen door. Toby stood his ground.

"Hurry up. The weather's coming in."

Toby barked, then, with a wag of his tail, bounded out into the yard.

The shrill ring of the telephone coincided with his departure, causing Sally to quickly close the door in his wake and run into the hallway to answer the call. It was the village constable checking to see if Alex needed any help shifting his herd to higher ground. Now the folk down Bridge Street were all moved to safety, attention had shifted to the livestock. Sally felt certain that Alex had the situation under control. He and one of the farm lads had set off at first light, and she was expecting them back any time now. She assured Constable Jones she'd let him know if any problems arose, then started to make her way back to the kitchen.

A sudden loud bang made her jump, and she hastened her step.

"Thomas!" she called, hurrying back into the living room to check on her son.

"Are you all right, Thomas?"

Building blocks lay strewn across the floor, but there was no sign of the little boy. Another loud thump caused her to spin around and run towards the kitchen, calling loudly for the child as she went.

"Thomas! Thomas! Where are you?" The note of panic in her voice rose to a fever pitch as she discovered the door that led out to the garden was wide open. It swung furiously back and forth on the wind, a sudden gust driving it hard against the wall with another angry thud.

"**Tommy**!" There was a sob in Sally's voice now as she stood on the threshold looking out across the little porch into the murk. He must have gone out there! Gone out in search of Toby! There was nowhere else he could be. The phone was in the hallway, and she'd have seen him if he'd left the living room that way. The kitchen was the only other way he could have gone, and she was certain she had closed the door securely after Toby, which meant that Tommy must have opened it.

Leaving the door to bang behind her, she turned and ran back through the living room, out into the hallway and up the stairs, hoping she was wrong… hoping it was *she* who'd left the kitchen door unlatched, and that Tommy had slipped upstairs unnoticed. She frantically searched the bedrooms and the bathroom, calling loudly as she went, but there was no response to her cries. Tommy was nowhere to be seen.

It didn't even occur to Sally to grab a coat as she ran back through the kitchen and out into the yard. She could think of nothing but Tommy.

The bitter wind stung her cheeks and tangled her hair as it whipped across her face, and the icy rain saturated her woollen dress until it clung around her legs with such a tenacious grip that she could barely move.

She stumbled over the stony path that led to the farm gate, calling for her son as she went. Surely, he would never stray from the path in this weather. The fields were quagmires of mud, and away to the north and west, the river Kenwater was joining forces with the Lug and the millstreams. Together, they were spilling over the land, their rising waters engulfing everything they met along the way. A small boy would be no match for their onslaught.

Sally's anguish grew with every step, and her vocal cords strained with the effort of calling for her son and his little dog.

"Tommy! Toby! Where are you?"

Her voice dropped away and ended with a sob. It was hopeless. They were nowhere to be found, and they'd never hear her calling over the noise of the wind and the rain.

Her hands closed around the top of the gatepost, and she bowed her head.

"*Please, God,*" she whispered. "*Please keep them safe. Please keep them safe.*"

As the two horses slowly picked their way along the path, Alex Morgan shifted in his saddle and reached up to wipe away the rain that had dripped onto his face and neck from the upturned brim of his sou'wester.

"Good Lord!" he muttered to himself.

"It can't be!"

He wiped the back of his hand over his eyes and peered ahead into the gloom. It was! There was a figure hunched over the gate ~ and it looked for all the world like his Sally.

Alex felt his heart skip a beat and his stomach churn over. Something was wrong. Something was terribly wrong. He kicked his heels to spur on the horse and, leaving his fellow rider to stare after him in wonder, took off at a gallop.

"Sal, Sal!"

Alex's voice rose above the dull thud of the horse's hooves, but the wind carried it away, and his wife offered no response until he was almost upon her. She looked up then, and even in the fading light, Alex could see that her eyes were red from crying.

"What is it, Sal? What's happened?"

Alex reigned in the horse and dismounted in one seamless movement. Sally was soaked through. Her dripping hair was plastered to her face, and her sopping dress clung to her body like a shroud.

"Sally!" Alex took off his coat and wrapped it around her.

"Look at you girlie! Look at the state of you! What is it? What's happened?"

"Tommy! It's Tommy! I can't find him." Great sobs racked her body.

"I'm so sorry, Alex. I'm so sorry!"

"There there, girlie, don't take on so. Just tell me what's happened, eh."

"I only left him for a minute to answer the phone. When I came back, he was gone. The kitchen door was open, but I knew I had shut it after Toby had gone out, so it had to be Tommy who opened it. It had to be."

"You searched the house?"

"Of course, I searched the house."

Alex nodded. It was a stupid question. He gave Sally a gentle, reassuring squeeze and turned to his farmhand, who had reigned in alongside them.

"I'm sorry to ask this of you, Chris, as I know you're ready to call it a day 'n' all, but if you wouldn't mind doing one last thing before you head home."

The young man nodded. He'd got the gist of the situation and knew what was required. They'd need to get a search party out right away if the child was to be found safe.

Alex was torn as to which way he should turn. On the one hand, he longed to stay and comfort his distraught wife, while on the other, he felt compelled to set off at once in search of the little boy who was the apple of his eye. If Sally was right and Thomas had wandered off across the farm, then there was not a moment to be lost in finding him. The flood waters were rising at an alarming rate, and half the lower paddocks were already underwater. Trees were down, and banks and bridges were washing away. On top of that, it was almost dark, and somewhere out there, all on his own was little Tommy.

The object of his parents' despair was tired of being cooped up indoors. He was bored. Tommy deliberately pushed over the castle he was building and watched the wooden blocks go flying in all directions. He could hear Toby barking at something outside and his mother talking on the telephone, telling someone that his father would be back soon. That must be why Toby was barking. He could probably see Daddy coming. It was then the idea struck him. He would go out and join Toby. See if he could spot his father making his way back across the farm or along the path that led from the road. Tommy Morgan clapped his hands together in glee at the idea, then carefully stepping over the scattered blocks, made his way to the kitchen.

As he stood on tiptoe and reached up for the doorknob, Tommy heard his mother put down the phone, and he could hear her calling after him as he slipped into the washhouse to find his Wellington boots and MacIntosh.

A little voice inside his head told him that Mother wouldn't like what he was doing, but just as he was about to give in to his better self and answer her, she disappeared back into the house, and the little voice in his head told him that now was the time to make good his escape. By the time Sally Morgan returned to the kitchen door and ran out across the porch into the yard, Tommy was gone, off in hot pursuit of his much-loved four-legged friend.

For his part, Toby was enjoying himself immensely. He spotted a rabbit and baled it up against the barn wall, then as Tommy ran to join him, the rabbit hopped off across the yard in a frenzy. Toby chased after it, wriggling his way under the fence and disappearing across the field. Tommy clambered over the fence and followed in their wake, jumping and splashing in puddles and sliding in mud patches along the way. This was much more fun than building blocks, even if his Wellingtons were getting heavier with every step as their cleats filled with mud.

"Wait, Toby," he called, struggling along after the little Jack Russell as it scampered down the hill.

"Wait for me!"

But Toby kept up the chase until the terrified rabbit bounded across a little stone bridge spanning the stream that ran through the lower fields and finally disappeared from sight.

Toby stopped then, sniffing at the ground for a trace of the rabbit's scent and a hint as to which direction it had taken.

"Naughty... Toby," puffed his diminutive owner as he finally caught up with the little dog.

Toby barked and took off again, the bedraggled and mud-spattered Tommy once more in pursuit. His little legs ached with the effort of keeping up with the energetic Jack Russell, and his Wellingtons rubbed up and down against the back of his calves, making them sore. He stumbled on, calling to Toby to wait up, until just as the little dog finally came to the realisation that the rabbit was long gone and turned to obey his young master, Tommy's foot caught in a tree root, tripping him up and wrenching his ankle so badly that he cried out in pain. The little boy lay on the ground trying not to cry, while Toby ran round and round him in circles, barking excitedly, until very slowly, Tommy pulled himself onto his knees, then tried to stand up. But he couldn't! His ankle hurt so badly that he fell down again, and this time, he didn't move. He lay perfectly still in a sea of mud while the rain washed over him, and Toby frantically licked at his face and his hands.

By the time Tommy came round again, it was getting dark and Toby had disappeared. The little boy gingerly pulled himself up and sat hugging his knees to his chest, shivering and whimpering with the cold and pain. He called out for the Jack Russell to come to him, but there was no reassuring bark. No sign or sound that the dog was anywhere nearby.

Tommy lowered his head onto his knees and started to sob. He hadn't meant to wander off so far. He only wanted to find his father, not to run off across the farm after Toby and some dumb rabbit. Now look what had happened ~ and Toby had gone off and left him! Tommy looked across the sodden ground in the direction from whence he had come, and his heart skipped a beat. The bridge had gone! Even the stream had gone! In its place, there was a river. A wide expanse of water rose up to meet him. A cold fear gripped at his heart, and his quiet sobbing gained momentum as, for the first time in his four short years of life, Thomas Morgan understood what it was to be truly afraid.

Despite his bravado and enthusiastic approach to the task at hand, Joshua Bates soon came to the realisation that the going was much harder than he had anticipated it would be, with great puddles that seemed to come halfway up the wheels, and driving rain that lashed at his face making it difficult for him to see where he was going. His feet slipped off the pedals on more than one occasion, and the bicycle nearly toppled over when he rode into a branch that lay almost submerged in a newly formed pothole. Joshua barely regained control of the cycle before it began to slither and slide wildly on a wide slick of mud that oozed its way over the road. He put a foot on the ground to steady himself and felt it sink into the mire, his shoe slowly filling with thick, slimy slush and squelching loudly as he pulled it free again.

Determined to continue on his way, Josh tightened his grip on the handlebars and pushed down hard on the pedals, but the bicycle refused to budge, and a quick downward glance soon revealed the reason for its obstinance. Despite the guard set in place to protect it from just such an occurrence, the chain was coated in thick, oozing mud, and Joshua was obliged to dismount. His shoes squelching with every step, he dragged the bike out of the quagmire and set it to rest against a tree while he searched around for something, he could use to dislodge the tightly packed sludge.

It was no more than three o'clock in the afternoon, but the light was already failing, and Josh knew he would need to hurry if he was to make it to the disused army camp at Baron's Cross and back again by dark. He broke a sturdy twig from the tree and used it to scrape away the worst of the mud, then hoping the rain would wash away the rest, set off again. It was heavy going, and he was forced to push the bike for some distance before the chain began to work freely, but he struggled on with dogged determination. Finally, he could just make out ahead of him the faint shimmer of the lights at Baron's Cross as they flickered through the driving rain. He peddled with renewed vigour then, his legs aching and his heart pounding with the effort of his exertions until, at last, he pulled to a stop outside the first of the barracks.

The inhabitants of Hut One were quite taken by surprise as the door suddenly flew open to admit a bedraggled and mud-splattered young man who stood on the threshold gasping for breath.

"Could someone... give me... a hand?" he panted.

"Bread... I have bread."

Nobody moved until Ted Green, who had been closely scrutinising the intruder, suddenly realised his identity.

"Lord! It's young Joshua Bates!" he exclaimed.

"You have bread, you say?"

"Bread," repeated Josh.

"C'mon, lads, let's give the young fellow a hand then!"

The stunned silence gave way to a bustle of activity. Joshua Bates had brought bread! The lad had to be barmy out riding a bicycle in this weather, but what a welcome sight his laden basket was!

With the aid of Ted and a couple of lads Josh recognised from school, the contents of the basket were soon emptied into the baby bath and spirited inside. The women took over then, opening the bundles and laying out the paper bags on a large wooden table, as a young boy was sent to round up the remainder of the camp's residents.

Joshua, now fully recovered from his exertions, leaned against the wall and watched in silence as the women distributed the bags around those assembled, and tired, hungry children pounced eagerly on his father's wares.

"You mind you thank Joshua over there now," one mother instructed her son, as the delighted six-year-old gleefully bit into a large, sticky bun, and Joshua felt suddenly overcome, as one by one, children and adults alike, came to shake his hand and extend their gratitude to him and his family.

The inhabitants of Baron's Cross were still discussing the Bates' generosity long after Josh took his leave. They offered him a bed for the night, but knowing his mother would be anxiously watching for him, Joshua declined and, despite the concern of those around him, ventured back out into the elements.

The delivery bike felt much lighter now and was a great deal easier to manage. The empty bath, wrapped snuggly in the groundcover, fitted neatly into the large basket, making the load far less cumbersome, and Josh felt certain his steady progress would see him well home by dark, in spite of the still driving rain and the wet, muddy condition of the road.

He grinned happily to himself as he rode along, feeling at once humbled yet proud of his part in his father's plan. He would enjoy describing to Matthew how gratefully his offerings had been received, and his mother would be pleased that she had agreed to the plan when he told her how excited and happy the children had been. Their eyes fairly lit *up at the sight of those Chelsea buns;* he thought with a chuckle as he took a rest from peddling to let the bike glide downhill.

He was almost back to the mud slick when it happened. A small dog suddenly darted out in front of him, and in his effort to avoid hitting the animal, Josh frantically applied his brakes and swerved sideways. The bike lurched and bumped its way over a tangle of debris on the roadside until it finally toppled into a ditch, taking a startled Joshua with it.

Every bone in Josh's body jarred and jangled as he landed with a heavy thud. His cheekbone scraped against a protruding gorse bush, and as the cycle crashed down on top of him, he felt the end of the pedal dig into his hip bone, and the back of his head engaged with something hard.

Stunned, and hurting from head to toe, Joshua slowly disentangled himself from the bicycle and pulled himself out of the muddy ditch. The small dog that was the cause of his collision stood alongside barking excitedly, then as Josh pulled the cycle back up onto the road, ran off in the direction from which it had come.

As Joshua looked after him, the dog stopped and ran back, still barking loudly.

"What is it, eh?" Josh asked as the animal took off again.

It ran a few feet, then stopped once more, looking anxiously back at Joshua and trading its bark for a pitiful whine.

Josh sighed. He was sore and tired and desperately wanted to go home, but the dog obviously wanted him to follow.

"Okay, you win ~ but it better be important."

Josh lifted his bicycle over the ditch, leaned it against a tree and followed after the little creature, who bounded off ahead, barking with renewed vigour.

There were several occasions when Josh wondered at the wisdom of his actions as he slid down the muddy hillside after the little Jack Russell, and when the animal set off to swim across the swollen stream, Josh looked after him in dismay. The current was carrying the dog downstream as it struggled valiantly to reach the opposite bank, and Josh realised it would be dangerous to follow him without a boat, yet something inside him told him that he must. Someone needed his help. The little dog knew that.

Josh could just make out the sound of his yapping, drifting eerily on the wind as it echoed across the water, sounding more and more like a cry for help until it gradually faded away. Joshua listened intently, his ears straining to catch the sound of the dog over the wind, but there was nothing.

"*Hello,*" he shouted,

"*Hello! Can anybody hear me?*"

There was no reply to his call. No answering bark. Nothing but the sound of the wind. Joshua didn't know what to do. Without the dog to guide him, he wouldn't know where to go if he crossed the water anyway. He sighed as his eyes scanned the thicket on the opposite side of the swollen millstream. It was hopeless. He turned to go, but as he started to walk away, a faint sound reached him, causing him to turn and look back.

"**Hello!**" he shouted again, and this time his call was answered by a weak cry for help.

Joshua ran back to the water's edge, his eyes once again scanning the thicket opposite. A slight movement caught his attention, and he stared intently until he could just make out what looked like a small boy sitting huddled under the trees.

"*Are you* all right? *Are you hurt at all?*" shouted Joshua.

"*I'm cold, and my foot hurts,*" came the faint, tearful reply.

Josh's mind raced. Somehow, he had to get the child to safety.

Then it came to him. He could use the rope from the delivery bike!

"Wait there!" he yelled over the wind as he turned to retrace his steps, *"And don't worry! I'll be back soon!"*

The child's frightened, frantic cries rang in Josh's ears as he slowly made his way back to the bicycle. It seemed to take him forever to climb back up the hill. His body still ached from his spill off the cycle and his feet slipped from under him, causing him to land on his hands and knees on more than one occasion, but eventually, he made it, and he wasted no time then in untying the length of rope that leashed the baby bath to the basket. He coiled up the rope and hung it around his neck, then he stood and stared long and hard at the baby bath before taking it firmly in his grip and setting off down the hill again.

Thomas Morgan watched anxiously for Joshua's return. What if he didn't come back? What if something happened to him? What if he did come back but still didn't come across the water? Tommy couldn't understand why he'd gone away in the first place. Perhaps he'd gone to look for Daddy. The thought cheered Tommy momentarily, and a glimmer of hope shone in the red, swollen eyes. Daddy would know what to do. He always knew what to do. Tommy rubbed his fists across his grubby, tear-stained face. He couldn't stop shivering now. He was so cold that his bones ached, and his sore, swollen ankle throbbed mercilessly. He wished Toby would come back and comfort him, but he had seen Toby being swept away. Silent sobs racked the child's body at the memory of the little Jack Russell struggling to keep his head above the swirling water. He wished he was back at home playing with his blocks by the fire, with Toby curled up on the hearth-rug in front of him. It was warm there and safe. Tommy's head fell back down onto his knees, and his eyelids drooped. He was too tired to watch for Joshua anymore. He was too tired even to cry.

Joshua looked around for somewhere to secure the rope. He could see the child still huddled up on the far side of the water. He called him, but there was no reply. The only sounds that Joshua could hear over the ominous, swirling river of water were those of the wind and the rain. He swallowed hard as he tied the rope to a nearby tree and tested its strength by pulling on it with all his might. He bit his lip as he bent down and tied the other end of the rope through one of the handles on the end of the baby bath. Then, checking that, too, was secure, Josh made his way to the water's edge. It was dark and scary, and Joshua shivered as he removed his shoes and coat and rolled up his trouser legs, but he never once thought about abandoning his mission. It troubled him that the child didn't answer when he called. Certain that he had only one course of action to pursue, Joshua Bates bravely gritted his teeth and stepped into the freezing cold water. He held the baby bath in front of him and used it as a flotation aid as he struck out for the opposite bank. The icy cold bit at him until his fingers and toes felt numb. The cuts and scrapes from his fall into the ditch stung madly, and his aching bones felt chilled to the core, but he battled on until he was able to touch the bottom with his feet.

He scrambled out of the water, then dragged the little bath up onto dry land and anchored it in place with the aid of a large stone. The current had taken him a little away from the child, and he had to make his way around the edge of the thicket to reach him.

Tommy was barely able to rouse himself by the time Joshua found him. His little body was frozen stiff, and his speech was incoherent. He opened his eyes and stared at Josh unseeingly. Somewhere deep inside, something told him that he'd be all right now, and the flicker of a smile crossed his lips as his head slumped over his knees again.

Joshua lifted the little boy up and carefully picked his way back over the debris that lay scattered along the water's edge. He put the child down as he removed the rock from the bath, then he gently put Tommy in its place. The baby bath was only just large enough to hold him, and as Josh carried it back into the water, he prayed that it would manage to stay afloat. It rocked wildly as Joshua set it down on the swirling current, and its dazed occupant whimpered with fear.

"It's all right," Josh reassured the little boy, "we'll be safe back on land soon."

Truth be told, Josh felt anything but assured that all was well. Once his feet were no longer able to touch the bottom, the bath wanted to drift away from him, and he struggled to control its movements, let alone guide it back to the other side of the river. He waited until the rope pulled taut, then slowly pulled himself along it with one hand while he gripped the bath with the other. It seemed to take forever to progress, no more than a few inches. His hands were stiff and numb with the icy cold of the water, and the baby bath seemed to weigh a ton as he struggled to coax it on against the current.

Josh could feel his strength ebbing. Every muscle burned with the effort of his exertions, and the gnawing cold made it harder and harder to catch his breath, but he refused to give in. He must have been in the water for a good ten minutes when, without warning, his frozen fingers let slip his grasp on the baby bath, and the swirling waters wrenched it away from him. It spun about wildly, causing the small child within to wake in a state of panic. His terrified screams echoed across the water while Josh grabbed frantically at the rope, at the same time calling to the little boy to calm him down; then, as the bath reached the end of its tether, Josh slowly pulled it towards himself again, urging the child not to move for fear he tipped the frail craft over.

By the time Josh's fingers closed around the handle on the end of the bath again, his energy was spent. It took him every ounce of effort to keep his head above the water, and he felt certain he would surely drown. He bobbed up and down, fighting for breath, his tired legs struggling to keep him afloat.

Alex Morgan threw down the telephone receiver in disgust. The line was dead. Why now, just when they really needed the wretched thing? It was so typical! He turned to his distraught wife and begged her not to worry. He would send young Chris into town to raise the alarm while he himself would head off in search of Tommy at once. He would make his way across the fields between Bargates and the Kenwater, following the higher ground to afford him a better vantage point.

The reassuring smile he bestowed upon his wife as he took his leave of her soon faded as he ventured back out into the storm. The wind seemed to be abating now, but the driving rain still lashed at him.

Alex could not for his life understand what might have induced little Tommy to stay out in this weather. He turned up his collar against the rain and shook his head as he led his horse through the gate at the bottom of the field. Whatever the reason, it made no difference. The child had to be found and found quickly.

Alex swung himself into the saddle and urged his mount on towards a small thicket of trees that bordered his land where it met the road. With any luck, Tommy and Toby would be up there, sheltering from the storm.

He called loudly, over and over, as he slowly picked his way along the path that ran between the trees, but the only sound that answered him was the creak and snap of branches being tossed in the wind. He came out of the thicket at the far end of the rise and looked out over the farmland stretching below him. The fields had all but disappeared under the swollen stream, which in turn had become a virtual sea. This land he knew so well had become a strange and alien place.

Alex dismounted and slowly led the horse down the hill towards the water, praying as he went that his son had not taken the same route. Even the horse struggled to keep its footing on the muddy ground, and Alex was about to turn and retrace his steps when a distant sound caught his attention. He froze on the spot, his ears straining. It sounded like a voice crying out in desperation, but he couldn't be certain. Perhaps it was just the wind playing tricks on him. As he stood poised, uncertain which way to turn, Alex heard the sound again. It *was* a voice. He was sure of that now. His feet slipped and slid under him as he hastened towards the sound, and his heart pounded as it filled with hope that the cries would lead him to Tommy.

Joshua felt himself sinking deeper and deeper into the icy cold water. The rope bit into his fingers as he clung to it in desperation, but he had no strength left in his arms to pull himself back along its length. Even Tommy's frightened cries failed to spur him on. The whole world seemed to be swirling about him, and the freezing water got darker and darker the further he sank. He bobbed up and down, his burning lungs gasping for breath as the sharp, searing pain of cramps bit hard at his frozen limbs, rendering him unable to move.

Joshua, certain now that his life must surely end felt a strange calm settle over him as he prepared to meet his fate. He closed his eyes and struggled to release his grip on the rope, but his frozen fingers refused to budge. He mustn't take the bath and the child down with him, or his efforts would be in vain. He could only hope that the little boy would have the sense to keep still until someone found him. He didn't even know who the child was, but surely someone must be looking for him by now.

A sudden sharp jerk on the rope shocked Josh back to his senses; then, he felt himself being pulled slowly back up towards the surface.

"Hold on! Hold on!" a voice was shouting, and over it, he could hear the child screaming,

"Daddy! Daddy! I knew you'd come and save us. I knew you would!"

Joshua coughed and spluttered and retched, until he finally managed to empty his stomach of its watery contents, then he looked up for the first time, at the man who had pulled him to safety.

He was a strong, solidly built man in his early thirties, and as their eyes made contact, Josh could have sworn there were tears running down Alex Morgan's weathered face.

"Thank you, thank you," he was murmuring over and over again.

"You saved my son. Thank you."

How he came to be lying on a sofa in a strange room, with Dr Edwards bending over him and a couple he didn't even know hovering anxiously nearby, was a mystery to Josh. His mind seemed to be filled with a jumble of nonsense. Chelsea buns and little dogs; small children, a tin tub, a length of rope and freezing cold, dark water that threatened to engulf him. None of it made any sense to Joshua as he shivered and tugged at a warm, cosy counterpane that was laid over him.

He gripped the quilt firmly around his shoulders and looked about in bewilderment.

"Where am I?" he asked in a voice that barely sounded like his own.

"It's all right, you're safe now," soothed Dr Edwards.

"You and the little boy, both."

"The little boy?"

"Tommy. Our Tommy."

it was the woman who spoke.

"You saved his life, remember?"

Joshua shook his head.

"No… that is sort of, I suppose," he replied vaguely as he drifted off once more.

It was morning when Joshua woke again, and he had a clear recollection then, of what had transpired the day before. As he opened his eyes to the dim morning light, he could see the man who pulled him from the water, was still keeping vigil in a nearby chair.

"Good morning, Joshua. I hope you're feeling better for a good night's sleep." He smiled as Josh swung his legs over the side of his makeshift bed.

"I'm Alex by the way," the man continued, "Alex Morgan."

Josh shook the outstretched hand.

"I'm Joshua Bates, but you seem to know that already."

Alex nodded.

"Dr Edwards and Constable Jones both knew who you were."

It was Josh's turn to nod.

"Thank you for pulling me from the water. I thought I was a goner until you came along."

"Thank you for saving our Tommy."

"I wouldn't have without your help."

"That's not how I see it, Josh. Without you, our Tommy would be dead. Even if the water hadn't got him, the cold would have. How did you find him?"

"There was a little dog that ran out on the road in front of my bike and made me fall off in a ditch. He wanted me to follow him. He led me down to the water, and then he got swept away, and I wasn't sure what to do next until your little boy cried out. I could see him then, huddled up under a tree on the other side of the water, so I went back up where I left my bike and fetched the rope and the baby bath. Lucky, I had them with me, really."

"Very lucky. Then what?"

"Well, you know what happened after that."

"You swam across a dark, freezing, swirling mass of water that you had just seen sweep a dog away to save a frightened child you didn't even know."

Joshua looked down at the carpet on the floor and started to count the roses in the pattern. Alex was making him sound like a hero, and he certainly didn't feel like one. He'd been scared and uncertain, not brave and fearless.

"You make it sound like I did something special, but I only did what anyone else would have done."

"I don't think so, Joshua. There are not many folks who would have found the courage to do what you did. Sally and I want to give you something, Joshua, to show our appreciation. Anything at all. Whatever you want. Just say the word, and it's yours."

Joshua shook his head. He was about to say that there was nothing that he wanted and that, after all, Alex had already saved *his* life when it came to him in a flash of inspiration.

"There is *one* thing I'd like," he said quietly.

Alex grinned broadly and nodded encouragingly.

"A job. I'd like a part-time job. You know, before or after school, or on weekends, maybe."

Alex's eyebrows flew upwards in surprise. He'd have happily given this lad a shiny new bicycle or even a car if he'd asked for it, and he lost no time in telling Joshua so.

"Well, that's really kind of you, sir, and it's not that I don't appreciate the offer; it's just that I wouldn't feel comfortable, you know, accepting something like that, but I'd really love it if I could earn a bit of money. Everyone says I'm the right build for a farm labourer."

Alex bit back the desire to tell Joshua he'd gladly *give* him money if that was what he wanted, but something told him it would be the wrong thing to do, so instead he promised to employ Joshua Bates for as many hours as he cared to work for, before and after school, and at weekends.

Joshua grinned happily as they shook hands on the arrangement. Perhaps he would make it to university one day, after all!

He was still grinning broadly as Alex Morgan delivered him home to the bakery later that morning. His mother, on the other hand, burst into tears the minute she set eyes on him. She felt her feelings of misgiving the previous day had been well and truly justified.

When Joshua failed to return from Baron's Cross, Matthew contacted the constable, who later found the abandoned bicycle under the tree where Joshua had left it. It was not, however, until some considerable time after that that Joshua himself had been located, and during the long and agonising wait for news, Margaret was beside herself with worry while Matthew blamed himself for coming up with the idea that they should send the bake to Baron's Cross in the first place. Now, here was Joshua breezing in through the door as if he'd been out for a day at the beach!

"Just look at you," admonished Margaret, "grinning like a Cheshire cat while I've been sat here all night, worried sick."

Joshua put his arms around his mother's neck and winked at his father.

"Now I happen to know that Constable Jones called round here last night to let you know that I was fine."

"Fine, you call it! Risking your life like that! Thank God you're safe." Sobbed his relieved mother, doing her best to admonish him.

"Oh, Joshua, I'm so proud of you!"

Chapter – 8

"Hilly! Hilly!"

Hilary St. Clair waved out gaily and tooted the horn on her much loved, little deep forest green MGB.

She had folded down the roof of the little car today, in order to enjoy the first warming rays of the summer sun. A long chiffon scarf, draped firmly over her head and around her neck, fluttered softly in the gentle breeze, prompting Hilly to comment how pretty it looked. Her Great Aunt was delighted at the compliment, though she brushed it aside with her customary air of self-dismissal.

Having Hilly's company on a regular basis, had taken years off the older woman. In fact, she enjoyed having Hilly and her friend Imogen around so much, she felt deeply saddened at the knowledge that her young relation's school days had now drawn to a close.

Hilary Anne's acceptance at Malvern Girls, had ultimately suited all three female generations of the extended Moncrieff family, most admirably.

Hilly's only regret was that she seldom got to see her old friends anymore. She heard about Josh's heroism on the day of the big flood, though. Even Mother grudgingly showed a degree of admiration over *that*, and Aunt Hilary helped Hilly pick out and post a card to congratulate him on his bravery.

Josh wrote back straight away, making light of the whole thing, which only served to make him even more of a hero in Hilly's eyes.

She longed to see him again, but because he was so set on saving up to pay for a university education, he was always working on the Morgans' farm when she visited home. In fact, *all* of her friends seemed to be busy these days. Lindy spent every spare minute she could find helping Dr Young, the vet, and Maisie was learning how to be a hairdresser. Mrs Bates and Susan were either busy designing and stitching ladies' wear, or they were working together selling their creations at their new market stall. Even John was grown up enough to take over Josh's chores, helping out in the bakery.

"Well then," stated Aunt Hilary, as Hilly tossed her bags into the back of the little car and hopped into the passenger seat,

"Your school days are over!"

Hilly smiled and bit her lip with an air of uncertainty.

"Yes." She smiled,

"Paris, here I come!"

"So, you've chosen L' Ecole des Beaux-Arts over Teacher's Training College!"

"I *have*. For now, at least. I love the idea of studying art in Paris, and it will be perfect for improving my French as well, although I think Mother may have preferred, I'd chosen a school in London. To be honest, I'd rather stay on here with you for a while first until my student accommodation is confirmed. That way, there would be less opportunity for arguments to arise!"

"Of course, my dear, I would love it if you *could* stay on, but we both know that your parents are looking forward to your returning home to the cottage for a short while at least."

Hilly sighed.

"Father perhaps, but I daresay it won't be long before I manage to upset Mummy again! I'll miss you, Aunt Hilary. I've never been so happy in all my life as I have these past few years."

"I know, child. I know. I shall miss you too."

The two women lapsed into a comfortable silence, each lost in her own thoughts, as the little car turned out of the school grounds and headed off, not in the direction of Leominster, but rather that of Ledbury instead.

"I phoned Elizabeth and told her that I was taking you to '*The Fountain*' before we headed home to *Elm Cottage*."

Hilly grinned.

"Oh, *thank you*," she enthused. "What a treat!"

The Fountain Hotel in Ledbury had become one of Hilly's favourite haunts over her years at Malvern Girls. About twenty minutes from Malvern and just a few miles from Aunt Hilary's manor house, '*The Fountain*' was renowned for its excellent teas. Aunt Hilary had very generously taken Hilly and Imogen there many times over the years, and they had never tired of it!

"It seems only right that we should celebrate your graduation in style," smiled Aunt Hilary.

"Just the two of us."

Hilly nodded in agreement.

"You will still have me to stay sometimes, won't you?" she enquired anxiously, suddenly worried that her regular visits to *Oak Manor* might now come to an abrupt end.

"Of course, you goose," laughed her aunt. "I've been rather afraid you may not want to!"

"*Not want to!*" Hilly was aghast!

She assured her great aunt that she would *always* want to, and they spent the remainder of their short trip reminiscing about some of Hilly's past visits.

"Do you remember that time years ago when Geoffrey Chatswood got stuck up the oak tree?" laughed Aunt Hilary.

"I'd rather not, if you don't mind. What a frightful child he was."

"He was indeed! You'll be pleased to know that he's actually turned into a rather charming young man. Works with his father these days."

"In London?"

"Yes."

"Excellent! We're not likely to run into him then!"

Aunt Hilary bit her lip.

"Thank you for letting me drive home," enthused Hilly a few hours later as she brought the little MGB to a halt outside *Elm Cottage*.

Helping Hilary Anne acquire her driver's licence was one of many things her aunt had done for her during her time at Malvern, and driving the little sports car was now a treat that Hilly relished.

She leapt out of the car as she spoke and rushed around to open the passenger door for her much-loved aunt.

"Least I could do!" smiled Aunt Hilary.

"I hope it hasn't upset your mother, though!"

Hilly laughed and nodded. It had not escaped the notice of either woman, that Elizabeth was standing at the window holding back the curtain, as she anxiously awaited their arrival.

She dropped the curtain immediately as the car turned into the driveway, but both of her relatives were well aware that she would have been there for ages, her anxiety mounting with every passing minute.

Elizabeth's nervous disposition had not improved over the years. It still got the better of her at the most inconvenient of times, and today, she had worked herself into a state of anxiety at the thought that Hilary Anne would likely be driving Aunt Hilary's precious little sports car. After all, it wouldn't be the first time!

She heaved a sigh of relief at their safe arrival and rushed to the front door to greet them, calling out to Robert as she went. It would be nice to have Hilly back at home for a while, even if it did mean she would be consorting with her old group of friends again. They were all getting quite grown up now, of course, just like Hilly, who, thanks to the efforts of her great aunt and the combined staff of Malvern Girls College, was now a very well-rounded, accomplished young lady. She had done the right thing by Hilly, sending her away to school, Elizabeth thought to herself as she threw open the door. Nobody could say otherwise.

A sense of immense pride and satisfaction washed over her as she watched her daughter, who was wreathed in smiles as she helped her aunt step from the car.

Hilary Anne was of average height, slender, graceful and every bit as pretty as Elizabeth herself. Her ringworm affected hair had recovered years ago, and its soft tones of pale gold shimmered in the late afternoon sun, as she flicked it back over her shoulders.

As Hilly looked up and waved hello, Robert burst through the open door, eager to join his wife as she greeted their visitors.

"I'll get that for you," he called to Hilary Anne as she reached for her luggage.

"Your trunk arrived safely. It's up in your room waiting for you."

Hilly nodded.

"Thank you, Daddy." She smiled happily as she threw her arms around him.

Robert hugged her back, his delight at having her home evident for all to see. As he finally let go of her and turned to warmly greet his aunt, Hilly made her way up the steps to where Elizabeth stood waiting.

"It's so good to be home, Mummy." She smiled, slipping an arm around her mother's waist and leading her inside.

"Oh, look! You've gathered cowslips for Grandfather's vase! How wonderful! I remember when I was very little, how I would pick them after school, and we would fill the vase together! They always grew in such great

116

drifts that the whole meadow looked alive! As though it was draped in a veil of shimmering golden organza that sparkled in the sun and billowed gently on the breeze. Is it still like that? Oh, I shall have to go and see!"

Elizabeth smiled. It pleased her that Hilly still remembered the times they spent together arranging flowers. Other than art, flowers were always the one thing they shared a passion for.

"We could go together if you like, Mummy. First thing tomorrow morning, perhaps. The dew is still sparkling, and the flowers are just opening up for the day. Maybe Daddy and Aunt Hilary would like to join us."

Hilary Anne's dreamily romantic enthusiasm prompted a ready response in the affirmative from her assembled relations, and she smiled happily as she made her way upstairs to unpack her bags.

She delved into the old leather trunk that had been sent on from school a few days earlier, searching out a large sketch pad and a box of soft, creamy pastels. *The pastels would capture the cowslips perfectly,* she thought to herself, as she put them aside on her old childhood desk. They would be easy to fetch from there in the morning.

She stood and looked about her then, remembering the years she had spent in the familiar little room before she went away to school. It was the best part of two years now since she had last come home to Leominster. Last summer was spent holidaying in the Lake District, and Christmas was enjoyed with Aunt Hilary at *Oak Manor.* Imogen had joined them for Christmas, too; her parents were en route to Australia at the time. Her father was to spend two years at a Staff College in the small seaside village of Queenscliffe, on the coast of Victoria. Now that school was over, Imogen had decided to join them there for the remainder of his posting.

Hilly sighed. She would miss Imogen the way she had missed Josh and Lindy and Maisie over her years away at school.

As she continued to unpack the trunk, her thoughts turned to how she should go about catching up with all her old friends again. A little smile played on her lips as fond memories flooded back.

Perhaps they could meet at the Sydonia, the way they had done so many times in the past. They would have a refreshing swim in the open-air pool, then huddle together at the kiosk that separated the pool and the lawn bowling greens, while sipping warming mugs of Oxo, and happily chatting until it was time to go home.

Hilly's smile widened with anticipation at the thought of such a reunion, then as she hung her favourite blue jeans in the old oak wardrobe, Elizabeth's voice drifted up the stairs calling her to go down and join them.

"Father has poured us all a small sherry in celebration of your homecoming," advised Elizabeth, her voice tinged with pleasure.

Hilary Anne pushed the cupboard door shut and closed the lid of the trunk on its few remaining contents. Then, she took one more contented look around the room before doing as she was bid and joining her family in the drawing room.

The morning dawned crisp and clear, and it felt to Hilly as she quickly washed, and pulled on her favoured denim jeans and a colourful striped jumper, that the air was filled with a delicious sense of promise.

She brushed her hair, tied it up into a ponytail, grabbed her art supplies from the top of the desk, and ran downstairs to see if the others were ready to go.

"What about breakfast?" asked Elizabeth as her daughter urged them to grab their coats.

"Oh, that can wait, Mummy, but the dew drops won't. We need to go right now if we're to catch the early morning sun rays. I want to make some sketches while the light is just right."

Elizabeth sighed and grabbed an apple from the fruit bowl on the table as her determined daughter led the way out of the door.

"She's quite right, you know," laughed Robert.

"Perhaps we could grab a treat for breakfast or brunch from Bates' Bakery on the way back. You'd like that, Hilly, wouldn't you?"

"Oh, absolutely, Daddy!"

"Sounds like a wonderful idea to me, too," enthused Aunt Hilary.

"Well, if that's what you all want. I suppose so."

If Elizabeth's voice was tinged with a slightly petulant air of annoyance at Robert's suggestion, her companions chose to ignore it.

This was Hilly's outing, and there was no place for Elizabeth's long-standing and totally unfounded dislike of Hilly 'cavorting with the Bates family' as she liked to put it.

Robert sighed inwardly, disappointed that his wife was so quick to poke the stick at the mention of Hilly's friends again, and Aunt Hilary cast an anxious glance in her niece's direction.

For her part, despite a deep pang of hurt and sadness that Elizabeth's attitude towards her friends was still so obviously hostile, Hilly stoically chose to pretend she didn't even notice her mother's familiar air of disdain at their mention. She would *not* let Mother spoil the day, and she would *not* ignore her friends because Mummy seemed to think they were in some way inferior and unsuitable to be her companions. It was as though she saw them as some kind of threat; Hilly thought to herself as she led the way to the meadow. Poor Mummy. She constantly worried about things that seemed so real to her, yet Hilly didn't understand at all. Perhaps something happened a long time ago that Mother was unable to forget, mused Hilly, completely oblivious as to just how close to the truth she was.

Time, it seemed, had done very little to ease Elizabeth's insecurities over her past. She carried with her an unfounded sense of guilt that her own upbringing was one of such privilege when, in reality, it could have been so much like that of many others in Leominster, the Bates family in particular.

Just as her own father had been a generation earlier, Matthew Bates was once a farm worker. Then, again just like her own father, Matthew was injured fighting for his country, and forced to start again. He worked hard, did well for himself, and earned the respect of the community. Together, he and Margaret provided well for their family and brought up four pleasant, well mannered, intelligent children. They beat the odds through their own diligence, courage and determination.

Elizabeth harboured a deep-seated feeling of discomfort that she, on the other hand, was offered a silver spoon. Her post-war visit to Bridge Street and the realisation of how very different her life would have been had not fate intervened on her behalf left Elizabeth with an irrational, unfounded fear that her background would be discovered and made common knowledge, that she would be exposed as a fraud, and people would snigger and point the finger at her. *Lady Liz*, as some of the townsfolk still called her, was no more than the mere daughter of a farm labourer! What a joke they would find it! Even if that farm labourer *was* also a much-respected local artist! Despite all her airs and graces, she was no better than anyone else, folk would say!

The very thought that she should suffer such humiliation was unbearable to Elizabeth, so while she knew deep down, that the Bates were decent, caring folk who would readily accept her for who she was, their very presence still reminded her of what might have been, encouraging her groundless, imaginary fears to cloud both her judgement and behaviour.

Elizabeth sighed, an unfamiliar sense of shame suddenly washing over her as she followed an exuberant Hilly to the meadow. It was all so complicated. She knew both Hilly and Robert would be disappointed in her. She had promised Robert only yesterday that she would not interfere in Hilly's life anymore and that she would be totally accepting of all her daughter's friends. It seemed, however, that old habits dyed hard, and she would need to make a greater effort.

In truth, the Bates, like the rest of the town's inhabitants, secretly admired Elizabeth. Her efforts during the war years, working as a member of the Land Army, gained her a great deal of respect in Leominster. She also willingly helped out whenever she could at the W.R.V.S. Clothing Exchange, where outgrown but still serviceable children's clothing was exchanged for points, which could, in turn, be used to acquire properly fitting garments. The Clothing Exchange was an essential service for mothers, both during and following the war, and Elizabeth's helpful advice and natural eye for style were much sought after by the local ladies. She had a knack for finding just the right shirt to go with a particular pair of pants or the perfect little jacket to pop over a simple dress.

Following the arrival of Hilary Anne however, Elizabeth retired into a little world of her own. A world that focused entirely on her daughter's future and well-being.

Where Elizabeth was concerned, that future included marriage to a well-educated, wealthy man, and try as she might, Elizabeth could not see Joshua Bates fulfilling that role. He may very well have managed to achieve his dream of attending university and studying medicine, but Elizabeth was quite certain, in her own mind, that he would never complete the full five-year course. Matthew and Margaret were in no position to offer the necessary financial support for that length of time, and surely no amount of farm labouring would provide sufficient funding either. It was all very commendable but obviously no more than an empty pipe dream.

Even if he did succeed, Elizabeth told herself, it would only be as a village G.P. He would surely never make the grade as a Harley Street Specialist. No. She wanted more than the drudgery of small village life for Hilary Anne! She wanted her daughter to be pampered and admired. To enjoy a life of privilege and luxury.

The main object of Elizabeth's thoughts had reached the meadow now and took off ahead, weaving through the cowslips just as she used to do all those years ago.

A huge smile and a girlish giggle of glee, accompanied by a graceful twirl and an arabesque, portrayed to her companions that Hilly was delighted with what she saw.

She found a small patch of clear grass and sat down, drawing up her knees and hugging them to her chest, as she closed her eyes and slowly drew in deep breaths of the fresh, sweet morning air.

She was home, and the meadow still glistened with its precious covering of golden blooms! It was several minutes before she stirred, then she reached into her bag, pulled out her sketchbook and pastels, balanced the book on her knees and began to draw.

Her eyes focused fully on each tiny detail of a single nearby cowslip, as she expertly copied the delicate beauty it displayed, onto the empty page before her.

"That looks even more beautiful now. Absolutely exquisite, Hilly."

The voice was familiar yet a little deeper than she remembered, and her heart missed a beat as she looked up to greet the young man who knelt down beside her as he spoke.

"Joshua! What are you doing here at this time of day?"

He grinned at her.

"I was just on my way to work when I saw a strange little nymph dancing in the cowslips and was drawn to come and investigate!"

Hilly blushed and giggled.

"Strange? What's so strange about dancing for joy?"

"Nothing at all."

He gave a playful tug on her ponytail as he spoke.

"It's good to see you back home, Hilly. Perhaps we could catch up later?"

"That would be lovely. What time do you finish work?"

"When the Priory bells ring at five o'clock."

"Then you should come for tea. Mother won't mind. Will you, Mummy?"

Hilly looked up at Elizabeth, who had just caught up with her daughter and stopped alongside the young couple.

"That sounds like a splendid idea."

It was Robert who answered as he and Aunt Hilary joined the little group. He looked pointedly at Elizabeth as he spoke, and recognising her chance for redemption, Elizabeth nodded enthusiastically.

"Of course, you must come for tea, Joshua. Perhaps Lindy and Maisie would care to join us too," she added, smiling sweetly.

"Hilly can pop into the hairdressers later to invite Maisie, and we are headed to the bakery when we leave here, so we can leave an invitation for Lindy with your parents. Shall we say six thirty for seven?"

"Thank you, Mrs Moncrieff. That's very kind of you. Give me something to look forward to all day."

Joshua rose to his feet as he spoke, wiping the wet grass from his hands and trousers and grinning happily at Hilly.

"Best get off to work now then, but I'll see you later, and we can have a good old catch-up."

Hilly nodded and smiled shyly back at him.

"I shall look forward to that."

Her soft brown eyes followed after him as he made his way back to the road, then as he disappeared from sight, she turned to a fresh page in her sketchbook. This time, she drew the whole meadow and there, between the softly swaying cowslips, strode the tall, imposing figure of a handsome young man. The figure was unmistakably that of Joshua Bates.

Aunt Hilary and Robert exchanged glances and smiled knowingly at one another while Elizabeth sighed inwardly. At least if Lindy and Maisie were to join them for tea as well, Hilly and Joshua would not be left alone.

Despite Elizabeth's best efforts to keep them apart and Joshua's long days working on the farm, Josh and Hilly managed to see each other almost every evening over the summer holidays.

They would meet in the meadow, or down by the River Lugg or the Kenwater, and take long walks together, as they shared their dreams and future aspirations… each of them secretly hoping that their future would be spent together.

Joshua had been studying at the University of Birmingham Medical School for three years already. To him, it was a dream-cum-true. The years of hard work on the farm and endless late nights of extra studying after leaving grammar school were all well worth it.

Margaret and Matthew were bursting with pride, and even a disbelieving Elizabeth had been gracious enough to congratulate him with genuine warmth.

"I went to Birmingham University myself before the war," she confided to Josh.

"I studied Art History and Antiquities."

"So that's where Hilly gets her talents from. Perhaps she should follow in your footsteps and join me in Birmingham."

Elizabeth froze. That was the very last thing she wanted.

"I don't think so, Joshua. As you know, Hilly is a very talented artist. We prefer that she attend a specialist art school. She has chosen to study in Paris. That way, she will learn to perfect her French as well. We are hoping for confirmation any day now that she has procured student accommodation at 'L' Ecole des Beaux-Arts', where she is to study.

"Yes. She has mentioned it."

"Where do you stay while you're in Birmingham, Joshua? Have you arranged student accommodation?"

"No. I'm renting a cheap room in a student flat."

"Oh, of course."

Elizabeth shuddered at the thought of an overcrowded student flat, with boys and girls cohabiting as seemed to be the way these days. No doubt, there would be wild parties, complete with loud music, alcohol and even drugs. She was not at all certain that studying would take any form of priority. No, a nice quiet room in organised university accommodation seemed far preferable. Not that she cared about Joshua's future anyway. Hilary Anne's feelings for the boy were surely no more than a schoolgirl crush. She would forget all about him when she got to Paris, then when she came back home, she would no doubt find work in London and hopefully meet a nice, respectable, well-educated young man from a good family, like that charming young Geoffrey Chatswood. He was working in the city for his father, and no doubt, one day, the business would pass to him.

Having convinced herself that she was right on all counts, Elizabeth decided to take Robert's lead and let Hilly go her own way for the next few weeks. Her conviction that Hilary Anne would forget all about Joshua Bates before long may not have been so unwavering, however, had she known that the young couple were hatching plans to travel through France and Italy together in a Combi Van, once their respective studies were complete.

123

Hilly thought it prudent to keep their plans 'undercover' as it were. Their own little secret, to be shared with no one. Josh was only too happy to agree. He would need to find time to do plenty of extra work on the farm during his holidays, and although he was quite sure that wouldn't be a problem, making enough money to carry out their secret assignment was something they both needed to work very hard at.

Somehow, the thought of spending a whole summer together when their studies were over made the blow of parting easier for both of them when the time came for them to go their separate ways again.

Joshua headed back to Birmingham to resume his studies a full week ahead of Hilary Anne's departure date. To help soften the blow of his absence, Hilly took herself off to stay at *Oak Manor* and spent a few happy days with her aunt, returning home to the cottage for the weekend in order to spend her last two days with her parents and catch a final chance to say goodbye to her friends.

It was all over far too soon for Hilly, and as she boarded the ferry to Calais and her journey to Paris began, she felt the same sense of nervous uncertainty wash over her that she had experienced on her arrival at Malvern Girls.

She wished more than anything that she could be sitting with Josh on the banks of the Kenwater, sketching the river in all its beauty, while Joshua studied some of his newly acquired medical journals. She wouldn't even see him over the Christmas break, as Mother and Father, along with Aunt Hilary, had decided to join her in Paris to enjoy this year's Christmas festivities, and next summer seemed such a long way off.

Despite her reservations however, Hilly settled quickly into life in Bohemian Paris. Her college dormitory was situated in the heart of the Latin Quarter, sitting directly above favoured student cafe, Le Contrescarpe, where passionate philosophical debates raged endlessly, amply fuelled with a generous accompaniment of cigarettes and cheap French wine.

Outdoor classes, seated on the banks of the river Seine, reminded her of sitting by the river with Josh, and she wrote to him regularly, describing her new French lifestyle in minute detail.

Joshua found her keen observations a wonderful distraction from his own more sobering studies and always made time to reply to her promptly.

Planning their proposed adventure gave them both a happy escape when the pain of separation washed over them, and as the months passed by, their long-distance relationship flourished.

Chapter – 9

Margaret Bates sat at one end of the table in her workroom, deftly sewing large bright yellow buttons to the bib top of a denim pinafore dress.

"There!" she exclaimed as she cut off the thread and laid the little garment to one side.

"That makes three each: small, medium and large."

She looked up and smiled at Susan, who stood at the other end of the large pine table, busily cutting out simple little miniskirts.

"I have just one more of these to cut, and once we run them up, we should be all set for the market tomorrow."

"Well, I think we deserve a cup of tea before we start stitching again." Her mother smiled. "I'll go and put the kettle on while you finish up here."

"Do you think Dad would find us a bun each? I'm famished."

"I'm sure he will. I'll pop along and see what he's baking this morning."

"I hope it's currant buns or date scones. One of each would be nice."

"You'll be going up a dress size if you eat too many of either," laughed Margaret as she made her way out of the room and headed to the kitchen.

She had set the kettle on the hob and was reaching down cups and saucers from the sideboard when a sudden commotion drifted up the hallway. It emanated from the direction of the bakery and prompted Margaret to hurriedly set down her china and run to investigate its cause. Susan also heard the racket. She put down her scissors and ran to join her mother at the bakery door. As they entered the shop, they were greeted by the pungent aroma of burning and clouds of smoke drifting from the bakery kitchen.

"Matthew! John!" Margaret's voice was filled with alarm as she rushed to investigate further.

"We're fine. We're fine," Matthew assured her as she appeared through the smoky haze.

"The oven, however, is *not!* It would appear the thermostat has given up the ghost!"

"Can it be fixed?"

"I hope so."

A worried frown settled on Matthew's brow as he extinguished the flames and removed the burnt remains of his daily bake of Chelsea buns from the large commercial oven. No oven meant no income. He had no idea how long it would take to fit a new thermostat or even if it could be done. If the rest of the oven was too badly damaged, they may need to replace the whole appliance.

"Try to keep the smoke out of the shop, John. It'll taint the rest of the bake if it hasn't already."

"Shut the bakehouse door, then open all the external doors and windows as wide as you can, John," advised Margaret, "while Susan and I look out for something to cover the display cabinets with."

She hurried up the stairs as she spoke, Susan following closely in her wake.

A large blanket box sitting at the end of the hallway relinquished a generous stash of bedding, and having laden up both herself and her daughter with as many blankets and counterpanes as they could possibly manage, Margaret then led the way back downstairs to the shop. As both Susan and John helped her wrap and seal the open shelves and glass cabinets as tightly as they could, Margaret's thoughts turned to Matthew. He had been under a lot of stress lately. She knew that he was missing Joshua more than he cared to admit. While they were all immensely proud of him, Josh's departure to university left a hole in the lives of the Bates family, each one of them missing him in their own way.

In Matthew's case, he felt he had lost more than his eldest son. He had lost a deeply loved friend and trusted confidant. He realised now just how much he had come to lean on Josh over the past few years, often sharing business concerns with him rather than troubling Margaret.

With the fire successfully extinguished, Matthew stood in the middle of his bakehouse and slowly looked around. It was as though he was finally seeing the big, outdated kitchen with fresh eyes. The familiar surroundings suddenly seemed drab and shabby. Joshua's sound, parting advice on the future of the family business rang in Matthew's ears. The lad was right. The bakery was old and tired. It needed to be upgraded and modernised, especially now that supermarkets were opening throughout the country. It was surely only a matter of time before one arrived in Leominster, and that would bring strong competition to small local businesses like Bates Bakery.

Matthew sighed. Josh was right when he suggested they should expand the business and perhaps even include a tea shop where customers could sit and relax while they enjoyed a cuppa with their fresh-baked wares.

"Think about it, Dad," Josh advised.

"I've already talked about it with John. You need to discuss it with him and Mum."

Perhaps the time was right to follow that advice, thought Matthew now, as he slowly made his way across the bakery kitchen and into the shop. He would put the idea forward to the rest of the family tonight.

While the state of the oven dominated an animated conversation over the tea table later that evening, Matthew sat in quiet contemplation, scarcely hearing what his family had to say on the matter.

Margaret cast an anxious glance in his direction. He was being unusually quiet, and it seemed to her that his mind was elsewhere. *It was out of character for Matthew,* she thought.

As though suddenly aware of Margaret's scrutiny, Matthew looked up and reached out his hand to her.

"Don't fret, love." He smiled wearily, "I have a plan."

"I could see there was something brewing in that head of yours," she replied.

"Hush now, children! Your father has something to say."

Matthew let his gaze fall on each member of his family in turn until he was satisfied, he had their undivided attention.

"I think the time has come," he said quietly, "for us to do more than just repair the oven. It's only been a few years since the last time it gave us bother. We didn't have the money to replace it then, and I'm not sure that the bank will help us out now, but I intend to make an appointment with Robert Moncrieff and put a business proposal to him. I'd like you to come along with me, John, as my business partner."

He paused and looked at his youngest son with an encouraging smile before he continued.

"Josh had an idea that he put to me before he left for university, and I know that was a few years ago now, but I've been a bit set in my ways and slow to realise the wisdom of his vision. That's why I need a younger man by my side. Someone to give me a bit of a shove when I need it. Would you do that for me, John?"

"Need you even ask Dad? You know I've always wanted to follow in your footsteps. So yes, of course, I'll stand by you. Josh and I used to talk about extending the bakery. Building a conservatory that opened to the garden and making it into a tearoom as well."

"Exactly so, son. A whole added stream of revenue. It will mean a lot more work for the two of us, and we may need to employ a waitress or two, but…"

"Nonsense!" burst in Margaret.

"The girls and I will be happy to help out when we can."

Matthew shook his head.

"You all have your own concerns to attend to." He smiled.

"This is for John and me to manage. As long as we have your blessings and you are happy with the proposal, that is all we need to ask of you ladies."

"You have the blessings of us all." Margaret smiled at him encouragingly, taking it upon herself to answer for her daughters as well. There was a spark in his eyes that had been missing for a long time. It filled her with happiness to see it return, to see the old, positive, jovial Matthew re-emerge, his enthusiasm bubbling over, as the family sat and exchanged ideas for the proposed venture until well after midnight.

As they finally retired for the night, their minds were still brimming with ideas, and an atmosphere of excited anticipation filled every nook and cranny of the Bates family home.

The next few days saw a sense of urgency prevail, as hasty repairs saw the old oven given a temporary reprieve. Matthew called on two local builders for advice and quotes, and a detailed business plan was drawn up. Josh was called home for the weekend to add his voice to proceedings, and when everyone was happy that nothing had been overlooked, Lindy helped Matthew and John type up their proposal for the bank.

Three days later, dressed in their Sunday best and with the completed proposal tucked safely into an old briefcase that Josh once used at Grammar School, Matthew and John presented themselves at Lloyds Bank. They arrived a full fifteen minutes ahead of the appointed time and sat nervously waiting for Robert Moncrieff to call them into his office. A large wall clock loudly ticked away the passing of each minute. Matthew ran a finger under the collar band of his shirt in an effort to release the unfamiliar pressure of his necktie, and John stared down at his shoes, hoping that Mr Moncrieff wouldn't notice that the heels were sorely worn down. He felt sure that *Mrs* Moncrieff would notice at once.

The door to Robert's office suddenly burst open, causing both Matthew and John to jump to their feet.

"Matthew. John. Please, do come in," smiled Robert.

"I hope you haven't been waiting long."

He showed the two men to his desk, then sat down opposite them. He knew there had been a fire at the bakery and guessed they were looking to raise a loan to cover any excess repairs not taken care of by their insurance policy.

As Matthew laid out their proposed plans and estimated costs, and John expanded on their ideas for the new venture, Robert Moncrieff listened with growing interest. This was no small repair job they were looking to undertake. This was a serious bid to grow their business. Their business plan was sound and made good sense. The alterations to the premises would certainly add value to the property. It was a proposal worthy of consideration. He invited the Bates' to leave all the information with him so that he could carry out due diligence. He assured them he would hold discussions with both his accountant and mortgage team over the proposal they had presented and that he would be in touch within a few days. Meanwhile, he suggested, that it would be wise to talk with both their solicitor and the Town Planners to be sure there would be no objections to the plan.

As they retraced their steps to the bakery, Matthew's tie seemed suddenly less restrictive, and John felt sure his worn-down shoes had gone unnoticed after all. They burst through the back door to the house, filled with boyish excitement, convinced there would be no problem with raising the loan.

"I think we've only gone and done it!"

Matthew grinned at Margaret, who came running as the sound of their voices drifted down the hallway.

She threw her arms around him, demanding to know everything that had transpired. What exactly Robert Moncrieff had said, and when they would know for certain. She led Matthew to their recently acquired telephone, and hovered anxiously, as he made an appointment with the Town Planners Office.

Suddenly, it all seemed so real. The thought of increasing their mortgage to such an extent terrified her, but she knew it made good sense.

True to his word, Robert Moncrieff sent confirmation to Matthew and John just three days later that the bank would increase their mortgage as requested. They should pop back and sign the documents at their earliest convenience. Matthew clapped John on the back and let out a whoop of delight.

"Margaret!" he called loudly, his voice resonating with undisguised excitement,

"Fetch down the sherry glasses, girl! It's time to celebrate!"

The mood in the Bates household remained buoyant for some weeks, but as those weeks turned into months of waiting for the council to grant planning permission, the excitement gradually turned to frustration.

"How much longer do they expect us to wait?" grumbled Matthew one day.

"This poor old oven won't go on forever, and I don't want to get the new one installed until the new kitchen is completed."

"I know, dear," sympathised Margaret, "it surely can't be much longer now. Perhaps you should contact them again."

Matthew sighed.

"I don't want to pester them. They'd probably just make me wait even longer. Or worse still, turn us down."

It was Margaret's turn to sigh. Matthew was right. They would just have to be patient, but she knew the long wait was playing sorely on his mind. He wasn't sleeping well, tossing and turning until the small hours, and he was quick to snap over little things. *It was so unlike Matthew,* she thought. He was generally possessed of such a happy, easy-going nature. She even found herself wondering if the end result would be worth it all.

Another several weeks passed by before the long-awaited approval was granted, but the ensuing excitement was short-lived once more. The architect was obliged to make some minor changes, and the builder had begun another project which he needed to complete before work on the bakery could begin. Bad weather then caused even further delays.

By the time the builder and his team finally arrived, the summer holidays were upon them once more. Settled weather meant progress was steady, but Matthew was keen to make up for what he saw as lost time. He pushed himself harder and harder, helping out wherever he could and causing Margaret concern for his well-being.

"You need to slow down, Matthew," she admonished him one evening.

"You're turning to skin and bone."

Matthew leaned against the broom he was using to sweep down the bakery kitchen and looked at her.

"We need the builders to be finished in the kitchen and hopefully the conservatory by the time they break for Christmas," he told her, "then we can get the new ovens up and running by the time we reopen in the New Year. That will give us time to decorate and arrange the finishing touches by summer. Then, we can throw the doors open wide, and our customers can enjoy the long summer days sitting in the garden when the weather's good!"

His excitement was palpable.

"It'll be a money spinner Margaret, and we need it. Meantime I just want to keep things shipshape, so we don't need to shut up shop for too long. Just for the Christmas break I hope."

"I know." She smiled. "But you need to take care of yourself too, Matthew. We need you."

He chuckled and shook his head at her.

"You worry too much, my love." He smiled as he picked up his broom again and carried on where he'd left off.

"I'm fine. John's pulling his weight, and Josh will be home in a couple of days."

"Then all three of you can work yourselves to the bone. Wonderful!"

Joshua Bates sat on the lid of his suitcase and firmly snapped the locks into place. All he needed to do after Christmas was to complete his final year and pass the last of his exams in style. Then, as he waited for his results to come through, he would apply to several hospitals for an internship and see what came of it. While he waited to hear on that score, he would go home, work for Alex Morgan on the farm as he always did, and help his father and John with the bakery.

Having locked the door to the little attic room that had been his home for so long, Joshua dragged his case down the stairs, then carried it out to the bright red mini that was parked in front of the house. Most of his flatmates had already departed for the Christmas break, but he had promised to drop fellow student Chrissy Sloane in Hereford on his way home, so went back indoors to search for her.

"Shake a leg, Chrissy," he called.

"It'll be next year before we get home at this rate!"

She appeared on the landing with a backpack almost as big as herself, threatening to tip her backwards at any moment.

Josh bounded up the stairs two at a time and took it from her.

"Let me take that." He laughed.

"Whatever is in it?"

"Just clothes and Christmas presents and a few books."

Josh shook his head.

"You're as bad as my sisters. They can't leave home without the kitchen sink either!"

He threw the bag over his shoulder, followed Chrissy down the stairs, and then, with a happy bounce in his step, showed her to the waiting car.

It would be good to be home for Christmas. Hilly was due back from France, too. It had been eighteen long months since they last saw each other. Mrs Moncreiff had done her very best to keep them apart since Hilly went off to France, but they had secretly arranged to meet the day after tomorrow at their favourite spot by the river so they could finalise the plans for their great summer escape. He hoped that Margaret and Matthew wouldn't be too upset about him going away again just as they were about to launch the new tearoom, but he felt sure they would agree he was due a break by then. It would only be for two weeks anyway, so he should still have plenty of time to help out at home. Though, of course, everything would depend on whether he picked up an internship. He may not get a summer holiday at all. Meantime, he would just enjoy catching up with everyone, especially Hilly, over the Christmas break.

Margaret was watching out for him and ran to greet him as he pulled up the little mini that Alex Morgan had so kindly loaned to him and brought it to a halt behind the assorted tradesmen's vehicles that were parked outside the bakery.

"Josh is here!" Margaret called excitedly, not waiting for the others to join her before she hurried outside.

Such was her delight as Joshua stepped from the car and hugged her warmly that she failed to notice how stooped over Matthew looked as he limped slowly and painfully towards them. Josh noticed, though, and felt quite alarmed at how much his father had suddenly aged.

"Mum told me you've been overdoing it," he chastised him soundly.

"Just as well I'm going to be here for a while."

"John!" he continued, as his youngest sibling loped up alongside them, "You look done in too. Why are you both burning the candle at both ends? I thought you'd employed someone else to do the revamp. What are all these vehicles for?"

Lindy and Susan joined them, and they dragged Joshua inside, chatting nineteen to the dozen and leaving John to carry the suitcase while their parents happily followed along behind.

"Happy now?" Matthew asked Margaret as he slipped an arm around her shoulders.

"Now that all your little fledglings have returned to the nest!"

Margaret beamed.

"It's been so long." She sighed with a contented smile.

"Isn't it wonderful?"

Matthew agreed.

"I'll join you all in a jiffy," he promised as he showed her through the door. "I'll just lock up the shop for the day."

"Well, don't be too long. Josh will have plenty of news, I'm sure."

"Like I said, I'll just be a jiffy."

He winked at her, delighted to see her so overjoyed, as she hurried off in the direction of the family kitchen.

Matthew turned over the 'closed' sign; then, as he reached up to bolt the shop door, he felt a sharp pain in his side. He caught his breath and doubled over until the pain began to ease. It had happened several times over the past few days, and it seemed to be getting worse. He must have pulled a muscle, he told himself. It would pass. Perhaps Margaret was right, and he needed to slow down for a bit.

He gingerly made his way to the kitchen to join his family, then sank thankfully into his favourite chair at the head of the table.

"Well!" He smiled,

"Who's volunteering to help Mum with the Christmas Tree then?"

John grimaced.

"I already decorated the shop tree by myself," he grumbled good-naturedly, "so bags I get to just sit and supervise this time."

"Good idea. We'll probably get it done much faster without you," suggested Lindy.

"Not to mention so much better," corroborated Susan, immediately taking sides with her sister.

"It's so good to be home," laughed Josh.

"Nothing ever changes, does it? Don't worry, Mum, we'll all help. John included."

John sighed, shook his head, and threw up his hands in a dramatic gesture.

Margaret smiled happily. Her first-born son was home, and the others were all falling in line as he took the lead the way he always did.

The house filled with laughter as the young ones trimmed the tree and hung their Christmas stockings from the mantle surrounding the big open fireplace in the front room.

The tradesmen working in the bakery finished up early, and Matthew invited them all to join the family for a quick tipple and a Christmas pie before they headed off for their holidays.

Then, as afternoon turned to evening and the family sat down to enjoy a light supper by the fire, Matthew suddenly found himself feeling exhausted. The pain in his side had returned, and his stump was throbbing. To add to his discomfort, he began to feel ill and a little feverish. He wanted nothing more than to retire to bed, but his family was happily chatting and setting up the Monopoly Board as they made plans for the next few days, and he felt unwilling to disturb their mood of excited anticipation.

He sat instead and looked around, a warm glow of pride and contentment washing over him, even as he simultaneously fought to overcome his ever-increasing nausea. The well-being and happiness of his family were what drove Matthew to always push himself, and he felt that now was no time to make an exception to that rule.

"I'm meeting up with Hilly in the morning," Josh was saying.

"It's our only chance to see each other this Christmas. Mrs Moncreiff is determined to keep her away from me again."

"Oh, Josh! I'm sure that's not so," chided Margaret, "she has simply made other plans for her family."

"She always has other plans for her family lately," sighed Joshua.

"I haven't seen Hilly since she went to France."

Margaret smiled.

"Never mind, dear," she soothed, stifling a yawn.

She gazed at him sleepily.

"You know, I think it's time I climbed the wooden hill to Bedfordshire. Are you going to join me, Mr Bates?" she asked Matthew.

"Mm? What's that? Bedtime, did you say? Wonderful idea. Been a long day."

His voice sounded strained with the sheer effort of replying. He took a deep breath and closed his eyes, steeling himself in readiness to evacuate the armchair and make his way upstairs. As he rose to his feet, the pain in his side also rose in intensity, causing him to let out an involuntary cry and fall back into the chair as yet another wave of nausea overcame him.

"*Matthew*!" The alarm in Margaret's voice caused the children to look up from their game.

"Dad!" The chorus of concerned voices seemed to Matthew to be drifting somewhere way above his head.

Joshua leapt to his feet and ran to his father's side, taking in at a glance the pallor of his skin and the sweat that was trickling down his brow. He reached for Matthew's pulse, then calmly suggested Susan and Lindy might like to fetch some flannels and a couple of buckets – one empty and one filled with cool water.

John helped Josh make their father more comfortable while Margaret hovered anxiously, demanding to know what she could do.

"Call Dr Edwards, Mum, while John and I get Dad upstairs."

Josh smiled at her reassuringly and shooed her off in the direction of the phone.

"Listen to Doctor Bates, Mum," chipped in John, "he knows what he's doing. Lucky he's home."

Josh shook his head.

"I'm not Dr Bates yet," he muttered, "but on second thoughts, I don't think we should move him upstairs just yet. Not until Dr Edwards says it's okay."

"What do you think it is?"

Matthew groaned.

"My side," he moaned.

"Pain. Feel sick."

"Is it your stump, Daddy?" asked Lindy as she handed Matthew the empty bucket she had retrieved from the laundry.

"That too," he replied, his voice no more than a whisper.

Susan returned with a bowl of tepid water and a small pile of flannels, and by the time Margaret returned, her children appeared to have the situation well in hand.

"The doctor's on his way," she said.

"John, can you go and wait for him please dear. I'd rather stay here with your dad."

"Of course."

As her youngest son left the room, Margaret turned to Matthew and took his hand in hers. She had told him that he needed to slow down. She had worried that something like this would happen.

"What do you think it is, Josh?" she asked.

"Is it to do with his leg?"

"It could be an infection in his stump, or it could be something entirely unrelated."

"Like what?"

"Something he's eaten perhaps, a bug that's going around, a kidney stone, or even his appendix. We'll see what Dr Edwards thinks, Mum."

Margaret nodded and reached for a cloth, dipping it into the water and gently wiping Matthew's face and hands.

Josh checked the time on his wristwatch. He hoped the doctor wouldn't be much longer. This looked serious to him.

"When did the pain start, Dad?" he asked his father,

"Was it just now, or has it been coming on gradually?"

Matthew moaned incoherently, and Joshua shook his head. He was both worried and annoyed with himself. He thought Matthew had looked as though he was in pain earlier when he came out to greet him home. He should have questioned him then and asked him if he was feeling all right. Of course, Dad would have just shrugged it off the way he always did, but that was no excuse for not enquiring. Josh sighed and checked his watch again as he felt once more for Matthew's pulse.

"Right." He looked at Margaret as he spoke.

"We're not waiting any longer, Mum. I'm going to call for the ambulance."

He strode to the door of the front room as he spoke, then made his way across the hall to the little telephone table. By the time Dr Edwards arrived, the ambulance was already on its way.

"You've done the right thing, Joshua," he approved.

"Well done, lad. Hospital's the best place for him to be."

Joshua nodded, and Margaret looked alarmed.

"Don't worry, Mum. He'll be fine."

Susan put a comforting arm around Margaret's waist.

"You should travel in the ambulance with Dad," she encouraged her distraught mother, "and Josh can bring the rest of us in his car."

"Excellent idea," approved the doctor.

"I'll not be far behind either."

He patted Margaret on the shoulder.

"Try not to worry, Margaret," he said in a kindly voice, "Matthew's a strong, fit man."

But he spoke with far more conviction than he felt. He agreed with Josh. This was serious, and there was no time to delay.

He voiced this opinion to the ambulance officers when they arrived, and as they carefully transferred Matthew from his armchair to the stretcher, and he cried out in pain as he simultaneously vomited into Lindy's empty bucket, they wholeheartedly agreed.

Despite their urgency, the trip from Leominster to Hereford Hospital took almost twenty minutes to complete, by which time Matthew's condition was grim indeed. Margaret stood and watched helplessly as he was rushed inside. Then Josh pulled up alongside and the children gathered around her. She took a deep breath to calm herself. All she wanted to do was run after Matthew, but she had to be strong for the young ones.

Why Matthew? she asked herself over and over. *Why should someone so decent and loving and caring be struck down like this?*

The Bates family sat huddled together in the waiting room for what seemed like an eternity. Dr Edwards sat with them, assuring them the hospital doctors would leave no stone unturned, and would get to the bottom of the problem as quickly as was humanly possible.

Margaret forced a smile.

"Thank you, Doctor. Of course, they will. I just wish it wasn't all taking so long."

"They're just being as thorough as possible, Mum. It takes time, that's all." Joshua smiled at her, hoping he sounded more convincing than he felt.

Another twenty minutes passed by before the duty doctor, Ewan Rossitor, finally approached them.

"We can't be absolutely certain just yet," he told them, "but we believe Mr Bates' condition may be due to an infection in his amputation wound. We'll know more when we get back the results of his blood tests."

"Can we sit with him?" asked Margaret.

The doctor frowned, then looked around the row of anxious faces and nodded.

"We prefer no visitors at times like this," he told them, "but as it's Christmas, I'll make an exception if you promise not to talk too much and you don't tire him out. We have given him strong painkillers and anti-nausea medication, so he's pretty groggy anyway."

"Just so long as he knows we're here. That's all that matters."

"Of course," nodded the doctor as he showed them through the door.

"Dr Edwards, a moment of your time, if you will."

William Edwards nodded. The hospital staff would want to know anything he could tell them about Matthew's amputation and his general health. He followed Dr Rossitor to his office, but he knew there was nothing he could say that would throw any light on the current situation. He wished desperately that he could put his finger on something, but like Margaret, all he could offer was that Matthew had been overdoing things lately.

Joshua too, was struggling to make sense of the situation, and as the others sat down, he picked up the chart that was hanging from the foot of Matthew's bed and studied it intently.

"Are you allowed to do that?" asked Lindy in a hushed voice.

Josh shrugged. He couldn't feel quite comfortable with what the doctor said. The diagnosis didn't sit right with him, and he wanted to know more.

Matthew was still moaning with pain, and his pulse felt erratic to Josh as he checked it yet again. Erratic and weak.

"Not my stump," whispered Matthew, his voice strained with the effort it took for him to speak as another wave of nausea washed over him.

"Not my stump."

Josh looked at him. His father had suffered a lot over the years with pain from his amputation, and if *he* felt it was something else that was troubling him now, then Josh believed him implicitly. Matthew cried out again, squirming and writhing in agony as another stabbing pain tore through him. It felt to him as though someone had set upon him with a hot, sharp knife.

"Those painkillers don't seem to be working at all." Margaret looked at her eldest son.

"Can you ask them to give him something stronger?" she pleaded.

Her face was pale and drawn with concern, and she fought to hold back her tears. She had never seen Matthew in such a state, and it frightened her.

Josh activated the bell to summon the nurse, and as they waited for her to appear, he pulled back the bedcovers and started an examination of his own. He may not be fully qualified just yet, but he felt sure, both instinctively and from past experience, that Matthew was right. His pain had increased to the point where he was lapsing in and out of consciousness, and as Josh checked the amputation scar, he could find no sign of ulcers or infection of any kind.

"What are you doing?" demanded the nurse as she bustled into the room.

"You can't do that! Cover the patient up at once!" she bristled with indignation.

"He's a doctor," John informed her. "Well, as good as. He is also the patient's son."

"I don't care if he's the King of Siam!" retorted the feisty little nurse.

"Mr Bates is *my* patient, and *you* will leave him alone."

"Just fetch the doctor please nurse," commanded Josh, ignoring her indignation and taking control of the conversation in a calm, measured tone of voice.

"And make it snappy, please, if you would."

The young girl looked at him, and he gave her a fleeting smile of encouragement.

"It is *very* urgent," he advised her firmly. She opened her mouth as if to retort again but thought better of it and turned to hurry from the room in search of Dr Rossitor.

Josh then turned his attention to his distraught mother, who was being comforted by his equally upset sisters.

"Try not to get too upset, Mum, "he encouraged her gently, "I'm sure the doctor will soon have it sorted."

As Margaret and the girls sat anxiously by Matthew's side, and John stood solemnly at the foot of the bed, Josh paced back and forth impatiently.

He had reached the conclusion that Matthew most definitely had appendicitis and informed Dr Rossitor the minute he arrived back in the room.

"There's no time to waste, Doctor. I don't believe his amputation wound is the problem. I think it's his appendix, and it needs to come out right now."

The concerned urgency in Joshua's voice caused the doctor to stop and eye him up with a measured look.

"I understand you are a final year medical student," he said, as he took another look at Matthew, "but I think I'll be the one to diagnose what's wrong here. Your diagnosis is a fair one given the circumstances, and I am inclined to agree with you, but we will have to wait for Mr Burrows, tonight's Senior Consultant Surgeon, to confirm our suspicions."

Joshua heaved an audible sigh of relief. At last, they were getting somewhere.

"How long will that take, do you think?"

"I believe he's in surgery right now, but I'll see what I can do to speed up the process."

"Thank you."

The doctor nodded and turned to Margaret.

"You will have to sign the surgical consent papers on your husband's behalf," he told her, "so we might as well get that underway."

"Of course," agreed Margaret, only too happy to be able to do something to help at last.

"See that Mr Bates is as comfortable as possible please Nurse, then fetch the consent forms for Mrs Bates to sign."

"Yes, Doctor," replied Nurse Templeton as she plumped Matthew's pillow and straightened his bedding.

"I'll look in again shortly," the doctor assured the Bates' as he hurried from the room.

Dr Ewan Rossitor wasted no time in ordering the Charge Nurse to prepare Theatre Two and arrange for theatre staff to attend at once.

"And if Mr Burrows is any more than two minutes away, find another surgeon immediately," he commanded, "and get an orderly to Room C right away." He turned on his heel and retraced his steps to Matthew's side.

"Are those consent forms ready yet?" he snapped at Nurse Templeton.

"Yes, Doctor."

She took them from Margaret's outstretched hand and thrust them at Dr Rossitor as she replied.

"Good. Thank you, Nurse. Now, where is that orderly?" he demanded impatiently. The little nurse was about to say that she would go and look for him as the rattle of an approaching trolley announced his imminent arrival.

"Get this patient to Theatre Two immediately, please," ordered the doctor. "Theatre staff should be on hand. Tell them I said they are to prepare for an emergency appendectomy."

As Matthew was carefully transferred to the gurney, Dr Rossitor advised the Bates family that they should move back to the waiting room.

"You'll find the facilities to make yourselves a cup of tea," he advised them kindly. "You might even find a biscuit if you're lucky."

He turned to Margaret then and gave her arm a reassuring pat.

"Try not to worry too much." He smiled as he hurried after the quickly receding trolley.

"Well done, young man," he called back over his shoulder to Josh. "I believe your diagnosis was spot on!"

As Christmas Eve dawned, the Bates family still maintained their vigil in the hospital waiting room. They had dozed fitfully through the night, stirring each time there was a sound to be heard in the corridor, but no one approached them to report on Matthew's progress.

As the rattle of breakfast trolleys disturbed the early morning quiet, Joshua rose slowly to his feet. He was stiff from head to toe and stretched his tall frame to loosen up his tight muscles, then glanced at his watch with a troubled frown. It was over five hours since Matthew had gone for surgery. They should have heard something by now. He walked quietly from the room so as not to disturb the others and made his way to the Emergency Department's reception desk.

"I'd like a progress report on one of your patients please," he said to the woman behind the desk.

"His name is Matthew Bates. Dr Rossitor admitted him to surgery some hours ago for an appendectomy, and we've heard nothing since. Is Dr Rossitor still on duty?"

"I'll check for you."

"Thank you. And if you find him, could you please let him know that Mr Bates' family is still gathered in the waiting room and anxious for news."

"Of course, sir."

"Thank you." Josh turned to walk away.

"And if Dr Rossitor has gone, I would appreciate it if somebody else could do us the courtesy of providing an update," he added as a rejoinder.

"Of course, sir," she repeated.

By the time he retraced his steps, the rest of the family was stirring, too. Susan and Lindy were making tea, and John had wandered off to search for Joshua. Margaret had been concerned to find Josh missing when she opened her eyes, but John was quick to console her.

"He'll just be in the bathroom or trying to get some news," he reassured her. "I'll go and have a look."

Margaret nodded her thanks, then sat with her troubled eyes fixed firmly on the door watching for her sons to return, as her daughters busied themselves with the teacups.

"Josh!" she uttered with relief as her eldest son made his way back into the room.

"We didn't know where you were. John's gone looking."

He smiled at her. She looked exhausted, and her anxiety was palpable. A wave of sadness washed over Josh. His parents had been together for so long. They were so close. Her anguish must be almost unbearable. It was wrong that she should be kept waiting like this. He suddenly felt angry at the whole situation.

"I've been looking for Dr Rossitor," he said, trying not to let his sudden sense of outrage get the better of him. Losing his temper with the hospital staff would help no one, least of all his distraught mother.

"Is he still on duty, do you think?"

"I don't know, but if they can't find *him*, they'll send someone else to see us."

He sat down next to Margaret and gratefully accepted a cup of tea from Lindy as she and Susan re-joined them, both carefully carrying a steaming cup in each hand.

"Where's mine then?" asked John as he, too, returned.

"On the tea trolley," replied Susan.

"You could bring the biscuits over, too, if you like."

John did as he was bade, and the family settled back down to resume their seemingly endless vigil.

This time, however, the wait was short. Dr Rossitor rushed in, full of apologies for their long wait. He was accompanied by a tall, gaunt, silver-haired man who exuded an air of superiority and self-importance. The man gave Margaret a cursory nod of acknowledgement, then turned his attention to Joshua.

"Mr Bates, is it? My name is Burrows, your father's surgeon."

"How is he?"

"It's pretty much touch and go, I'm afraid. The appendix had already burst before we operated. Obviously, I did all I could, and I have transferred him to the Intensive Care Ward in the hope that he may recover."

Josh's heart dropped. Matthew was a strong, determined man, but peritonitis was deadly serious. He looked at Margaret, wondering if she understood the implications of what Mr Burrows had said. The tears streaming down her face confirmed that she understood exactly what the surgeon meant.

"Why didn't you find the problem sooner?" she wept.

"Just because his leg was amputated, you jumped to the conclusion that *that* was the problem. You didn't even check him over properly."

Margaret was beside herself.

Mr Burrows turned to her.

"I understand your distress, Madam," he said in a voice devoid of emotion, "but I can assure you both Dr Rossitor and I gave Mr Bates a thorough examination on his admission. We are not miracle workers. We have, however, done our best, and now perhaps we should all hope for a Christmas miracle."

He turned abruptly then and left the room. The truth was that Margaret had hit a nerve. He struggled with her accusation that *he*, of all people, could have made such a basic error, though he knew she was right. Rossitor even called it at the time, but as senior physician, he had overruled the younger, less qualified man.

Damn it! He thought. He was exhausted and angry with himself. It had been a long, difficult night, and he had taken his eye off the ball. Only momentarily, he told himself, trying to justify his actions, but he knew his momentary lapse could well cost Matthew Bates his life and leave his family without a husband and father.

As Matthew lay unresponsive in the Intensive Care Ward, Margaret sat stoically by his side, each of her equally devastated children taking turns to support her. The constant beep of machines troubled her, and each time they altered their rhythm, her heart fluttered with fear. She held Matthew's hand and gently encouraged him to wake up. Several more hours lapsed before she suddenly sat bolt upright and called out in excitement.

"He squeezed my hand!"

Lindy, who was sitting with her, had dozed off, but as her mother called out, she woke with a start and looked intently at her father. His eyelids flickered, and as the nurse swiftly made her way across the room from the desk where she had been working, both Margaret and Lindy were filled with hope that Matthew was going to recover.

"I'm sorry ladies, I'd like you to wait outside with the rest of your family now if you don't mind." The nurse was all efficiency.

"Is he going to be all right then?" asked Margaret.

"It's too soon to say."

"It is a good sign though, isn't it?

The nurse checked Matthew's vital statistics and pressed the call button to summon the doctor. She looked at Margaret and Lindy and nodded.

"Yes. Now, please, ladies. The doctor will check Mr Bates and we'll give you an update when we can".

She gently steered the two women from the room as she spoke, and they quickly made their way to the waiting room to pass on their news to the others.

The mood in the waiting room lightened perceptively, and a row of hopeful, expectant faces greeted the doctor as he entered the room fifteen minutes later.

"He's not out of the woods yet," he informed them, "but he's fighting. I suggest you all head home now and get some sleep," he continued.

"There's nothing you can do here. We're keeping him under sedation and under constant surveillance. We'll contact you at once if there's any change."

"Thank you, Doctor, but I'd rather stay."

Margaret looked done-in, but the thought of leaving Matthew was inconceivable to her.

"No, Mum, the doctor's right. There's nothing we can do here. We all need to get some sleep and a good meal to keep our strength up. Dad won't want to see us all looking like this, will he?"

Josh smiled wearily at his mother, and Margaret looked from him to the rest of her brood in turn. They all looked thoroughly worn out and dishevelled. How could she not have noticed the effect this was having on them? Josh and the doctor were right. She needed to get them home.

"You'll be in touch *immediately?*" she asked the doctor. He nodded.

"Immediately," he promised.

Margaret sighed and rose slowly to her feet.

"All right," she agreed, though in her heart, she felt she was letting Matthew down. She had loved him from the first moment she met him, and they had been inseparable ever since. To leave him here alone in the hospital did not sit comfortably with her.

It was almost teatime when they arrived back at the bakery. It was dark outside, and the house seemed cold and uninviting. The ashes from last night's fire sat in the grate, and the Monopoly set lay on the floor where they had left it.

Margaret stooped to start tidying it away, but a chorus of

"We'll take care of that." Met her ears, as her children joined her.

"Come on, Mum, I'll run you a nice hot bath," Susan smiled, taking her mother by the elbow and steering her in the direction of the bathroom.

By the time Margaret had bathed and donned her nightwear and slippers, there was a fresh fire crackling in the grate. The girls had tidied the front room and turned on the Christmas Tree lights for a little extra cheer while the boys, having cleared the grate and re-lit the fire, made their way to the kitchen.

As John busied himself heating soup and toasting crumpets for a quick, easy tea by the fire, Josh set five supper trays, then went to telephone the hospital. There was no further news on Matthew's condition. He was sleeping and comfortable, the nurse assured him.

"You *will* contact us the minute there's any change, won't you?"

"Yes, Mr Bates."

"Thank you."

The family ate their meal in silence. It didn't feel like Christmas Eve. The atmosphere in the room was heavy and sombre. A loud banging on the door knocker made them all jump.

146

"Maybe it's Hilly," suggested Lindy, rising to her feet and making her way from the room. "Weren't you supposed to be meeting her this morning, Josh?"

"Lord, yes!" Josh felt his stomach turn over. Poor Hilly! She wouldn't even know what had happened, why it was that he had failed to turn up! She would have waited there alone in the cold. He should have phoned her from the hospital to let her know what was happening, but his concern for his father had been so all-consuming he had been unable to think of anything else.

"She will have left for London by now," he called after Lindy in a flat, despairing voice.

"I've missed her."

Margaret looked up at him. The sorrow in his voice tugged at her heartstrings.

"She'll understand, dear. Drop her a line at the Art School."

He looked back at her and nodded as the sound of carol singers drifted down the hallway. It was odd that carol singers would knock, and it seemed there were more than just children's voices raised in song. Curiosity getting the better of them, they all rose slowly to their feet and followed Lindy to the front door. The two little carol singers, it turned out, were not alone. There on the doorstep, singing with them, were Alex and Sally Morgan, along with young Tommy, who grinned broadly when he caught sight of Josh. They were all wearing Santa hats, and eight-year-old Tommy was hopping excitedly from foot to foot.

"We've come to wish you Merry Christmas," he called out happily, "and to help Uncle Matthew play Santa Claus!"

The Bates family stood rooted to the spot and looked at him as Alex stepped forward to shake hands with Josh and John.

"So, where's that husband of yours?" he asked Margaret as he gave her a hug and a kiss on the cheek. Margaret burst into tears and Alex stepped back, still holding onto her shoulders. He looked at her in alarm.

"Whatever is it?" he asked.

Lindy and Susan had tears in their eyes, too, and both the boys were visibly upset as they filled the Morgans in on what had happened over the past twenty-four hours. Sally hugged each of the Bates family in turn, then led Margaret and the girls back to the fireplace. Josh handed the bemused little carol singers a shiny sixpence each.

"You still need to make Matthew's delivery for him," Sally said to Alex.

"Get the boys to help you."

Alex nodded and led the boys out to his little farm truck. A large object, carefully covered over with an oilskin and a tarpaulin, sat in the tray. With Tommy's help, Alex removed the protective covers to reveal a huge parcel wrapped in Christmas paper and topped off with a big red bow.

"You chaps should carry that, and I'll bring the other one," instructed an excited Tommy as he reached into the cab and produced another carefully wrapped gift.

"I helped Mum and Uncle Matthew wrap them up," he declared proudly as the two packages were carefully placed under the Christmas Tree.

"Thank you, Tommy." Smiled Margaret, regaining some of her usual warmth and hospitality.

"You're welcome. Are you going to open them now, or will you wait till Uncle Matthew comes home?"

"I think we'll wait for Uncle Matthew."

"I wouldn't if I were you. I know what's in them!"

"Thank you, Tommy!" His parents spoke in firm unison to bring the conversation to an end before their over-excited son let the cat out of the bag.

"Well, I think we should all have a glass of sherry." Smiled Margaret.

"Do the honours, will you boys?"

John fetched out the glasses from the cabinet, as Josh reached down the sherry bottle, but as he started to remove the cap, he was interrupted by the shrill ring of the telephone. He quickly placed the bottle down on the sideboard and ran to the hallway to answer the phone.

By the time he returned, John had finished the job for him. He looked up as Josh stood motionless in the doorway, his face as white as the snow that had begun to fall outside.

"Josh?"

He handed his brother a glass of sherry.

"What is it?" he asked, though he feared he already knew the answer. His voice echoed strangely in his ears, mingling with the heart-wrenching sound of his mother's anguished cry and desperate, uncontrollable sobbing.

"*No!*" she wept. "*No! No! Not my Matthew!*"

Josh nodded slowly, the tears flowing freely from his own dazed eyes as he spoke in a voice that was choked with emotion.

"He couldn't fight it anymore, Mum. The poison in his blood went to his brain. There was nothing more the doctors could do."

Chapter – 10

Hilary Anne deliberately placed her alarm clock on the little desk by the window rather than on her bedside table. That way, she would need to get out of bed in the morning to turn it off and wouldn't be tempted to go back to sleep after it woke her. Not, of course, that she was at all likely to do that, Hilly thought to herself with a wistful smile. Tomorrow would be her only day at home over the entire Christmas Holidays. It would be only half a day at that, and her one chance to see Josh.

Since returning from Paris, Hilly had spent two happy days at *Oak Manor* with Aunt Hilary, and while she thoroughly enjoyed her visit as always, just this once, Hilly felt she would rather have been home in Leominster, catching up with her friends.

Aunt Hilary's friends, the Chatswoods, had invited the entire Moncreiff family to spend Christmas in London as their guests. Their kind invitation sent Elizabeth into transports of delight as she endeavoured to impress upon her daughter what a privilege it was to receive such a generous invitation. A privilege that would afford them a wonderful opportunity to see the sights and enjoy the many entertainments on offer in London.

Hilly, on the other hand, felt she would far rather spend Christmas in Leominster with her own friends. Quite apart from anything else, that awful Geoffrey boy was sure to be home for the holidays, and she would be obliged to be nice to him.

As she snuggled down for the night, Hilary Anne banned Geoffrey Chatswood from her mind and turned her thoughts instead to Joshua Bates.

Joshua was still the only subject on her mind as she swung her legs over the side of the bed the following morning and made her way to silence the noisy alarm clock.

Her bag was already packed in preparation for the two p.m. departure. That way she would have more free time to spend with Josh. They had arranged to meet at ten, which gave her plenty of time to dress and have breakfast, but she wanted to look her very best for Josh, not just throw on any old thing.

She carefully pulled on a pair of warm woollen tights, a snuggly long-sleeved camisole, and a cosy, deep red, polo neck sweater, before donning a sweet little dark navy blue, corduroy mini skirt. A pair of soft tan, knee length leather boots completed her stylish ensemble. To add a touch of French flair, she then plaited her hair over one shoulder and popped on a jaunty red beret.

Having enjoyed a plate of scrambled eggs and bacon, washed down with a steaming hot cup of back coffee, and endured a lecture from her mother, over her lack of manners on wearing a hat at the table, she then politely excused herself and dashed upstairs to collect a little water colour of the Champs Elysee, which she had painted for Josh as a Christmas gift.

"See you all later," she called as she slipped into a warm woollen camel coat, wrapped a navy and red tartan scarf around her neck, and pulled on a pair of tan kid gloves.

"Where are you off to now?" demanded her mother.

"I'm just going to see my friends before we leave for London."

"Well, make sure you keep an eye on the time, please, Hilary Anne."

Elizabeth's voice reached her from the kitchen. It was tinged with its usual tone of disapproval over anything she suspected involved Joshua Bates, and Hilly rolled her eyes as she tucked the beautifully wrapped little painting into a crocheted carry-all, which she then slung over her shoulder.

"Of course, Mother. I'll be back in plenty of time," she replied sweetly as she hurriedly slipped out of the front door.

In truth, she wished it would start to snow so heavily that by two o'clock, the road to London would be closed, and they would have to stay at home. It was certainly cold enough for snow, and the leaden grey sky looked dark and threatening.

As she hurried along Ryelands Road on her way to the Kenwater, the cold air bit at her face and made her eyes water, and Hilly began to wonder if the decision she and Josh had made to meet by the river was entirely wise. Perhaps somewhere indoors, or even at The Sydonia, may have been a better idea, though nowhere near as private, of course. In the end, the only thing that really mattered, she decided, was that they would be together again. A happy smile touched her lips, and she quickened her pace, eager to reach her destination as quickly as possible.

It was only a quarter to ten when she arrived at their secret rendezvous. Hilly thrust her hands into her pockets and hugged the warm, woollen coat a little more closely to her person. Josh would probably be early too, she told herself, but when a full hour passed by and there was still no sign of him, she began to worry. *It was so unlike him,* she thought. *Something must be wrong.* Her toes and her knees were stinging with the cold, and she couldn't even feel her nose any more. She would give him ten more minutes, she decided, and then she would go in search of him.

As the minutes ticked by, her mind began to run riot as to where he could possibly be. Perhaps he had suffered an accident and lay injured on the ground somewhere. There was no one else around who would be able to help him. *No, she couldn't wait any longer, just in case,* she thought, as she began to carefully retrace her steps.

Hilly kept her eyes keenly peeled for any sign of Joshua as she slowly picked her way back along the river bank, but he was nowhere to be seen. As she reached the outskirts of the town, another awful thought popped into her head. Perhaps he just didn't care enough to venture out in the cold; he didn't feel as deeply for her as she felt for him. She pushed the thought from her mind. Why would he have kept in touch when she left for France if he didn't have feelings for her? Josh was busy at university, and yet he always found time to write regularly. Anyway, he still seemed keen to join her for their secret summer getaway to Italy and France. No. There was no reason to believe he didn't care for her anymore.

Hilly trudged on in the direction of the bakery, increasingly worried as to what she might find when she got there. A growing feeling of uneasiness washed over her as Elizabeth's voice rang in her ears.

"Nice girls don't chase after boys, Hilary Anne. Let them do the chasing and don't be too keen. Boys feel things differently from girls."

Hilly slowed her pace. What if Josh really didn't want to see her? What if he felt she was chasing after him?

Her mind filled with doubt, but her heart urged her on. She could still catch up with Lindy anyway, she told herself. There was nothing wrong with that, and she could buy some fresh baked fruit mince pies to take to the Chatswoods for Christmas.

Having reassured herself that her behaviour was perfectly acceptable, she continued on to the bakery, only to find the 'Closed' sign hanging on the door. There was no sign of life anywhere, but she plucked up her courage and made her way through the building materials that lay abandoned in the yard until she reached the side door.

She banged loudly on the door knocker, but no-one answered. Hilly took a deep breath and knocked again with all her might, but there was still no reply, and the house seemed strangely quiet and cold.

Hilly sighed. Something didn't feel right. She slowly turned away and walked pensively back to the street. She could hear a choir joyfully singing Christmas Carols, their voices drifting from The Corn Square, and it filled her with melancholy as she remembered the days of her childhood when she Lindy and Maisie went carol singing together to make money for Christmas. Anything left over after buying presents, they would save for next year to put towards the May Fair, with all its delights. The Dodgems, the Noah's Ark and the Merry-go-Round had always been their firm favourites. A little smile momentarily lightened her mood as she remembered.

She decided to stop by the hairdressers and see whether Maisie had seen Josh or Lindy, but Maisie hadn't seen any of the Bates family for several weeks.

"Sorry, Hilly, I can't help you," she said.

They chatted briefly, but Maisie was busy, and Hilly was anxious to be on her way.

"Merry Christmas," she called as she stepped back out into the cold.

Hilly desperately wanted to go and see if Susan was working at her market stall in The Corn Square, but a quick glance at her watch told her it was time to head home. She was just wondering whether she dared incur Mother's wrath by being late when a young man's voice interrupted her thoughts.

"Hello Hilly, Merry Christmas."

She looked up to see who it was and identified the voice as belonging to an old Leominster Primary School classmate, Jimmy Jones.

Jimmy had been in love with Hilly for as long as he could remember and had been deeply envious of Joshua Bates for just as long.

"Where's Joshua today?" he asked.

Hilly looked at him.

"I don't know. You haven't seen him anywhere, have you?" she asked hopefully.

"No. I saw him yesterday, though, in Hereford. He was driving a little red Mini and had a rather attractive girl with him. They were parked at the bus stop. Sitting there in the car, kissing each other, like they were more than just friends if you know what I mean."

Hilly felt the ground open up under her feet, her heart dropped and the colour drained from her face. Her whole world fell apart in one sickening moment of utter heartbreak. At the same time, Jimmy Jones, seeing the reaction his words had wrought on Hilly, felt a sudden pang of conscience. He had exaggerated the bit about the kiss, hoping it might encourage Hilly to forget about Josh and look at *him* for once. In truth, the girl was just getting out of the car and leaned over to give Josh a farewell kiss on the cheek. Hilly, though, was so obviously upset by his exaggerated description of events that, for one fleeting moment, Jimmy felt an uncomfortable pang of guilt. *Perhaps he should confess and tell her the truth,* he thought, but that would only serve to make Hilly think badly of him, and he didn't want that. Josh would laugh and tell her the truth soon enough, he decided, as Hilly took her leave of him.

"I have to go," she said.

"I'm off to London after lunch."

Hilly tried to sound excited at the prospect. She would never let Jimmy Jones know how deeply his words had cut. She had too much pride and self-respect for that.

Hilly held her head up high and walked slowly on, blinking back the tears that threatened to overcome her. She felt so stupid. Everyone else probably knew there was another girl in Josh's life. They were either being kind by not saying anything, or they were laughing behind her back. It was humiliating, but if Josh wasn't interested in her any more, then she would just have to accept it. She wished she knew where he was so she could talk to him about it. Ask if it was true. The thought of losing him was more than she could bear, but she would never make a fuss or stand in his way. As long as he was happy, that was all that mattered. She would quietly stand aside and see what happened.

Mother, at least, will be delighted, Hilly thought sadly as she opened the front door of *Elm Cottage* and quietly made her way upstairs. She needed more time to regain her composure before she faced the family. In the end, she decided that nobody else need ever know what had transpired this morning. Especially not Mother.

Hilary Anne removed her gloves, coat and beret, freshened her makeup, re-plaited her hair, then sat on the side of her bed, staring blankly at the pastel drawing of Josh in the cowslips, which hung on the opposite wall. Large tears spilt over her eyelashes and splashed onto her skirt, leaving big, damp splodges on the corduroy. She angrily wiped them away, took several deep gulps of air, swallowed hard and carefully dabbed at her eyes. No one must know she had been crying. No one must *ever* see her cry. She rose to her feet, took one last look in the mirror to check her eyes were not red, collected up her outdoor garments, and made her way downstairs. She would gather her dignity, go to London, and try to enjoy herself, then she would write to Josh as soon as she returned to Paris.

Elizabeth placed a pot of home-grown vegetable soup on the table for lunch, and Hilly sipped at it slowly, enjoying its comforting warmth. She was unusually quiet, but if anyone noticed her withdrawn manner, Elizabeth's endless, excited chatter gave them no chance to comment or ask awkward questions that Hilly was in no mood to answer.

"Just think Hilly," Elizabeth enthused, "we can go and see all the Christmas Lights on Oxford Street and take a stroll through Hyde Park. Even go to see Buckingham and Kensington Palaces!"

Hilly forced herself to smile. Two whole weeks of listening to Mother's excited prattle was a daunting prospect, but it would be nice to see her enjoy herself.

The journey to London was uneventful. Hilly sat in the back of the car with Aunt Hilary. She closed her eyes and pretended to sleep as her mother continued to chatter on.

The Chatswoods owned an attractive townhouse on Wrights Lane in Kensington, and as Robert brought the car to a halt outside, Elizabeth's excitement spilt over as she took in the elegant facade.

"Oh, how beautiful!" she gushed.

"If you were to take a job here in London with William, Robert, we could live somewhere like this too!"

Robert closed his eyes and said nothing. They hadn't even stepped from the car, and Elizabeth was already riding her favourite hobbyhorse! He was, of course, fully aware that she would use the holiday to push him about moving to London, but he hoped he might at least get a few days of peace before the nagging began. He gritted his teeth and opened the car door.

"Wake up, Sleeping Beauty," he called to Hilly, who was still snoozing in the back seat. "We're here!"

Hilly opened her eyes and blinked a few times.

"Golly, it's a bit grand," she commented,

"It's all sandstone and marble and wrought iron. No wonder Geoffrey didn't know how to climb a tree; he'd probably never seen one before!"

"For heaven's sake, Hilary Anne! What a ridiculous thing to say! There are trees everywhere. Not to mention the fact that Hyde Park is just down the road."

"I don't imagine he'd be allowed to climb the trees there."

Aunt Hilary suppressed a chuckle and smiled quietly to herself as she alighted from the car, while Robert gave his daughter an amused shake of his head as he helped his wife to her feet.

"I hope you don't intend to continue like this, Hilary Anne."

"Of course not, Mother. I was only teasing. The house is very handsome."

Elizabeth sniffed and sailed up the marble stairs that led to the smart black door like a woman on a mission of great importance. She banged three times on the shiny brass knocker, then stood back admiring the smart black planter boxes with their neat topiary buxus balls.

Daphne Chatswood was waiting expectantly for her visitors to arrive and opened the door with a flourish.

"You've made it!" she gushed with a welcoming smile as she reached out to hug each of them in turn.

"Was the traffic too awful? It does tend to be quite frightful on Christmas Eve. We wondered if you might decide to avoid it and catch the train!"

Elizabeth laughed.

"Even worse, I imagine," she replied, "and so many small children!"

"Of course!" agreed Daphne.

"They do tend to be frightfully noisy and over-excitable at this time of year!"

She ushered her guests inside as she spoke. William appeared from a room on the right of the grand entrance hall and called for Geoffrey. Hilly's heart sank. She had hoped he would not be there, but he sailed down the stairs, wreathed in smiles and oozing charm from every pore.

"Can I fetch your bags in for you?" he enquired politely.

"You could certainly give me a hand. Thank you, young man," replied Robert.

"Very good of you to offer." He smiled as he led the way back to his car with both Geoffrey and William in tow.

Daphne, meanwhile, led the ladies upstairs to freshen up before they gathered back down in the formal reception room to partake of light refreshments.

Hilly looked about with interest. The interior of the house was every bit as elegant and gracious as the exterior. *Right up Mother's alley,* she thought to herself, as the three men re-joined them.

"Now, Hilary Anne," Daphne interrupted her thoughts, "you remember Geoffrey, of course?"

Hilly looked at her and smiled sweetly.

"Of course," she agreed.

"Poor girl's not likely to forget, is she," William laughed.

The older members of the party all joined in his laughter as Hilly and Geoffrey eyed each other up for the first time.

"I trust you are feeling quite well after your journey?" he enquired with a hint of sarcasm.

"You don't require the coal scuttle?"

"Geoffrey! Hilly was just a little girl!" Daphne frowned at him.

"Yes, but I'm quite grown up now and no longer suffer from travel sickness. Thank you, Geoffrey. Have you managed to overcome your fear of heights yet?"

It was Elizabeth's turn to frown.

"Well countered, young lady," laughed William, "and now that the niceties are all out of the way, who's for a little Christmas tipple before dinner?"

Christmas Day came and went with a flurry of festive activities. A great number of gifts changed hands, Christmas Carols played endlessly on the stereogram, while a succulent ham on the bone, and a large roast turkey with all the trimmings, were washed down with several bottles of fine French wines.

The housekeeper having left early to join her own family, Hilly and Geoffrey volunteered to clear the table and do the washing up, while the others enjoyed a glass of port.

"How lovely to have a daughter," smiled Daphne.

"Geoffrey would never have thought of that without Hilly's input! I do believe he's rather taken with her!"

Elizabeth smiled back happily.

"They do make rather a lovely couple, don't they?" she enthused.

"They do," agreed Daphne.

Aunt Hilary closed her eyes and quietly shook her head. Would Elizabeth never learn? Unless Hilly had undergone a sudden change of heart, there was only one young man on her mind, and that young man was *not* Geoffrey Chatswood.

Geoffrey, on the other hand, was smitten, and Hilly was indeed the absolute object of his desire.

Hilly, meanwhile, was finding Geoffrey's sudden charm attack a little overwhelming. He seemed rather too interested in her personal life, asking endless questions she had no desire to answer while at the same time telling her more about himself than she had any desire to know. All she really wanted was to be on her own while she tried to make sense of what Jimmy Jones had told her about Josh and the other girl.

Geoffrey's persistent unwelcome attentions began to make her feel distinctly uncomfortable.

"Why don't we see if the others would like to play charades," she suggested in a desperate attempt to escape from him.

As she reached up to return the last of the crockery to the kitchen dresser, he suddenly put an arm around her shoulders and roughly spun her around to face him.

"I thought you and I would spend some time on our own," he said suggestively, gazing intently into her eyes and pinning her arms to her sides.

He took her by surprise then, leaning into her, pushing her roughly against the cabinetry, and forcing his kisses on her.

Hilly felt a moment of panic. She tried to wriggle free from him, but he held her in a vice-like grip, and she found it impossible to move at all. Every time she moved a muscle, his grip tightened even further. It was as though he was obsessed with controlling her, determined to possess her.

Hilly's panic rose, and she summoned all her strength to kick him in the shin, which thankfully had the desired effect of making him let go.

"I don't think so, Geoffrey. I already have a boyfriend."

As she ducked from his grasp and ran out of the room, a pained expression of disbelieving, hurt and anger flashed across Geoffrey's brow, but he convinced himself that Hilly was only playing hard to get. Oh well, she could play games all she liked, but he'd win in the end. He always did.

Hilly made a concerted effort to keep her distance from Geoffrey over the next few days. She enlisted Aunt Hilary's unknowing aid as a chaperone and stayed close by her side at all times, ensuring Geoffrey could not get her on her own.

At first, he found it mildly amusing, but as the days slipped by, he began to feel annoyed. How dare she keep behaving like this? It was boring him now.

For her part, Hilly was still struggling with Josh's disappearance, as well as Jimmy Jones' story about the other girl. She wanted to talk to Aunt Hilary and see what she made of it all, but the opportunity did not arise because just as *she* was determined to stay away from *him*, Geoffrey Chatswood was equally determined to stay close to *her*.

He would appear as if from nowhere, sit or stand as near to her as possible, and stare at her in a manner that made her feel decidedly uncomfortable, but she held her ground and continued to ignore him, other than to reply with short, sharp comments when the conversation demanded it.

Chapter – 11

"You do realise you're making a fool of yourself now, don't you," Geoffrey spat at Hilly a week later, on the morning before New Year's Eve.

Their parents had planned a walk around Hyde Park, and Hilly was waiting out of Geoffrey's way on the front step for the adults to appear, but he got there ahead of them. She resisted an urge to slap him and, instead, infuriated him even further by smiling sweetly and saying nothing. In truth, she was a little afraid of him. He was moody and unpredictable, like a predator stalking its prey. There was no telling how he might react if she said what he perceived as the wrong thing.

She heaved a sigh of relief as the front door opened, and their fathers stepped out to join them.

"Hello, you two. You're keen, aren't you?" smiled William Chatswood.

"I don't think the other ladies will keep you waiting much longer my dear," he assured Hilly kindly, and she smiled back at him, as his son muttered darkly under his breath, that keeping people waiting was the favourite pastime of the females in this house.

William frowned at him but had no chance to retort as the ladies made good their appearance, and the group sallied forth.

The walk proceeded pleasantly enough as they enjoyed a leisurely stroll around the park and The Serpentine before wandering onto Oxford Street in search of a hot drink and sustenance. They stopped at the iconic Lyons Oxford Corner House Tea Shop, where Geoffrey promptly made it his business to arrange the seating, and as he sat down beside her, trapping her in the middle of a deeply buttoned bench seat, Hilly felt an overwhelming need to escape him.

Determined not to spend one moment more than necessary in his company, she suggested to the other ladies that perhaps they should leave the men to their own devices and go to investigate the shops. She was keen to look at Liberty's beautiful fabrics and artworks, then some of the fashion shops, and perhaps even Carnaby Street.

To her horror, Aunt Hilary quite unexpectedly professed to be in need of a rest, especially as they were going out to the theatre later and opted to return to Wrights Lane with the menfolk.

Geoffrey gave Hilly a supercilious smile, then turned his attention to Aunt Hilary with all the charm he could muster. As they left the Corner House, he took her by the elbow and offered to find a taxi in order to spare her from walking any further in the cold. As luck would have it, an empty cab happened by almost immediately, and as he raised his arm to hail it, his actions received hearty approval from all but Hilly.

"How thoughtful, Geoffrey," gushed Elizabeth.

"He's such a credit to you, Daphne. Do you know, I think I might head back for a rest too," she continued, "How do you feel? There's room for another." She smiled encouragingly.

"Oh, I shouldn't want Hilary Anne to miss out on browsing around the shops. It's her last opportunity, really."

Geoffrey saw his chance and pounced.

"I'll escort Hilary Anne," he volunteered enthusiastically.

"Oh, there's no need for that! I'm perfectly happy to go alone. You'll just be bored!"

"That's very gallant of you, Geoffrey. Thank you," beamed Elizabeth.

"He really is a lovely young man, Daphne," she purred as the taxi pulled away from the kerb.

"Thank you," Daphne smiled.

"He can be quite charming when it suits him."

Hilly stood frozen to the spot as the taxi disappeared from sight.

"That didn't go to plan then, did it?" smirked Geoffrey.

"I have no idea what you mean," she replied.

"You don't have to escort me, you know. I'd really rather potter about on my own. You will get bored very quickly, and I intend to be all afternoon."

"Oh, come on, Hilly. Forget the other chap. Your mother doesn't like him anyway. Says he's a baker's son or something."

"What's wrong with that? Mr Bates is a lovely man, and I've loved his son forever."

"Huh! Puppy love! Is *he* a baker, too?"

"No. He's a medical student, if you must know. Not that it's any of your business!"

161

"Oh, come on, Hilly," he repeated, though her revelation had taken a little of the wind out of his sails.

"We may have to go out to 'Wait until Dark' with the old folks tonight, but tomorrow I'll take you out for dinner, then we can go and welcome in the New Year at Trafalgar Square. It'll be fun. Or we could just stay in alone," he suggested hopefully.

Hilly was already aware that the older generation was headed to a dinner party to see in the New Year, and she would be left alone with Geoffrey.

She closed her eyes and sighed. Geoffrey seemed so lonely and desperate that she almost felt sorry for him.

"Oh, all right. Tomorrow night you can take me for some hot chips, and we'll see in the New Year at Trafalgar Square."

After all, she was headed back to Paris the following day, she thought. It wouldn't hurt her to be nice to him for one night. What harm could come of that?

Geoffrey smiled and inclined his head. She might be about to leave London, but he had finally won! He would take her around the wretched shops this afternoon, and as he did that, he would use all his charms on her, then tomorrow night, he would wine, dine and woo her, and she would be putty in his hands! The baker's son would be forgotten!

It was late afternoon by the time Hilary Anne and Geoffrey returned to Wright's Lane, and the adults were partaking of a high tea in the conservatory before dressing to go to the theatre.

"How were the shops?" asked Elizabeth.

"They were wonderful! I could have spent hours at Liberty's, and Carnaby Street was a great lark! I bought a sweet little feather boa to wear to the theatre tonight. We went for a walk too, by the Houses of Parliament, over Westminster Bridge, along the Thames path, and back over Tower Bridge."

"Heavens, my dear, you must be exhausted!" exclaimed Daphne.

"Not to mention ravenous," suggested William.

"Not really," smiled Hilly. "I seem to have done nothing but eat all week. Perhaps I might just have a quick cup of coffee and a sandwich; then, if you'll excuse me, I still have a little packing to take care of before we head out.

Honor Blackman's performance in *Wait Until Dark* was outstanding, but the evening was spoiled for Hilly by Geoffrey sitting beside her and constantly touching her. He brushed her leg with his hand as he offered her a box of After Eight mint chocolates, reached for her hand as soon as the lights were dimmed, and put an arm around her shoulders when the play got a little scary.

She pulled herself away from him and tried to push him off, but he tightened his grip, sensing she would never make a fuss in public.

By the time the final curtain fell, Hilly had endured quite enough. She wished she hadn't agreed to spend New Year's Eve with him but could see no way out. She felt utterly trapped, just like the blind lady in *Wait Until Dark*.

A feeling of deep foreboding hung over Hilly all the following day. Elizabeth, on the other hand, was delighted to hear that her daughter was seeing in the New Year with Geoffrey. Perhaps she was coming to her senses at last. Seeing the kind of lifestyle that a nice young man like Geoffrey could offer her.

Hilly, on the other hand, felt no interest in anything that Geoffrey had to offer. She desperately wished she could go back to Leominster and see Josh and Lindy and Maisie before she returned to Paris. To see in the New Year with her own friends. She felt so comfortable when she was with them. Geoffrey scared her. He may well be all smiles and charm on the surface, but there was something lurking deep inside him that she simply could not trust. Her own instinct warned her to take care whenever he was near.

"I'm pleased to see you're resting, Hilly" commented Geoffrey, sauntering into the conservatory, where she sat browsing through a copy of the latest *Vogue* magazine, which she had found lying on the coffee table.

"You'll need plenty of energy later to enjoy what I have in store for you tonight."

"I thought we were going to have fish and chips and watch the fireworks."

"Oh, we can do much better than that. You're in London now, remember, not sleepy little Leominster," he sneered.

"But I only want to see the fireworks, and I don't want to be up too late. I'm travelling back to France tomorrow, remember."

"Oh, grow up, Hilly!"

She closed her magazine with a snap and rose to her feet, ready to make good her exit, but he stood just inches in front of her, barring her way.

"Where are you going now?" he asked.

"I came to spend some time with you."

"Well, I'm sorry, but I'm going for a walk."

"I'll come with you."

"No, thank you. I need to be on my own to get my thoughts back on track for my studies," she lied as she reached for her handbag, which was lying on the floor beside her.

"No, you don't. You're just trying to avoid me again." A wounded, forlorn look flickered across Geoffrey's face, causing Hilly to feel a very brief moment of guilt. She had decided to make her way to the public telephone box and ring Josh. She needed to hear the truth from him about the other girl. Jimmy Jones' words still haunted her every waking moment, and while she dreaded Josh saying it *was* true, that he *had* found someone else, somehow, not knowing, seemed even worse.

Hilly determined that if it was indeed true, she must somehow find the courage to wish Josh well and find a way to move on without him. Her heart would be broken, but she would never let it show. Never stand in the way of his happiness. She loved him too much to do that.

The one thing she knew for certain was that she did not want Geoffrey Chatswood hanging around while she made the most important phone call of her life.

"I'm sorry, Geoffrey, but I must insist."

Hilary Anne bestowed upon him a warm, winning smile.

"I'll be back in plenty of time for our fish and chips," she added, annoyed with herself for feeling that she must, in some way, appease him. Make him feel better about himself. He was, after all, a grown man, and he was behaving like a spoiled little boy.

Hilly made her way to the front door as quickly as she could and pausing only to collect her coat and hat from the hall stand, made her way out to the street, leaving Geoffrey to advise the others of her where-abouts.

She hurried past the phone box on Wrights Lane, making her way to the High Street in search of another that would be well out of the way of Geoffrey's prying eyes. She felt sure she could feel them burning into her back as she walked along and even turned to check he wasn't following her. She had only to make her way to the Tube Station to find another telephone.

Hilly stepped inside the phone booth, fetched a handful of pennies from the outer pocket of her bag, dialled the number, and waited in nervous anticipation for her call to be answered, but the phone simply rang and rang. She hung on for what seemed like an eternity until, with a deep sigh of disappointment, she replaced the receiver on its cradle.

She called the hairdressing salon where Maisie worked but was told Maisie had the day off. When she tried to contact Lindy at Dr Young's Veterinary Clinic, the receptionist told her very brusquely that Miss Bates was not in attendance today, and she couldn't say when she might return.

Feeling very much the way she did when Mother chided her for no good reason, Hilly hung up the phone yet again. Hot tears pricked at the back of her eyes as she stepped back onto the High Street. It was as though her entire world had disappeared. She needed so desperately to hear the familiar sound of a friendly voice. To be reassured that all was well, especially where Josh was concerned.

Feeling unable to return to Wrights Lane and Geoffrey, Hilly slowly made her way in the direction of Holland Park, and as she walked along, lost in her own unhappy thoughts, a deep-seated, uncomfortable feeling that something was horribly wrong gradually crept over her.

Hilly wandered aimlessly for a good hour or more before settling down on a park bench. She still felt no desire to head back to Wrights Lane, no desire to spend the evening with Geoffrey, and even no real desire to return to Paris tomorrow. Her attention was taken for a short time by a pair of little squirrels scurrying about in search of food, but as even *they* deserted her, she finally rose stiffly to her feet and trudged slowly back to the High Street. As she reached the telephone box, the temptation to ring Josh one last time overcame her. She held her breath and crossed her fingers as she listened to the phone ringing at the other end of the line, but there was still no reply. She hung on until the line cut out, and then she sadly hung up the receiver and made her way back to the house.

Geoffrey waited impatiently for Hilly to return. He had become completely obsessed with her over the past few days and felt slighted and more than a little sorry for himself when she made it so abundantly clear that she did not want his company on her outing this afternoon.

He sat at the kitchen table and pouted. She was obviously up to something. Why else would it be so important to her that she went out alone? His imagination ran riot until he thoroughly convinced himself that *'the baker's son'* was catching a train to London, and the two of them were meeting up to spend the day together. His eyes narrowed, and he set his mind on planning his revenge.

How dare she? he thought to himself. Well, he'd show her who the best man was for her tonight. Hilary Anne Moncrieff would never look at *Joshua Bates again.*

He went for a walk himself then, searching the High Street for any sight of her. None being forthcoming, simply stood to convince Geoffrey even further that he was correct in his assumptions. He then returned home to lick his wounds and await her eventual return. He felt further offended when none of the older generations seemed to even notice that he was sorely vexed about the fact that Hilary Anne had sauntered off without him. How they could sit there by the fire, discussing politics and every day matters when he was so obviously suffering, was quite beyond his comprehension.

Geoffrey fumed silently to himself until the sound of the front door closing and Hilly's voice calling out 'hello', made him jump to his feet and run to the hallway.

"There you are!" he exclaimed in an accusatory tone of voice.

"You took your time, didn't you?"

"I had a lot to do."

"What? Clearing your mind?" His voice was filled with sarcasm.

"That's right." Hilly felt quite alarmed and taken aback.

"Of course, excuse me! Obviously, art school is extremely taxing on the brain!" Geoffrey hissed.

Hilly looked at him in disbelief. A feeling of disgust washed over her. Who *did* he think he was?

She threw him a disdainful look and pushed past him, making her way to the lounge and taking a seat on the settee alongside her aunt.

"Have you all had a lovely day?' she asked politely, trying hard to regain her composure.

"We certainly have," replied Aunt Hilary.

"We took a little fresh air while the two of you were out, and since then, we have simply relaxed in preparation for a late night this evening. What have you been up to since you sent poor Geoffrey home alone?"

Hilly bristled.

So Geoffrey followed her. How dared he?

She threw him a scathing look as he lurked in the doorway listening.

166

"Oh, she didn't want my company," he informed them all, "Hilary Anne had her own agenda."

"Hilary Anne?" Elizabeth's voice had an edge to it.

"I simply wanted to clear my head and get my thoughts back to my studies."

"So, where *did* you go then?" asked Geoffrey in an accusatory tone.

"You were nowhere to be seen when I went to check on you."

"Check on me?"

"I just wanted to be sure that you were all right."

"You wanted to spy on me, more like."

"Hilary Anne!" Elizabeth was horrified.

"What a terrible thing to say. Poor Geoffrey is doing his best to be gallant, and the perfect host, and you speak to him like that. Where were you, anyway?"

"That is *my* business." retorted a frustrated Hilly.

She had no wish to tell Mother what was going on in her private life. Mother *or* Geoffrey Chatswood!

"Please don't speak to your mother like that, Hilly."

Robert's voice was calm and measured.

"You have a right to your privacy, I agree, but I think you owe both your mother and young Geoffrey an apology. Don't you?"

Hilary Anne did *not* agree, but she bit her tongue the way she had learned to do from a very early age and took a deep breath. She had no wish to upset Father or Aunt Hilary or Mr and Mrs Chatswood, so she resolutely smiled her sweetest, most penitent smile and apologised.

"I'm very sorry," she offered in a soft, sad, little voice.

"I think I must be a little tired. However, that is no excuse, of course! I walked for such a long time; you see. Then I sat for a rest and watched two dear little squirrels gathering food for ages until I got so cold, I could scarcely move." Her voice faltered, and a concerned Daphne leapt to her defence.

"There, there, my dear. Don't distress yourself."

She threw her son a disparaging look.

"Geoffrey will put the kettle on and make you a nice hot cup of tea to warm you up. You must be hungry, too. I shall make you a fresh ham sandwich, and you must sit beside the fire and warm your feet."

Hilly felt suddenly overcome with guilt. She had been so horrible to Geoffrey, yet here was his mother being kindness itself.

She fought back the urge to cry. Why must her own mother always make her feel that she was in the wrong? She felt so miserable. She was devastated that she had failed to contact Josh. Where could he possibly be? She convinced herself that Jimmy Jones was right. Josh had another girlfriend now and had forgotten all about her. She drank her tea and ate her sandwich in heartbroken silence, paying no mind to the conversation that carried on around her.

"Don't you think, Hilly?"

The mention of her name brought her out of her reverie.

"Mmm? Sorry, I was miles away," she apologised quietly. "I think I should go and have a lie-down before Geoffrey takes me out on the town tonight."

She paused and turned her attention to Geoffrey.

"That is, if you still have a mind to take me out tonight?" she asked him.

"Well, of course," he replied.

He felt no qualms over the way he had spoken to Hilly. How was he to know she was only watching a pair of silly squirrels? If she hadn't been gone for so long, he wouldn't have been suspicious of her whereabouts in the first place. No, he had no reason to apologise. So, what if he was wrong? He certainly felt no need to change his plans for this evening.

Chapter – 12

As Joshua Bates opened his eyes on Christmas morning, he thought for one moment that the awful events of the past two days had been nothing but a bad dream. He could hear someone moving about downstairs in the family kitchen, just like every other Christmas Day for as long as he could remember.

From the time he was a small boy, Dad would be up bright and early, making French Toast with strawberries and maple syrup as a special Christmas breakfast treat. *He'd come and get them all up in a minute,* thought Josh, *when everything was ready for them.*

He tucked the counterpane under his chin and closed his eyes again. Slowly, the cold, factual reality that it was not Matthew in the kitchen crept over him like a damp, thick, chilling fog. Matthew's passing was not a bad dream. It was a terrible, unbearable truth. Josh felt a veil of deep, suffocating sadness fall over him. It must be Mum or one of his siblings in the kitchen, trying to keep things as normal as possible.

He dragged himself from the comforting warmth of his bed and dressed quickly, in order that he might go downstairs and help whichever of them it was. The aroma of percolating coffee greeted his nostrils as he stumbled his way down the stairs in the dim morning light.

"Good Lord, Josh! You look awful. Are you sleepwalking?" asked his brother as Joshua almost fell through the kitchen door.

"I should have known it was you," Josh replied, ignoring John's opinions on his dishevelled appearance.

"Dad would be proud of you, John. You get more like him every day, you know."

John gave him a wry smile.

"Thank you," he said quietly. "That's the best thing anyone ever said to me."

Sensing his brother's pain to be the equal of his own, Joshua reached out and wrapped his arms around him.

"He'll be a hard act to follow," he consoled the younger man, "but if anyone can do it, you can."

They held their embrace for several minutes, choking back their sobs until the familiar sound of Margaret's footfall on the stairs caused them to hurriedly break their embrace and roughly wipe their faces dry before their mother could see their grief.

Margaret came through the kitchen door with a smile on her face, but her sons could see that she, too, had been crying.

"Oh, it's you two!" she exclaimed. "The smell of cinnamon and coffee reminded me that it was Christmas Day."

"I was just telling John how proud Dad would be of him for keeping up the family tradition."

"So, he would," agreed Margaret, hugging each of her sons in turn.

The girls joined them then, still dressed in their nighties and cosy winter dressing gowns.

"I almost forgot for a moment," confessed Susan. "The smell of Christmas breakfast made me think that everything was normal."

"Me too." Sighed Lindy.

They settled themselves down at the table, each one trying hard to find a little Christmas Cheer, but the meal was eaten in uncommon silence, and the empty chair at the head of the table haunted them all.

"Right!" Josh looked at each of them in turn. "All these long faces are not what Dad would want. I suggest we clear the dishes and head to church as usual. I'm sure you ladies all have pretty new dresses to wear."

"We do, but it wouldn't be right for us to dress in anything other than black." Margaret sighed. Her thoughts were in a jumble. A Christmas Service with cheery carols and excited children keen to discover what Santa had placed under the tree would be so comforting right now, but how could they turn up in black and spoil the day for everyone else?

"No," she said, "for the first time I can remember, we won't be going to church this Christmas. It wouldn't be right somehow."

Josh reached out and squeezed her hand.

"Whatever you think, Mum. We'll just have a nice quiet day to ourselves."

He stood up and started clearing the plates as he spoke, but the sound of the phone ringing caused him to put them down again, wondering out loud as he did, who would be calling so early on Christmas Day.

170

The familiar voice of Alex Morgan greeted him.

"Sorry to call so early, Josh," he apologised, "but me and Sally would like it if you all came to us for Christmas Lunch. There's more than enough to go around and we thought you could do with a bit of company today. We'll be eating around one o'clock, but come nice and early, any time you like, and we'll drink a toast to Matthew."

The Bates family was delighted with the invitation.

"Alex is quite right," agreed Margaret. "Church might be a struggle today, but some nice, understanding company is just what we need."

"Yes, and I think Dad would want you ladies to wear your new dresses, so why don't you go and put them on while John and I finish up here."

"Good idea, and I bet we'll have this done *and* be dressed to leave before you girls are anywhere near ready," grinned John.

Christmas Day passed in a far more pleasant manner than any of the Bates family could have hoped for, and by Boxing Day, they all felt a little more able to cope with what lay ahead. Word of Matthew's passing travelled quickly, and Margaret found herself overwhelmed by the tributes and offers of help that arrived daily. It seemed everyone who had ever known Matthew wanted to send their condolences.

Josh took it upon himself as the eldest son to make all the arrangements for Matthew's funeral, though he took care to consult with Margaret at every step along the way. John was determined that he would prepare all of his father's favourite refreshments to offer to those who came to pay their respects, and while Susan and Lindy lent him a hand in the kitchen and arranged the floral tributes, Alex Morgan kept a fatherly eye on them all.

The day dawned cold and blustery, and Josh felt it echoed the frigid emptiness he felt in the pit of his stomach.

He offered his arm to Margaret and solemnly led her to the family pew, making sure she was comfortably settled before turning his attention to his siblings. The three of them sat in silence, their teary eyes focused on the casket that lay before them. As he took his own seat, a tiny, muffled sob stabbed at his heart. Lindy sat beside him, shaking with the effort of trying to control her desire to burst into a loud, lusty fit of tears. She twisted a sopping wet handkerchief round and round in her trembling fingers. Josh put his hand on her arm to comfort her, and Sally Morgan, who was seated behind her, leaned forward to offer a large box of tissues. Having whispered her thanks, Lindy set about blowing her nose as quietly as she could and wiping away the flow of tears that she seemed unable to control.

She passed the tissues to her mother who was struggling with her own efforts to stem the tears, and as Susan also helped herself to a good supply from the proffered box, both Josh and John gritted their teeth, and stoically blinked furiously, in order that their own tears be kept under control, and they should show strength and resolve to their distraught mother and sisters.

The boys both spoke of their father with touching tributes, as did many others. His strength of both body and mind concerning his disability had been apparent to all. His cheerful banter and kindness were appreciated by all, and how could those evacuated to Baron's Cross on the day of the flood ever forget his thoughtful generosity?

As the service drew to a close, Margaret sat and sobbed uncontrollably. Her tearful daughters did their best to console her as her sons joined Alex and three of Matthew's closest friends to carry their father on his final journey.

The next few days passed in a blur for them all. Joshua found it difficult to concentrate on his books, and the usually cheery John was quiet and subdued.

Matthew's last gift to them all became the centre of their world. It was a coloured television set that offered a wonderful respite from their sadness.

Nobody wanted to plan ahead, but with the holiday season coming to an end, they were forced to make an effort to do just that. The builders were due to return, the Veterinary Clinic would revert to normal hours, and following the Christmas rush, Susan and Margaret were low on stock.

"You know I'll have to leave you all to your own devices the day after tomorrow, don't you?"

Josh looked anxiously at his mother as he spoke. He felt like a rat leaving a sinking ship. He knew his siblings would care for Margaret, but he had no real heart to return to Birmingham, while the pain of losing Matthew was still so raw for them all. He consoled himself with the thought that maybe one day, he might be in a position to spare another family from suffering the way they were now.

Margaret seemed to read his thoughts.

"Of course, you need to get back to university." She smiled.

"The country needs good doctors. I'm so proud of you, Josh, for speaking up the way you did at the hospital, and I know your dad was too.

There's nothing more you can do here, but there's plenty you can do when you graduate."

Josh sighed.

"Thanks, Mum. I knew you'd understand how I feel. You always have."

He gave her a hug and a kiss on the top of her head.

"Do you know, I think I might go for a walk," he announced. "Anyone care to join me?"

His question was answered by a chorus of "No thanks," he looked around his assembled family and shook his head.

"Lazy, the lot of you!" he quipped, though in truth, he was happy to go alone. He was hoping to catch up with Maisie in case she had heard from Hilly, but when he called at the Cowan's cottage, her mother shook her head.

"I'm sorry, Josh, you've just missed her, I'm afraid. Gone off somewhere with Jimmy Jones and some of their other friends, I think, though she'll be sorry to have missed you."

Josh nodded and turned to walk away.

"How are you anyway?" she carried on.

"We're all in shock over what happened to your dad. It was a beautiful send-off you gave him. He'd have been proud."

"Thank you."

Josh smiled politely, then quickly made good his escape. He wanted to forget the stress of the funeral. Put it out of his mind for a few hours at least and focus on the future.

He slowly made his way to the river Kenwater, to the spot where he had planned to meet Hilly just two weeks earlier. *It seemed like months ago, yet only yesterday, all at the same time,* he thought. So much had happened. All his plans, everything he held dear to him, seemed to have been caught in a huge, dark storm. Torn to shreds and blown away by a cruel, vicious wind.

Josh turned up the collar on his coat and sat down under the large, gnarled old tree that was his and Hilly's secret meeting place. He wondered where she was and what she was doing. Whether she was thinking about him, remembering the precious moments they had spent here together. If he closed his eyes, he could almost feel her soft, warm embrace and taste her sweet, passionate kisses. He sat perfectly still, afraid that any movement would break his trance. It was mid-afternoon and threatening to turn dark before he finally stirred.

It suddenly occurred to him that Hilly would not even know about Matthew's death. She was always so fond of him that Josh even teased her one day that she felt more for his dad than she did for him. He knew that news of Matthew's passing would upset her deeply, and he wanted her to hear about it from him, not some stranger on the street.

He strode back towards the town with a real sense of purpose.

Hilly would be back in Paris now, so he would write to her at once before anyone else beat him to it. He was almost back to The Corn Square when the unmistakable figure of Elizabeth Moncreiff suddenly appeared before him. A few long strides took him to her side.

"Good afternoon, Mrs Moncreiff," he greeted her politely, "I trust you had an enjoyable holiday in London?"

"We certainly did, thank you, Joshua."

"And Hilly got off back to Paris, all right?"

"She did, thank you." Elizabeth Moncreiff turned and looked at him. A strange, supercilious smile flickered across her face.

"Yes," she said, "her young man escorted her to the boat train and saw her off. We have high hopes they'll get engaged in the spring when Hilary Anne graduates. He has an excellent job in the city and so much to offer her. I know the two of you have always been very good friends, Joshua, but I do believe Hilly has come to realise that Geoffrey is in a far better position to give her what she wants in life than you will ever be."

"Geoffrey? Really? You do surprise me. I thought she always found him to be nothing more than a sulky, spoiled brat."

Josh threw her a scathing look and strode off, leaving Elizabeth to bristle with indignation. She may have embellished the truth a little, but where she was concerned, Geoffrey *was* a far better suitor for Hilary Anne, and she did, after all, have good reason to believe that Hilly was finally seeing things *her* way. From the moment Hilly was born, she had strived to provide the very best for her, and that best was not the son of a small-town baker. A tiny pang of conscience hit her as she saw the pain in Josh's eyes, but she swept it aside. There was no shame in wanting Hilly to have all the things that she herself had longed for. Robert was a handsome man who was kind, pleasant, and intelligent, but he lacked drive and ambition. He had always failed to understand her desire to live the way the Chatswoods did.

Elizabeth did not believe that she had spoken out of turn but decided, nevertheless, not to mention her conversation with Joshua to Robert. He would doubtless be annoyed, or angry even, and say that she was interfering in Hilly's life again.

The nerve of that Bates boy, though, to imply that she was lying. How dare he!

For his part, Joshua struggled to believe that Hilly could be interested in *that Geoffrey boy*, as she always called him. Elizabeth Moncreiff could be an unpleasant woman when it suited her, but why would she even say that?

Even though he struggled to believe her, Josh felt strangely unsettled by her words. What if she was telling the truth? What if Hilly had undergone a change of heart and really had fallen for Geoffrey Chatswood?

As he opened the door and stepped inside, Josh's mind was in turmoil, and the pain in his heart was almost too much to bear. If it *was* true, he had lost both his father and his soulmate in just two terrible weeks.

As Elizabeth Moncreiff opened the door to *Elm Cottage*, she was surprised to find that Robert had beaten her home.

"Goodness. You're home early today," she gushed. "How lovely."

"Sit down, Elizabeth." Robert looked at her. The strain on his face and the tone of his voice told her that all was not well. He seemed quite out of sorts and more than a little upset about something. Her stomach churned as uncomfortable feelings of panic and guilt swept over her. Surely, he couldn't already know about her conversation with Joshua. That was not possible. Was it Hilly? Had something happened to Hilly? She took a seat at the table and waited in trepidation for him to speak again.

"It's Matthew Bates," Robert said. "The most dreadful thing. Poor chap died on Christmas Eve. Burst appendix by all accounts. We've missed the funeral, but we must send our condolences at once. Thought we might even pay Margaret a visit tonight."

The colour drained from Elizabeth's face as feelings of remorse washed over her. She began to feel quite unwell. Poor Margaret. Poor Joshua. What had she done?

Chapter – 13

Hilly sat on the side of her bed and slipped on her new, shiny black patent leather shoes. She pulled the little loops on one side, over the sparkly buttons, to the hooks on the other side and smiled. The resulting row of twinkling diamante buttons running down the centre front of each shoe was just right. The sparkle would perfectly reflect the fine lurex thread in her little dark navy-blue dress. Happy with her choice thus far, she reached into the wardrobe and fetched out a heavily embroidered sleeveless jacket lined with soft fake fur. It was cold out, and she would need to wear something warm if she and Geoffrey were to see in the New Year out of doors. He insisted she should wear something chic and classy and hinted that he had a special evening planned for her.

Hilly's smile suddenly faded and she sighed deeply. She wished for the millionth time today, that she was home in Leominster, and seeing in the New Year with Josh.

She thought about what her friends would be doing tonight. They usually made a big bonfire down by the river Lugg and cooked sausages and roasted chestnuts. Then they would share all their fireworks, and when the last of their skyrockets fell to the ground, they would join hands and make a huge circle around the bonfire to sing *Auld Lang Syne.*

"Get a move on, Hilly." Geoffrey's voice wafted up the stairs, bringing her out of her reverie. She sighed again as she ran a brush through her hair and applied a little shiny, hot pink lip gloss. She popped the gloss into a small black bag, then slowly made her way downstairs to where Geoffrey waited impatiently.

As she slipped on her camel-coloured duffle coat for extra warmth and reached for her beret, scarf and gloves, Geoffrey eyed her up appreciatively. As usual, she looked stunning, and he was looking forward to showing her off to his friends tonight.

"Come on then," he urged her, opening the front door and stepping out into the cold night air, "We don't want to miss all the fun!"

He grabbed hold of her gloved hand and pulled her through the door, then, without releasing his overly tight grip, marched her down the street in the direction of the Underground Station.

The tube was packed tight with revellers headed into the city, all keen to join in the midnight celebrations, and Geoffrey took the opportunity to put his arms around Hilly and hold her close. Hilly stood stock still and glared at him. She was not about to lose her balance and neither needed nor wanted his support. She wished he would let go of her.

"Wouldn't do to lose you in the crowd, would it?" he smirked as if reading her thoughts, and Hilly spent the remainder of the short trip wondering if she might, in fact, find a way to get lost in the crowd once they reached their destination.

Geoffrey however, had no intention of letting Hilly slip from his grasp and as they stepped from the train, he placed his arm firmly around her shoulders, leading her up the escalator and out onto the street beyond. Hilary Anne Moncreiff was with *him,* and he was determined everyone should know it.

"Where are we going?" asked an irritated Hilly.

"You'll see. You didn't really think we were coming out for fish and chips, did you? You're not in Leominster now, Hilly, hanging out with baker boys and silly little hairdressers. We do things with a little more panache than that in London, don't you know."

"At least my friends have good manners," spat Hilly, "and I'd thank you to let go of me, please, Geoffrey."

She was furious that he should belittle her friends that way. Make fun of the honest, hardworking lives they led. How dare he!

"In fact, I think I'll just go back now," Hilly continued, "I happen to fancy fish and chips."

"Oh, come on Hilly, don't be like that. I was only joking. We're here now anyway, and I'm sure we can get you some fish and chips if that's what you really want."

'*Here*' turned out to be '*The Limelight Club*', situated on Shaftesbury Avenue.

"I want you to meet *my* friends and see how *we* celebrate the New Year in London. I didn't mean to upset you. Honestly."

He looked at her in a way that was designed to portray to Hilly that she had totally misunderstood him, and that he was hurt to the quick, that she should believe otherwise.

"Come on," he reiterated. "You'll love it."

Hilly suddenly found herself feeling that she was the one at fault. That she was being unkind. Geoffrey was doing his best to entertain her, and it wasn't his fault that she was missing Josh so much. As a sense of guilt washed over her, she took a deep breath and gave him a small, half-apologetic smile.

"Of course," she said, then against her better instincts, she followed him inside, as the all too familiar feeling of being unable to trust him washed over her once more. She told herself she was being silly and that Geoffrey was perfectly harmless. She was leaving for France tomorrow anyway, and she would have nothing more to do with him after that.

"Geoffrey!" Waved out a young man, as they stepped into the dance hall.

"Over here!"

They threaded their way through a throng of young people, to where two couples sat sipping at their drinks, chatting and laughing loudly.

As Geoffrey introduced her to his old school chums and their girlfriends, Hilly felt very much that she was on display. Like a trophy being held up to be admired. She fought back the urge to run and, in answer to Geoffrey's enquiring what she would like to drink, replied she'd have a Coke.

"Like the other girls are having, thank you, Geoffrey," she said politely.

"That'd be a Black Russian then, would it?" he asked with a sardonic grin.

"It would," agreed Poppy, with a happy smile, "and this is my third already, so Hilly has a little catching up to do."

"Absolutely!" he called over his shoulder as he made his way to the bar.

"What did you say your drink is?" Hilly asked.

"It's a Black Russian. Very yummy," giggled Poppy.

"Kahlua and Vodka and Coke," offered Stella. "Don't you drink cocktails in Leominster then?" She laughed, lighting a cigarette as she spoke.

Her grating laugh and condescending tone, set Hilly on edge again. *She wasn't having it,* she thought, with a rare flash of anger.

"I live in Paris these days," she returned in a haughty voice that could well have belonged to her mother.

"We generally prefer fine French wines and champagne."

Hugh, who was Poppy's boyfriend, looked at her.

"I say! Well met, Hilly!" he approved as Stella narrowed her eyes and blew a long plume of smoke in his direction. Hugh blew her a kiss and advised her partner, Nigel, to keep her under control. Hugh had never really understood what Nigel saw in Stella anyway. She was too high-maintenance and pretentious for his liking.

Poppy, on the other hand, was sweet-natured and very biddable. *Just the way he liked them,* he thought, as Geoffrey returned to the table, closely followed by a waiter carrying a tray laden with beverages.

"Right, my man," Geoffrey declared in a voice designed to display his own importance,

"Black Russians all round for the ladies, ales and whiskey chasers for the gents."

"Of course, sir," replied the waiter with a slight inclination of his head. "We seem to have an extra cocktail however, sir. What would, sir, like me to do with that one?"

"You will, of course, hand that one to my very beautiful young lady! It has already been noted that she has a little catching up to do."

"Of course, sir," agreed the unflappable middle-aged man, handing the extra glass to Hilly, who threw him an apologetic look and thanked him quietly.

"It's me you should be thanking, not him," snapped Geoffrey, as the waiter made a grateful retreat. He looked at the miserly tip Geoffrey had left on the tray, and wondered what a pompous cad like that was doing with such a charming young lady in tow. *She didn't seem any too happy about the situation*, he thought. *Perhaps he should keep an eye on her as the evening progressed.*

As the waiter suspected, Hilly found the evening to be more of an uncomfortable endurance than an enjoyable occasion. The three boys, particularly Geoffrey, lined up cocktail after cocktail in front of their dates while they themselves imbibed in far more beer and whiskey than any of them was able to handle.

Stella amused herself, making unpleasant remarks about the attire of almost every other young woman in the room, and Poppy became so intoxicated that Hilly felt genuinely concerned for her well-being.

"Do you feel quite well?" she asked as Poppy struggled to set her glass back down on the table.

"I feel wonderful," giggled Poppy. "My head is like a whirly gig, going round and round! Is your head going round and round like a whirly gig, too, Hilly? Only I think I might take mine to the little girl's room."

She tried to stand as she spoke, tumbling back into her seat with a puzzled expression on her face.

"How did that happen?" she asked as the three equally intoxicated male members of the party roared with laughter.

"You never could hold your drink, Poppy," commented Stella. Poppy looked at her.

"Yes, I can! I can hold it very well, thank you. I just can't put it down!" She dissolved into another fit of giggles, prompting Hilly to intervene.

"Come on, Poppy," she offered, "I'll help you get to the powder room."

"Thank you. You are very kind, you know Hilly. Much kinder than Stella. You are even kinder than my lovely Hughy is."

Hilly helped Poppy to her feet and carefully led her to the Ladies room, as Poppy regaled her every step of the way with the names of many others, she felt Hilly to be kinder than.

Having waited patiently as Poppy sorted herself out, Hilly then suggested that perhaps they should ask the barman to call them a taxicab and call it a night.

"But we haven't welcomed in the New Year yet," complained Poppy, "and Stella said she had a special treat for us all at midnight."

Hilly sighed. She didn't particularly care about welcoming in another year, but she felt unable to leave Poppy with the others.

Stella apparently cared about no-one but herself and all the boys, even Hugh, seemed past caring about anything.

As she delivered Poppy back to the table, Geoffrey stumbled to his feet and put an arm around her waist.

"Come on, Hilly," he slurred, kissing her and letting his hand slide down her back in order to squeeze her bottom.

"You owe me a dance."

"I owe you nothing, Geoffrey. Take your hands off me, please." Hilly pulled away from him, but Geoffrey half pushed and half pulled her onto the dance floor.

"I'm going home," declared Hilly, treating him to her most frosty glare.

"Oh, really!" he mocked, "and how exactly do you propose to get in? I have the key," he gloated, fishing it from his waistcoat pocket and brandishing it in Hilly's face.

"See!"

"Your mother very kindly showed me where she keeps one hidden for emergencies," rallied Hilly.

"Perhaps she knows what you're like!"

Geoffrey grabbed her wrists and forced her arms behind her back.

"Let go of me, Geoffrey!"

The friendly barman, who had been keeping a weathered eye on proceedings, decided that things had gone far enough.

"Excuse me, sir, I believe the young lady has asked you to unhand her."

He placed a firm hand on Geoffrey's shoulder as he spoke, and

Geoffrey spun round with a wild stare, at the same time shoving Hilly into the path of another young couple dancing nearby.

As Hilly apologised to the couple who had broken her fall, Geoffrey set upon the hapless waiter. His arms flailed wildly, but the waiter had seen it all before and expertly stopped him in his tracks.

"I'm sorry, sir, but I shall have to ask you to leave."

Hugh and Nigel stepped into the fray, and as Nigel tried to placate Geoffrey, Hugh assured the barman that the two of them would keep Geoffrey under control.

"It's only five minutes until midnight," he cajoled, "and the young ladies are all frightfully keen to welcome in the New Year." He smiled as Poppy and Stella joined them, keen to see what all the fuss was about.

"You are very naughty, Geoffrey," scolded Poppy.

"Don't you treat my friend Hilly like that! She might have fallen down and been hurt." She wagged a finger at him, and Geoffrey glared at her with ill-concealed disdain.

"I'm fine, thank you, Poppy," smiled Hilly sounding considerably calmer than she felt. They had attracted quite a crowd of interested onlookers, and she felt distinctly uncomfortable. Geoffrey's anger frightened her, but she was determined not to let it show.

She turned her attention to the barman, who still gripped Geoffrey firmly by the scruff of his neck.

"Thank you for your assistance," she said in a calm, controlled voice. "I wonder if you would be so kind as to order a taxi for us, for half past midnight. I'm sure he can behave for that long, at least. If not, you can call the police instead."

"If you're quite sure that's what you want, Miss."

"Thank you."

The man let go of Geoffrey's collar with a little warning push of his hand, and the two men glared at each other with undisguised hostility until the barman thought better of making matters worse and made his way to the telephone, which sat at the back of the bar.

Having made his call, he returned to advise Hilly that the cabs were snowed under tonight and that he was unable to take any further bookings.

"I'm sorry, Miss, but apparently, you will have to wave a cab down or take public transport."

"Thank you for trying," Hilly smiled. "We should have thought to make prior arrangements." The man apologised again, and gave Geoffrey, one final warning.

The countdown to midnight began, and as the final second ticked over, a loud cheer filled the nightclub, closely followed by a rowdy, enthusiastic rendition of *Auld Lang Syne*. The air was electric, as the cacophony from the dancefloor mingled with the confusion of car horns and raucous revellers that drifted in from outside. Someone started a conga line that led the patrons round and round the dancefloor and out into the street beyond, where the sky was exploding with fireworks for as far as the eye could see, and the air was acrid with gunpowder.

"Oooh." Sighed Poppy. "It's sooo exciting!" She threw her arms around Hugh and kissed him firmly on the lips.

"Don't you think it's exciting, Hilly?" she asked. Hilly smiled at her.

"I think it's very exciting," she agreed, "but it's also very cold."

"Geoffrey will collect our coats from the cloak-check, won't you, Geoffrey, and then Stella will give us our special treat, won't you, Stella?" continued Poppy, "and we can sit here on the steps and watch the whole world pass by until a taxi comes along!"

She sat down as she spoke, pulling Hugh down next to her on one side and Hilly on the other.

"And hurry up, please, Geoffrey, so we don't have to wait forever for Stella's treat."

Geoffrey looked as though he was about to argue the point and tell Poppy she could fetch her own coat when Stella caught his eye and inclined her head to one side in order to direct his attention to what she was extracting from her handbag. He understood at once and bounded back up the stairs with a great deal of purpose.

"Come on, Nigel! You can give me a hand!" he shouted over his shoulder, "and make sure we have everyone's coat tickets!"

Hilly was a little bemused at Geoffrey's sudden urge to make himself useful. *It seemed so out of character,* she thought, but the reason for his sudden burst of agreeable behaviour became instantly apparent on his return.

He pulled on his own overcoat, then sat himself on the stair beside her, solicitously placing her coat around her shoulders.

"Is that all right for you, Hilly?" he asked, "or would you rather stand up and put it on properly?"

"I'll wear it properly, thank you, Geoffrey. I'm sure you don't want to hold it around my shoulders all night."

"No. You'll need a free hand for this, won't you?" agreed Stella, handing Geoffrey a handmade cigarette as she spoke.

"There's one each, by the way," she said, passing them around with one hand and reaching for her cigarette lighter with the other.

"Not for me, thanks Stella," smiled Hilly, pulling her coat tightly around her slender form.

"I don't indulge."

"I'll have hers," offered Geoffrey, taking it from Stella's outstretched hand.

"I'm sure you have plenty more where this came from."

"Don't they smoke pot in Paris, either?" asked Poppy, with a sad little shake of her head. "It must be a very boring place if they don't drink cocktails and they don't get high."

"Of course, they do. It's just me. I don't."

"Well, maybe you should," suggested Stella. "Might make you a little less uptight! What do you think, Geoffrey?"

"Oh, I couldn't possibly say," commented Geoffrey, taking a long drag and inhaling thoroughly.

"Wouldn't dare. Would I, Hilly?" He laughed, narrowing his eyes and slowly exhaling the smoke in her direction.

"We need to find a way to get home, Geoffrey," Hilly replied pleasantly, ignoring his snide remark.

"It'll take far too long to walk, so perhaps we need to catch the tube again."

By the time they eventually arrived back at the house on Wrights Lane, Geoffrey had smoked both his joints and all but finished the contents of a hipflask, which he had secreted in his coat pocket. He stumbled up the stairs and fumbled in his pocket for the front door key, cursing loudly as he dropped it on the ground. Several attempts to reach down and pick it up failed.

"Well, don't just stand there, woman!" he spat at Hilly.

"Make yourself useful and pick the damn thing up!"

Hilly glared at him.

"It is not my fault that you have drunk and drugged yourself into a stupor, Geoffrey! And you will not speak to me like that!"

Hilary Anne opened the door and marched inside, discarding her duffle coat and accessories on the hall stand before making a beeline for the stairs. There was no sign that the adults had returned, so she threw a rejoinder to Geoffrey, saying that he should make himself some very strong black coffee and sort himself out before they came back to spare them from finding him in his present disgusting state.

Geoffrey, who was feeling more than a little queasy, made a mad dash for the downstairs lavatory, leaving Hilly to make her way upstairs unimpeded.

She closed the bedroom door firmly behind her and changed into her night attire, noting as she did that her clothes reeked of smoke and alcohol. She found a discarded shopping bag and popped the offending garments into it before hanging the bag by the open window to help remove the clinging aroma; then, she gingerly made her way across the landing to the upstairs bathroom. She felt no desire to run into Geoffrey. His mood had turned more and more amorous and possessive on the trip home, and he had continually tried to kiss her on the lips.

With any luck, thought Hilly, *the others would be home before she finished washing, and Geoffrey would slink quietly off to his attic room to avoid detection.*

Her ablutions completed, Hilly cautiously opened the bathroom door and looked out. There was no sign of Geoffrey, so she crept quietly back to her own room and slipped inside with a sigh of relief, placing her toilet bag on the nightstand and turning back the bed linen. A sudden movement behind her caused her to spin around in alarm.

"Well, get in, then." Geoffrey grabbed her, throwing her down on the bed and tearing at her clothes.

"Get off me!" she screamed over and over, but her cries were muffled by his mouth pressing roughly down on hers.

She tried desperately to break free of his hold, but he was stronger than he looked, and the alcohol and drugs seemed to have increased his self-belief that he was superior and, as such, entitled to help himself to anything he wanted.

Right now, what he wanted was Hilly, and she was going nowhere. As he forced himself on her, Hilly found herself feeling repulsed and strangely detached from her body. She tried again to scream at him to get off her, but her efforts were in vain. As the sound of their parents' voices finally drifted up the stairs and he pulled himself off her, making a beeline for the door, she lay trembling with horrified fear and angry disbelief, her terrified mind trying to come to terms with what had just transpired.

Chapter – 14

Elizabeth talked non-stop on the journey home from London. She recalled every moment of their holiday like an excited child, enthusing over everything from the Chatswoods' stunning townhouse to the exceptional people they met along the way, as well as the wonderful hospitality and attractions they enjoyed.

Both Robert and Aunt Hilary sat in silence, perfectly poised for the inevitable culmination of her dialogue. It came with a rush of words carefully designed to convince Robert that her desire to live that lifestyle at all times was, of course, only to ensure they were in a position to provide for Hilly's future happiness.

"I really do wish you would reconsider William's employment offer, Robert. It would be so good for all of us to live in London. Especially Hilly. She's had such a wonderful time, and she and Geoffrey have become very close, you know."

"I think she behaved admirably, Elizabeth and put up with Geoffrey purely to keep us happy. She couldn't wait to head off to France this morning."

"Yes, with Geoffrey."

"He was only taking her to catch the boat train, not going with her to Paris, for goodness sake, and I suspect she would have been more than happy to go to the station on her own."

"You're wrong, Robert! I suspect she didn't want to go at all, and I'll wager that as soon as she finishes up at art school, she'll head straight back to London – and not only in search of employment!"

Robert took a deep breath and shook his head. He exhaled slowly while Aunt Hilary bit her lip to stop herself from speaking out of turn.

Elizabeth, however, simply turned to gaze out of the car window, a secretive smile playing on her lips. She knew something they didn't know, she told herself. She was quite sure she had seen Geoffrey let himself out of Hilly's bedroom last night and saunter off up to his attic room, dressed in nothing but his shirttails, his trousers slung over his shoulder.

No, Hilary Anne appeared to have come to her senses at last and realised that Geoffrey was the right man for her! Not that she approved of what they were so obviously up to last night, but their generation had different ideas about that sort of thing. *Robert, of course, would be furious,* she thought, though she had no intention of telling him. She would keep their secret safe for the time being.

By the time the Moncreiffs had returned Aunt Hilary to *Oak Manor* and arrived home in Leominster, Elizabeth was already planning her daughter's imminent wedding to Geoffrey Chatswood, and by the time she ran into Joshua Bates the following day, she was thoroughly convinced that her own dreams for Hilly, were indeed, about to come true.

Joshua's feelings were irrelevant to Elizabeth, and it was not until she returned home and Robert advised her of Matthew's death that she felt any guilt over speaking out of turn. Even then, she told herself, it was inevitable that Joshua would find out about Hilly and Geoffrey sometime. It might as well be now. Of course, she would not have chosen this afternoon to tell him had she been aware of his current circumstances, but what was done was done, and there was no point in crying over spilt milk.

As Joshua Bates let himself through the side door at the rear of the bakery, Elizabeth's words were still playing over and over in his head, like a record stuck in a groove.

For the first time in a very long while, he felt unable to decide on a course of action. He wanted so badly to write to Hilly, to explain why he had not come to meet her as planned, and to assure her he still wanted to spend summer with her in France and Italy, but every time he tried to put pen to paper, he saw Elizabeth's face and heard her words ringing in his ears over and over again. What if she was right and Hilly really did want to marry Geoffrey? The choice must obviously be hers, and he was in no position to marry anyone at the moment, least of all Hilly. He had nothing to offer her. Geoffrey, it seemed, had it all.

Josh dropped his head into his hands and looked at the blank piece of paper that sat in front of him. *It looked just the way he felt,* thought Joshua. Empty, and devoid of feelings!

There was so much he wanted to say to Hilly, and yet nothing he wrote down seemed right. Whatever he put down on paper sounded selfish and self-pitying, as though he was trying to justify leaving her standing alone in the cold on Christmas Eve. Perhaps Lindy or Maisie could write to her about Matthew, and he would wait to hear from Hilly before he wrote to her himself. Let Hilly make contact first. See if she corroborated Elizabeth's story.

He picked up the blank sheet of writing paper and angrily screwed it up into a tight ball which he threw with as much force as he could muster in the direction of the closed bedroom door.

If his mother or his siblings found his mood to be uncharacteristically sombre at the tea table, they made no comment. Of course, he was quiet. Josh had a lot on his mind. The death of Matthew, the fact he had not caught up with Hilly as planned, his return to Birmingham, and his anxious wait to hear which, if any, of the hospitals he had applied to for his internship were willing to offer him a position.

"Could you do me a favour, Lindy?" Joshua blurted out suddenly, "And let Hilly know about Dad. I can't find the right words. I've tried and tried, but I just can't get it right, and I think it's best that she hears the news from us. Tell her I'm really struggling with everything at the moment, but I'll write to her soon."

Lindy was about to reply that she was quite sure Hilly would far rather hear from *him,* but something in his demeanour held her back. Something was not right with Josh tonight, she thought. Was there something going on between him and Hilly that she didn't know about? A lover's tiff, perhaps? Was that why he seemed so preoccupied and melancholy? Perhaps Hilly would tell her what it was.

"Yes, of course, I'll write to Hilly," she assured him. "I owe her a letter anyway."

Margaret, too, found it a little odd that Josh would not want to write to Hilly himself and wondered what was wrong with him tonight. He had come in from his walk earlier and made a beeline for his room without so much as a single word. Something must have happened while he was out, though she could not for the life of her, think what that something might be.

It wasn't until the Moncreiffs called by a little later in the evening that she began to get a real inkling of the situation.

They sat around the fire talking, and while Robert Moncreiff, whose condolences were both warm and sincere, talked to John about the business, Elizabeth sat on the edge of her seat, looking decidedly uncomfortable. She seemed unable to look Josh in the eye, and when Lindy inquired about their trip to London and whether Hilly had enjoyed herself, Elizabeth simply replied,

"Yes, thank you, Lindy; we all had a lovely time."

"What did you all do on New Year's Eve?" asked Susan.

"I know Hilly was quite excited about seeing all the fireworks. Did she wear the little navy-blue lurex dress that I made for her? She looked so pretty in it."

"I'm not sure what Hilly dressed in to celebrate New Year's Eve. We went our separate ways, you see. Hilary Anne and her lovely young friend Geoffrey went off together to a very upmarket nightclub in the city."

She threw a challenging glance in Josh's direction.

"So you told me, when I ran into you yesterday," he said.

"She wore your dress to the theatre though, Susan," Elizabeth continued, ignoring Joshua's interruption, "and you're right, she does look very pretty in it. Geoffrey certainly thought so," she added quite unnecessarily.

Robert sensed Joshua's reaction to Elizabeth's comments and decided it was time to intervene. The poor chap had enough to contend with at the moment without Elizabeth adding salt to his wounds with her ridiculous notions.

"Hilly and Geoffrey went out as part of a group, of course," he offered. "There was half a dozen of them in all, and I'm not sure Hilly found the situation was entirely to her liking. She had her heart set on joining the crowds at Trafalgar Square."

Margaret looked at her eldest son, and her heart went out to him. Josh threw Robert a grateful look, and Margaret wondered why such a kind, caring man would put up with someone possessed of Elizabeth's airs and graces. It was all about appearances with Elizabeth, she thought, and she always made it obvious she did not consider Josh was good enough for her daughter.

Margaret took another anxious glance at Joshua. He looked upset and deflated, as though he had the weight of the world on his shoulders. She might have known when he came home so unhappy earlier on that Elizabeth Moncreiff had something to do with his state of mind. Poor Josh and poor little Hilly. Well, they had both herself and Robert on their side.

Robert Moncreiff rose to his feet.

"It is time we left, Elizabeth," he said in a stern voice.

"Margaret, John, my door is open at all times."

He led his wife to the door in silence, then drove her home in silence.

It was not until he closed the door of *Elm Cottage* behind them that he soundly berated Elizabeth for her behaviour.

Elizabeth stared back at him and took a deep breath. Perhaps now was as good a time as any to let him in on her secret.

"Never mind *my* behaviour," she snapped.

"Your precious daughter has been sleeping with Geoffrey Chatswood behind our backs. I saw him leaving her bedroom with no trousers on, with my own eyes. Perhaps I should tell Joshua Bates about that!"

Chapter – 15

As the train pulled away from the platform, Hilary Anne Moncreiff closed her eyes and heaved a deep sigh of relief. She was free of Geoffrey Chatswood at last. There would be no more having to pretend in front of their parents that she found him to be a pleasant companion. No more feeling that he was constantly lurking, watching her every move.

By the time she boarded the ferry to Calais, she felt safe, and by the time she opened the door to her little dormitory room above 'Le Contrescarpe', she could almost believe that the last two weeks of her life were, in fact, nothing more than a bad dream.

Hilly placed her suitcase on the bed and set about unpacking it. The shopping bag containing the clothes she wore on New Year's Eve caused her a moment of distress as her mind flashed back to the horror of it all. She loved the little navy-blue dress and the embroidered jacket but wondered if she would ever be able to wear them again, given the memories they would now evoke forever.

She hated Geoffrey Chatswood! How dare he destroy her life! She had never met anyone as self-entitled as Geoffrey. *It was an unpleasant trait and one that she could not abide,* she thought, as she picked up the bag of dirty clothing and thrust it into the laundry hamper she kept sitting by the washstand. She loved those clothes, and Geoffrey Chatswood would not put her off ever wearing them again, she told herself defiantly! He would have no further control over any part of her life! She would tell Josh what happened in London, and she would tell him what Jimmy Jones said to her about the other girl. Then she would wait for a reply and see what Josh had to say about it all.

Hilly lifted the empty suitcase onto the top of the old wooden wardrobe and turned to the little desk that sat under the window. *There was no time like the present,* she thought, as she sat down on a rickety old upright wooden chair, to write her letter to Josh.

The desk drawer stuck fast as she tried to open it to retrieve her writing pad, so she jiggled it as hard as she could in an effort to free it.

"Come on you silly thing," she muttered, as it still refused to budge, then without any prior warning that this small frustration would affect her so badly, Hilary Anne Moncreiff burst into tears and buried her head in her hands as her courage failed her.

What was she going to say to Joshua anyway? That she had been too physically weak to fight off Geoffrey Chatswood? Unable to scream? Too afraid to make a fuss?

There was nothing Josh could do about it, she thought. She wanted to throw herself at him. To beg his forgiveness for what she had done. She felt so ashamed. So unworthy of him. Anyway, would he even care what had happened to her, or how she felt, if what Jimmy Jones told her was true? After all, Joshua did not keep their rendezvous on the morning of Christmas Eve.

Hilly sat at the desk and wept until her eyes were red and swollen and her body began to ache all over; then, she slowly dragged herself to her feet and, very stiffly, made her way to the washstand.

As she splashed her eyes and her face with cold, soothing water, sporadic heartbroken sobs shook her body. *It was over,* she thought. Her dreams of a future with Josh were spread in tatters before her. Geoffrey Chatswood had won.

The next few days passed in a perfunctory haze for Hilly. She attended her classes and mingled with her friends the way she did before, but somehow, all the fun and excitement had disappeared. There was nothing to look forward to any more. No purpose to saving the few francs she earned at the market each week from the sales of her artwork. There had been no word from Josh, and his lack of correspondence only served to convince her that Jimmy Jones was right all along. She could scarcely believe that Josh would just drop her like that. She was convinced his feelings were every bit as strong as her own, and he had seemed so keen they should travel together come summer. Something was wrong! It *must* be. What if he'd heard somehow about what happened between her and Geoffrey? She was overcome with despair and plagued with constant stabs of unbearable guilt.

In the end, Hilly was back in Paris for ten days before she heard anything. Returning home from an afternoon life drawing class, she stopped to check her mailbox in the entrance foyer, the way she did every day, and her heart leapt at the sight of the envelope sitting inside. She reached for it with eager anticipation, but her hopes that it was from Joshua faded the moment her eyes scanned the handwriting. The letter was from Lindy, not Josh. She swallowed her disappointment and made her way upstairs. *At least it seemed that Lindy was still happy to be her friend,* she thought. Perhaps she would even throw some light on Josh's silence.

It was not until after she put away her oversized art satchel and turned on the room's tiny, one-bar heater that Hilly permitted herself to sit down on the side of her bed and rip open the letter she still clutched tightly in her hand. It was three pages long, and as she carefully unfolded each of them, Hilly could immediately see that Lindy had been crying as she wrote. Tear stains and ink smudges spattered the pages, making some of her words virtually impossible to decipher. As she carefully scrutinised the first page, the chilling words *'died on Christmas Eve'* leapt out at Hilly, causing her heart to miss a beat and her stomach to churn over and over.

Who died on Christmas Eve? Not Josh! Oh no! Please, not Josh! She closed her eyes and took a deep breath, steeling herself in readiness to scrutinise Lindy's words more closely.

She could scarcely bear to look again, and when she finally found the courage to do so, a large black ink splodge all but obliterated the most important word of all. She tried desperately to decipher the name hidden beneath the huge dark smudge. Hilly's heart raced, and her eyes strained as she struggled to make out who it was who had passed away.

She read the alarming sentence over and over. *No! It wasn't Josh,* she decided, a great surge of relief rushing through her body. The name wasn't long enough, and it definitely started with a 'D'.

'Dad'! The word was Dad. It was Matthew Bates who had passed away. For Hilly, the news that it was Matthew who had died was almost as heart-breaking as if it *had* been Josh. She loved all of the Bates family, but she loved Matthew almost as much as she did his eldest son.

No wonder Josh had not turned up on Christmas Eve. He would be devastated, along with Mrs Bates and all his siblings; and Josh being Josh, she told herself, he would be trying to be strong and console the others, while his own heart was breaking too.

Great sobs engulfed her once again. *Poor, poor Josh. What had she done?* On top of all he was going through, she had let him down so badly just when he needed her most. *She could never forgive herself for this,* she thought, and she most certainly could not expect Josh to forgive her, either. She wondered why it was he hadn't written to tell her the dreadful news about Matthew himself. *The pain must be more than he can bear*, she thought sadly.

Lindy went on to assure her that Josh had asked her to say that he would write to her any day now, but as another week passed by and Joshua's promised letter failed to eventuate, Hilly became more and more depressed. She sent a beautiful, hand-crafted bereavement card to the whole Bates family, but still unable to find the words she wanted to say to Josh, simply slipped a little personal note to him in with the card, saying how truly heart-broken she was to hear about his dad, and that she understood how devastated he must be feeling, and that, of course, she perfectly understood why he had been unable to meet her on Christmas Eve. She did not mention Jimmy Jones, and she did not mention London or Geoffrey Chatswood. Hilly then concluded by saying Lindy had mentioned that he intended to write, so in order their letters did not cross paths, she would wait to hear from him before she wrote again. It was delaying the inevitable, perhaps, but it left the ball in his court, which, in Hilly's mind, meant he need feel no pressure to reply to her note at all if he didn't want to. And then, too, if he *had* found someone else and didn't want to stay in touch, she would never need to tell him what had transpired in London.

The days dragged by for Hilly. No word came from Josh or from Lindy. Even Maisie seemed to have forgotten her. She received a card from Aunt Hilary to see if she would like to visit *Oak Manor* for Easter, but before she had time to reply, a letter came from home saying Mother and Father were going to spend Easter in Paris with her. Hilly sighed. *Oak Manor* would be far preferable where she was concerned, but of course, there was no stopping Mother once she set her mind to something.

A restless night's sleep did nothing to soothe Hilly's agitated state of mind, and the following afternoon, she sat at Le Contrescarpe with her friend Madeleine, lamenting.

"I do wish Mother would ask me first before she made such plans." She sighed. "I know she means well, but it would be nice to be asked what I would like to do and be able to make my own decisions."

"Poor 'illy. Per'aps she worries for you that you are alone and that you do not eat well." Madeleine had been worried about Hilly herself since school resumed after Christmas. She looked pale and had lost weight. Even more troubling was that she often looked as though she had been crying.

"What 'appened at Noelle to make you so sad, 'illy?" she asked. "You do not speak always of Joshua, 'ow you did before. You 'ave 'ad, a tiff, per'aps?"

Hilly's eyes welled up and she stared blankly into her coffee cup.

"It's much worse than that," she confided, "Josh has found someone else... and I didn't even get to see him over Christmas."

A large tear rolled down her cheek and splashed into her untouched coffee.

"You know for certain there is une autre femme?"

"Yes... No... I think so. Jimmy Jones told me."

Hilly sadly shook her head. Should she tell Madeleine about Geoffrey? About what she had done to Joshua? Perhaps it would help to talk to someone else.

"It's more complicated than that, though," she said hesitantly. Her courage failed her, and she lowered her head.

"Ow so?"

"Josh's father died on Christmas Eve, and all I could think about was that he didn't keep our rendezvous."

"Did you know 'is papa 'ad died?"

"No, but I should have known that something was wrong. It was not like Josh to stand me up. I went to his house, and there was no one at home, and my friend Maisie wasn't at work, so I couldn't talk to her either. Then I ran into Jimmy Jones, who was in Josh's class at school, and he told me he had seen Josh the day before. He was in his car, and he was kissing another   girl."

"Bah! I do not like zis Jimmy Jones, 'illy. You must 'ear zis from Joshua 'imself, not from zis Jimmy Jones person! You 'ave written to Joshua, yes?"

"No. I can't."

"Sacre bleu, 'illy. Pourquoi?"

"Because there is more, Madie. So much more, and I don't know how to tell him or even how to tell you. I don't know where to start."

Madeleine looked at her distraught little English friend and shook her head, at the same time, reaching for a packet of long, slim cigarillos she had been given for Christmas. She pulled two from the pack and lit them both. One was rolled in hot pink paper, the other in a pretty aqua blue.

"Ici, m'amie," she said, handing the blue one to Hilly, "zis is for you, and you will not say to me zat you do not smoke. It will 'elp you to be calm." She smiled encouragingly at Hilly, waved the pink cigarillo in the air and called across the room to the cafe owner.

"Henri, une carafe de vin s'il vous plaît, et deux verres!"

Henri nodded.

"Mais oui, Mademoiselle Madeleine," he replied as Madeleine turned her attention back to Hilly.

"We will do zis ze French way, m'amie," Madie informed her English friend. "We will drink de vin, we will fume un cigarrillo, and we will talk. Yes?"

"I don't smoke, remember?"

"Now – you do!"

Henri placed a carafe of the house red wine on the table and poured a glass for each of them.

"I 'ope this makes you 'appy again, Mademoiselle 'illy."

"Merci, Henri."

Hilly took a sip of her wine, looked at the pretty blue cigarillo she was holding between her fingers and took a tentative puff.

Perhaps it was time to reinvent herself, she thought. Perhaps this was the answer. She would immerse herself in French customs and stay in Paris forever. Without Josh, there was nothing for her in England any more. She would visit her parents and Aunt Hilary occasionally, and that would be that. She looked at Madeleine and smiled a sad, wistful smile.

"Okay," she agreed, "we will do it the French way." She took another sip of wine and eyed up the cigarillo with a great deal of suspicion.

"Not this, though," she apologised as she stubbed it out in the ashtray. "It is too bitter for me, and it makes me feel dizzy."

Madeleine laughed.

"Le vin and conversation, then. Oui?"

"Oui."

Despite Madeleine's patience and concerned encouragement, Hilly found it difficult to unburden her soul. They were onto their second carafe of wine, and Hilly had even smoked the offensive cocktail cigar before she finally began to open up.

Madeleine's green eyes flashed with passionate anger when she heard about Geoffrey's assault.

"And you spoke to no-one about zis pig? Zat is rape, 'illy. You should 'ave reported Geoffrey to ze police!"

Hilly shuddered and shook her head.

"No! I just want to forget about it all. Everything that happened. But I can't. I thought when I got back to Paris, it would all go away, like a bad dream, but it hasn't. It haunts me, Madie, like an endless nightmare. I can't eat, and I can't sleep. I feel sick."

"Oh, 'illy, what is it we can do?"

Madeleine lit two more of her pretty cigarillos and poured another glass of wine for each of them.

Despite the fact that she was feeling ill and developing a headache, Hilly accepted them both with a wan smile.

"When we 'ave fini with zis," announced Madie, raising her glass and taking a large gulp of her wine, "we will go to your chambre and we will write to Josh, and we will say to 'im, what 'as 'appened. 'E will report Geoffrey to ze police. 'E will be your 'ero!"

"NO, Madeleine. No! I don't want Josh to know about any of this. It is my problem, not his. It is just better this way. If he still cares for me, he will be hurt that I could let it happen. He is hurting enough with his father's sudden death. He has his final exams and his internship to worry about, too. Anyway, if he does have another girlfriend, he won't even care. Why should he? He hasn't written to me either like he said he would, so it's probably true that he has someone else. All I know for certain is that I have let him down, Madie. Don't you see? I hate myself!"

Madeleine didn't see at all, but her friend's pale, woe-begotten little face and agitated state of mind stopped her from saying any more about writing to Joshua.

"'illy, 'illy," she consoled, "do not be so 'ard wiz yourself. We will zink of un autre idee. Oui?"

Hilly swallowed hard and nodded.

"Thank you. I am sorry to be such a sad sack." She wiped her eyes and tried to smile.

"I think I have had too much wine," she confessed, "perhaps I need to eat. Voulez-vous les moules et frites?"

Chapter – 16

Talking to Madeleine, Hilly decided, definitely helped her to feel less alone with her misery, and to see the situation with a little more clarity.

At Hilly's request, Madie agreed to mention the incident to no one, and as the girls talked over their meal of mussels and chips, Hilly began to slowly come to terms with all that had passed.

Madeleine was right. She should hold her head up high and move on with her life. She only wished, above all else, that she would hear from Josh, and it would transpire that Jimmy Jones' story was wrong and Joshua had not passed her over for someone else. Quite obviously, he failed to keep their Christmas assignment because of poor Matthew's passing. What's more, she would forgive Josh anything, she told herself the next morning as she dragged herself from the warm comfort of her bed. How could she not? Yet despite Madie's efforts to convince her that she was not to blame for what happened with Geoffrey, Hilly still felt that she had let Josh down and could not expect him to forgive her.

She swung her legs over the side of the bed, shivering as her toes touched the bare wooden floorboards; then, as she rose to her feet, the room started to spin around wildly, causing her to quickly *sit* back down before she *fell* down.

It took several minutes before the dizzy spell passed, and she gingerly attempted to stand once more. She must have drunk far too much wine last night, Hilary Anne thought as she tied back her hair and brushed her teeth, or perhaps it was the strong tobacco in the cigarillos. After all, she had never smoked any kind of tobacco before, and the cigarillos were very strong and bitter.

Every little movement she made caused her head to throb, and she felt she might be sick at any moment.

In reality, the room was cold and draughty, but to Hilly, it felt both hot and airless, making her feel faint again. Tiny beads of perspiration settled on her upper lip. She threw open the pretty little casement window above the desk and gulped in the cold morning air, but the smell of cooking food drifting up from Le Contrescarpe below increased her feelings of nausea.

Hilly swallowed hard as she fought to overcome her desire to rush to the bathroom. This would *never* do! Perhaps she was not suited to the French lifestyle after all; she thought as she poured herself a large glass of water. She could not afford to feel unwell every day because she was drinking too much wine! There were assignments to finish before Easter, and she needed a clear head to decide what she would do following her graduation in August. It had all been so clear to her before, but now, without Josh in her life, her future seemed nothing more than a dark, empty void.

As another wave of nausea washed over her, she slowly sipped her glass of water, then telling herself she would be fine, donned her coat and hat, slung her art satchel over her shoulder, and ventured out in search of Madie. With any luck *she* would be making *her* way to school now, too. But Madie was nowhere to be seen.

Despite her warm coat and knee-length leather boots, the cold morning air nibbled at Hilly's fingertips and toes, and the damp, chill wind that blew across the Seine and along Rue Lacepede, cut right through the fibres of her duffle coat, causing her to shiver.

A stop at her favourite little Patisserie for a warm croissant and a cup of sweet, steaming hot chocolate to enjoy along the way revived her spirits, and by the time she reached l'Ecole des Beaux-Arts, Hilly finally felt ready to face the day ahead.

It was not until later that afternoon after she returned to the college dormitory and retrieved her mail from the box, that she began to feel unwell again.

The writing on the envelope she had withdrawn from the mailbox was unfamiliar, causing her heart to sink once more. She stuffed the solitary letter into her coat pocket and turned to greet Madeleine, who walked through the door just moments after her.

"Eet ees not from Joshua, zen, your letter?" enquired Madie as the two girls made their way upstairs together. She had seen the disappointment on Hilly's face.

"No. I don't know who it's from. I'll open it later. Do you want a coffee?" Hilly asked, "Only no wine, I think. I felt quite unwell this morning."

Madeleine laughed.

"You 'ad no more zan zree glasses, 'illy. You 'ave 'ad more zan zat before!"

"Then it must have been the cigarillos... or perhaps it was the combination."

Madie rolled her eyes and shook her shiny auburn hair in mock disbelief while Hilly laughed and marvelled at the way Madeleine's hair fell neatly back into place. She admired the sleek new page cuts that the French women were sporting. She had noticed they were popular in London, too.

"Do you think my hair would suit a page cut like yours?" Hilly asked.

"But of course. We will go tomorrow to ze salon of Vidal Sassoon and make for you, ze appointment."

Hilly smiled. That would be fun! She wondered momentarily what Elizabeth would think but decided she didn't really care. How she wore her hair was not up to Mother any more, and anyway, she would use her own money to pay for the haircut, so that would be that. It was time Mother stopped trying to control her!

"You will look very French," approved Madeleine with a big, happy smile.

It was not until after the two girls had enjoyed a light supper of chicken soup with fresh, crispy baguettes and Madeleine had returned to her own little room that Hilly remembered about the letter she had popped into her coat pocket earlier.

She sat back down at the tiny table and eyed it suspiciously. There was no sender's name or address to be seen, and the handwriting was not familiar to her. The envelope contained nothing more than a single page, yet its content filled her with considerable alarm.

My Dearest Hilly,

Your mother most kindly agreed to give me your address in Paris, in order that I could keep in touch with you while you are away.

You have been constantly in my thoughts since our night of passion together, and I am hoping to arrange a business trip to Paris, so that I can come to see you. I cannot tell you how happy I am to hear that Joshua Bates has moved on. Now I can have you all to myself. Just the way I like it. I hope your bed is big enough for two, Hilly. I will be there to share it with you soon.

With all my love and in ardent anticipation,
Geoffrey

Hilary Anne dropped the sheet of paper onto the table and jumped to her feet, all in one horrified movement. The chair she had been sitting on clattered to the floor, and she left it lying where it landed.

How dare her mother encourage that loathsome boy to contact her, and what did he mean about Joshua 'moving on'?

It was too late to talk to Madeleine about it now, but first thing in the morning, she would seek her help in scripting a letter that would get rid of Geoffrey Chatswood from her life forever.

Hilly spent the night tossing and turning. The spectre of New Year once again haunted her over and over and the ensuing lack of sleep left her feeling listless and ill when she rose the following morning.

Madeleine, who was still cocooned in her cosy, patchwork quilt and enjoying a deep, peaceful sleep, woke with an abrupt and sudden jolt as Hilly banged furiously on her dormitory door at the unfashionable hour of six thirty a.m. She dragged herself from her bed and pulled on her warm, sheepskin slippers. Then, she quickly made her way to the door, pulling a long, silken floral shawl around her shoulders as she went.

She had been more than a little shaken by the frantic knocking, but when Hilly then burst through the door as though the devil himself was chasing after her, Madie's alarm turned to genuine concern. Despite the early hour, Hilly was already fully dressed, and it was immediately apparent to Madeleine that her friend was in a state of considerable distress.

"I'm sorry to wake you so early," Hilly apologised, waving her letter in the air, "but I really need your help right now before we go to school. I haven't been able to sleep a wink! It's this letter that arrived yesterday," she explained, thrusting the single page in Madie's direction.

Madie's eyebrows shot up, and she exhaled loudly as she read Geoffrey's letter.

"Non, non, non 'illy," she exclaimed, "zis will not do!"

"No. I knew you would understand. I need you to help me write back to him at once. To help me make him understand that I do not want to see him ever again! I have to post the letter on my way to L'Ecole, Madie, or I will not be able to work all day for fretting."

"Of course, 'illy. Do not worry so. Eet will be good to send to 'im ze message! 'E will see zat 'e must not come 'ere!"

Hilly let out an audible sigh of relief.

"The trouble is," she confided, "that I can't really say what I'd like to because I have to be nice about putting him off. Mother thinks that he and his family are wonderful because they are wealthy and his parents are old friends of Aunt Hilary's, so I can't tell him what I really think. I have to be diplomatic."

"Bah! Zat is a shame, 'illy. 'E does not deserve for you to be polite."

"No. The funny thing is that Mother is always so concerned about what other people think. I wonder what *she* would think if she knew what Geoffrey is really like."

"You 'ave not told to 'er what 'appened?"

"No!" Hilly was horrified at the thought of telling Elizabeth.

"She must never know. She would never believe me anyway. She thinks Geoffrey is perfect!"

"Poor 'illy. Do not worry. We will tell 'im zat 'e is not welcome 'ere and zat you do not care for 'im."

"Nicely, though."

"Oui. We will tell 'im nicely," sighed Madeleine.

Hilly waited impatiently for Madie to dress, then dragged her back along the hall to her own little room. She set her writing pad down on the table, then sat and stared at it blankly. She wanted to write to Josh, not to Geoffrey. She had tried so many times, but the words always failed her, and now, the longer she left it, the harder it seemed to be to write anything at all. She wondered for the umpteenth time why he had not acknowledged the card she sent or even replied to her note. She wished she had not said that she would wait for him to write first. What was stopping him? Was Jimmy Jones right, and Josh unable to find the right words to tell her himself that he had found someone else? It seemed so unlike him. The thought was almost too much to bear, yet the alternative was even worse. What if he had somehow found out about Geoffrey? She couldn't even deny that it was true, and yet, despite how it had come about, she felt too ashamed to admit it to Joshua. She hung her head and sighed in anguish as Madie sat down opposite her.

"Be strong, 'illy." She smiled kindly. "We will fix zis Geoffrey first and zen we will find why Josh, 'e does not write to you. Oui?"

Hilly nodded sadly as Madie took the pad from her and began to write.

Geoffrey,
I do not wish to be rude, but you must not come to Paris. I am very busy, and I do not wish to see you,
Hilary Anne Moncrieff.

"Zere! Zat is all you must say!" Madie handed the pad back to Hilly with a big, triumphant smile.

"It is true. It is not rude. It is perfect. We will go togezer now to post it. Oui? Zen we will 'ave un café et croissant, avant nous attendons l'école! Ce soir, we will meet for un vin a La Contrescarpe, and zink what must be told to Joshua!"

Madeleine was enjoying her new role as confidant to Hilly. She had no one special in her own life at present and felt she could, therefore, fully commit to Hilly's predicament. Her natural French passion for love and romance was stirred by Hilary Anne's plight, and as she made her way to class later, her adored lessons in textile design took a back seat to Hilly's problems. She was determined to happily resolve the situation and was still mulling over what must be said to Joshua as she walked home alone at the end of the day.

Hilary Anne's still life lesson ended earlier than she expected, and she was surprised as she returned to her room shortly before three p.m., to find a single red rose attached to her door handle. There was no message. No clue where it had come from or who had left it there. It hung from a velvety, deep red ribbon, which she found necessary to untie in order to fit her key in the lock.

"I hope you like it, Hilly."

The man's voice made her jump, and she spun around to see Geoffrey Chatswood standing before her. She froze with horror as he pushed her into the room, then, still gripping her by the elbow, forced his way in after her.

"I'm sorry, Geoffrey," she said, handing the rose back to him, "but I do not want to see you, as I explained in a letter, I sent to you this morning. I am not interested in seeing you at all, Geoffrey. I am far too busy, and what's more, I am expecting a friend at any moment."

She gave him a frosty stare and indicated that she would like him to depart. Geoffrey stood his ground.

"I have come all this way just to see you, Hilly." His voice was plaintive, and a wounded look settled on his face.

"I wrote to tell you to expect me."

"Yes. And I wrote back to say, please, do not come."

"Well, I didn't get your letter."

"Of course not! *Your* letter only arrived yesterday! I replied at once and as I just said, I told you not to come. I'd like you to leave now, please, before my friend arrives."

"Your friend can wait, Hilly. I am taking you out for a meal tonight," he insisted, holding out the rose stem again. "Let me put this in some water for you."

He opened the cupboard above the sink and reached down a glass.

"I have to go back to London tomorrow evening, Hilly. Tonight's the only chance we have to spend time together."

Hilary Anne Moncrieff clamped her teeth together and closed her eyes. Why would he not get the message? She did not want to go anywhere with him. She did not want to see him.

Geoffrey Chatswood refused to believe that Hilary Anne had no interest in him. It was surely obvious to her that he was the perfect catch. She was just playing her silly games again! Well, he would win. He always did! He was going to marry Hilary Anne Moncreiff, whether she liked it or not. Her mother certainly liked the idea. He had already spoken to her about his plans for the future, and she fully backed him up when he declared his intention to ask Robert's permission to propose to Hilly. A secretive smile crossed his lips as he placed his rose in the glass of water.

"I can see I need to buy a vase for you, too," he said as he placed the glass on the little table.

"Please don't."

"Hilly!" He strode towards her and grabbed her arm again. "Why are you always so unkind to me?" he asked.

"Why won't you leave me alone?" she asked in return. "I already have a boyfriend."

"Do you?" he asked with an unpleasant sneer.

"Oui. She does!"

Geoffrey pulled up with a start.

"Who are you … and what business is this of yours?" he asked, eyeing up the attractive auburn-haired French girl who had suddenly appeared at the doorway.

"I am 'illy's friend, Madeleine. "oo are you?"

"This is Geoffrey," Hilly answered on his behalf.

Madie tossed her head and treated Geoffrey to her most haughty stare.

"Hrmph! 'Illy does not want you 'ere," she told him, "I zink you must go. 'Illy and me, we 'ave ze important work to do."

"Well, so do Hilly and I, so *you* can go!" Geoffrey glared back at her but Madie stood her ground.

"Just go, please, Geoffrey. Madeleine is right. We have an important assignment to work on. You cannot stay."

Geoffrey redirected his glare in Hilly's direction and snorted.

"Go where? I intend to stay here. You know I do."

"Well, you can't. You will have to find a hotel room. I don't want you here… and anyway, it's against the rules," Hilly added firmly before he could press the issue any further.

"Just go! Now!"

"And do not return," added Madie, as Geoffrey finally realised, he was getting nowhere and grudgingly began to move away. He stopped to throw one last look of loathing in the direction of the two girls, who stood watching to see that he really did leave them alone, and then he stormed down the stairs in a huff.

"No, no, no, 'illy. 'E is not for you!"

Hilary Anne agreed wholeheartedly.

"Thank you for helping me get rid of him." She smiled. "Let's go, in case he comes back!"

The two friends quickly followed after him, hurrying down the stairs and making their way to Le Contrescarpe, then, armed with a large glass of wine each to help inspire them, sat down to the task of writing the perfect letter to Joshua.

"Do you 'ave to tell 'im about Geoffrey? You did not want to be wiz 'im. You were not in ze wrong. Does 'Joshua 'ave to know? Per'aps 'e will not want to know."

"I have to tell him, Madie. I feel so grubby. So unworthy of him. I have decided to be honest and bare my soul and hope he will understand."

"And if 'e does not?"

Hilly looked at her. That was her greatest fear.

"I know he might not, but if Geoffrey starts talking… makes sure it gets back to Josh, about what happened on New Year's Eve, he won't know what to think, and if Jimmy is wrong and Josh does not have a new girlfriend, he will want to find someone else if he thinks that I would just happily treat him like that."

Hilary Anne bit her lip.

"What else can I do, Madie? I have to tell him my side of the story. I don't want him hearing rumours. And I need to hear it from Josh himself if Jimmy Jones is right. It's all such a nightmare."

"You told to 'im zat 'e must write first, oui?"

"Yes."

"Zen, you must wait."

Hilly sighed and put her pen back down on the table. It never got any easier and it never would. She just wanted to see him. To hold him. To hear him say that everything would be all right. She wished that Christmas and New Year had never happened. Nothing would ever be the same again.

Chapter – 17

Joshua Bates was the last of the flat's inhabitants to return to Birmingham following the Christmas break, and the others were already unpacked and settled back in by the time he turned up. He found them gathered together in the lounge, exchanging stories of their holidays.

"There's no food in the place," smiled Chrissy apologetically as she welcomed him home.

"We thought we'd grab a pub meal tonight and do a food shop at the market tomorrow."

"Sounds good to me," Josh replied, giving both Chrissy and her friend Kate, who also shared with them, a quick hug and a kiss on the cheek.

"Good to see you've all returned safely," he continued, shaking hands with the two boys who made up the rest of the group sharing the rambling old house together. "I'll just take my bag up; then I'll be with you."

"There's some mail waiting for you on the kitchen table, old man. You might want to grab that too," offered Malcolm McLeod as Josh wandered back into the hallway.

He dropped his case at the foot of the stairs and made a beeline for the kitchen. There were several letters waiting on the table. Malcolm had placed an elastic band around them to keep them neatly contained, and Josh smiled in appreciation as he picked up the little bundle and made his way back to the staircase. *It was so typical of Malcolm,* he thought, *to keep things all ship shape and Bristol fashion.* It was an attribute that would stand him in good stead for his chosen career as a pharmacist.

"We're ready to go when you are Josh!" Chrissy's voice drifted up the stairs after him.

"Be right with you!" he called back, placing his bag on the bedroom floor and quickly flicking through his bundle of mail. There was no sign of a French postage stamp. No trace of Hilly's handwriting. He heaved a deep sigh of disappointment and tossed the mail onto his bed. It could all wait until later. He was hungry, and he wanted to catch up on his friends' gossip. Anyway, he reminded himself that Hilly had asked him to write first so their letters didn't cross. He had tried, but for the life of him, he could not find a way to broach the subject of Geoffrey Chatswood without sounding churlish and without sounding angry with Elizabeth, whose attitude had, after all, been rather unpleasant. She obviously felt that she had triumphed in getting Hilly away from him.

Perhaps Chrissy and Kate could help steer him in the right direction. Lindy had most unhelpfully said that it was time he wrote his own letters to Hilly. She had already sent the bad news about Dad, and that was one thing, but when it came to writing about his feelings for Hilly, *that* was entirely up to him.

He knew she was right, of course, but argued that it was Hilly's feelings for Geoffrey he was worried about, not his own feelings for Hilly. He wanted to know how to ask Hilly about Geoffrey without sounding as though he owned her and she had no right to see anyone else. He would never do that to Hilly.

"So, what did you get up to over Christmas, Josh, my friend?" asked fellow Med student Daniel Smither as they waited for their fish and chips to be brought to the table.

"Spent endless hours with the gorgeous Hilly, I suppose?"

"No. Not even one single second, as it happens." Josh's voice sounded flat and empty. It echoed in his ears like a hollow, tuneless bell.

"In fact," he continued, the strange voice still ringing in his ears, "it was a pretty ghastly Christmas all around."

Four pairs of eyes gazed at him intently.

"How so?" asked Malcolm.

An air of solemn silence fell over the table as Josh briefly outlined the events that had overrun his life since the last time the five friends had gathered together here at the pub. They had all been so happy then. Their term exams were behind them and they were enjoying the anticipation that came with a trip home for Christmas. There were no expectations that any one of them might be facing a holiday break filled with horror and heartache, such as that which had befallen Joshua.

Kate reached out and took Josh's hand.

"I'm so sorry, Josh," she said softly. "What happened to your dad was tragic."

"Sounds as though it should never have happened at all," offered Daniel as Chrissy moved closer to Josh and placed a comforting hand on his arm.

"Of course, it should not have happened," agreed Josh, "and I have to admit it's left me doubting myself. I should have spoken up sooner. Called the G.P. sooner. Put Dad in my mini and rushed him to the hospital the minute I suspected something, but I just waited to be sure. Didn't want to be seen as trying to be too clever. So instead, I let my own father die."

"That is a ridiculous thing to say, Josh," scolded Chrissy. "It sounds to me as though you did more than could or should have been expected of you."

"I thoroughly concur, old man," agreed Daniel.

"Yes. Me too. What did your family have to say about it all?" asked Malcolm.

"I imagine they were very proud of you, and more than a little thankful that you were there." Kate gave Joshua's hand a squeeze as she spoke and feeling overwhelmed by his friends' warm support, Josh looked around them all with a grateful smile.

"Thank you. You're all very kind," he said simply as a waitress arrived with the fish and chips. "At least I still have *some* friends who care about me."

"Joshua! I take it that *that* remark has something to do with Hilly!"

"It does." Josh took a bite of his battered fish and looked from Kate to Chrissy and back to Kate again. "Talking of Hilly," he continued, "I've been hoping you girls may be able to give me some advice where she's concerned."

"Lord, Josh, old man, do I sense *more* trouble in your life?"

Josh nodded, and four pairs of eyes studied him closely once more.

Malcolm shook his head and raised a quizzical eyebrow.

"Don't do things by halves, do you?"

"I haven't done anything."

"Maybe that's the problem," suggested Chrissy. "I imagine there was a reason that you didn't manage to see Hilly at all?"

"Yes. The situation with Dad. And Hilly's mother."

"*What?* Well, obviously, you were totally unable to leave your father's side when he was ill or your mother's side after he'd passed. That much we can all understand. I'm sure Hilly understood, too."

209

"Hilly didn't know about Dad. Her mother rushed her off to London the minute she returned from Paris. Elizabeth Moncrieff doesn't approve of me. She goes out of her way to try to keep Hilly from seeing me. It happens all the time, but this time, it worked. She kept Hilly in London until it was time for her to go back to Paris. Then, yesterday, quite by chance, I came across Elizabeth in Leominster, and she couldn't wait to tell me that over the course of the holidays, Hilly had fallen in love with her old childhood friend, Geoffrey Chatswood and that she and Hilly's dad, are expecting an engagement to take place when Hilly graduates at the end of term. She was positively gloating about it."

"*No!* Has Hilly confirmed any of this?"

"Has she ever even mentioned this Chatswood chap before?"

Joshua patiently answered the barrage of questions that were flung in his direction, before returning his attention to Chrissy and Kate.

"The thing is," he explained to them, "I need some help with writing to Hilly. A considerable amount of help, as it happens. I keep trying. Just keep messing it up."

Malcolm's eyebrow shot up again.

"Messing it up?" he quizzed.

"How can you possibly mess up a simple letter?"

"It's not though, is it? If it was that simple, I'd have done it by now. I need to be a little careful how I word things. I can't suggest I see her mother as a pretentious interfering snob or come across as the jealous, jilted monster."

"No! Certainly not," agreed Chrissy and Kate in one voice.

"Of course, we'll help you. Won't we, Chrissy?"

"Absolutely. The minute we get home, we'll get right on to it."

It took several hours and a lot of wasted Basildon Bond writing paper, before Joshua and the girls felt they had cracked it, and Josh found it necessary to read the letter over just one last time the following morning, before he headed out to the post box to send it on its way.

Dearest Hilly,

The letter read,

I am sorry to be so long replying to your beautiful card and note. I have found it challenging to choose the right words. I know you understand now why I failed to keep our Christmas rendezvous, and I'm sure you also realise, given the fact I needed to enlist Lindy's help to convey to you the heart-breaking news about Dad, that I have found it more than a little difficult lately, to put pen to paper. I have tried and failed miserably on several occasions. Please forgive me.

Forgive me too, Hilly, for what I must say next.

While my feelings for you have not changed in any way, I am unable to continue with our summer holiday plan. If I am not required to commence an internship, I will be very much needed at home. I'm sure you understand my situation.

Perhaps, if what I have heard is true, you will be more than happy to call it off. I won't pretend that I am not deeply hurt and confused, but if what I heard is indeed the truth, please know I will never stand in the way of your happiness, Hilly.

Accordingly, I wish you and Geoffrey the very best for your future together, and I sincerely hope we can remain the best of friends, always.

With all my love,

Joshua.

As he stood in the cold morning air, gripping the envelope in his gloved hand, Josh closed his eyes and took a deep breath. What more could he have said? He had explained his own situation, conveyed his feelings, and not even mentioned Elizabeth Moncrieff's behaviour. He raised the envelope to his lips, then he slowly dropped it into the appropriate slot.

The next hand to touch that little letter would be Hilly's; he thought sadly as he turned in the direction of the university and trudged slowly on his way. The cold wind that chilled the air seemed to reach right into his soul. *Would he ever see Hilly again,* he wondered, *now that he had set her free?*

He should have been feeling relieved that his letter was finally on its way, but he still felt hurt and confused. Surely, Elizabeth was wrong about Hilly and Geoffrey. Hilly had never liked Geoffrey before, so why would she suddenly change her mind now? He could only hope that Hilly would write back at once and set his mind at rest. It would all turn out to be more of Elizabeth's nonsense, and Hilly still cared for him and had no intention of getting engaged to Geoffrey Chatswood.

Chapter – 18

Hilly was overjoyed when Josh's long-awaited letter finally arrived.

She ran up the stairs to her room, eagerly tearing open the envelope as she went, then as she drew out the single page contained within, she threw herself on the bed and eagerly read its content, over and over.

That there was no mention of another girl filled her with an overwhelming sense of relief, and of course, while she was disappointed that their holiday plans needed to be abandoned, she perfectly understood Josh's situation.

What she did not understand, and what chilled her to the core, was why he would think she was planning a future with Geoffrey Chatswood.

Her worst fears on that front must have eventuated. Geoffrey must have made it his business to seek Josh out and fill his head with some fantasy of his own making.

Hilly's blood ran cold at the thought of Geoffrey boasting that she had gone to bed with him. He would not have told Josh the truth of the matter. He would never admit to himself, let alone Josh, or indeed anyone else, that she had not been a willing participant in that encounter.

Hot tears of humiliation ran down her face as she held Josh's letter to her lips.

"I love you, Josh," she whispered out loud. "Please forgive me."

She knew then that she must reply to him at once. She must find the courage to tell him the truth of what had happened with Geoffrey and assure him that she saw no future for herself with that awful boy, that she could think of nothing worse, and that if Josh was no longer interested in her, she would understand, and she would simply spend the rest of her life on her own.

How she managed it, she really did not know, but two nights later, Hilly finally sealed her letter to Josh and placed it on the table, ready to be uplifted and posted on her way to school the following day.

The next morning, however, Hilly once again woke up feeling quite out of sorts. She was forced to make a mad dash along the hallway to the lavatory to be sick, and as she returned to her room to wash and dress, she felt drained of energy… listless and utterly exhausted. She told herself that she was simply suffering from weeks of reliving the nightmare of New Year's Eve. The horror of it all still played over and over in her mind. Surely, she could have done more to stop Geoffrey. Why had she frozen in horror and fear the way she did? She thought she was stronger than that. Josh would be disappointed in her too when he read her letter.

As Hilary Anne stared at her reflection in the mirror, she barely recognised the thin, pale girl who looked back at her. She had become some kind of insipid creature she could not even begin to understand, let alone live with anymore. She was unable to eat or sleep. Of course, she felt ill all the time, she told herself. She needed to take herself in hand and get over it. Otherwise, Geoffrey Chatswood would have won.

But even as her mind worked overtime to convince herself that she was right, Hilly knew in her heart of hearts that her malaise was due to more than her recurring nightmare and self-disgust. She knew full well what the real problem was. The cold hand of fear gripped her, and she could feel a rising panic overwhelm her as she finally admitted the truth to herself. She was pregnant. She was carrying Geoffrey Chatswood's child.

Hilly did not make it to school that day or the day after.

Worried that her friend had apparently gone to ground, Madeleine decided it was time to go in search of her.

"'Illy!" she gasped as Hilary Anne eventually opened the door in answer to her persistent knocking, "Qu'est ce que?"

Hilly gulped.

"You'd best come in, Madie," she said quietly, "there is something I have to tell you."

"Do not say to me zat you are sick. Zat, I can see."

Madeleine took in Hilly's drawn, pale face and the dark rings that had appeared under her sunken eyes. She had lost weight this term, and her disposition was that of a deeply troubled person struggling to cope with a great burden of nervous tension and despair.

Hilly took Madeleine by the hand and led her to the table.

"Sit down, Madie," she said, "there is something I have to tell you." Madie nodded and took the proffered seat, suggesting that perhaps Hilly needed to sit down, too.

"I 'ave ze great concern for you, 'illy."

213

"No. Please. I'm not sick. Not really. That is, well, what I think it is, is that, well, I think that I am pregnant."

"You are pregnant? Wiz ze bebe of Geoffery Chatswood?"

Madie's words rang over and over in Hilly's ears.

"The baby of Geoffrey Chatswood." She slumped forward, rested her throbbing head in her hands, and stared blankly back at her friend.

"I don't know what to do, Madie. I really don't know what to do. I can't believe I am having his baby. I hate him."

"Zen, you must 'ave ze abortion."

"*Abortion!*" Hilly's soft, troubled eyes widened in horror at the very mention of the word. "I can't do that, Madeleine. Kill my own baby? No. No."

She looked dazed and completely unable to even comprehend the idea of abortion, and as she looked across the table at Madie in sheer desperation, yet more huge, salty tears ran down her tragic, pale face. She lowered her eyes and let them rest momentarily on the letter still waiting to be posted to Joshua. Madeleine followed her gaze.

"You 'ave written ze letter to Joshua! What 'ave you told to 'im? Zat Geoffrey Chatswood raped you and now you are 'aving ze bebe?"

"No! Oh Lord, no! I told him about New Year's Eve but not about the baby. I wasn't sure, you see… I didn't want to believe it, I suppose. It's all such a nightmare, and why should Josh want anything to do with me now anyway? No. I have lost him forever." Hilly's anguished cry came from somewhere deep inside her, and Madeleine felt suddenly overwhelmed as she realised she was at a total loss to know how to help resolve her friends' unthinkable dilemma. The answer was obviously not as simple as she had believed.

"I zink zat we will talk wiz ma mere. She will know what is ze best for you to do. She is very wise and very kind, ma mere. Oui. Zat will be ze best. We must go now to Le Contrescarpe, where Henri, 'e will let us use 'is telephone."

"No. I have one idea that might work, Madie. I will have the baby, and I will bring it up on my own. What do you think?"

"'Ow, 'illy? 'Ow, will you live? Where will you live?"

"I will sell my paintings and sketches at the market. The baby can come with me in the daytime, and I will rent a room where I can work and where we can sleep at night."

"Non, 'illy. Zat, ce n'est pas une bonne idée!"

Hilly sighed and shook her head. What else could she do? She could not kill her own baby, and anyway, abortion was illegal, and she would probably die, too, at the hands of a back-street abortionist! She could not marry Geoffrey Chatswood, either. That was unthinkable. She would rather die.

"Come, 'illy. We will speak to Maman. Or we will speak to votre maman."

Mother! A shudder ran through Hilly's entire body at the very thought. Of course. She would have to tell Mother and Father. It was nearly March, and they would be here for Easter. Mother would guess at once what was wrong with her, and she would blame Joshua. She would never believe that Geoffrey Chatswood was to blame. In her eyes, Geoffrey was perfect.

"I 'ave ze solution!" Madie's voice was triumphant, and her eyes sparkled as she grabbed hold of Hilly's hands.

"Adoption, 'illy! You can find for ze bebe a new mama et papa."

Hilly looked at her. *It would be so hard,* she thought, *to give away her own baby, but perhaps Madie was right.*

Two weeks later, Hilary Anne was still mulling over the idea of adoption. It did seem to be the most sensible solution to her problem, but just as she started to come to terms with the idea, Easter arrived, and along with it came her mother and father.

As Hilly had predicted, Elizabeth guessed at once that her daughter was with child.

"Is there something you have to tell me, Hilary Anne?" she asked the day after they arrived. Hilly swallowed hard. There was no point in trying to hide the truth. Mother had guessed, just as she knew she would.

"I suppose that Bates boy is the father and no doubt he wants nothing to do with either you or the child? I warned you about him, but no, you had to moon around after him like a love-sick puppy! You will not ruin your reputation and your life like this, Hilary Anne. You will return to London at once, and you will have an abortion. Father and I will take care of everything the way we always do. We will arrange it today."

"No, Mother. I will not have an abortion. I do not want this baby, but I will not kill it either. I will place it for adoption. If it *was* Joshua Bates' baby, I would feel very differently. I would have it, and I would keep it, but it is not Josh's child. He would never do this to me."

Elizabeth's eyes narrowed. How dare Hilary Anne take that tone with her. She would do as she was told. Did she even know who the father was? She had obviously been sleeping around with lord knows who. She had definitely slept with Geoffrey Chatswood. *After all*, thought Elizabeth, *she herself had been witness to that!*

A sudden, delicious thought popped into her head. *Could the baby belong to Geoffrey? That would be too good to be true!* Geoffrey already wanted to marry Hilly. He had said as much! They could marry at once, and nobody need ever know that Hilly was already pregnant.

"Who *is* the father, Hilly?" she asked keenly. "Do you even know?"

"Yes, Mother. Of course, I know."

"Well?"

"It doesn't matter, Mother. I do not love him. I have no feelings for him at all other than deep loathing."

"Oh. But you were happy enough to go to bed with him?"

"I was not! He was drunk, and he forced himself on me."

"Well, if that is true, that is grounds for abortion. It is also a matter for the police. I demand to know who this man is, Hilary Anne."

"Very well! I will tell you, but you are not going to like it, Mother, or then again, knowing what you think of him, perhaps you will! It is your precious Geoffrey Chatswood, Mother, and no, I will not marry him, so don't even suggest it."

"Yes, you will. You will not return to Leominster looking like this. What will people think? What will your father think, and Aunt Hilary? No, Hilary Anne, you will not bring shame on your family. I am quite sure that Geoffrey will be more than happy to marry you. Whatever you think about him, I believe he will make the perfect husband for you. He adores you. He has already asked for your father's permission to propose. Does he know about the baby?"

"No, he does not, and he will not."

"If he is the father, he has every right to know."

"He has no rights at all, Mother. He is very lucky that I have not been to the police and charged him with assault."

"And you will *not* go to the police. You said that he was drunk. He would never have behaved like that otherwise. Not Geoffrey!"

"And if Josh was the father, what would you be saying then? Geoffrey is not who you seem to think he is, Mother. He is arrogant and self-entitled.

216

A spoiled little brat who is used to getting everything he wants! I will *not* marry him. The baby will be placed for adoption."

Hilary Anne tossed her head defiantly, and Elizabeth stormed from the room.

"You will have to speak to her, Robert," she demanded moments later as she apprised Robert of the situation. "She never listens to me!"

Robert looked at his wife in horrified disbelief.

"I cannot believe that our little Hilly is pregnant, and I find it difficult to believe that Geoffrey Chatswood is the father. I know the boy is smitten with her and keen to marry her, but in all honesty, I thought that Hilly had eyes for no one but young Joshua Bates and that Geoffrey was in for a very big disappointment."

"Well, it doesn't matter, Robert. If Geoffrey is the father, he needs to be told at once, and we'll just have to hope he still wants to marry her. Daphne and William must be advised of the situation too, though goodness only knows what they will think of Hilary Anne now."

A sudden thought struck her.

"If we act quickly enough, perhaps they don't even need to know. *Oh, Robert.* How could she do this to us? After all that we have done for her!"

"She has done nothing to us, Elizabeth, but she has made her own bed, and you're quite right; now she must lie in it."

Despite a great deal of sobbing and pleading with her father, Hilly was unable to change his mind. She would marry Geoffrey Chatswood, he told her, and that was that. She had a responsibility to the child, and she would not throw away her own life and her reputation by becoming a single mother. No other man would want her with someone else's child in tow. Not even, he wagered, Joshua Bates. Abortion, he reminded her, was both illegal and a highly dangerous gamble to take. She would marry Geoffrey.

He looked at his distraught daughter, and to her absolute horror, tears welled up in his eyes, then slowly began to roll down his cheeks.

"I am so disappointed, Hilly. Not *in* you, but *for* you."

"Please, Daddy," she pleaded one last time.

"He forced himself on me. I didn't want to do it. I can't marry him. *Please,* why can't the baby be placed for adoption?"

"Because your mother is quite right. You cannot return to Leominster in this state, and you cannot remain in Paris by yourself when you graduate. Where and how will you live? You cannot accuse Geoffrey of assault or prove after all this time that he forced you into anything, so you cannot have a legal abortion. You will just have to live with the consequences of your actions, Hilly. You will ring Geoffrey tonight and tell him about the baby."

"He might not want to have anything to do with it. He might not want to marry me, either."

"He will marry you, Hilly. He needs to take responsibility for his actions, just as you do. No, Hilly. I'm sorry. My mind is made up, and you will do as you are told."

As she listened to the phone ringing at the other end of the line, Hilly hoped in desperation, that there would be no reply, and she would have more time to think of another plan. Her parents hovered over her, waiting to make sure that she carried out their bidding, while she herself believed she now thoroughly understood how it felt to be standing in front of the firing squad.

The ringing suddenly stopped, and as the receiver was raised from its cradle, Hilly's legs buckled beneath her, and she collapsed quietly to the floor.

Things moved quickly after that. While Elizabeth fussed over her daughter, Robert picked up the abandoned telephone receiver and calmly advised a stunned William Chatswood, who had answered Hilly's call, of the situation that had arisen with their offspring.

All four parents were in one mind as to the action that should now be taken, and Geoffrey declared himself only too happy to oblige as he reacted like the cat who got the cream.

He assured both sets of parents that he had been thoroughly determined to marry Hilly, even before he knew about the baby, and as Hilary Anne sunk even further into the depths of utter despair, Geoffrey made it his business to return to Paris at once. He placed a diamond solitaire ring on her finger and strutted around like a triumphant peacock. He had won again! Daphne and William accompanied him and at Robert and Elizabeth's bidding, a concerned Aunt Hilary arrived three days later.

Elizabeth and Daphne set about arranging a small but elegant Civil Wedding Service, while Aunt Hilary did her best to persuade them that perhaps they should consult with Hilly, before they rushed into making any arrangements on her behalf.

Madeleine, realising that the matter had been taken completely out of Hilly's hands and that she was to have no say in the matter, somewhat sadly agreed to be her bridesmaid.

"I am not 'appy 'illy, zat you are ordered to marry Geoffrey," she declared.

"Eet is like ze dark days in ze 'istory books! Eet is not so bad aujourd'hui to 'ave ze bebe wizout ze 'usband. C'est la vie! Eet 'appens!"

"Not in Mother's world," sighed Hilly, who was living in a permanent daze. She felt like a rabbit caught in the headlights, with her life taken over and the situation spiralling completely out of her control.

"I am so grateful that you agreed to be my bridesmaid, Madie," she said as the two friends talked over a coffee at Le Contrescarpe.

"But zis is not 'ow you want your life to be, 'illy."

"No, but I realise that it is what I have to do, and it will be just a little bit easier with a friend by my side. A friend who understands."

Madeleine shook her head. She would never understand ze British and zere 'stiff upper lip'.

A week later, as the two girls followed Elizabeth and Robert into the Registry Office, where Aunt Hilary and the Chatswoods waited for them, Madeleine looked at her friend in wonder. Hilly was wearing a beautiful midi-length cashmere woollen dress in a pretty shade of soft, dusky rose pink, which seemed to be reflecting a slight blush onto her otherwise pale cheeks. She wore a matching soft pink cloche hat, which was adorned on one side with a spray of deep, dusky pink fabric roses. She looked beautiful. Far too fetching for the likes of Geoffrey Chatswood.

How could she bear it? wondered Madeline. *How could she be so calm and serene on the outside when inside, she must be in such a terrible state of turmoil and distress?*

"What are you zinking, 'illy?" she asked quietly.

"I am thinking that I am doing the right thing. By my parents, by my baby, and by Josh."

"By Josh?"

"Yes. Most of all, by Josh. I was weak. I am pathetic. I am unworthy of him."

"'Ow do you know zat zis is 'ow he zinks?"

219

"How can he possibly think anything else? No. This is how it has to be, Madie. I love him too much to expect his forgiveness. The most I can ever do for him now is to walk away and set him free to follow his dreams."

"Wizout you?"

"He will find someone else he can be happy with."

"And you, 'illy? 'Ow about you?"

"It will be the best for everyone."

"For ze ozzers per'aps, 'illy. Not, I zink for Joshua, and not I zink, for you."

"I will have my baby to love."

Hilly took a deep breath, drew herself up, and forced a smile to her lips. Then, she turned to Geoffrey, who was nattily clad in a morning suit he had hired for the occasion. He smiled back at her triumphantly, and as her heart broke into a myriad of tiny, shattered pieces, Hilary Anne Moncrieff solemnly made her wedding vows.

Chapter – 19

Hilly looked at the smartly framed certificate she held in her hands, and a wistful little smile flickered briefly on her lips. Despite the heartbreak and upset of her final term in Paris, she had passed her Diploma of Fine Arts with Honours.

William Chatswood decided that Geoffrey should work from their small Parisienne office, until such time as Hilary Anne completed her studies, and she was grateful to him for making it possible for her to at least see her course through to the end. The resultant Diploma had given her back a tiny scrap of self-esteem. Something to be proud of.

Hilary Anne Chatswood placed the framed certificate on the floor of the tiny box room that was her temporary studio, leaning it carefully against the wall. She had collected it from the framers on her way home earlier and would ask Geoffrey to hang it for her when he came in from work; she thought as she made her way downstairs to the little kitchen that served as both cooking and laundry space in their bijou London flat.

They had been back in London for three weeks now. The flat they were renting was small but adequate, offering them a lounge, kitchen and bathroom on the ground level, along with one bedroom and a box room, at the top of a precariously steep flight of stairs. It was a temporary arrangement while they looked for a property to buy.

Both sets of parents, as well as Aunt Hilary, had gifted them generous sums of cash on the occasion of their marriage, and together with meagre savings of their own, they had put together enough for a small house deposit. Meanwhile, the little flat in Brixton was handy to the city for Geoffrey's work and to West Dulwich, where they were looking to purchase.

Despite the day being hot and sticky, Hilly had spent the afternoon trudging around what transpired to be several totally unsuitable properties with their Real Estate Agent, returning home feeling hot, tired and thoroughly despondent. Her feet were burning, and all she really wanted to do was sit down and rest, but Geoffrey would be home from work soon, and would expect to find her in the kitchen cooking his evening meal.

The thought of standing over a hot stove was too much for Hilly, so she decided to prepare a nice crispy salad instead, with cold chicken left over from the roast dinner they had enjoyed the night before.

Despite the fact that every single window in the tiny flat was already opened as widely as possible, it still felt airless, and the close, muggy atmosphere was causing her to feel feint and rather unwell. Her hair was sticking to her face and clinging around her neck, and she could feel small beads of perspiration sitting uncomfortably on her top lip. Concerned that she may pass out from the heat at any moment, Hilly staggered to the bathroom, where she ran a flannel under the cold tap and slowly wiped her face and hands with it before wrapping it around the back of her neck in an effort to cool and refresh herself.

She learned from day one of her marriage, that just like her mother, Geoffrey expected her to look immaculate at all times, and he would not appreciate the way she looked at the moment, she thought, as she continued on her way to their diminutive kitchen.

No wife of his would look like something the cat had dragged in, he once told her sharply. *Scruffy jeans and hair tied back in jaunty scarves may be all very well for Parisienne art students, but he had an important job in the city and he expected his wife's appearance to reflect that.*

She would not sit around in her brunch coat for hours after breakfast either, and he didn't care if she was suffering from morning sickness. There were standards to be maintained at all times, as he was quite certain Elizabeth had raised her to understand.

As she laid their little table for two and placed a small, crystal bud vase filled with pansies in its centre, Hilly wondered, as she did so often throughout the day, what Josh was doing right now. She wished it was him who was coming home to her. She dreaded the sound of Geoffrey's key in the lock. She could never be sure these days how he would greet her. For the last week, in particular, he had been in a dark mood that frightened her.

During their time in Paris, he had been charming and considerate for the most part, and she had begun to believe that even though she could never love him the way she did Josh, perhaps things might not be quite as frightful as she had feared.

Since their return to London, however, Geoffrey had reverted to the selfish, demanding person she had always found him to be in the past.

While Hilly had no idea, what brought on his bouts of dark, broody behaviour, Geoffrey always managed to make it quite plain to her that *she* was somehow the underlying cause of every problem.

The door slammed loudly, causing Hilly to jump. Her heart skipped a beat, and then she froze to the spot, waiting to see what would happen next.

"I hope you've cooked a decent meal for me tonight, Hilly. A big, juicy steak with mushrooms and onions and eggs and chips, perhaps?"

"I thought that as the weather is so hot, we would have a nice crispy salad with cold chicken and some lovely fresh bread,"

"Salad and fresh bread! I'm not looking for a picnic lunch, Hilary Anne. I'm looking for a decent, wholesome meal that will fill me up! I've been out, slaving away at work all day so that you can spend your day swanning around looking at properties and a million things you seem to think no baby can live without. Did you find anything you think I should look at?"

"No."

"No. You never do. You're obviously expecting far too much. You need to tone down your ideas."

"Perhaps we need to look a little further out of the city."

"If you hadn't gone and got pregnant, you could be earning a living too, and we could save more and buy something decent!"

Hilly wanted to scream at him. To point out that if either of them was to blame for her pregnancy, it was him and that he was the one picking fault with every property they had viewed together. The truth was that Geoffrey wanted to live on the Northern side of the Thames, in areas like Kensington or Mayfair, where property prices were well beyond their means. He was a snob with grandiose ideas. Hilly despaired of ever moving out of their current accommodation and wondered how she would manage with the steep stairs and tiny rooms if they were still living there when the baby arrived.

She would not even be looking for a home with Geoffrey were it not for the baby, she thought bitterly, so he had no right to complain at the cost of cribs and prams. She took a long deep breath, clenched her teeth and swallowed hard, determined not to let Geoffrey have the satisfaction of seeing that she was upset.

"Here you are," she said in an even, pleasant voice that portrayed no hint of the anger and hurt that was raging deep inside her.

"Would you like steak and chips for tea tomorrow night, then?"

Hilly placed their salads on the table and sat down as she spoke, but Geoffrey was having none of it.

"I am **not** a rabbit, Hilary Anne, and I am **not** eating nothing but a wretched salad for my tea. You can eat it on your own. I'm going out for a decent meal!"

He picked up his plate and emptied its contents onto the kitchen floor in a fit of petulant rage, then stormed from the house, once again slamming the door behind him.

While Hilly sat and stared after him in stunned silence, Geoffrey made his way to nearby Brixton Road, where he eagerly flagged down a passing taxi and requested the cabbie deliver him to a well-known gentlemen's club in St James's Street.

His plan to pick a fight with Hilly and escape for the evening had succeeded admirably, and as the taxi made its way over Westminster Bridge, he sat in the back and congratulated himself on his ingenuity.

As the cabbie pulled to a halt outside the Carlton Club, Geoffrey wasted no time paying his fare and alighting. His late maternal grandfather had put his name down at the Club the day after he was born, and he had been a regular visitor there from the day he turned twenty-one.

Since returning from Paris, Geoffrey valued his membership more than ever. It gave him a bolthole where he could escape the unexpected realities of married life. Having achieved what he set out to, in respect of prising Hilly from the arms of Joshua Bates, it was only now that Geoffrey realised that married life brought with its responsibilities he had never dreamed of. He was tired already of discussions around baby names and nursery furniture, and Hilly appeared to give no thought whatsoever to *his* needs. Everything in her world seemed to be centred around the baby.

A sardonic smile crossed his lips as he made his way into the club. Hilly had no idea that he had been coming here after work most days since their return to London. In fact, she had no idea he was even a member, and he was determined it would stay that way.

Geoffrey knew full well that Hilly would not like him frittering away their money on alcoholic beverages and gambling, but as far as he was concerned, it was none of her business. Gentlemen's clubs were a man's domain, designed for the very purpose of giving a chap a place to enjoy himself away from the drudgery of married life and the prying eyes of females.

He had said as much to his old friend and fellow club member, Nigel Fortesque, the last time he called in, which led to a marvellous stroke of luck.

Having been recently dumped by his girlfriend, Stella, a wounded Nigel agreed wholeheartedly, declaring that women were to be avoided at all costs. He then bet Geoffrey two hundred pounds that a certain gentleman, however much he was enjoying himself, would throw the contents of his glass down his throat and obediently rush off home to his wife at the dot of eight o'clock, as he always did.

Geoffrey, in turn, declared that despite his being a creature of habit, who was apparently completely under the thumb of his very controlling wife, the chap would surely stay on beyond eight o'clock if they purchased him another whiskey or two. Nigel laughed.

"I'll bet you two hundred pounds that he won't," he stated, and Geoffrey was only too happy to take him on.

The bet was duly recorded in the book, and the whiskey was delivered to the bemused but never-the-less delighted gentleman in question.

Nigel was then forced to pay out when it transpired that due to the fact the fellow's wife was out of town visiting family, he had, in fact, booked a room and was spending the entire night at the club!

Geoffrey promptly put the resultant two hundred readies in his wallet, determined to keep them for his personal enjoyment, and he was hoping now, that tonight would offer the opportunity to expand his little cache of ill-gotten gains.

Having signed the member's book to acknowledge his arrival, he strode into the hallowed club rooms with a great deal of purpose and made his way directly to the bar, where he had arranged to meet up with both Nigel Fortesque and their friend Hugh Oldfield.

A quick glance at the handsome clock on the wall told him he was almost twenty minutes early, so he procured a table suitable for the three of them, ordered himself a large whiskey to be getting on with, and sat down to await his friends' arrival.

By the time Nigel and Hugh turned up some thirty minutes later, Geoffrey was enjoying his third glass of the amber liquid.

"About time you turned up," he complained jovially.

"I was just contemplating whether I might find it necessary to imbibe the whiskeys I got in for you chaps, as well. Would be a shame to waste them!"

"A thought that troubled you deeply, no doubt!" returned Hugh as he shook Geoffrey's hand and took a seat at the table.

"Now, before I forget and get into all sorts of trouble with Poppy, she has charged me with inviting you and Hilly to come for tea on Saturday night. You're invited too, old man," he continued, turning his attention to Nigel, "but I warn you in advance that since you and Stella are together no more, Poppy is determined to find you a new lady. I understand she's planning to set you up with a childhood friend who has just moved to London."

"Oh? So, what's she like, this friend? Would I be wise to stay away?" asked Nigel, with feigned disinterest. He would not readily admit to himself, let alone his friends, that he would rather enjoy some new female company in his life.

"Poppy tells me she's quite the looker. Never met her myself, mind you, though I understand she's moved to London to be a model, so she can't be too bad, eh!"

"Oh well. A man has to do what a man has to do, and if it will help to keep Poppy happy, well, of course, I'll oblige."

Geoffrey shook his head.

"I'd just enjoy being a free man if I were you."

"Says the man who now goes home every night to the delicious Hilary Anne."

"Harrumph!"

"Good Lord! Do I detect trouble in paradise already?"

"*Paradise?* I barely exist in Hilly's world! All she thinks about is spending my money and where we're going to live. Anyway, I came here to get away from all that, so come on. Drink up, and let's hit the gaming tables! I'm feeling lucky tonight!"

As Geoffrey pushed all thoughts of Hilary Anne from his mind, threw caution to the wind, and enthusiastically embarked upon a night of heavy drinking and reckless gambling, Hilly sat alone in their little flat, wondering how she could possibly get away from him.

Her situation was beginning to become untenable. She did everything that Geoffrey asked of her without complaint, but his demands were becoming more imperative every day, and he seemed to be going out of his way to upset her and make her feel worthless.

It was as though he believed he owned her and pleasing him should be her only concern. He appeared to be completely disinterested in the baby. Her pregnancy was nothing more than an inconvenience to him. Perhaps Madeleine was right, and she should simply have refused to marry him. After all, her parents had refused to acknowledge how she felt. That they preferred to take Geoffrey's side still hurt her deeply. She felt lonely and abandoned, just as she thought poor Josh must be feeling. She almost hoped it was true that he had found another girl because then he would be spared the hurt that she must surely have otherwise thrust upon him. She couldn't bear to think that Josh was feeling as miserable as she was.

Hilly decided not to waste her time, sitting up and waiting for Geoffrey to come home. She even wished that he would not. He would no doubt be drunk and either want to pick another fight or demand sexual favours, depending on his mood. Either way, she didn't want to know. She was hot and tired, and she would not lose sleep on account of Geoffrey Chatswood.

As she dragged herself upstairs to bed, she wondered for one brief moment where Geoffrey might have gone but quickly decided that she really didn't care. She simply could not cope with his unpleasant behaviour tonight. She was exhausted, and all she wanted was to sleep. Perhaps things would look better in the morning.

As Hilly struggled to accept the unhappy life that fate had cruelly thrust upon her, Elizabeth Moncrieff rejoiced in her daughter's situation. Hilary Anne had apparently grown up at last. She recognised how fortunate she was to be married to a man like Geoffrey, who would provide a comfortable roof over her head and happily come home to her every night.

There was not a smidgen of doubt in Elizabeth's mind that Hilly was living the perfect dream, and she was only too happy to say so to anyone in Leominster who was of a mind to listen.

On returning home from Paris, Elizabeth made it her business to ensure that every one of Hilly's friends was aware of her marriage to Geoffrey. She even booked an extra shampoo and set at the hair salon in order to be sure that Maisie Cowan was privy to the fact and aware of how well Hilly had done for herself. That way, word was sure to get back to Lindy and Joshua Bates as well.

Elizabeth knew that Joshua was still completing his education and that Lindy, too, was away, studying to become a vet. She was a little irked, however, to discover that even Maisie Cowan was making something of herself and was, in fact, now residing in Birmingham, where she was fortunate enough to have gained employment and training at the salon of the famed Vidal Sassoon.

Determined, however, that Joshua Bates should be made aware that he could no longer chase after her daughter, Elizabeth invited Margaret and Susan Bates for afternoon tea at Elm Cottage. She ran into them at church the Sunday following her return from Paris and insisted they must come for tea at four o'clock that afternoon so she could show them all her wonderful holiday snapshots.

"You ladies will be very interested in the current Parisienne fashion trends, I'm sure." She smiled.

Having shown her visitors several photographs of herself, Hilly, Madeleine, and a group of family friends visiting favoured tourist attractions in Paris, Elizabeth then proceeded to deal her trump card and produce an expensive leather-bound album containing photos of Hilary Anne's wedding.

"I'm sure you all knew that Hilary Anne decided to marry Geoffrey while she was in London for Christmas. They have been lifelong friends, of course, and Robert and I always hoped their friendship would blossom into something more, though we did feel they might wait until Hilly completed her degree. I'm sorry, by the way, if Joshua is upset by this turn of events. I know that he and Hilary Anne were always very close. I did try to warn him off, mind you, before he went back to university, and I'm sure Hilly would have written to him to let him know what she was planning."

Margaret and Susan looked at each other in stunned silence, and Elizabeth smiled at them in feigned innocence as she pretended not to notice the shock on their faces.

"They decided against a big church wedding," she continued in a honey-sweet voice.

"They very wisely felt the money it would cost would be better spent helping them to secure a property in London when they return. Geoffrey is working in Paris until Hilly finishes her art degree, you see," she prattled on, but neither Margaret nor Susan was listening anymore.

Margaret's mind raced. No wonder poor Josh had been so utterly miserable since Christmas. He had just lost his beloved father when Hilly had gone and done this to him! How could she? It seemed so unlike her. Did Josh really know? Was Hilly really happy? Perhaps Elizabeth and Robert had forced Hilly's hand somehow.

As her mind raced, Margaret politely offered Elizabeth her congratulations, then with as much grace as she could muster, rose to her feet, reminded Susan that they had work to complete, and led her equally stunned daughter out of the door.

"How dare she! We should have known Elizabeth Montcreiff had an ulterior motive for inviting us to tea," Margaret commented to her equally upset daughter as they walked home to the bakery.

"She simply couldn't help herself! She just had to rub it in!"

Susan agreed. "I'd like to know why she has never thought that our Josh was good enough for Hilly," she added.

"She has always tried to come between them!"

They walked on in silence for a few minutes, each of them grappling to come to terms with what they had just learned.

"Oh, Mum." Sighed Susan, her voice filled with emotion, "poor Josh. Do you think he really does know? It might explain why he has seemed so distant and so sad of late. I thought he was just feeling inconsolable about Dad. He even thinks he's responsible for what happened to Dad. That he should have been able to diagnose the appendicitis straight away, even though the doctors didn't. I think he's lost confidence in his own ability to be a doctor over that."

Margaret sighed.

"Yes," she agreed sadly. "I think you're right. For him to have lost Hilly as well…" her voice tapered off.

He was strong, her Josh, she thought, *just like her Matthew had been. He would find a way to overcome his pain and no doubt be all the stronger for it.*

229

Chapter – 20

A little rush of excitement rippled through Joshua Bates as he stood on Denmark Hill, taking in the sight of the large, weathered, red brick edifice on the opposite side of the road.

So that was King's College Hospital, where he would both work and continue to learn for the next several years at least. He hardly dared to believe it was true when he received his letter of acceptance. Of the hospitals Joshua approached, King's was the one that interested him the most, and as he stood before it now, he realised his acceptance there had given him a much-needed boost of confidence and a renewed sense of purpose in life.

Joshua was hit hard by the news that Hilly's correspondence contained when it eventually arrived just a week before Easter.

With a great deal of encouragement from Madeleine, along with agreeing Josh deserved to at least know what had transpired in London and why she felt she must now end their relationship, Hilly finally found the courage to post her letter, and its contents shook Josh to the core.

He was all set to travel to Paris and console her the minute he could get away.

Hilly was quite obviously not to blame for what had happened on New Year's Eve. To think she felt unworthy of him as the result of Chatswood's despicable actions left him yearning to go to her, to comfort her and reassure her that where she was concerned, his feelings were still just as they had always been.

He also felt a deep yearning to travel to London and sort out Geoffrey Chatswood once and for all.

To then learn, shortly after Easter, that Hilly was now married to the man left him stunned and struggling to understand why.

His immediate reaction on learning of her ordeal on New Year's Eve, had been to cancel his plans for Easter, and go to her at once. He had known, though, that his mother and siblings needed him home for Easter, and he had also promised to give Alex Morgan a hand on the farm.

Joshua had felt stretched in so many different directions that he was torn over which way to turn, and he agonised for many long, painful hours over where he was needed the most.

His heart ached to be with Hilly while his previous commitments weighed heavily on his mind, and in the end, he had felt obliged to return home to Leominster. At the same time, he determined he would travel to Paris to console Hilly as soon after Easter as he could possibly manage. Meanwhile, he would write again to reassure her that all was well between them.

Then, before he could even put pen to paper, he had received the devastating news that Hilly was now Mrs Geoffrey Chatswood!

Josh had fallen in love with Hilly the very first time he saw her.

He was only six years old and Hilly, barely three, when Elizabeth brought her into the bakery to choose a treat, and Josh thought she looked just like the little angel they hung on top of the Christmas tree.

He had loved her for all those years, and now he had lost her. To Chatswood, of all people! He still wondered if he could have stopped the wedding had he followed his heart and gone to Paris for Easter. But how could he possibly have foreseen what would happen next?

Joshua sighed deeply as he crossed the road and made his way to the hospital's main entrance. *It was all too late now,* he thought. He would never know what might have been.

The following evening, as an excited but nervous, newly appointed Dr Joshua Bates proudly reported for a night shift at the Accident and Emergency Department of King's College Hospital, Mr Geoffrey Chatswood once again signed into the Carlton Club on St James's Street, looking to enjoy a night of serious drinking and gambling.

Geoffrey's new-found pleasures had become a regular pursuit, and he could now be found at the Carlton Club several nights a week.

Hilly still had no idea where it was he disappeared to, on his frequent evenings out with his friends. When she timidly dared to ask him over tea one night, Geoffrey coldly advised her it was none of her business. That he would go wherever he wanted, whenever he wanted, with whomever he wanted, without needing any sort of permission from her. The dark scowl and threatening, intimidating stare that accompanied his words left Hilly in no doubt that there would be trouble should she ask again, and after that night he would often not even bother to come home to eat.

Daphne Chatswood insisted the young couple join them for a meal in Kensington every Monday evening, and while they were visiting the house in Wrights Lane, Geoffrey was always at his charming best. He fussed over Hilly as though she was all that mattered in his world.

He knew she would say nothing to his parents about his all too regular nocturnal activities. She was too afraid he would move on and leave both herself and the baby homeless. He had already threatened to take that course of action, and had also put a sudden stop to her searching for a property in Dulwich.

"This house-hunting lark is all just taking far too long, Hilary Anne," he informed her in a sullen, disgruntled tone one Saturday morning when she suggested they go house-hunting together.

"It appears there is nothing suitable in Dulwich, and I am bored with the whole thing! We will continue to live here until we can afford a suitable residence in Kensington or Mayfair. The sprog can sleep in the box room. You don't need a studio."

Hilly felt at a loss to understand Geoffrey's attitude. He had been so keen to marry her and provide for both herself and the baby. They were the centre of his universe in Paris. All he could talk about was their future together and how much he loved them and wanted to provide for them.

Now, it was as though he loathed them both. That having got what he wanted, as usual, he had quickly lost interest in them. Stealing Hilly from the 'baker boy', as he persisted in calling Josh, was a fait accompli, and now he was bored with the whole situation. A wife and baby were nothing more than a tiresome millstone around his neck.

It was the speed with which his attitude towards buying a house changed that perplexed Hilly the most. One minute, he was berating her for not doing enough to find somewhere suitable; the next, she was ordered to call a halt to the whole thing!

"You are useless, Hilary Anne," he snarled at her.

"Most women would be falling over backwards to find a home for their family. But not you! Obviously, I'll have to take care of that too, the way I have to do everything around here. You are pathetic."

Hilary Anne desperately wished she had someone to talk to about the way Geoffrey was treating her. A friend she could turn to and confide in, the way she had with Madeleine, but there was no-one.

Poppy was the only friend Hilly had in London, and while she was always kind and delightful company, Hilly felt her connection to Geoffrey was a little too close for her to become a trusted confidante, and despite the wonderful relationship she shared with Hugh, it appeared that Poppy too, was in the dark about what the boys got up to.

She did however, confide to Hilly in a conspiratorial tone on the night of her little dinner party, that she was convinced Nigel was the ringleader of their gang. He was constantly badgering Hugh to join himself and Geoffrey on some 'boys night' out.

"I've decided he needs a new girlfriend to keep him in line," she giggled to Hilly.

"Patsy will be perfect. She is very pretty, and she is much nicer than Stella. I thought Stella could be very unpleasant when it suited her. She never cared about anyone but herself. Did you like her, Hilly?"

"Not really," Hilly replied with simple candour.

"I like you, though, Hilly," Poppy assured her. "Sometimes, I think that you're too good for Geoffrey. He can be very selfish, too. Just like Stella," she commented with a flash of insight that took Hilly by surprise.

"I'm worried that Patsy is too good for Nigel, too," she added with a worried little frown as that particular young man put an arm around her friend's shoulders and kissed her on the side of her head.

"Perhaps introducing them was a bad idea."

Hilly gave her a reassuring smile.

"Don't worry. I'm sure Patsy can handle him," she said quietly, though she found herself remembering that she had believed she could handle Geoffrey too, and she had been so wrong. She unconsciously placed her hand on her stomach as she spoke, which was a habit she had acquired over the past few weeks. It was almost as though she was trying to protect her unborn child.

Poppy looked at her. Hilly did that quite often these days, she thought, *and she had gained a little bit of weight lately, too.*

"Hilly, are you pregnant?" she blurted out as she was struck by another sudden flash of insight.

"Good grief! Are you?" Hugh looked stunned, and Hilly looked from him to Geoffrey like a rabbit caught in the headlights. She wasn't supposed to tell anyone, and Geoffrey might think it was her fault that Poppy had guessed.

It was decided on the day they became engaged that they would keep the pregnancy secret for as long as they possibly could. Elizabeth had been adamant that no one needed to suspect there was an ulterior motive for their marriage, especially as Hilary Anne didn't yet look pregnant. After all, what would people think? The prospective parents happily agreed. Hilly because she couldn't bear it if any of her friends, particularly Josh, were to think badly of her, and Geoffrey because he didn't want people believing Hilly only married him because of the baby, even though he knew in his heart that it was true.

"Yes," he said now, answering Hugh's question on behalf of his wife.

"We've only just found out," he lied.

"Well!" exclaimed Hugh, "That is wonderful news! Congratulations to both of you. You must be very excited!"

As he proposed a toast to the expectant parents and Poppy gave Hilly a delighted hug, the mother-to-be forced herself to smile.

"Well, we've known for a little while," she confessed. "Only we decided to wait for a few months before we said anything, just in case something goes wrong."

"Of course," smiled Poppy. "Very wise. Oh, I shall have to arrange a baby shower for you! What fun!"

"Thank you," replied Hilly shyly, "that would be lovely."

"A baby shower?" questioned Nigel. "Can't babies use normal showers? I didn't know that!"

Poppy giggled.

"A baby shower is a party ladies give for their pregnant friends, Nigel," she explained. "Everyone brings gifts. Babies need lots of stuff, you know. Nursery furniture and clothes and nappies and toys. All sorts!"

"Crikey! All sounds a bit expensive if you ask me," Nigel replied.

"No wonder you've been pushing up the odds of late old man," he commented to Geoffrey, "Sounds like you'll need every penny you can lay your hands on!"

Hilly gave him what Aunt Hilary would describe as an 'old fashioned' look, and Geoffrey glared at him.

What the hell was Nigel playing at? He knew that Poppy and Hilly were in the dark about the Club and the gambling nights. Both he and Hugh had told him that they didn't want the girls to know for fear they would put

234

a stop to it. Not that Hugh really needed to worry. He wasn't married. He didn't have to explain himself to anyone, least of all Poppy.

In truth, Geoffrey knew that Hilly would have very good reason to complain. He reluctantly admitted to himself that he had possibly been getting a little carried away, but only, he tried to convince himself because he wanted to raise enough money to buy a decent home for Hilly and the baby. The only flaw with his plan, as he saw it, arose from the fact he was using their property account to fund most of his gambling, and having lost rather heavily of late, they could no longer even afford to buy in Dulwich.

As Hugh brought out the whiskey bottle and Poppy fussed over Hilly, Geoffrey sat in an unhappy state of growing despair. He owed hundreds of pounds in unpaid gambling debts, and only today, he had his bookie place a large sum of borrowed money on a 'sure thing' at Ascot that failed to deliver. Instead of winning, the wretched horse drifted back through the field and came in second to last.

Not even Hugh and Nigel knew the extent to which his gambling was out of control, thought Geoffrey, as he threw back a large glass of whiskey and gazed across the table at his wife.

She was so beautiful and gracious, he thought. Despite her constant bouts of morning sickness and heartburn, she still managed to look stunning, and to remain graceful and serene.

He knew he had been treating her badly of late. A rare feeling of guilt washed over him, and he felt sick with worry. He knew, too, that Hilly hated his constant nights out and was upset over his decision to halt the house hunt. If she ever discovered the reason why he was in financial trouble, she would surely leave him. He couldn't go on misappropriating funds from their property account to pay his debts. There must be another way.

As the evening progressed and the conversation carried on around him, Geoffrey sat lost in his own little world. He quietly knocked back glass after glass of whiskey, his mind churning over and over as he desperately tried to find a way to quickly resolve his current financial nightmare. It would only take one stroke of good luck, he told himself. Just one big win at cards or on the horses. Then suddenly, it hit him! The solution to his problems had been there all along!

He didn't need to play poker or baccarat for high stakes. He didn't need to visit his bookie and take a chance on the nags or the dogs!

He was a financier with ready access to money!

He could easily find a way to make a few pounds in a hurry! Why hadn't he thought of it before? If he could return the money to their joint account, perhaps with a little extra, and reinstate the property search, Hilly would be happy again, and all would be well. As a plan he saw as daring but fool-proof began to formulate in his mind, Geoffrey heaved a great sigh of relief and downed another glass of Hugh's excellent whiskey.

There was an extra bounce in Geoffrey's step as he entered the premises of the Chatswood & St. Clair Financial Investments Company the following Monday morning. He quickly made his way to his desk and directed his young personal assistant to bring him Mrs Hilary St. Clair's investment portfolio at once.

One tiny wave of uncertainty and guilt washed over him as he planned his next move, but he promptly swept it aside. When all was said and done, he assured himself minutes later, as he opened the file the obliging Miss Sandra Balfour had placed before him, Aunt Hilary's investment funds were as good as *his*, anyway. Robert Moncrieff and Hilary Anne were her only living relatives. They would inherit her considerable wealth when she died, and as Hilly's husband, he too would surely benefit. What difference would it make if he borrowed some of that money now? The old lady had given him the authority to control her investments on her behalf, and she would never suspect a thing.

Ignoring the nervous butterflies in his stomach and the little voice in his head telling him that what he was about to do was wrong, Geoffrey Chatswood boldly took it upon himself to contact his broker. He then arranged for the immediate sale of a small bundle of Great Aunt Hilary's shares.

They should easily fetch the tidy sum of three thousand pounds, and as soon as the proceeds were paid into the investment company's trust account, he would write out a cheque for the full amount. He would not, however, return the proceeds to Mrs St Clair's investment account. Instead, he would make that cheque payable to his very own fictitious company, Mayfair Holdings.

Three nervous days later, his clever plan carried through to a successful conclusion; Geoffrey informed Miss Balfour that he had pressing business to attend to and would be out of the office for the next hour or two. With the fraudulent cheque tucked safely into the inside pocket of his suit jacket, Geoffrey Chatswood then calmly made his way to The

Haymarket, where he had visited the Bank of New Zealand just two weeks previously and opened an account for himself in the name of Mayfair Holdings.

As he paid the cheque into his bogus company account, Geoffrey congratulated himself on his foresight. He planned to use the account to keep his own secret stash of pocket money and hide any ill-gotten gambling gains from Hilly. Little did he know how soon his secret account would become an invaluable asset! No one would question him selling off shares and transferring the proceeds to Mayfair Holdings. He would use the money he had borrowed from Aunt Hilary to pay his creditors and reimburse his joint account with Hilly, adding a little extra to the latter as a sweetener.

His plan was successfully executed, and Geoffrey decided to walk the short distance back to the office. He felt a great load had lifted from his shoulders and he strutted along quite happily, convinced that no one would ever discover what he was up to. No one he knew had dealings with the Bank of New Zealand, and no one would connect him with Mayfair Holdings. There was enough money in the Mayfair Holdings account now for him to repay a debt or two and take a few decent wagers. He would soon win the money back. Then he would reimburse Aunt Hilary's investment account, and all would be well!

So pleased was he with his morning's work that he stopped at a little public house he passed along the way for a self-congratulatory whiskey. His next stop was at a little flower stall, where he bought a large bunch of flowers each for Miss Sandra Balfour and Hilary Anne. He would buy some chocolates for Hilly, too, on his way home from work, he told himself. She deserved a little treat.

Chapter – 21

"Would you mind dreadfully, Geoffrey, if I invited Madeleine to stay for a few days? We could put her up on the sofa bed, and she could help me with searching for a suitable house. I know she'd love to come, and I would truly appreciate her help."

Hilly looked at her husband and smiled hopefully. *Geoffrey had been so much more pleasant of late,* she thought, *ever since Poppy's dinner party.* Before then, she would have never dared to suggest that she invite Madie to visit them. Even now, she felt a little apprehensive at making the suggestion for fear it would bring on one of his moods. For some reason, Geoffrey seemed to dislike Madie.

Geoffrey closed his eyes, pursed his lips and bowed his head.

"Of course, if you'd rather not, that's fine," added his wife hurriedly.

"No. Actually, Hilly, that's a splendid idea."

"Oh, Geoffrey, thank you. I shall ring her tonight."

"Mm. I'm out tonight, by the way, so don't bother cooking for me."

Hilly's delight at his agreeing to have Madie stay faded a little. Geoffrey's nights out had been less frequent of late, and his drunken outbursts had been fewer, too. She felt no desire to see him return to his old ways. He saw the anxious look on Hilly's face and smiled.

"Don't worry, I won't be too late. Enjoy talking to Madeleine," he said as he turned and made his way to the door.

"Tell her she needs to come right away," he added with a wink. "We need to move before the baby arrives."

Hilly heaved a sigh of relief. Geoffrey seemed to understand how she felt about their housing situation. He agreed that they would be better off financially, living in Dulwich for a while and putting money into a home of their own, than they would be paying rent to someone else. They could easily move to Mayfair or Kensington later when they managed to save a little more. He had increased the amount of their deposit by five hundred pounds, too, which would make such a difference to what they could afford. She wondered where he found such a large sum of money so suddenly, and the thought that it may well have been won on a horse race or a card game left her feeling a little apprehensive. If he could win that much, surely, he could lose that much, too. Hilly sighed, pushed the nagging doubts from her mind and settled down to telephone Madie.

Three days later, Hilary Anne stood at St Pancras station, eagerly awaiting the arrival of the train from Portsmouth. As it finally approached and shuddered to a halt alongside the platform, she watched keenly for the familiar figure of Madeleine to alight. Her wait was short-lived. The train barely stopped moving before a carriage door was flung open with great exuberance, and the irrepressible Madeleine emerged, her bright auburn hair falling neatly back into place as she jumped from the last step onto the platform and looked around expectantly.

"'Illy!" she called out, waving excitedly as the two young women caught sight of each other. Hilly waved back enthusiastically and ran to greet her with a hug.

"Thank you so much for coming, Madie. I have missed you. There is so much to talk about, and I really do need your help with finding a house."

"I am so 'appy to see you m'amie, and Geoffrey, 'e does not worry zat I come?"

"Of course not! Why would he?"

"'E does not like me, 'illy, par ce que 'e knows I do not like what 'e 'as done to you," came the frank reply. "Does 'e treat you now, 'ow 'e should?"

"Not always, perhaps, but at the moment, he is trying very hard to be a good husband."

"Bah! 'E should be always ze good 'usband."

Hilly laughed.

"Come on," she urged, "Never mind Geoffrey. Let's get you home and settled in."

Geoffrey turned on the charm for Madeleine, determined not to give her any cause to question his movements. She was too sharp for his liking. Quick to see through things that Hilly would quietly accept or ignore. He had not yet managed to refund even one penny of the three thousand pounds he had borrowed from Aunt Hilary, but a grand plan was forming in his mind. It would require him to go away for a few days, and if he could encourage Madie to stay on, it would ease his conscience about leaving Hilly alone. If he did *that*, she might even take it into her head to go and visit Aunt Hilary rather than be at home by herself, and that would never do. It did not suit him to have any unnecessary dealings with that particular lady at present.

Both Madeleine and Hilly were delighted at Geoffrey's suggestion.

"I have to go to Bristol on business," he explained. "I have a client there who is anxious for me to visit. I'll only be gone for two nights."

Having convinced his father that he was going to Bristol in order to visit an important existing client and meet up with a prospective new one, Geoffrey set off two days later for Paddington Railway Station. He had removed a large sum of cash from his Mayfair Holdings Account to tide him over while he was away, and his hotel room was most obligingly being paid for by Chatswood & St. Clair Financial Investments Company in the guise of a business expense.

Feeling very pleased with himself that his cleverly executed plan had worked out so well, Geoffrey sauntered down the platform; his eyes peeled for any sign of Nigel Fortesque. It was a great pity, he told himself, that Hugh had decided not to join them. He was getting far too serious and conscientious of late, was Hugh. Not good old Nigel, though. A chap could always rely on *him* to skive off work and enjoy a bit of a lark! Truth be told, this little jaunt was all down to Nigel in the first place!

Nigel had caught wind of the fact that a new casino was opening in Bristol, and the two of them immediately set about planning a way to spend what they saw as some well-deserved time there. Geoffrey's carefully trumped-up work commitments could be easily taken care of in the mornings so as not to raise suspicion at the office, and the afternoons, evenings and wee small hours could be enjoyed at the bar and gaming tables.

It was the perfect ruse, thought Geoffrey, as he caught up with Nigel, who he spotted standing on the platform waiting for him. He gave his old chum a clap on the back.

"I'll wager this is the earliest you've been up and about in a while!" he quipped.

"How much are you willing to put on it?" laughed Nigel as the two of them boarded the train and claimed their seats.

At the exact same time as the London train pulled into Temple Meads Station in Bristol, Hilary St. Clair parked her little car in the driveway of Oak Manor and made her way into the manor house.

Several letters sat waiting for her on the beautiful mahogany hall console, and she stopped to gather them up, glancing casually through them to ascertain their origins.

An American postage stamp immediately caught her attention, and she quickly made her way to the conservatory, where she placed the mail on a small octagonal table, which sat beside her favourite chintz-covered armchair.

She rang the butler's bell to attract the attention of Mrs Biddle, the housekeeper, removed the scarf from her head, picked up the correspondence from America, and settled herself down to read.

The letter was from her old school friend, Rose Beaufort, who had married a very charming young American and moved to New York shortly after the Great War finally came to an end. Her husband Harry went on to make a large fortune as a very successful entrepreneur, and along with their two sons, they enjoyed a lavish New York lifestyle until the inclusion of America in the Second World War tore their family apart.

Both of Rose and Harry's sons lost their lives fighting in the Pacific, and the distraught couple then threw themselves into charitable works to help ease the unbearable pain of loss.

Now, with the passing of Harry a year ago, Rose was once more struggling with that same burning sense of emptiness. The thought of spending a long, dreary winter alone in New York prompted her to write to Hilary in the hope she would join Rose on a luxury cruise down the Nile. The riverboat departed from Cairo two days before Christmas, and Rose had already taken the liberty of procuring two first-class tickets in anticipation of Hilary's agreeing to accompany her.

Hilary St. Clair picked up the cup of tea that Mrs Biddle had placed on the table beside her and took a long, invigorating sip.

Her eyes eagerly scanned Rose's letter again, her mind racing and a delicious feeling of impending excitement creeping over her as she read.

A cruise along the Nile, she thought, sounded like a wonderful adventure and Rose would be the perfect companion for such an undertaking. She would contact Rose at once to confirm her acceptance, though despite her kind offer, she would not allow Rose to bankroll her participation in the proceedings. She was in no need of charity. She would simply use some of the money that was currently tied up and sitting idle in her investment portfolio with the Chatswood & St. Clair Investment

Company. There was an old shareholding in a small Australian Opal Mine that she would not miss!

Aunt Hilary downed the remnants of her tea in a single gulp and leapt to her feet with all the agility of a woman many years her junior. A quick glance at her exquisite Swiss wristwatch told Hilary she should still be able to catch Geoffrey at the office if she phoned right away.

Her mind raced as she waited for the call to be answered. There would be several things to organise before she left, and although the cruise was still nearly five months away, she would need to arrange sufficient funds to cover not only the cost of the cruise itself but also such expenses as travelling to Cairo and any side trips they should decide to undertake along the way. In fact, she thought it might be prudent to set herself up with a travel account. If she and Rose enjoyed this adventure, they may well decide to make such excursions a regular occurrence!

By the time Miss Sandra Balfour answered Geoffrey's telephone, Aunt Hilary had decided she would try to realise the sum of around three thousand pounds in anticipation of her needs. With any luck, that should be just about the current value of her shares in the Opal Mine.

The revelation that Geoffrey Chatswood had left London this very morning to spend several days tending to business in Bristol left Mrs St. Clair momentarily deflated.

"Never mind, Miss Balfour, my dear," she responded, quickly recovering her poise,

"I shall speak to Mr William Chatswood instead."

"Of course, Mrs St. Clair, I'll transfer your call to him at once."

"Hilary! What a pleasant surprise to hear from you," enthused William Chatswood.

"I understand from Miss Balfour that you were wanting to talk to Geoffrey."

"I was, but I hear he is away in Bristol for the rest of the week."

"He is indeed. He has clients there to keep happy, and as Hilly has Madeleine visiting from Paris for a few days, now seemed the ideal time for him to take a business trip."

"Of course, and I am sorry to disturb you in his absence, William, but I have some business of my own that I am anxious to get underway immediately. I would be most obliged if you were able to get the ball rolling for me today, William. If I wait for young Geoffrey to return, I fear it will be next week before anything happens."

William Chatswood raised his eyebrows and scratched his head. It was not at all like Hilary St. Clair to be impatient.

The unbridled excitement with which Hilary then outlined her plan to William quite took him by surprise. Her friend's suggestion seemed to have ignited a spark in her, one that was beginning to burn brightly in the depths of her imagination.

In truth, since Hilly had left school and moved away from Malvern, Hilary St. Clair's life had been both lonely and tedious. Now, at last, she had something wonderful to look forward to again.

"I would like to realise a small bundle of shares I have held for a very long time and transfer the proceeds into my cheque account with Lloyds Bank without delay, please, William," she explained, "as I wish to reimburse Mrs Beaufort immediately, for her outlay in securing the cruise on my behalf."

"Of course, Hilary. Which are the shares you have decided to sell?"

"The very small parcel I took out all those years ago in the Australian Opal Mine. In truth, I have been meaning to ask Geoffrey to do something with them for some time now."

"I shall get onto it at once, Hilary. Leave it with me."

"Thank you, William; I shall look forward to hearing back from you."

Aunt Hilary replaced the phone on its cradle and made her way upstairs, a huge, happy smile on her face and an extra bounce in her step.

Next, she flung open her wardrobe doors and took a critical look at the contents within. *It had been such an age,* she thought, as her eyes took in a rack of tired, old-fashioned garments, since she acquired anything new and elegant to wear. She would get Mrs Biddle to help her sort through her clothes at the earliest possible convenience, then she would take a trip to London and get Hilly to help her choose what she would need for her great adventure.

Perhaps Elizabeth would care to join them, too. She possessed such a wonderful eye for fashion. A natural flair that she had passed on to Hilary Anne, who was just like her mother when it came to putting an outfit together. In fact, Hilly was more like Elizabeth than she cared to admit, with her exquisite taste in fashion and her passionate love of fine art and all things botanical. That was where the similarities ended, though, thought

Aunt Hilary with a rueful smile and a nod. The child had inherited none of her mother's airs and graces.

The shrill ring of the telephone broke into her thoughts, and she hurriedly made her way back downstairs to answer it.

"Hilary. William Chatswood here," came the response, as she answered with a cheery hello.

"William! How wonderful to hear back from you so soon!"

An awkward silence greeted her before William cleared his throat and resumed the conversation.

"Hmm, um, I'm afraid we seem to have struck a small hitch, Hilary. I'm afraid Geoffrey seems to have traded your Opal Mine shares just a matter of a couple of weeks ago. It appears he has already reinvested the proceeds into a company by the name of Mayfair Holdings."

It was a stunned Hilary St. Clair's turn to fall momentarily silent.

"No!" she responded, quickly recovering both her voice and her poise, "how very extraordinary that we should both think to relinquish that little bundle of shares at the exact same time! Who are Mayfair Holdings? I don't believe I've heard of them before. Have you? Perhaps I should leave my money invested with them and look at relinquishing something else instead."

Mrs St. Clair was obviously a little nonplussed by William's revelations. Having been quite certain of her way forward, it now seemed that young Geoffrey had put a spanner in the works. Not that he had done anything wrong, of course. He had her full authority to buy and sell on her behalf. He had simply taken the wind out of her sails.

"Why don't I make some enquiries on your behalf, Hilary? Meanwhile, give some thought as to where you would like to go next, should the Mayfair Holdings purchase prove to be worthy of retaining."

"Thank you, William."

The timbre of Hilary's voice was a little deflated.

"That certainly sounds like the best course of action. Perhaps I shall need to wait for Geoffrey to return after all."

William Chatswood put down the phone and frowned. The disappointment in Hilary's voice, that her plan could not proceed as immediately as she hoped for, had not escaped him. Despite her having given his son carte-blanche to control her investments, he himself had told the boy several times that he must always refer to Mrs St Clair before he acted on her behalf. It was common courtesy!

William pushed down the button on his intercom and asked his secretary to drop whatever she was doing and fetch him Mrs St. Clair's portfolio.

An hour later, having acquainted himself with its contents, the senior Mr William Chatswood then telephoned the junior Mr Geoffrey Chatswood's broker.

As their conversation drew to a close, William's stomach churned in a sickening manner. His frown deepened, and his mind whirled with a thousand questions.

What was that boy up to? It was quite obvious that it was not only Hilary St. Clair who had no idea what was going on. William wanted answers and he wanted them now.

Chapter – 22

Geoffrey Chatswood stepped from the train at St Pancras Station, feeling almost as dismal as the weather. He took his leave of Nigel Fortesque and made his way outside in search of a taxi.

His time in Bristol had failed to deliver the results he so fervently hoped for, and while he did not lose heavily at the casino, he had barely broken even, and his debt to Aunt Hilary was no closer to being discharged.

He climbed into the back of a familiar black London cab, thankful to be out of the steady rain that was engulfing the city, and sat gazing unseeingly at the constant stream of passing headlights as they glistened in the rain.

The comforting sounds of slapping windscreen wipers and the swish of tyres making contact with sodden roads were strangely soothing, and by the time the cab pulled up outside the office, Geoffrey managed to completely reassure himself that there was nothing at all to worry about. He was no worse off than before he went to Bristol, and he had, after all, secured a new client for Chatswood & St. Clair Investments, which would please his father immensely.

He was, therefore, somewhat puzzled to find William Chatswood waiting for him with a less-than-pleased expression on his face.

"In my office now, please, Geoffrey."

William's tone of voice echoed the visible displeasure on his countenance.

Geoffrey's stomach lurched, as he was overcome with sudden, unfamiliar feelings of guilt, and his recently regained air of self-assurance began to ebb once more.

It was unlike his father to take such a stern tone with him. Warning bells jangled in his head, and he nervously prepared for the worst. His rakish air of self-confidence dissolved even further as he caught sight of Hilary St. Clair's portfolio sitting open on his father's desk.

"Sit!"

William all but barked the word, and Geoffrey instantly obeyed the command. Somehow, he had been rumbled! But how? He had been so careful to cover his tracks, and why would anyone other than himself have been looking into Mrs St. Clair's investments?

He perched anxiously on the edge of the chair, his stomach churning over and over, and his clammy hands gripping the armrests so tightly that his knuckles turned white.

William Chatswood sat bolt upright behind his desk; his eyes firmly fixed on the open file before him.

"Tell me, if you would be so kind, please, Geoffrey, about Mayfair Holdings." His voice was perfectly controlled, but there was an edge to it that caused Geoffrey a sense of deep-seated alarm. He sat motionless, gazing at the floor, his previous air of cocky self-assurance all but deserting him. His mouth opened and closed like a goldfish, but no sound emanated. For the first time in his life, Geoffrey Chatswood was rendered mute.

"I am waiting, Geoffrey."

William Chatswood did not choose to wait for long.

Failure on his son's part to offer even one word of explanation, he roared, left him with no choice other than to draw his own conclusion as to the truth of the matter. That conclusion, he continued, was deeply disturbing.

"Please tell me I am wrong, Geoffrey."

William lowered his voice, and the expression of rage on his face turned to one of desperate hope.

Geoffrey slumped in his chair and dropped his head onto his chest.

"I'm sorry, Father. I didn't know what else to do." His voice was thin and hollow.

"I only wanted to find a way to get some money in a hurry so I could provide for Hilly and the baby. I started to place a few bets and play the tables at the Club. It all went very well at first, then suddenly I began to lose. I thought my luck would change again, but it never did. I had to use some of the money we put aside for the deposit to buy a house, in order to clear my debts. My bookie turned out to be quite an unpleasant sort of chap. Threatened to hurt Hilly if I didn't front up with the money. Well, I couldn't let that happen, could I?" he whined.

"Then I didn't know how to explain to Hilly why we couldn't look for a house anymore. I didn't think Aunt Hilary would mind if I borrowed a few thousand for a while. It's not like she'd miss it."

"Arrgh! And how, Geoffrey, did you intend to repay Mrs St. Clair? By continuing to gamble, no doubt!" William Chatswood threw his hands up in the air in a gesture of horrified despair.

"I'm sorry, Father."

William looked at his son with undisguised contempt.

"I am disgusted, Geoffrey. I am also deeply ashamed that I have not seen the kind of man you are turning into. Hilary Anne was telling the truth about you assaulting her, too, wasn't she? That poor child. You happily destroyed *her* life in order to get what *you* wanted, and now you have happily stolen from Mrs St. Clair, once again, to satisfy your own unbridled desires! I would happily do the right thing and call in the constabulary, Geoffrey, if I did not believe that to do so would break your poor mother's heart."

William threw another look of undisguised contempt in his son's direction, and Geoffrey, whose countenance had now turned quite ashen, squirmed uncomfortably in his chair. His familiar air of self-important arrogance turned to one of subdued uncertainty.

"What *are* you going to do?" he asked in a small, timid voice.

"It is what *you* are going to do that should concern you now, Geoffrey!"

"I don't know what I can do. I don't have the three thousand pounds I borrowed from Mrs St. Clair at the moment. I paid off my bookie and replaced what I'd borrowed from our joint account, along with an extra five hundred pounds to make Hilly happy; then I re-invested the remainder."

"Re-invested! Gambled, you mean?"

Geoffrey nodded miserably.

"Yes," he admitted in a subdued voice.

"I'm sorry, Father. I was desperate. You must surely understand."

"I understand nothing other than the fact that you are a complete and utter disappointment."

"I'm sorry Father," Geoffrey reiterated, "what can I do to make it right? Anything. I promise I'll do anything. Please just tell me what I can do."

William closed his eyes, bowed his head, and said nothing for several minutes as Geoffrey sat in nervous anticipation of his father's response.

"Tomorrow," said William, finally breaking his silence, "Mrs St. Clair is coming to London to ascertain why her shares in an Australian Opal Mine have seemingly evaporated into thin air. Shares she had decided to relinquish in order to enjoy a well-deserved holiday with an old friend."

Geoffrey once more squirmed uncomfortably in his chair.

"What is going to happen, Geoffrey," continued an irate William, "is that you are going to tell Mrs St. Clair what you have just told me. She will then decide what action she will take. She may want to call the auditors to investigate your past activities, in case this has happened before, or she may choose to call the police herself. I will not discourage her from taking either of those courses of action. You have brought shame on yourself, your mother and me, the Company and your wife. You will go home now, Geoffrey, and explain yourself to Hilly if you can. You will then report back here on the dot of eight thirty tomorrow morning. Now get out of my sight. I cannot bear to look at you for one moment longer."

Geoffrey rose slowly to his feet, picked up his overnight bag, which lay discarded on the floor, and walked numbly to the door.

Why was Father treating him like this? It was only one little loan, after all, and he had done it for Hilly and the baby, not for himself. Surely Father could see that? But no, it seemed that rather than take a perfectly logical look at the facts, he was deliberately looking to find fault and create dishonest intent where there was none.

Apparently unable and thoroughly unwilling to accept his father's outrage, Geoffrey's thoughts rambled on with a jumble of self-pitying excuses. Hilly would understand, wouldn't she? She knew how much he loved her and that everything he did was for her benefit.

Feeling much maligned and misunderstood, Geoffrey slowly trudged his way in the direction of Soho, oblivious of the rain that was running down the back of his neck and causing his shoes to squelch. He suddenly felt desperately alone and uncertain of his next move.

The only certainty in Geoffrey's tortured mind was that he could not bring himself to face Hilly right now. What if she didn't understand, and she took as dim a view of his actions as Father? Then what would he do? Anyway, she was not expecting him home until this evening. He had all day to plan what he would say to her. He just needed to have a strong drink and devise a good, convincing story.

The loud blare of a car horn as he stepped carelessly into the road without looking brought Geoffrey back from his self-pitying reverie. He waved apologetically to the startled driver and stepped back onto the pavement, only to add to his chagrin by stepping into a puddle that spilt over the top of his shoe, drenching his sock and splashing muddy water up his trouser leg.

Geoffrey cursed under his breath and quickened his stride until he finally arrived at the public house, which was his chosen destination.

According to Nigel Fortescue, if he played his cards right, he could purchase more than just alcohol here, and a joint or two was just what he needed right now.

He dropped his sodden carry bag on the floor by the bar and clambered thankfully onto a secluded bar stool that was tucked neatly away in a dimly lit corner.

"Was you after a drink or a towel then?" quipped the cheery cockney barman. Geoffrey gave him a withering look and ordered a pint of best bitter along with his customary whiskey chaser. Having downed both in an alarmingly short period of time, he then ordered a repeat, and as the barman obliged, Geoffrey took a good long look around him.

Two elderly gentlemen sat reminiscing at a small table on the far side of the room, and a tarty-looking woman was brazenly seducing a middle-aged man at another table nearby. The barman followed Geoffrey's gaze.

"Not too many geezers out in this," he offered, indicating the inclement weather. "You lookin' fer someone in particular?"

"I was rather hoping Mary Jane might be here if you get my drift," replied Geoffrey, holding out a ten-shilling note. The barman shook his head.

"She don't come out fer that," he said.

The custom was slow, and this geyser looked well-heeled.

"She might be hidin' in the 'lost and found' though. I could take a gander fer yer."

He held out his hand as Geoffrey replaced the ten shillings with a pound note.

"I'll see if I can find 'er then," nodded the barman, slipping the 'nicker' into his trouser pocket and disappearing through a door at the rear of the bar.

Some hours, several drinks, and a second joint later, Geoffrey finally decided he was sufficiently fortified to face Hilary Anne. He still had no idea what he would say to her, but he was supremely confident that, unlike Father, even if she didn't applaud them, she would at least understand his actions.

"Thank you, Albert, my friend," he said to the barman, with whom he was now on first name terms, "you are a jolly fine chap."

He held his hand over the breast pocket of his suit as he spoke.

"And I can assure you my very good friends, Nigel and Hughie, will agree with me wholeheartedly, Albert."

One last remaining 'deep sea diver', carefully folded and discovered lingering in the depths of his wallet, had been replaced with a small plastic bag containing a sufficient amount of marijuana to enable Geoffrey to share with both Nigel and Hugh the next time they met.

As he rose to his feet to take his leave, Geoffrey found his balance to be strangely lacking, and he giggled stupidly as he grabbed wildly at the edge of the bar to steady himself.

"Whoopsy!" he exclaimed, as he stooped to pick up his bag. He laughed out loud again, then gingerly making his way to the door, Geoffrey stepped out into the elements.

The earlier relentless downpour had dwindled to a light yet constant drizzle, but it was still steady enough to wet him through, and as he staggered aimlessly down the street, it occurred to him that he needed to get home and out of his wet attire. His suit was still damp and uncomfortable from his earlier drenching, and he could do without the added discomfit of another dowsing.

He came to a sudden halt in the middle of the footpath, causing a fellow pedestrian following closely behind him to curse loudly.

"Oi!" exclaimed the man as he swerved wildly to avoid crashing into Geoffrey. "Watch it!"

"Sorry. Sorry," slurred Geoffrey, offering the man an exaggerated salute and a bow in apologetic acknowledgement.

"A thought just occurred to me," he offered by way of explanation to the thoroughly disinterested man, "which requires a little research. Had to stop, you see, to check the financial implications of the situation."

The disgruntled man shook his head and hurried on his way as Geoffrey fished into his pocket in search of his wallet.

"Wrong pocket!" he admonished himself with a drunken guffaw.

The elusive wallet finally located and inspected, the realisation then dawned on Geoffrey that he had insufficient funds left to pay for a taxi home. He did, however, have just enough to take a bus.

He walked on in the direction of The Haymarket, chuckling foolishly to himself as he sidestepped and jumped over the numerous puddles along the way.

By the time he manoeuvred the short distance required and the Brixton bus finally made an appearance, the rain had started to fall in large, steady droplets once more, and Geoffrey's drunken giggles had given way to wallowing self-pity. He clambered unsteadily aboard and sank thankfully into an empty seat obligingly situated on the downstairs level of the familiar double-decker. Then, as the big red bus lumbered its way through the busy streets, he held on tightly to the back of the seat in front of him in order to keep himself in an upright position. His head, however, seemed to take on a life of its own. It wobbled and flopped around most alarmingly, and as the bus stopped and started and jolted its way through Trafalgar Square, past Big Ben and over Westminster Bridge, Geoffrey began to feel horribly queasy.

It wasn't fair, he told himself, as the nausea began to take hold and the effects of the alcohol and drugs began to diminish. It was all Hilary Anne's fault. He was only trying to make her happy. She was never satisfied with anything. It didn't matter what he did; it was never enough, and she never acted as though she loved him, either!

By the time the bus finally reached Brixton and lurched to a halt at his regular stop, Geoffrey was in a dark mood indeed. His high had all but deserted him, and he had convinced himself that Hilary Anne was to blame for his entire, unpalatable situation.

He emptied the contents of his stomach into the gutter, then staggered wildly down the street, muttering darkly under his breath, until he finally reached his front door.

"Hilary Anne!" he shouted loudly as he flung the door open wide and dropped his sopping wet bag onto the floor, "I'm back!"

"You're early!" Hilly's reply drifted down the stairs to greet him.

"You don't have to sound so damn unhappy about it!"

"Geoffrey! I am just surprised! I didn't expect you until teatime!"

Hilly put down her pencil and closed her sketchbook. She was designing a series of Christmas cards which she hoped to sell to Hallmark, in order to generate an income.

She stepped from the box room where she had been working since seeing Madie off earlier in the day and collided with Geoffrey as he finally managed to drag himself up the last of the stairs and step onto the narrow landing.

"Geoffrey! You're soaked through! You need to get out of those wet things before you catch your death! I'll go and make you a nice hot drink while you get changed, and then I can tell you about the house that Madie and I found. I'm sure you'll love it. I do!"

"Too bad! It's a pity you don't love me, too, isn't it?" Geoffrey's words were slurred, and he glared at Hilly with an angry scowl.

"There will be no house, Hilary Anne. Forget it!"

"Geoffrey? I don't understand. Whatever has happened? Did your meetings not go well? Here, let me help you."

Hilly reached out her hand to help divest him of his wet jacket, but he roughly pushed her away. The unmistakable odour of alcohol and cigarettes mixed with vomit assailed her nostrils.

"Where have you been, Geoffrey?"

"None of your business," he snorted, grabbing hold of her shoulders and giving her another angry shove. This time, he pushed her with such violence that it caused Hilly to lose her balance.

As she began to topple sideways, Hilly reached out, desperately searching for something to grab hold of, but there was nothing there to help break her fall. She felt herself painfully twisting and turning and bouncing over and over and heard herself crying out to Geoffrey for help; then everything went black.

"Hilly! Hilly! Wake up! I'm sorry. I didn't mean to hurt you! It was an accident. It was! I promise! I love you!" Geoffrey's voice was a strange mixture of penitence and panic.

253

His words were still slurred, and as he bent over Hilly, searching frantically for a pulse, he felt sick to the pit of his stomach. She lay perfectly still, her arms and legs twisted on the stairs at odd angles while her head and shoulders rested on the living room floor at the foot of the stairs. She had landed headfirst.

What if she had broken her neck? What if she was dead? If he had killed her? Geoffrey's panic and nausea increased. What would he tell people? He would just have to say that he found her like that when he got home. Nobody could say otherwise. After all, it *was* an accident. He didn't push her down the stairs deliberately. She just lost her balance, that was all, he reassured himself. Yes! Of course! That was all he had to say! She had come out on the landing to greet him and tripped. Hilly moaned softly, and Geoffrey felt a great flood of relief rush through him. She was alive!

"It's all right," he whispered hoarsely, "don't try to move in case you've broken something. I'll call for an ambulance."

Hilly opened her eyes and looked at him.

"Don't move!" he repeated. "I'll be back in a minute."

"Why?" she asked in a groggy voice.

"Why did you push me? What did I do?"

"I didn't push you. You fell," he replied. "Don't worry. You'll be fine."

Hilly heard him make his way to the telephone. She heard him say his wife had tripped and fallen down the stairs and that she was pregnant. Then Hilary Anne was engulfed in darkness once more.

Chapter – 23

Hilary Anne opened her eyes and looked around the strange, clinical surroundings that greeted her. She was in pain from head to toe, her tummy hurt and she felt decidedly unwell. Her neck was restrained by a large, cumbersome brace, the bed on which she lay was moving swiftly down a long corridor, and she was surrounded by people she didn't know.

A young woman dressed as a nurse hurried alongside her, patting her hand while smiling kindly and telling her in a soft, comforting voice that she was not to worry.

"Where am I?" asked a disorientated Hilly.

"What happened?"

"You had a fall, remember, down the stairs at home. Nothing to worry about. You're safe now," came the reassuring reply. "Your husband called for an ambulance, and now you're in the A&E Department at King's College Hospital."

Fractured memories of Geoffrey pushing her, then feeling herself tumbling over and over, flashed through Hilly's dazed mind.

"Aarrgh," she moaned, grabbing hold of her stomach and writhing with pain.

"My baby." She sobbed. "Is my baby all right?"

"Try not to worry, Mrs Chatswood. The doctor will check everything for you," soothed the nurse as she threw a questioning look at the ambulance technicians.

"When is the baby due?" she asked.

Both the accompanying paramedics shook their heads. Hilly had been drifting in and out of consciousness and too distressed to answer their questions, while Geoffrey, who had travelled with them in the ambulance, seemed to be in a world of his own and was no help at all.

"We think she's about six months gone, and there is some bleeding," offered one of the men.

All eyes turned to Geoffrey.

"Can you confirm that Mr Chatswood?" asked the nurse.

"When is the baby due?" she asked again.

"Sorry."

Geoffrey lowered his eyes and stared at the floor.

"Sometime in late September, I think," he mumbled.

"Is it all right then, the baby?" he asked, almost as an afterthought.

"Geoffrey. Why?" Sobbed Hilly. "Why? I don't understand."

Another pain shot through her, and she cried out, causing the nurse to ask Geoffrey to go and sit in the Waiting Room.

"I'd rather stay with her," complained Geoffrey.

"No. Go." Hilly's voice had an agitated edge to it.

"I don't want you here." She sobbed. "Just go!"

"It's just down there and round the corner." The nurse pointed down the corridor.

"Don't worry. We'll let you know what's happening as soon as we can."

She watched until he disappeared from sight. There was something about Mr Geoffrey Chatswood that she found strangely disquieting. He reeked of alcohol, and while she couldn't be absolutely certain, she was pretty sure he had a faint aroma of marijuana about his person as well. She was about to ask the paramedics whether they agreed with her when Hilly moaned again, and the nurse returned her full attention to her distraught patient.

"Don't upset yourself, Mrs Chatswood. I understand that you're concerned for the baby, but you must try to stay calm."

"Yes. No. You don't understand." Hilly sobbed. "Help me. Please, help me."

"We'll do everything we can," appeased the nurse as the duty doctor made his appearance and added his reassurances to those of the nurse.

"I hear you've been trying to take the stairs in a hurry," he said in a light, kindly voice as he quickly ran his eyes over Hilary Anne's notes. Then, as he looked up at his patient for the first time, he drew in a sharp breath and let out an audible gasp.

"Hilly!" he exclaimed. "Good Lord! It *is* you!"

"Josh!" Sobbed Hilary Anne, as she felt a great sense of relief flooding through every inch of her being. She would know that voice anywhere. Everything would be all right now that Josh was here. Hilly opened her eyes and looked at the doctor, who stood at the side of her bed.

"You've grown a beard!" she whispered. "It suits you."

"Huh!" Joshua grinned as he handed his clipboard to the nurse. He reached out and gave Hilly's arm a gentle squeeze.

"Try not to worry, Hilly," he said quietly, "You're safe now. We'll check on the little one and make sure that you haven't broken any bones when you fell."

"But, Josh." Hilly found herself struggling to speak. Struggling, too, to stay awake. She was still in a state of shock and drifting in and out of consciousness. Dr Bates turned to the nurse, and Hilly, afraid that he was about to leave, felt her sense of panic return.

"Don't go, Josh!" she pleaded as she fought to shake off the darkness that threatened to engulf her once more.

"Please. Don't go. Need to tell you wh…"

It was sometime later that Mrs Hilary Anne Chatswood regained consciousness. The young nurse who had been looking after her had gone, and a different, more senior nurse sat at a small desk on the opposite side of the room. She rose to her feet as soon as she saw Hilly stir, then quickly made her way to check on her patient.

"Welcome back, Mrs Chatswood." She smiled as she reached out and pressed a button on the wall.

"Dr Goode will be here to talk to you soon," she said as she checked Hilly's pulse and vital statistics.

"Dr Goode?" Hilly was confused. "Who is Dr Goode? I want to see Dr Bates. Dr Joshua Bates."

"Dr Goode is your obstetrician, Mrs Chatswood, and I'm afraid Dr Bates is with another patient now."

"No. He wouldn't leave me. I know he wouldn't."

"Your husband is still here, though," smiled the nurse. "He refuses to go home until he has seen you. He's very dedicated to you."

Hilly froze. She didn't want to see Geoffrey. She wanted to see Josh. She had a horrible, empty feeling inside. A feeling that something was horribly wrong. The baby! She had lost the baby! Hot tears welled in her eyes and ran down her cheeks as she asked the nurse if she was right.

"There, there," the woman soothed her, "Doctor will tell you everything as soon as he gets here."

She handed Hilly a glass of water, then looked up, an expression of relief on her face as Dr Goode entered the room with Geoffrey at his side.

Her patient, however, seemed anything but pleased to see them.

"I want to see Dr Bates." She sobbed as the nurse and Dr Goode did their best to console her.

Geoffrey stood rooted to the spot. Dr Bates? No! It couldn't be. The 'baker boy'? What were the chances that he would be here and involved in caring for Hilly? Was he even qualified to be a doctor?

"Please," she insisted. "I want to see Dr Bates."

Dr Goode seemed a little puzzled that his patient should be so insistent about seeing a junior intern rather than himself, and asked the nurse if she had any explanation as to the reason why.

"They went to primary school together," spat Geoffrey, "and I would prefer he stays well away from her, thank you!"

Dr Goode raised an eyebrow. The tension in the air was palpable, and his patient's blood pressure had spiked with Geoffrey's intervention.

"I want to see him," she repeated, "and I want you to go, Geoffrey!"

"I think perhaps you should go back to the Waiting Room, Mr Chatswood," suggested the nurse.

"Your wife is a little distressed at the moment."

"Ha! My wife! I am a little distressed, too, in case you haven't noticed. This is my baby as well, remember," raged Geoffrey as he spun on his heel and stormed from the room.

It was all about Hilary Anne, as usual, he ranted to himself as he charged angrily down the corridor. It was never about him. He barged his way past an orderly pushing a trolley, who, deciding he didn't like Geoffrey's behaviour, followed after him. Then, as he careered wildly around the corner, Geoffrey ran head-on into a doctor who was approaching from the opposite direction.

"Woah, woah!" The doctor reached out to steady Geoffrey as he all but lost his balance and very nearly toppled over.

"What's up, sir? Can I help at all?"

The startled doctor looked closely at the young man with whom he had collided. He was obviously in a state of extreme distress, and he had equally obviously been drinking rather heavily. The man's clothes and breath smelled strongly of alcohol and tobacco, and unless he was mistaken, there was a distinct smell of marijuana on his breath as well. "Come and sit down," the doctor urged Geoffrey, steering him into the Waiting Room. "I'll find someone to come and help you." *He had better things to do right now than deal with a drunken drug addict,* he thought, as he guided Geoffrey into a chair and asked the reception staff to get him some assistance.

"I don't want assistance; I want to see my wife." Geoffrey's raised tone of voice was angry and belligerent. The doctor threw him a disparaging glance.

"Call Security if he gives you any trouble," he advised the receptionist, "meantime, find him a good large cup of strong black coffee."

"Yes, of course, Dr Bates."

Bates! Despite his heavily intoxicated state of mind, the name rang loud and clear in Geoffrey's befuddled brain. The doctor turned to leave the room, but as he stepped away, a wound-up Geoffrey suddenly reached out and grabbed hold of his arm.

"So! It's you, is it?" raged Geoffrey, his wild, erratic behaviour rising to a crescendo.

"You're the bloody 'baker boy'! The wonderful Dr. Joshua Bates! I suppose you're scuttling back to my Hilly, are you? Trying to save her precious baby. Well, you know what? That's *my* baby too! That's right. Hilly is *my* wife! Not yours, you loser. You stay away from her, you hear me. Stay away!"

Joshua wrenched his arm from the man's vice-like grasp and did his utmost best to remain calm. So, *this* was Geoffrey Chatswood! This despicable, drunken creature was the monster who had defiled his Hilly! Joshua clenched both his fists and his jaw. He drew in his breath and closed his eyes, drawing on every ounce of self-control that he could muster in an effort to control his urge to strike the man.

No, he told himself firmly, it was not worth losing everything over a cretin like *that!* Geoffrey Chatswood had caused him more than enough heartache already.

Geoffrey's threatening behaviour and raised voice sufficiently alarmed both the orderly following on behind, who had been witness to the whole extraordinary event, and the Emergency Department's Reception Staff, that they jointly saw fit to alert Security, and as Joshua Bates gave him one last withering glare, Geoffrey Chatswood was escorted from the premises, still loudly warning Dr Bates to stay away from his wife.

Now even more determined than before to do all he could to help Hilly through her ordeal, Josh strode urgently back to her room, arriving just in time to hear Dr Goode gently explaining to her that there was no longer a foetal heartbeat. That there was nothing more they could do. She would deliver the baby in the normal way, but she needed to understand that, sadly, the child would be stillborn.

"I'm so very sorry, Mrs Chatswood," he said quietly. "We'll do all we can to help you."

Hilly gave him a blank stare. Her baby was dead. Killed by his or her own father. She let out a heart-wrenching, guttural cry.

"Nurse will go and fetch your husband to be with you," offered the kindly Dr Goode.

"No!" screamed Hilly. "No! No! No! I don't want him near me. He's the reason my baby is dead." She sobbed hysterically.

"I didn't fall down the stairs. He pushed me! He was drunk, and he was angry, and when I tried to soothe him and calm him down, he pushed me."

She sobbed uncontrollably.

"I want to talk to Dr Bates," she wept, reaching out to Josh, who she had just noticed standing in the doorway.

"It's all right, Hilly," soothed Josh as he strode across the room. "Geoffrey's gone. He has been sent packing for creating a ruckus, and he won't be allowed back in for now. You're perfectly safe. My shift ends soon, and then I'll come and stay with you if that's what you want."

"If that's all right with you, of course, sir," he added, looking at Dr Goode.

"Of course. I'd prefer it if you could stay now. You seem to have a calming effect on my patient."

Joshua nodded and settled himself in for a long night.

Elizabeth Moncrieff tied back her hair with a long silken scarf and reached for a wide-brimmed straw hat. She was going to prune the dead heads on her roses this morning, and then after lunch, she was going to make a start on turning Hilly's bedroom into a nursery, ready for when her grandchild came to stay.

It was only three months until the baby was due, and she would need time to redecorate the room. Perhaps she would take a trip to London to

260

visit Hilly, and they could shop together for a pretty cot and some toys for the little one.

She took a long, hard look at herself in the mirror as she pulled her hat into place. Was she really old enough to be a grandmother, she wondered? *No*, she decided. She was only forty-six years old, and her close scrutiny in the mirror had not revealed any particularly noticeable grey hairs or wrinkles. Surely, she would be able to pass as an aunty.

The sound of Robert's voice calling her made her jump. Why was he home at this time of day? He had barely left for the bank.

"Elizabeth. Where are you?" He sounded upset and agitated.

"We have to leave for London right away," he called, running up the stairs and joining her in their bedroom.

"Pack a few essentials as quickly as you can," he advised. "Enough for us both for a few days."

"Robert? What is it?" Elizabeth was alarmed.

"It's Hilly. She needs us. She's lost the baby. She's at King's College Hospital. Joshua Bates phoned me at the bank to let us know."

"Joshua Bates!" Elizabeth bristled. "What does he have to do with this?"

"He's one of her doctors, Elizabeth. I'll tell you everything while we're on the way. It's terrible. Terrible!"

He threw a small suitcase at his wife and urged her to pack it quickly.

A shocked Elizabeth removed her gardening hat, and hurriedly did as she was bidden, while Robert phoned to book a London hotel room, then hurriedly backed the car out of the garage.

"We should have listened to Hilly," he said to his wife as they drove away from the house.

"She was right about Geoffrey Chatswood. We should never have forced her to marry him. He's a monster, Elizabeth!"

"Whatever are you talking about, Robert?"

"By all accounts, Geoffrey pushed Hilly down the stairs."

"Nonsense! Who says so? That Bates boy? Geoffrey would never do such a thing. Hilly would simply have lost her footing and fallen. That upstairs landing of theirs is so narrow. Why haven't they bought a house yet? They have plenty of money for a deposit. They could have moved on weeks ago. I hope Hilary Anne hasn't set her expectations too high."

Robert Moncrieff wanted to scream at his wife. He could not for the life of him understand why she thought Geoffrey Chatswood was so wonderful or why she held such disdain for Joshua Bates.

Despite his overwhelming frustration with Elizabeth, he bit his tongue and said nothing. Instead, he tightened his grip on the steering wheel and pushed his foot down a little harder on the accelerator. Hilly was his only concern right now, and the sooner they got to London, the better.

At the same time, Hilary St Clair was a woman on a mission. She alighted from the black cab that had carried her from her hotel to the premises of the Chatswood & St Clair Financial Investments Company and briskly made her way inside.

Clutching firmly onto a worn leather briefcase, she exuded an air of wounded dignity mixed with a good degree of obvious concern and fierce determination. If young Geoffrey Chatswood thought he could pull the wool over her eyes, he was sadly mistaken! His father would doubtless take a dim view of matters, too! It was just as well her beloved Winston was not here to witness this. He would be turning in his grave!

Mrs St Clair was a good half hour early for her appointment with William and Geoffrey, but she turned down the receptionist's kind offer to fetch her a cup of tea and made her way directly to William's office. Once there, Hilary St Clair opened her briefcase and drew out a bulging manila folder, which she placed on William's large walnut desk.

Next, she opened her folder at the first of several page markers she had strategically placed within, and then she sat herself down on William's comfortable deep-buttoned leather chair and stared stonily at the office door, mentally preparing herself for what she could only foresee as the unpleasant conversation that lay ahead.

William Chatswood burst through the door just minutes later. His usually calm, immaculate, unruffled appearance had deserted him. His hair was untamed, his chin unshaven, and his shirt collar undone.

"Hilary!" he exclaimed. "Have you heard? No! I dare say not. Unless Robert telephoned you, but no. You'd have been travelling."

"For goodness sake, William. Have I heard what?"

"About Hilly! Poor little thing has lost the baby."

"No!" Hilary St Clair froze. "What happened? I was talking to her only yesterday. She had just returned home after seeing Madeleine off at the railway station, and she was very excited about a house the two of them had been to see. There was no hint that anything was wrong with either her or the baby!"

"No. Nothing was. She fell down the stairs later in the day. Fortunately, Geoffrey was there when the accident happened and called for an ambulance. Daphne and I have only just been informed. She's waiting in the car, by the way. We're on our way to the hospital. Thought you'd want to join us."

Chapter – 24

The sudden influx of visitors was overwhelming for Hilly. Elizabeth and Robert were the first to arrive.

"Hilly!" exclaimed a perturbed Elizabeth. Her beautiful daughter had a swollen black eye and a graze on her cheek. Her left arm was in a plaster cast and sling, and the bed sheet was folded back, revealing the fact that her right ankle was heavily bandaged and her leg was covered in scrapes and bruises.

"How on earth did you manage to fall down the stairs? Were you not watching where you were going? Just look at what you've gone and done to yourself! And the baby! That poor little baby! How does poor Geoffrey feel about it all?"

Elizabeth finally paused for breath, pulled up a chair and sat down.

"Poor Geoffrey, nothing!" Hilly's voice was strained with emotion as she struggled to maintain control of her frayed nerves and temper. How typical of Mother to berate her and be more concerned about how Geoffrey felt than how *she* felt.

"I did not fall or trip, Mother, and I was not being careless! Geoffrey *pushed* me. He came in, reeking of alcohol and drugs and vomit! He was sopping wet from being in the rain, and he was in an ugly mood. I reached out to try to help him take off his wet jacket, and he just grabbed me and pushed me down the stairs. And if you don't believe me," she wept, "just look at the bruises his fingers have left where they dug into my shoulders and arms!"

Hilary Anne slipped the hospital gown down over the top of her arms as she spoke, revealing the angry marks that Geoffrey's attack had left. "And, *NO, Mother, I did NOT provoke him!*"

"No. I am afraid that would have been me!" came William Chatswood's voice from the doorway as Hilly tried desperately to control her tears.

"I'm afraid I angered him earlier in the day. Instead of going home to Hilly as I advised, it would appear the stupid boy went off on some kind of wild binge! Where is he, by the way?" he asked as he ushered Aunt Hilary and Daphne into the room before entering closely in their wake.

"Nobody knows," sobbed Hilly. "And I don't care!" she added defiantly between sobs.

"I hope he went and jumped in the river!"

"Hilary Anne!" Elizabeth was horrified.

"What a terrible thing to say!"

"Well, it's the truth! And I hope no one pulled him out!" replied her upset, unrepentant daughter.

"Apologise to Daphne and William at once!"

"No, I will not!"

Hilly felt unable to even look at the Chatswoods. They might love their son, but she did not. He was a bully who only ever thought about himself.

"I don't ever want to see Geoffrey again."

"Don't be so silly."

Hilary Anne looked at her mother and glared.

"It's quite all right, Elizabeth. Hilly is understandably upset at the moment, and between you and me, I'm not sure I ever want to see him again myself!"

"William!" This time it was Daphne who was agitated.

"Everybody, please! We did not come here to upset Hilly, yet that seems to be all we have succeeded in doing." Robert spoke with measured authority.

"Robert is quite right," agreed Aunt Hilary, seating herself on the opposite side of the bed to Elizabeth.

"Hilly needs our concern and sympathy, not a lot of wild accusations and berating. She has been through a terrible ordeal, and if Geoffrey is an innocent party in this event, why is he not here supporting his wife?"

She raised an eyebrow and looked frostily at each member of the assembled group in turn.

"Excuse me." A young nurse stood in the doorway.

"There are far too many of you in here, I'm afraid. We have a policy of no more than two visitors at a time. If you'd like to decide who should visit first, the rest of you can sit in the waiting room until it's your turn. Only please, none of you stay for too long. Mrs Chatswood needs her rest."

She eyed the assembled visitors sternly, then stood her ground, waiting for them to respond to her request.

"Robert and Elizabeth must stay, of course," stated William.

"Hilary and I have some business to discuss anyway," he continued, "so we can go back to the office and get on with that. At least we've seen Hilly, and she knows we are concerned for her wellbeing. We can come back when she's feeling a little more chipper." He smiled.

"Must you go back to the office, William? Perhaps we can take Hilary somewhere nice for a cup of tea."

"No, Daphne. Business first, I'm afraid, and as it's something you need to hear about too, you had better join us."

He escorted his wife and Hilary St Clair from the room under the watchful eye of the feisty little nurse.

"I don't want Mrs Chatswood being upset either," she said pointedly to Elizabeth and Robert. "She has suffered a great deal of trauma."

An hour later, as his father and Mrs Hilary St Clair, sat discussing his fraudulent behaviour, while his mother listened in stunned disbelief, Geoffrey Chatswood finally stirred from his drunken slumber. His head thumped, and his stomach was still churning over and over. He tried several times to open his eyes, but when he eventually succeeded, they stubbornly failed to focus.

For just one moment, he wondered where he was, and then it slowly came back to him, bit by bit, like the fractured clips of an old-time movie. The drinking, the drugs, the fight with Hilly. He remembered her tumbling down the stairs. The ambulance, the hospital. The fight with Joshua Bates.

Then, he finally remembered it all, as the whole nightmare scenario came flooding back to him. He recalled staggering to a telephone box and calling Nigel, but as there was no reply, he had then phoned Hugh for help instead.

"Why aren't you staying at the hospital with Hilly?" asked a dumbfounded Hugh. "Surely she wants you there?"

"No. Nobody wants me here. They've thrown me out."

"They've thrown you out? Don't tell me. You're drunk, and you picked a fight with someone. Not the doctor, I hope."

"He asked for it! It was the bloody 'baker boy'. Can you believe it, Hugh? Of all the doctors in London, my Hilly ended up with him. And then, she refused to see me. Wouldn't even talk to me. She said I pushed her. As if! I love her and the baby!"

By this time, Hugh had built up a pretty clear picture of what was going on.

"I'm sorry, old man, but you need to go home and sober up."

"Can't go home. No money for the fare. Anyway, they might have set the 'plods' on me by now."

"What! Why would they do that? What exactly have you done?"

"Nothing. They think I've been smoking Mary Jane. That's all."

"And have you?"

"It was hours ago, but I got some to share with you and Nigel, too, and I don't want them finding that in my pocket, do I? Can't find Nigel either." Geoffrey complained. "Thought *he* might help me, but he's not at home."

"That's because he's here."

"Oh, good. One of you can come and get me then."

Poppy, having listened with growing concern as Hugh repeated the conversation to both her and Nigel, put her foot down very firmly.

"He is not coming here, Hugh. I won't have it! I don't trust him, and I don't like him! Poor Hilly. He probably did push her. He can be so moody and aggressive."

"Well, we can't just leave him hanging around the hospital grounds. He *will* get himself arrested, especially if he's carrying weed."

"I'll go and fetch him," offered Nigel.

"Sorry, Poppy old girl, but a friend in need and all that. He can have my sofa for the night. Better than kipping in a phone box, and you know he'd never leave Hugh or me in the lurch if we were in trouble."

"No," agreed Poppy. "Only poor Hilly!"

Dr Joshua Bates tapped quietly on the door as he entered Hilly's wardroom. The nurse who had seen fit to clear the room of visitors had also gone in search of Dr Bates.

"I think you might be needed, Doctor. There were raised voices, and Mrs Chatswood was still very agitated. I sent some of her visitors packing, but her parents stayed with her, and I think her mother was the one upsetting her. I understand you know the family, and I was wondering if you might be able to help."

Joshua nodded.

"Of course. I'll see what I can do."

He stood at the foot of Hilly's bed and looked sternly at Elizabeth.

"I hear you have been upsetting my patient, Mrs Moncrieff. I'm sure you didn't mean to. I'm sure you yourself are very upset seeing your daughter in this state, but you must understand that Hilly cannot suffer any further stress right now."

Elizabeth sniffed and glowered at him. How dare Joshua Bates talk to her like that. Joshua smiled apologetically.

"We must work out a plan together," he continued in an encouraging, conspiratorial tone, "first to help her recover and then to keep her safe."

"Quite so," agreed Robert. "I must say it is a great relief to me that she has you here to watch her back."

"Nothing will happen to her here at the hospital," Joshua assured him. "Geoffrey has been banned from visiting unless Hilly wants to see him, of course."

"Never!" Hilly was adamant. *"Never again!"* I *hate* him, and I'm scared of him. I'm not having his baby anymore, so I'm going to divorce him."

Elizabeth flinched. Divorce! What would people think?

"Then we must arrange for you to go somewhere other than your own home when you're discharged," encouraged Joshua. "Somewhere you can feel safe."

"She will come home to Leominster with us, of course."

Elizabeth slowly began to comprehend the situation.

"No, Mother. He'll just come after me. It has to be somewhere he can't find me. Perhaps I could go back to France and stay with Madie. She'll help me. I know she will."

"We'll all help you, Hilly." Joshua patted her arm.

"Don't worry. We have time to sort something out. You'll be here for a few days yet, and you are perfectly safe."

Robert agreed, and Hilly sighed with relief. She felt a little happier now she knew that Josh and Father were going to help her. Aunt Hilary was on her side too, and Mother would support her in the end. She always did.

William Chatswood squared his jaw and looked Hilary St Clair straight in the eye.

"I don't really know where to start this conversation, Hilary. I never thought the day would come that I would be apologising to one of my oldest friends and a business partner to boot for the appalling and dishonest behaviour of my own son."

His voice faltered; he lowered his eyes and sadly shook his head, lost in an unfamiliar world of uncertainty.

"I cannot believe Geoffrey would do this to anyone, least of all you. He has known you all his life, and now, with his marriage to Hilly, you are family as well. Where did we go wrong, Daphne? We gave the boy everything he ever wanted, including the best education money could buy. Did we give him too much? Overindulge him? Why would he do this? Why?"

Daphne Chatswood was confused.

"Do what, William?... Hilary? Will one of you please tell me what is going on?"

Daphne looked from one to the other of them with a puzzled frown and a blank stare. William seemed to have suddenly aged right before her eyes. He appeared broken and deflated. His face was drawn with anxiety, and his shoulders slumped forward. Hilary on the other hand, exuded strength and dignity. She sat bolt upright, her eyes flashing with righteous indignation.

By the time they enlightened her with the whole, upsetting story of Geoffrey's dismal, fraudulent behaviour, Daphne Chatswood's puzzled demeanour had changed to one of shocked disbelief.

"No," she stated firmly, in fierce defence of her son,

"Geoffrey would never do that!"

"Don't try to defend the boy, Daphne. He *has* done it. He has stolen from Hilary, and now it appears he has pushed Hilly down the stairs and killed his own child. He is out of control! A dishonest monster and a coward! He has even run off rather than face the music!"

"William! How can you say that about your own son? Do you have any actual proof that he has done these dreadful things?"

"Yes, Daphne. Of course, we have proof of his financial shenanigans, and why would Hilly say he pushed her down the stairs if he didn't?"

"Because we know she only married him for the sake of the baby. Now that the poor little thing is no more, she won't want to hang around, and if she blames Geoffrey for her fall, then she'll have the perfect excuse to leave him. Poor Geoffrey! He hasn't even had a chance to defend himself. I won't have everyone blaming my son like this. It's not fair. He loved that baby, too. The baby *and* Hilary Anne."

Hilary St Clair drew herself up and waded into the argument.

"That is quite enough, Daphne. I will not sit by and listen to you talk about Hilary Anne like that. We all know her side of the story about her pregnancy. And yes, you're right. She did only marry Geoffrey because of the baby. That, and Elizabeth's paranoia about what other people might think about her daughter being single and pregnant. Poor Hilly tried to do the right thing for everyone. I also believe she is quite frightened of Geoffrey. He likes to control and manipulate her. I've seen him do it, and I think he actually enjoys upsetting her. He seems to have some strange idea in his head that it makes him more of a man, and anyway, if he is so innocent, Daphne, where is he now? Skipping the country on my money, no doubt! My poor Winston will be turning in his grave!"

"Ladies. Please. We are all upset. We need to calm down and decide what is to be done for the best. So far as your money is concerned, Hilary, Daphne and I will personally reimburse you at once, and of course, we will help Hilly in any way we can."

"Thank you, William. I shall need that holiday more than ever now. However, I am sorry, but I must insist Geoffrey is dismissed from the Company with immediate effect. I am also considering whether to lay charges with the constabulary. I will see how Hilly feels about that. She may want to charge him with assault as well."

William looked at her.

"Hilary. What can I say? My father, too, will be turning in his grave. As you know only too well, before Winston came on board, the Company was struggling. Father was filled with gratitude and admiration for the way Winston helped turn things around. For his only grandchild to now be bent on destroying everything that he and Winston worked so tirelessly to build is more than flesh and blood can bear. That he has stolen from you, of all people, Hilary, is unthinkable. I agree he must be dismissed at once, and you and Hilly must make your own decisions considering taking any further action."

William's anguish was plain to see. His face was ashen, and his voice shook with emotion. Hilary's anger began to abate, and her expression softened. Despite everything, William and Daphne were her friends, and regardless of his behaviour, Geoffrey was still their son.

"Find him, William. Find him, and we will hear his side of the story, as Daphne wishes. That is only fair."

"Thank you, Hilary. It is more than he deserves."

William shook her hand, and Daphne's eyes filled with tears of gratitude.

William Chatswood lost no time searching for his wayward son. His first port of call was the Carlton Club. It made sense to him that Geoffrey would hide out there, where no awkward questions would be asked. He was not, however, prepared for the news that greeted him there.

They had not seen Mr Geoffrey for several weeks, and his monthly account payments were in arrears. The sum total outstanding came as a shock to William, but he paid it nevertheless before continuing on his way.

Geoffrey, he decided, was out of control. He needed to be found at once. Perhaps a phone call to Hugh Oldfield or Nigel Fortescue would throw some light as to his whereabouts.

To his profound relief, this avenue of enquiry proved fruitful, as Hugh obligingly enlightened him as to where Geoffrey had spent the night and, a little less obligingly, revealed Nigel's address.

The constant ringing of the doorbell and loud banging on the door startled Geoffrey. What if it was the Police? What if they had found out about the drugs or the fraud? Maybe Hilly had charged him with assault. He froze with dread.

"Geoffrey! I know you're there! Open the door at once!"

Hilly held tightly to Joshua's hand, afraid that were she to let go, he would disappear again. He was off duty now and had come to spend some much-longed-for personal time with her. He sensed she wanted to talk, and he was more than willing to listen.

"Has your girlfriend moved to London with you?" Hilly took a deep breath and steeled herself for his reply.

"My girlfriend?"

"Yes. Jimmy Jones told me about her on Christmas Eve."

"Really? What did he say?"

"That he had seen you with her in Hereford. That you were in your car together, and you were kissing."

"You believed him?"

"Yes. Why would he lie to me? I had been waiting by the river for you for ages and ages. I had to go home because we were going to London, and

271

I was cold and upset that you hadn't come, so I went to look for you, but the bakery was closed, and no one was home, so then I went to check if Maisie or anyone else knew where you were, but nobody else had seen you either. Then I had to go home because we were leaving for London, and as I was walking by the Corn Square, Jimmy called out to wish me Merry Christmas, so I asked him if he'd seen you, and that's when he told me."

"Oh, Hilly. Jimmy Jones would say or do anything to try and get you away from me. He has fancied you since primary school. He hates that we were always so close. He hates me!

The girl in the car that day was one of my flatmates. She was going home for Christmas, and I was dropping her off to catch her bus home from Hereford. She gave me a peck on the cheek to say thank you. That's all. Her name is Chrissy Sloane. You'd like her. I'll introduce you, and you can ask her if you like."

"No. I mean, I would like to meet her, but I don't need to ask her. I know now why you didn't keep our rendezvous, and I am so truly sad about what happened to your dad. I know how much you loved him. I did, too."

"He loved you too, Hilly. We all love you."

"I don't love Jimmy Jones, though."

"I should hope not!"

"I don't love Geoffrey Chatswood, either."

Hilly haltingly told Joshua then about New Year's Eve and Geoffrey raping her. Her voice faltered as she carried on.

"I felt so cheap and nasty. So pathetic and useless. So unworthy; especially of you. I was actually glad to think you had already found someone else who wouldn't be so stupid or let you down like me. Then I realised I was pregnant, and I didn't know what to do. I didn't tell Geoffrey, but he had decided I belonged to him anyway. He came looking for me in Paris, and I told him to go away, but he just laughed and got nasty. He only found me because Mother gave him my address. Then she and Father came for Easter, and Mother guessed that I was pregnant. She was furious. She thought you were the father. She wouldn't believe what Geoffrey had done. She always thought he was so wonderful and would be such a catch for me. Anyway, she told the Chatswoods I was expecting their grandchild, and they ordered Geoffrey to 'do the right thing by me', which was what he wanted all along. Mother and Father insisted it was the right thing for both me and the baby, and that was that. We were married within days, and Geoffrey got what he wanted, yet again."

"Poor Hilly. I had no idea what was going on, or I would have come and rescued you."

"I tried to write and tell you, but I couldn't get the words right. I had no right to expect you to help me or to understand how trapped I felt. How much I hated myself. I thought you had another girlfriend anyway, so why should you care? In the end, I just did what I thought was right for my baby and everyone else. My parents, the Chatswoods and most of all for you. I would quietly set you free to be with the other girl. I was unworthy of you anyway, so if I couldn't be with you, it didn't matter who I married. At least you would be happy, and I would have my baby to love. I knew I could never love Geoffrey, but I have tried really hard to be the perfect wife in every other way."

Hilly looked at Josh, her eyes filled with hurt and sadness.

"He hates me now, though. I think he just decided I was something else he wanted. That I was going to be another of his possessions. Then, like everything else in his life, once he had what he wanted, he just lost interest. He says cruel, hateful things to make me feel small and stupid, and then he goes out gambling and drinking with his friends till all hours. Sometimes, he stays out all night. Not that I care."

Large, hot tears trickled down her face, and then she took a deep breath and pulled herself together.

"I'm so sorry, Josh. For everything. Thank you for listening. Please don't hate me. I really couldn't bear that. I hope we can always be friends."

"Oh, Hilly, you goose!" Josh gently wrapped his arms around her.

"I still love you. I always have, and I always will. I will make sure Geoffrey Chatswood never comes near you again."

"How can you possibly forgive me? I have been so stupid."

"No, Hilly. I should have realised something was wrong. I should have written to you and explained about Dad right away. Not asked Lindy to write. Lord knows I tried. It was so hard, and there was so much going on in my life; then when your mother said she and your dad were expecting you to announce your engagement to Geoffrey Chatswood when you finished studying, it was as though a part of me just shut down."

"What? When did Mother say that?"

"Right after Christmas. When she got back from London. I ran into her by chance, and she told me then. Gloated about it, really. Then, when I didn't hear from you, apart from your lovely condolence card, I thought it must be true."

Hilly looked at him.

"What are we like?" She smiled. "Me listening to Jimmy Jones, and you believing Mother? No wonder she was so keen that I should marry Geoffrey for the sake of the baby. It was exactly what she wanted all along. She refused to believe that he assaulted me."

Josh looked at her.

"Do you remember when we were very young, that we made a pact, along with Lindy, that we would be best friends forever?"

"I do."

"Well, I think it's time you and I made another pact that from here on in, we don't listen to other people. We talk to each other instead."

"I agree."

Chapter – 25

William Chatswood marched his disgraced son through the front door and into the lounge, where his mother and Hilary St Clair sat waiting. Any hopes Geoffrey was harbouring that Mrs St Clair might treat him with leniency were dashed immediately. One look at her stony countenance informed him at once that she was not about to be trifled with. Even Mother looked at him as though he was a stranger.

News of Geoffrey's drinking, drug consumption, and out-of-control gambling rocked Daphne to the core. She looked at him now as though she was seeing him for the first time. The little boy she once cherished and adored had turned into a weak, self-entitled young man, completely lacking in self-control and principles. How could she not have seen what he was becoming? She always believed his bouts of sullen pouting and his frequent temper tantrums were just part of growing up. That if she ignored them, he would grow out of them. She could not have been more wrong, she thought now, as he stood defiantly before them.

"Your father has very generously reimbursed me with the money you misappropriated, Geoffrey, and it is now entirely up to him as to whether or not you pay *him* back," Hilary St Clair was saying.

"It is, however, entirely up to me to decide whether I choose to take legal proceedings against you. That decision will depend, in part, on the findings of the internal auditors, who are currently investigating all of our company accounts with a very fine-tooth comb. Should they find any further discrepancies, I will not delay in bringing in the police.

I have also spoken to Hilary Anne about your fraud and deceit, as I believe she has as much right as any of us to decide what your punishment should be. I was more than a little concerned to hear that she believes you have also been dipping into your joint bank account without consulting her in order to fund your addictions."

"Geoffrey!" Daphne Chatswood was visibly shaken, and Geoffrey's arrogant stance began to crumble.

"Is it *all* true, Geoffrey?" asked his distraught mother. "Did you also assault poor Hilly on New Year's Eve and push her down the stairs yesterday, as she says?"

"Well, she agreed to go out with me and to marry me. She didn't have to. I thought she was in love with me, and I was in love with her. I thought she was beautiful. She's not, you know. She threw herself at me and got pregnant on purpose to make sure I would marry her because she and her mother thought I was such a good catch. I didn't want to get married and have a child. Not yet, anyway. I'm not ready for all that."

"Stop talking nonsense, Geoffrey. You spent the whole of the Christmas break following Hilly around like a lovesick puppy. She did not throw herself at you. Quite the opposite, in fact. I never thought I would say this, Geoffrey, but I am deeply ashamed of you."

Geoffrey hung his head.

"I'm sorry, Mother. I didn't mean to hurt her, or you, or anyone. It's the drink and the drugs," he whined pathetically, "I don't seem able to handle them."

"Then stop using them," advised his father.

"Perhaps he's an addict," suggested Daphne, "and rather than be angry, we need to get him some help."

William snorted with rage.

"Do not try to make excuses for him, Daphne," he roared with vexation, "Geoffrey is not a child anymore. He makes his own decisions. He will have to live with the consequences."

Daphne swallowed and nodded in reluctant agreement, as Geoffrey, realising that his 'poor little me' act was getting him nowhere, reverted to his air of sullen, misunderstood, arrogance. He looked defiantly at Hilary St Clair.

"The money in that joint account is as much mine as Hilly's," he stated belligerently.

Hilary St Clair looked back at him with undisguised loathing.

"Hilary Anne has also told both her parents and me that she wants a divorce."

"Well, she hasn't told me that, and I'm not giving her one. I suppose the 'baker boy' has put that idea in her head. She's upset, and she's not thinking straight."

"You are the one who is not thinking straight, Geoffrey. You just this minute said you don't want to be married, and why on earth would Hilly want to stay with a weak, selfish, controlling creature like you? It is my belief that you see Hilly as your possession, and you would rather harm her than relinquish her!"

"Hilary!"

"No, I am sorry, Daphne, but it is true. If Geoffrey wants any chance of staying out of jail, he will agree to a divorce at once. He will also agree, should the audit prove unsatisfactory, to leave this country on a permanent basis, without delay. The alternative is that both Hilary Anne and I will press charges."

"I think those demands are more than fair." William eyed his son with disdain while Daphne struggled to come to terms with the fact that one way or the other, she was about to say goodbye to her only child.

Geoffrey swallowed hard and looked at his parents in disbelief. How could they let Mrs St Clair make such demands without speaking up for him?

"Why should I believe you that Hilly wants a divorce or wants me to leave the country? She hasn't said anything to me about it," he spat at Aunt Hilary.

"Hilly has no desire to speak to you about anything ever again, Geoffrey."

Hilary St Clair reached into her handbag and produced an envelope, which she all but threw in his direction.

"She asked me to see that you got this letter instead."

"Harrumph!" Geoffrey crushed the envelope in rage, stuffed it in his pocket and stormed from the room. William followed after him, watching his son clamber wildly up the stairs to the sanctuary of his childhood bedroom before returning to comfort his unhappy wife and assure his disgruntled friend and business partner that he would see to it that the boy did exactly as she and Hilly wished.

Geoffrey, meanwhile, removed the crumpled envelope from his pocket and eyed it with a mixture of suspicion and trepidation. He flung himself down on the bed and angrily tore open the envelope.

Geoffrey,

I will not see you face to face, but I believe you need to be certain that what Aunt Hilary tells you is the truth. You have the right to know that I have requested Father to arrange for me to see a Lawyer today in order that I can start divorce proceedings against you without delay. Should you make any attempt to block our divorce in any way or come anywhere near me ever again, I will charge you with rape, domestic violence, and the manslaughter of our unborn child.

I am not a naturally vindictive person, Geoffrey, and I have no real desire to see you in prison, but I will not be assaulted, controlled or intimidated by you any more. I have no feelings for you other than disgust, and I believe it will be in your best interests to leave the country permanently, with immediate effect. Failure on your part to comply with my wishes will leave me with no choice other than to lay charges.

Should Aunt Hilary and your own father be obliged to do that anyway, I will add my voice to theirs in order to keep you away from me for as long as possible.

Hilary Anne Moncrieff

Geoffrey screwed Hilly's letter into a ball and hurled it into the wall with as much force as he could muster. *Her name is Chatswood, he thought* angrily, *not Moncrieff. She is still my wife, whether she likes it or not, and I will not agree to a divorce! That bloody 'baker boy' will be behind all this nonsense!*

Geoffrey stared angrily into space. How could she say those things about him? He suddenly jumped to his feet and strode to the wardrobe, where he searched frantically through some old belongings left stored on the top shelf. Having found the solid silver money box he was looking for, he emptied its considerable contents into his pockets, then shoved the handsome, antique moneybox into an old canvas satchel, along with his late grandfather's prized fob watch and an extensive collection of exquisite Parker fountain pens.

Geoffrey then slipped silently from his room. He crept down the stairs and quietly let himself out of the front door.

Having successfully executed his escape without drawing attention to himself, he scurried down Wrights Lane to High Street Kensington, where he jumped on the first passing bus that would take him in the direction of Chelsea and The Kings Road. Once there, he quickly sought out a pawn shop, where he exchanged his sack of precious items for some good old-fashioned, hard cash. The pawnbroker also showed considerable interest in the gold Rolex watch Geoffrey wore strapped to his wrist, and for one fleeting moment, Geoffrey was tempted to leave that with him as well. It had been a twenty-first birthday gift from his parents, and while he currently felt no attachment to it for that particular reason, the watch was still his most prized possession. In his mind, it showed the world that he was a man of substance. A man not to be trifled with.

He declined the pawnbroker's generous offer, tucked the handsome sum of cash he had already acquired into his wallet, and sallied forth, feeling immensely pleased with himself. With the first part of his plan having worked so well, Geoffrey sauntered down the road, his eyes peeled for a Public House in order that he might partake of a whiskey or two to celebrate his newfound riches.

Having stumbled across the perfect establishment, he settled himself down in a private booth and reached into his jacket pocket for a cigarette. As he opened the cigarette case, his eyes fell on the three marijuana cigarettes he had placed there the day before, and he immediately pounced on one with eager delight. It seemed to be a day for rediscovering hidden treasures, and he was going to make the most of it. He took a long, lingering toke, then reached for his double whiskey, savouring every moment of what he considered to be pure enjoyment.

Having indulged in two further double whiskeys, along with a pint of best ale, Geoffrey then convinced himself that Nigel and Hugh would perfectly understand if he didn't share the Mary Jane with them and decided to have one last toke before heading home to Brixton.

Once there, he determined he would take a bath, find some fresh clothes, then go back to the hospital to have it out with Hilly. Losing the baby was a terrible shock to them both, but they still had a future together.

He would take her an enormous bunch of roses and a bottle of champagne, and he would make her see that he still loved her, and she would change her mind and not divorce him after all. He might even promise to stop gambling if that's what she really wanted. Satisfied that he had devised a flawless plan to win Hilly back, he took his last puff of marijuana, downed his last gulp of whiskey, and signalled to the proprietor.

"I would like one bottle each of fine French champagne and malt whiskey to take with me, please, good, sir." He smiled happily. "And would you also be so good as to direct me to the nearest florist shop."

Geoffrey carefully placed his two precious bottles into the now-empty canvas bag and made his way back outside. His earlier anger had given way to a wonderful mellow feeling of deep self-belief that he was invincible. He chuckled happily to himself as he purchased a beautiful bunch of deep red roses sprinkled with drifts of dainty, snow-white gypsophila from the bemused florist.

Thanking the young woman profusely, Geoffrey then continued on his way, immensely enjoying the sensation that with every step he took, he felt that he was floating through the air on a soft, billowing cloud of happiness. He was surely indestructible. Nobody, least of all Joshua Bates, would stand in his way. Hilary Anne was his wife, and that was how things would stay. He must go to her straight away and make her see that he was the only man she would ever need.

A feeling of intense urgency suddenly overcame him. He needed to reach Hilly before her father reached the hospital with his lawyer in tow.

Geoffrey's previous state of elated euphoria deserted him, and in its stead, an uncomfortable feeling of rising panic crept over him. He quickened his step, determined to make haste as he made his way back in the direction of the Underground Station.

He could see the familiar underground sign just yards away on the opposite side of the street before it occurred to him that a taxi would be more expedient. He paused to look around for one and could scarcely believe his luck as a recently vacated cab pulled away from the kerbside a short distance off.

This was definitely his lucky day, thought Geoffrey Chatswood as he frantically waved out to attract the driver's attention.

With his eyes firmly fixed on the familiar black taxi and his mind firmly fixed on his overwhelming sense of urgency to reach Hilly, Geoffrey's distracted and befuddled brain ceased to function with any sense of normality and oblivious to everything else around him; Geoffrey Chatswood stepped from the footpath, straight into the path of the rapidly approaching traffic.

Screeching brakes, raucous horn blasts, and the horrified gasps and cries of warning from fellow pedestrians were the last sounds Geoffrey Chatswood ever heard.

The startled driver of a small delivery van tried desperately to swerve and brake in time as Geoffrey dashed out in front of him, but the sickening thud of his van making contact with the young man, followed by the sight of Geoffrey flying in the air, then landing briefly on the bonnet before disappearing from sight and sliding under the wheels, told the shaken man that his evasive efforts had been in vain. As the van finally came to a halt, he sat frozen with shock, his hands still gripping the steering wheel, his face as white as a sheet, and his eyes staring straight ahead in blind horror as equally shocked passers-by gathered around to see if they could help in any way.

Geoffrey Chatswood, though, was beyond help. He lay disturbingly still in the middle of the road. His hand still gripped the remnants of Hilly's roses, and his canvas bag lay beside him, its shattered contents spreading wine and whiskey under his lifeless, broken, blood-spattered body.

Chapter – 26

Hilary Anne sat up in her hospital bed, eagerly awaiting the arrival of her father and Mr Marlow, the lawyer. She was feeling a lot better today and was keen to get the divorce proceedings underway. It would be such a relief to be free of Geoffrey and start her life afresh. She could put his selfish, unpleasant behaviour behind her and move on, happy in the knowledge that Joshua still loved her, and she was free to love him back.

Hushed voices in the corridor alerted her to the arrival of her visitors, and as Robert entered the room, she smiled warmly.

"Father?" Her bright smile faded. There was no sign of Mr Marlow, and her father was accompanied instead by Mother and Aunt Hilary. Their faces were drawn, and Mother looked as though she had been crying.

"Whatever is it?" demanded Hilly.

"From the looks on your faces, something terrible has happened. Is it Mr Marlow?"

"Marlow? No, no, Hilly. Mr Marlow is fine." Robert hesitated and looked at his daughter with uncertainty.

"Tell her, Robert," encouraged Elizabeth. "She has to know."

Robert nodded.

"I'm sorry, Hilly, but you have no need of Mr Marlow. There is no easy way to tell you this, and I know you had little time for the fellow, but I expect you will be sad, regardless, to hear that Geoffrey has passed away."

"Geoffrey is dead?" Hilly looked from one to the other of her visitors in stunned disbelief.

"How? What happened?"

"He was run over. Stepped out in front of a delivery van. By all accounts, the poor driver had no show of avoiding him."

"Where did it happen?"

"The Kings Road. Apparently, he was trying to flag down a taxi and just suddenly charged out into the middle of the road."

"Was he high?"

"High?"

"Yes. You know. Drugs and alcohol."

Robert shook his head.

"I imagine there will be an autopsy to answer that question."

"And Daphne and William, how are they?"

"As you would expect."

"They are very upset, of course, Hilly," offered Elizabeth, her eyes filling with tears once more.

"They thought poor Geoffrey was up in his attic room, lying down and coming to terms with the consequences of his behaviour. You can imagine their shock when the police arrived to inform them of the tragedy. They think he was most likely coming to visit you, Hilly. He had a bottle of champagne in his bag and was holding a big bunch of red roses. He didn't want to lose you, Hilly. He loved you."

It was Hilly's turn to shake her head.

"Not really, Mother," she said sadly.

"He was in love with the whole idea of having a wife and family, but he had no idea how to love anyone other than himself."

"How can you say that? He adored you, Hilly. They found a receipt from a pawn shop in his wallet, and it seems he had just pawned his childhood treasures to find the money to shower you with gifts."

"No, Mother, he would have done that to buy alcohol and drugs. He was an addict Mother. I'm sure that once he had indulged his habits, the guilt set in, hence the champagne and roses. He always turned on the charm for *you*. He was good at that, but you never saw the real Geoffrey. He was possessive, cruel, and controlling. The most self-entitled person I have ever met. He didn't love me; he just wanted to own me, to show me off to his friends, and use me as he saw fit."

"I'm afraid Hilly is quite right, Elizabeth," agreed Aunt Hilary. "Don't waste your time mourning him. I shan't. I feel for Daphne and William, of course. Whatever else he was, Geoffrey was their son."

"Of course," agreed Robert, "and we must all respect that, but we must also remember what Geoffrey has done to our Hilly."

He turned his attention to his daughter.

"You are our priority, my dear." He smiled fondly. "And all that matters. Your future happiness is our only concern."

The conversation turned then to where Hilly would go when she was discharged from the hospital. She lay back and listened as her visitors decided on a plan of action. In the end, it was agreed that Elizabeth and Robert would collect her belongings from the flat, and Robert would take them back to Leominster for her. He had to return to work, while Aunt Hilary needed to stay in London until the auditors had completed their task. She would then sort out her finances, and once that was done, Hilly and Elizabeth would travel home to Leominster with her.

"I do think we should attend poor Geoffrey's funeral though before we leave," insisted Elizabeth, "if only for Daphne and William's sake."

Hilly agreed that she would comply with her parents' wishes this one last time, but only if Joshua was happy with the arrangement. Elizabeth bristled, but Hilly looked at her defiantly.

"You will understand, Mother, that I will no longer tolerate your disapproval of Joshua and his family. I have never understood your attitude towards them. In fact, Mother, I will no longer tolerate your interference in any part of my life. I have loved Josh since we were children. He is the best friend I have ever known, and he has always been there to protect me. Even now, after the appalling way I have treated him, he is standing by me. If I am forced to choose between the two of you, Mother, Josh will win."

"Thank you, Hilly."

None of them had noticed Dr Bates enter the room.

"Don't worry, Mrs Moncrieff, I'm sure it won't come to that." He smiled kindly as Elizabeth sniffed and threw a wounded look in the direction of her daughter.

Hilly's unrepentant, frosty glare had a sudden, unexpected impact on Elizabeth. Hilary Anne was no longer a child, she realised. She was a young woman with a mind of her own. Elizabeth looked at Josh then as if she was seeing him for the first time. He was tall and handsome. A strong young man with a good heart. She remembered the day he brought Hilly home with her grazed knee and torn dress and how he had stood by her when she caught ringworm and her hair fell out. He had ridden his bicycle through the storm to provide food to the folk taking shelter at Baron's Cross, and he had saved little Tommy Morgan's life. On top of all those things, Joshua Bates was now a doctor. Of course, Hilly loved him. How could she not?

Geoffrey Chatswood had been born to a life of financial wealth and privilege, but Joshua Bates, had been born to a life that offered far greater riches.

For the first time, Elizabeth Moncrieff understood. She apologised then, not only to her daughter but also to Joshua Bates.

As the chilly winds of winter began to make themselves felt and Christmas approached once more, both the Moncrieff and Bates families found themselves looking to the Festive Season with mixed feelings.

On the one hand, the familiar sights and sounds of Christmas were strangely comforting, and the promise of a New Year brought with it hope for happier times ahead.

On the other hand, both families struggled with memories of the events that had befallen them over the previous year.

Hilly sat at the kitchen table with Aunt Hilary, looking over the glossy travel brochures that offered enticing photographs of the many wonders to be found along the Nile. With her departure date just days away, Hilary St Clair's excitement was palpable. Hilly smiled at her.

"I'm sure you and Mrs Beaufort will have a wonderful time."

"I hope so, Hilly, because I have quite made up my mind that in future, I shall travel somewhere new every year, and I am hoping that Rose will agree to join me."

"Well, I think that is an excellent idea, and from what you tell me of her, I'm sure Mrs Beaufort will, too."

Hilly gathered up their teacups and made her way to the kitchen sink, remembering the plans that she and Josh had made to travel together.

One day, she thought ruefully, carefully placing the pretty bone china cups in the sink and gazing dreamily out of the window. A little squeal of delight suddenly escaped her as she caught sight of the object of her thoughts, wending his way along the garden path.

"It's Joshua," she informed her amused aunty as she rushed to the kitchen door to let him in.

"You're a day early!" she exclaimed, reaching out to hug him.

"Well, I can go away and come back tomorrow if that's what you'd prefer," he teased.

Hilly laughed.

"Come in," she grinned. "Would you like a cup of tea?"

"No thanks. I've just had one at the bakery, along with one too many of John's rather delicious cream buns. Thought I should walk it off and wondered if you'd care to join me."

"Of course. I'll just wash up these cups and grab my coat."

"Leave those," laughed Aunt Hilary. "I'll see to them."

Hilly thanked her aunt, grabbed her coat and hat, and made good her escape.

Aunt Hilary stood at the kitchen sink, watching the young couple walk arm in arm down the garden path, and smiled to herself.

It was good to see Hilly looking so happy. It was as though Geoffrey's death had given her back the life, he had so selfishly stolen from her. She deserved to be happy again after all she had been through.

Joshua Bates thought so too. He led Hilly down Ryelands Road, past the school, and down to the river Kenwater and their secret meeting place.

"I won't leave you waiting here alone this year." He smiled, taking her in his arms and kissing her.

"In fact, I think we've both waited long enough, Hilly."

He reached into his coat pocket and pulled out a small box covered in deep red velvet.

"Will you marry me?" he asked, flipping open the box to reveal its contents. Despite the gloomy winter's day, the diamond solitaire ring within sparkled brightly as a delighted Hilary Anne softly whispered her reply.

"Yes." She smiled happily, "of course I will, Josh. To be with you is all I've ever wanted."

Joshua took the ring from its box and slipped it on her finger.

"I was worried you'd feel it was too soon after Geoffrey."

"Geoffrey has been dead to me for a lot longer than six months. I know it's an awful thing to say, but I have never felt able to mourn him. If I am honest, his death was more of a relief than anything."

Josh nodded. He knew better than anyone how frightened of Geoffrey, Hilly had been. How lost and trapped in a nightmare she had felt. He held her close, and she snuggled her head into his shoulder.

"I know!" she said suddenly, "I should wear the ring around my neck and hide it under my clothes until Christmas Day and then slip it back on my finger after church. Then, we can announce our engagement to everyone at lunch. Hopefully, it will take their minds off the sadness of last year for a bit, though we'll all wish your dad was still here, of course. Would he approve of me being his daughter-in-law, do you think?"

"He would love it." Josh laughed. "I'm more concerned about how your mother will feel about having me as a son-in-law. Your father approves, by the way. I asked for his permission."

"And your mum and siblings?"

"Oh, I'm not so sure about them," he teased.

Just as Hilly hoped, everyone was delighted with their announcement on Christmas Day. Even Elizabeth smiled with genuine pleasure. She turned to Margaret, who was seated beside her and gave her a totally 'out-of-character', impulsive hug.

"I am so pleased," she said graciously.

"Joshua is a tower of strength to Hilly. He has always stood by her, no matter what. I'm so sorry to have disapproved of their friendship in the past. I see now how wrong I was."

Margaret smiled. She knew how hard it must have been for Elizabeth to apologise.

"The past is just that, Elizabeth," she said kindly. "Theirs, yours and ours. We must put it all behind us now and move forward together."

The happy couple set a date in the middle of May for their wedding to take place, and the months flew by. As Josh continued his internship and studies, Hilly returned to London with him and set up a little studio where she could both work and teach. Their mothers, meanwhile, happily joined forces to help with the wedding plans, as both Hilly and Josh were adamant they would marry in Leominster, surrounded by everyone they cared about.

By the time the big day arrived, everything was arranged to perfection.

Hilly opened her eyes and looked around. Pale sunlight filtered through the window, where she had sat so often as a child, and it spread a soft, comforting glow across the familiar little room.

A sweet, contented smile played on her lips, and her eyes shone with sheer pleasure as they rested on her wedding dress, which was hanging under a protective plastic cover on the outside of the wardrobe door.

Susan Bates had designed the dress specially for her. Elizabeth had travelled to London to help Hilly choose the perfect fabric, and Susan and Margaret had happily stitched away together, laughing and reminiscing as they worked not only on Hilly's dress but the bridesmaids' outfits too.

Hilly stretched. She was too excited to stay in bed, and the morning air was fresh and inviting. A glance at the pretty little carriage clock sitting on the bedside table told her there was plenty of time to take a stroll to the river before Lindy, Maisie and Madie came to join her, and the day was filled with pre-wedding, girlie fun. *It was all so different from last time,* she thought to herself as she took in the sweet, fresh air and let her mind wander down memory lane. *This time, she was in love, and she was happy. All was as it should be.*

Joshua stood at the altar, impatiently awaiting the arrival of his bride.

His student beard had gone, revealing his strong, masculine jaw. He was handsomely dressed in a dark blue serge suit and a plain white shirt, offset with a fashionably wide, blue and white floral tie. As he nervously fingered the knot on the latter, the sudden joyous strains of organ music announced his wait was over. He momentarily closed his steely blue eyes and took a deep breath to steady his nerves as John, thoroughly embracing the role of best man, looked at him and nodded encouragingly.

Josh's student friends, Malcolm and David, along with Alex and little Tommy Morgan, deserted their posts as groomsmen and took their seats next to Margaret, Susan and Sally, as a delighted Margaret whispered proudly to Susan that their efforts in the sewing room had been worth every minute.

Elizabeth smiled across the aisle at Margaret and mouthed the words "thank you". *Margaret and Susan had done them all proud,* she thought.

Hilary St Clair sat beside her, smiling with pleasure, and as they watched Hilly walk serenely down the aisle on Robert's arm, her three best friends following happily behind in pretty blue and buttercup floral peasant dresses teamed with sweet, short-cropped, laced denim jackets, Elizabeth felt strangely content, in the unfamiliar knowledge, that all was now right in her world.

Hilly's radiant smile filled the church with joy while Joshua stood stock still, grinning adoringly back at her. *She looked even more stunning than usual,* he thought. Her dress was perfect. Maisie had bobbed her hair and applied her make-up with true professional skill, and Lindy and Madie, with help from Elizabeth and her stunning garden, had fashioned a garland of fresh spring flowers and fine blue ribbons, which Hilly wore in place of a veil. Over her arm, on a wide blue ribbon, she carried a huge floral ball, spilling over with the same glorious spring flowers that adorned the garland on her head.

Margaret happily informed Susan that the simple yet charming wedding dress she had designed was perfect. Hilly and Elizabeth had chosen a soft lawn cotton fabric in a dainty cream and white Laura Ashley print. The pretty, midi-length dress was fashioned with a demure ribbon and pin-tuck trimmed bodice, which joined to the softly gathered skirt with a wide, elegant waistband, while gently gathered sleeves drawn into soft, deep cuffs sat just below the elbows. *It really was perfect,* thought Margaret happily, as she watched her eldest son reach out to fondly take his bride by the hand.

The simple, traditional ceremony passed flawlessly, and as the groom kissed his bride and the organ played, loud cheers and happy laughter filled the church.

As The Priory bells pealed happily over the town, the busy photographer, who Elizabeth had hired for the day, plied his trade with cheery gusto until, happy that all the necessary group photos had been completed, Elizabeth, Robert and Margaret, rounded up the guests and directed them back to the bakery, where under the guidance of John, a splendid High Tea had been prepared.

Anxious to return to the bakery and ensure that the staff he had employed for the day were carrying out his instructions to the letter, John temporarily handed over his Best Man's duties to a delighted Malcolm McLeod.

"The new Dr and Mrs Bates would like to visit Dad's grave, then go on to Elizabeth's garden at Elm Cottage and down to the river for more photos before they join us," John told Malcolm.

"Give them exactly an hour and a half, no more, then drag them to the bakery," he grinned, handing over the car keys.

"We will be ready then and waiting."

As Malcolm sat in the car and watched from a respectful distance, Alex Morgan, who was ushering his young son into his own car, watched too as Joshua and Hilly knelt before Matthew's headstone.

If not for Josh, he thought, *our Tommy would have been there too, right alongside poor Matthew.* He knew that Joshua still felt he had failed his father, and it saddened him. Josh had done all he could, and now it was time for him to move on and be happy.

289

Malcolm smiled, as Hilly took the garland from her head, removed two beautiful red roses from deep in the heart of it, and placed them gently on the ground in front of the headstone. She turned to kiss her husband, and the two of them embraced before rising slowly to their feet and making their way back to the waiting car. *Hilly is perfect for Josh,* thought Malcolm. *They understand each other so well.*

Determined not to let anyone down, Malcolm McLeod performed his duties with his usual meticulous precision. He kept a close eye on the time, urging on both the newlyweds and the photographer, and he delivered them to the bakery with a full five minutes to spare.

The bakery's new Tea Shop looked like a picture from a glossy magazine. The ladies had spent the whole of the previous day setting it up to perfection. On the main table, a soft, floaty white organza tablecloth was adorned with pretty bone china, sparkling crystal wine glasses, and delicately embroidered napkins. A large, deep blue vase filled with stunning, fresh spring flowers from Elizabeth's garden took pride of place in the centre of the table.

On the wall above the table hung the letters J & H, perfectly fashioned from huge displays of Hilly's favourite wildflowers – bluebells, forget-me-knots and golden cowslips.

The smaller guest tables were similarly attired, but in their centres, small crystal vases filled with Hilly's favourite fresh spring wildflowers echoed the display on the wall.

The bride and groom's parents, along with Susan and Aunt Hilary, greeted each guest at the door, while the bridesmaids, happily assisted by David Smither, graciously escorted them to their tables.

John and his hired help worked tirelessly in the kitchen, and each tasty delicacy was perfectly presented on elegant platters and tiered bone china cake plates.

Once the guests were happily seated, wine in hand, John stood watch in the doorway, and as soon as he saw the car approaching, he signalled to Robert, who tapped a spoon against his wine glass to let everyone know the guests of honour had arrived.

As Malcolm McLeod ushered his charges through the door and the happy couple stepped inside, John Bates shook his hand and thanked him profusely for his assistance.

John then cleared his throat and proudly resumed his duties as Best Man.

"Ladies and gentlemen," he announced with great relish,

"Please be upstanding to welcome Dr Joshua and Mrs Hilary Anne Bates."

As the assembled guests rose to their feet, and loud claps and cheers echoed around the room, Robert put one arm around Elizabeth and the other around Margaret.

"Our children," he said simply, "make a beautiful couple indeed."

The bride and groom, meanwhile, stood rooted to the spot, gazing straight ahead in stunned disbelief. As John turned around to usher them to the table, Hilly felt Joshua freeze and gently took hold of his arm. There, before them, large as life, stood not John but Matthew Bates, a huge, happy grin on his face, his arms outstretched, holding a jam tart in each hand, the way he had so often greeted them when they were children. Hilly blinked.

"I think I'm seeing things," she whispered.

"I think I am, too," returned Josh, placing his arm around his new wife's waist. "I also think he approves."

Hilly nodded and smiled.

"I hope so."

Then, as the vision gradually faded away, and the bride and groom slowly followed John to their places at the head of the table, a sudden single puff of wind carried a handful of rose petals through the open door. They drifted and floated gracefully overhead, and as a delighted Hilly reached her hands up towards them, two perfect, deep red petals settled gently on her palm. Her eyes shone with happy tears as she held them out to Joshua.

"One last gift from Matthew," she whispered softly.

Josh smiled as he gently closed his hand over her open palm and nodded in happy agreement.